Sex, Wine & Chocolate | B. Martin

This book is a work of fiction. The names, characters, places and incidents are all products of the author's imagination and are used fictitiously. Any resemblance to actual events, locations, or persons living or dead, are completely coincidental.

ISBN: 978-0-9994773-3-5

Cover design by Magali Torres of Estratosphera Designs

Written by Brandi S. Martin
Edited by Tenita Johnson of Soitiswritten.net

Chapter | 1

It was 7:30 a.m. when the wind whistled outside of her window. As the sun began to rise, small rays of sunlight fell onto her sleeping eyelids. She had forgotten to close the thick red curtains, which usually covered the large windows in her bedroom, the night before. The illuminating light woke her just enough for her to roll over and face the clock on her nightstand. She smiled as if the early hour was a treat. Glancing back at the window and letting out a small yawn, the sun seemed to be merely a thin line in the sky. It was as if God was peeking before fully opening His eyes to say, "Good morning."

Not only had the light crept in, but a slight chill was in the air. It hinted to Alana that her favorite season, autumn, was in bloom a little early this year. The summer hadn't been a very hot one, so it wasn't unusual that the beginning of September, especially in the Midwest, was so cool. She couldn't wait until everything began to change. The autumn aesthetics was what she liked most about the season. Autumn really made her marvel at the beauty of nature and showed her what life was really all about: seeing and enjoying all that surrounded her.

The chilled breezes, accompanied by the warm sun on her face, always seemed to awaken her senses. The howling winds lifted their voices, demanding that all who heard them recognize the arrival of fall and all of its splendor. Her favorite part, oddly enough, was the leaves. The brilliant colors, in which they changed into as they began to age, were beauty at its best. The crisp sound they made while crashing into one another sounded like waves in the middle of the ocean every time the wind blew. When enough of them had fallen from their branches, they made a scraping sound as they rustled down the concrete sidewalks, transforming them into nature's wind chimes. She absolutely loved it!

After getting out of bed and completing her morning stretches, Alana cracked one of her bedroom windows to determine the outside temperature. Goosebumps spread up her arm as a cool current rushed in through the small opening.

"Whoa! Chilly!" she said as she rushed to close the window. She walked out of her bedroom and stood there for a moment, staring out into her immaculate loft. Her beautiful home, which took up the entire top floor of the four-story building she owned, was a far cry from what it was the first time she saw it. But even in its previous decrepit state, she saw its potential. She had a knack for seeing greater possibility in things that appeared desolate to others. After spending a pretty penny to have it renovated and upgraded, it was now one of the nicest buildings on the block. She sashayed across the room in a sexy swift stride before arriving at the big brown double doors across from the bathroom. She flung them open like she was sneaking up on someone before whispering to what stood before her.

"I've been waiting to have you on me all summer long," she said, wrapping her arms around the fall wardrobe that hung in her closet.

Fall fashion, in her eyes, was definitely the most fabulous. Thick tweed blazers, long skirts, knee-high boots, faux or even real furs became a part of her everyday life. Even casual clothing looked dressy when she paired it with the right leather jacket or stylish driver's cap. She pulled out a crisp white, form-fitting tuxedo shirt with black stone buttons, sleek black slacks, and black stiletto pumps with gold heels. She reached up on the top shelf where her jewelry box sat and retrieved her gold cuff links, a gold and ruby necklace and matching stud earrings.

She laid her ensemble on the dining room table to the left of her and retreated to the bathroom to get ready. After her shower, Alana went to the vanity in her bathroom to apply her makeup. Every time she looked in the mirror, she felt like a lighter, younger version of her grandmother was staring back at her. Alana shared a lot of her grandmother's features: high-defined cheek bones, small almond-shaped eyes, naturally long dark lashes and a deep dimple in her right cheek. The only difference was Grandma Marra was a beautiful brown, and Alana was what her aunt from down south called "High Yella." She didn't take after her mother much. Alana had only seen her mother in pictures because she died when Alana was an infant. And if she had any sort of resemblance to her father, she wouldn't know it. Bad blood between her grandmother and him had kept him out of Alana's life.

Alana had brown hair, which she'd recently cut into a sassy bob, with auburn-colored highlights in the front. She stood about 5 feet, 6 inches tall, with a petite figure that had curves in all the right places. After applying her makeup, she looked in the mirror again for one last look. She smiled and turned off the lights as she thought to herself, *"Something good is going to happen today!"* Looking over her place once more, she realized it was now 9:30 a.m. She sprayed on some perfume and finally exited the loft. She opted for the stairs, which were right next to the old-fashioned cage elevator. It was the one feature that convinced her to buy the building in the first place.

On her way down the echoing staircase, she ran into one of her tenants. The third floor of her building had been converted into four spacious lofts, which she rented out. Unit 3A was occupied by Carolyn, an elementary school teacher. Unit 3B was rented out to a young medical student from India named Samir. In unit 3C was a newly married couple, Sarah and Mike, who had a small dog named Sophie. Finally, unit 3D was rented out to a ballroom dance instructor and widower named Bill.

"Hi, Carolyn!" Alana said as she came up behind her on the stairwell. "How are things?"

"Well, Alana, I'm okay for a Monday. But Friday I'll be even better. I love my students, but there is nothing like getting a break from them."

Both women laughed as they walked out the door into the private parking area in back before encouraging each other to have a good day. A couple of steps away from the secured entrance to the lofts was the back door to Alana's business. On the second and main floor was her restaurant, which had two levels. It was a very popular cappuccino and wine bar in Midtown called The Cocoa Marra. It carried some of the finest exotic coffee, espresso, wine and cognac.

The menu consisted of gourmet dishes, one-of-a-kind hors d'oeuvres and appetizers. More than anything, the establishment was well known for the chocolate-covered, wine-infused strawberries, which were served with every bottle of wine purchased. Customers in a romantic mood could also order the strawberries separately. The atmosphere was usually that of a melting pot, filled with businessmen in suits, hipsters with pink and blue hair, college students and couples. It had become the spot where people of different cultures and occupations converged to mingle and socialize. It was a hit from the moment it opened.

As she entered the back door, which led directly into the kitchen, she could hear the sounds of Carlos Santana's "Smooth" blaring from the radio. There she found Diego, the sous chef, who was already preparing for the early lunch crowd. He was always the first one in.

"Good morning, boss," he said in a long drawn out voice, as if he was teasing her. As usual, he was bearing a big, bright smile. Diego was one of Alana's first employees and one of the few who still remained with her from the very start. He came highly recommended by a friend who worked with him before. He was a stocky Mexican in his late thirties with short, dark, thick spiked hair, dark thick eyebrows and a neatly trimmed goatee. He was a hard worker who always strived for perfection, which made him a pit bull in the kitchen.

He had the gifted ability to fix a problem before it had time to spread. But even through his intensity to have a well-ran kitchen, he had a very welcoming, funny side. He was never late, and he'd only missed work twice in the five years of his tenure at The Cocoa Marra--both being the days his children were born. He was extremely dedicated to his wife, Carla, who was his high school sweetheart. That was something Alana always admired about him. Every year, he and Carla celebrated their anniversary with friends, family and the staff at the restaurant, where he always made her a signature dish.

"Diego, my sweet! Bright and early as usual, I see. Nice weekend, I presume?"

"Of course! Gigi is waiting for you with her morning coffee, and here is yours," he said, handing her a cup. Alana inhaled the fresh beans deeply before smiling and offering assistance.

"Ahh, bless you! Need any help?" Diego looked at her as if the question were the most ridiculous thing he had ever heard.

"Are you kidding me? My stooges will be here shortly to take all of my orders in an attempt to impress me. Go!" he said, waving her off with a knife.

Alana put up her hands in retreat and continued through the kitchen into the restaurant. The room was large with dark hardwood floors and exposed brick walls. On the first level were small tables with little candles in the middle of them. The tables for two were mostly aligned along the six large windows that were in the front of the restaurant. The tables set for four were in the middle of the room, spaced perfectly for staff to maneuver during rushes. By the front door was a small waiting area sectioned off by a glass partition. Written on it in gold were the words, "The Cocoa Marra." Red velvet window benches provided seating for customers while they waited. In front of the waiting area was the hostess' podium and, behind the podium, was one end of the bar, which stretched all the way down by the kitchen door.

The wooden bar, which had grapevines carved into it, was custom made. Matching custom shelving lined the brick wall behind the bar and surrounded a painting of Alana's grandmother, Marra. Each shelf displayed the top wine choices of the week, as well as the featured cognac. Small wine fridges were tucked away discreetly under the countertops, helping to cut down on the trips staff had to make to the wine cellar in the basement. In the left corner behind the bar was a shiny silver and gold espresso machine with an old-school pressure gauge and lever, which added a touch of character to the bar.

In front of the bar were multiple round bar stools with red leather seating. Larger parties usually required the booths along the back wall. The shell-shaped booths were blood red velvet upholstery, with the option of adding chairs to the outer side of the table to accommodate even larger parties. One end of the booths started at a wooden partition, which separated it from the kitchen. At the other end of the booths was a spiral staircase that led to the second level. On both levels, the restrooms with uniformed attendants could be found by the stairs.

Unlike the first floor, the second level was more intimate. Only the outer perimeter of the room was aligned with tall, two-seater tables, which were good for drinking and mingling. The middle of the room was completely open, allowing patrons to see down to the first floor or up to the second. Dark metal railing, which matched the spiral staircase, provided a barrier to protect patrons from falling and acted as a post for the string patio lights that stretched from one side of the room to the other. It created an almost star-like ceiling for customers on the first floor. In addition, on the second level, two sets of red velvet chairs sat by the windows, each with a coffee table in the middle. This provided a more laid-back atmosphere for those wanting to engage in a more personal interaction. Large murals decorated the walls on each side of the room. They were hand-painted by a local graffiti artist. One mural featured people of all races dining and drinking, and the other reflected those same people dancing.

On the second level was a small corridor, which was used by staff. In it was a small wooden door that, when lifted, revealed a dumbwaiter elevator. Alana had it installed so servers would not have to struggle to bring trays up the staircase. Her favorite feature, of course, was the wine cellar in the basement. It was large and exquisitely stocked with both expensive and rare wines. Her place was beautiful and one of a kind. It could best be described as "high end meets hipster."

She continued through the dining area until she reached her best friend, Gigi, who was sitting at a table by the window. Gigi hadn't even looked up yet; she continued sipping her coffee and reading her newspaper. Alana took a seat across from her for their usual morning chat.

"Ms. Campbell," Alana said as she sat down.

"Ms. Jones. Could it be?" Gigi asked as she looked at her thin gold wrist watch. "Did I beat the early bird this morning?"

"Well, G, some of us require more beauty sleep than others. We can't all be as naturally beautiful as you."

"So true! So true!"

They laughed in unison as they continued sipping their coffee. Gigi and Alana had been best friends most of their lives. Alana's grandmother, who raised her, and Gigi's parents had them both enrolled in the same daycare when they were children. After a small squabble over cookies, the girls were inseparable. There was nothing they didn't know about each other and nothing they wouldn't do for one another.

When Gigi graduated from school for fashion design, Alana surprised her by leasing the small business space across the street from hers for a full year so that Gigi could open Cloth. The boutique featured clothing by well-known designers, as well as original designs from her up and coming line called "Chocolate Couture." She was a beautiful woman who could have modeled her own clothes, as she stood at 5 feet, 9 inches tall with beautiful, flawless skin the color of dark chocolate. She was very slim with shoulder-length curly hair and hauntingly beautiful hazel eyes. Her beauty seemed almost unreal.

She was wearing a lime green, long-sleeve satin blouse with a deep plunge. The color accentuated her skin tone all too perfectly. Her skinny gold necklace with matching dangling earrings, skin-tight, knee-length black pencil skirt and black stilettos made her look like a true diva. Gigi tapped her thumb ring against the coffee cup until she got her friend's attention. Alana stared at her thumb for a moment before rolling her eyes and asking her, "What is it?"

"Well, Brian has this friend and he saw a pic-"

"No! No! No, Gigi! I don't want to meet any more of Brian's friends," she said, cutting her off.

Gigi smacked her lips and continued drinking her coffee. She had been with her boyfriend, Brian, a handsome bank manager, for almost two years. Ever since they'd got together, she often tried to hook Alana up with either one of his friends or business counterparts. Unfortunately, after previously agreeing to go on a few of the dates, and later regretting it, Alana was no longer eager for their failed matchmaking skills.

"And why not?" Gigi questioned with sass.

"Do you really have to ask?"

"Oh, come on! They have not been *that* bad. What about David?!"

"Ah! The uggo. Did you ever pay attention to his face? It looked like his mother should have used birth control."

"And Henry?"

"The mama's boy? Instead of ordering a martini, he should have just asked for her breast milk in a glass--shaken, not stirred!"

"Nelson?"

"Mr. Dull! The man's idea of an exciting weekend is how many pieces of lint he can pull off of his sweater!"

"And I guess there was something wrong with Ryan, too?"

"As a matter of fact, there was! The man's breath was so bad that it seared off a nice chunk of my hair. Why do you think I got this haircut?"

"Girl, stop it!" Gigi said, laughing.

"I'm serious. You aren't complaining because you got the coolest one in the group!"

"Well, don't say I never tried. I sure do wish I knew what you were looking for," Gigi said.

"I'm looking for someone that will make me want *him* more than I want sex, that I'll love more than wine, and that I'll need more than chocolate!"

"Honey, please! If you meet someone like that, we'll both be amazed."

Alana skimmed through the paper while her bestie went over the morning schematics. Suddenly, they heard the rumbling of a motorcycle coming down the block. With a smirk, Gigi announced, "Here comes Mr. Perfect," as the ladies continued sipping. After a while, the ladies heard Diego confirming the day's menu with Simeon, the head chef, whom had just entered the back door. Moments later, heavy footsteps crossed the room and, before long, he was standing at the table. Without hesitation, he set down his espresso and bent over to kiss Alana's temple.

"Good morning, boss," he said before turning his attention to Gigi. In their usual silly, but flirty banter, he grabbed her hand and kissed it. "And good morning to you, too, my chocolate enchantress."

"Well, hello, my sexy sushi roll!" Gigi responded with spunk.

Simeon and Alana had been friends since college. Besides being a very talented and sought after chef, he was, in a word, *beautiful*! He stood at about 6'1" with a slim, but chiseled, build. He looked like he could have been a spokesperson for a cologne advertisement. He was the result of a Japanese father, and a mother who was half black and half French. His skin, which looked like it had been lightly kissed by the sun, masked his fiery, and sometimes hard to deal with, personality. In addition to English, he was fluent in Japanese, French and Spanish. If that wasn't enough to make him popular with the ladies, his skills in the bedroom could only be rivaled by his talent in the kitchen. If one didn't fall in love with his looks or his charm, tasting his cooking would surely seal the deal.

He and Alana had a brief fling when they were twenty, but nothing that she took too seriously. They were better off as friends, in her book, and she couldn't ask for a better one. After Simeon sat down, he sipped his coffee with a smirk as he looked back and forth between the ladies, hinting that he wanted one of them to ask him something. Alana peered over her paper and noticed his attempt to gain attention. She rolled her eyes again, this time at her other best friend, and giggled. She finally decided to ask him the question he seemed so desperate to answer.

"What's going on with you? Is the Victoria's Secret fashion show in town or something?"

"Nope," he answered.

"Let me try. Another woman vowed to be your faithful, dedicated love slave?" Gigi asked.

"Come on now. It's only Monday. That usually happens on Wednesdays," he shot back sarcastically.

"Well then, do us a favor; spare us the guessing game already. What has you as giddy as a preteen at a boy band concert?" Alana demanded.

"I'm in! I'm going to Le Cordon Bleu in Paris!" he exclaimed.

Both women gasped while beaming with pride. They were overjoyed for their friend's accomplishment. Gigi clapped her hands and smiled, while Alana jumped up from her chair to give him a bear hug. She knew how important this was for Simeon. He was already a successful chef who was often praised by food critics. Despite the fact that his friends and family probably thought he was crazy for leaving in the midst of such a successful run, he felt like the only thing that would make him feel truly untouchable was if he obtained the esteemed "Le Grand Diplôme."

The three of them chatted back and forth for a while about the good news before Alana grabbed his hand. She suddenly realized that, not only was one of her best friends going away for nine months, but she also needed to find a head chef to take over for him. Simeon revealed that he had already given it some thought. He felt Diego was ready and capable of taking over in his absence. He had been grooming him for the past couple of years and was confident about leaving his growing legacy in his hands. However, Alana would need to find a sous chef. Unfortunately, Simeon didn't feel like any of the other kitchen staff was responsible, nor skillful enough, to take Diego's spot. Alana agreed and decided that after making the announcement of Simeon's departure, she'd start the hunt for a new sous chef.

At 10:30 a.m., Gigi headed across the street to open the boutique. Once the entire staff arrived at The Cocoa Marra, Alana called an emergency meeting. With everyone gathered around the dining room, she announced that Simeon would be going to Paris in four months to attend Le Cordon Bleu and that Chef Diego would take his place as head chef. As expected, Diego was overcome with gratitude. He hugged Simeon and Alana before rushing off to the office to call Carla.

The response to Simeon's leaving was bittersweet. The staff, especially the female staff, liked him very much. Everyone soon dispersed to their stations as Alana, Simeon and Diego had one more quick pow wow in the office. The three discussed their concerns about the need for a qualified sous chef, who could keep up with the fast pace, high expectations and occasional overtime. But Diego was certain that he had the perfect solution. Just that quickly, he thought of an old friend and colleague he'd met in culinary school, Alex.

Chapter | 2

The following day went by swiftly for Alana. It had officially been 24 hours since Simeon delivered the news that would change his life and her business. The weather couldn't seem to make up its mind, having changed from sunny to cloudy, then back to sunny again. The cool, uneventful Tuesday gave her some time to herself, which was rare. All day, she'd been thinking about the things she needed to get in order. To clear her mind, she decided to go to Donnie's Basement, her favorite second-hand store, to see about some old records. Over the years, she'd built up quite the collection.

It started the year her grandmother passed away. Among many other keepsakes, she left Alana three crates full of her favorite records. Most of them were jazz and soul, with a few other genres thrown in. She figured a little wine and music was sure to help her relax and make her thoughts more lucid. After a short drive, she arrived at Donnie's, excited to see what he would surprise her with today. The owner, a retired roadie who stayed true to his Rock 'n' Roll flare, often had people come in off the street to either sell or donate items they found or inherited. Their unwanted gems were treasures in his eyes.

He carried everything in his store: old clothing, figurines, ancient electronics and more. His regulars always got first dibs. He put aside small boxes with items for those whom he knew were collectors. A few days earlier, he'd called Alana to let her know that a young woman had brought in some records if she wanted to come check them out. As she walked through the door, Donnie was eager to greet her with a smile.

"Hello, love," he said with his thick English accent.

"Donnie, my sweet," she said as he kissed her hand. "What you got for me today?"

"Let me grab them from the back."

As he disappeared through the door, Alana figured she could do some browsing until he returned. In the clothing section, she came across a 50s style dress that reminded her of the feminine-looking women she saw in old magazines. She quickly removed her leather jacket, and grabbed the navy blue and white dress off the hanger. She held it up to herself in the mirror as she tilted her head from side to side, the way she often did when trying on clothes. She wondered if the dress looked as good on her as it had on the ladies back then.

"Perfect!" she heard a deep voice say behind her.

"You think so?" she asked, turning to face the source of the compliment.

Standing before her was one of the sexiest men she had ever seen. Who the hell was he, and why hadn't she ever seen him before? The question swirled in her mind as their eyes locked briefly. She sized him up, her eyes scanning his body from head to toe. *"He is the perfect serving of milk chocolate,"* she thought to herself. *"A real feast to behold."* She nibbled on her lip, unable to refrain from admiring his smooth brown skin. It looked like it would melt if the sun rested on it for too long.

He wasn't extremely tall, but just tall enough to make him well worth the climb. The thin, light grey sweater and black jeans he wore showed off his physique quite nicely. With his build, it was evident that he was no stranger to the gym. His broad tapered shoulders and chiseled chest looked indestructible through the thin layer of clothing. His low-cut hair and scruffy beard, which was neatly lined up and trimmed, accentuated his ruggedly handsome face. It was hard to put a finger on his age because he looked mature, yet still youthful. And those eyes! His dark brown eyes looked like pools of honey when they caught the right light. They appeared somewhat intimidating with the dark, sharp brows that hovered above them. But, when he smiled, the intensity melted away, transferring itself to the feeling that radiated through her entire body. He *literally* made her hot!

"I can assure you that you and that dress were made for each other."

They stared at each other for a moment, both obviously taken aback by the sight of the other. Alana turned back to the mirror, trying to play it cool, although her instant attraction to him set her soul on fire. He watched her boldly, not once breaking his stare, as if he wanted to make it known that he couldn't take his eyes off her.

"Have you ever fallen in love at first sight?" he asked her, smiling. Alana laughed lightly before hanging the dress back up. "How do you know if I've ever fallen in love *at all*?"

Although she came off as simply playing coy, Alana really hadn't been as lucky with love as one would think--and it wasn't for lack of trying! She dated here and there, dating every kind of guy from corporate executives to high school basketball coaches. But, for some reason, the relationships always reached a certain point and she'd suddenly lose interest. There was always something missing. If they had a great friendship, the sexual chemistry was off. If they had great sex, the communication was off. If they had great communication, he was off! She started to wonder if she just hadn't found the right person yet, or if something was seriously wrong with *her*. She had yet to find the complete package. She had yet to reach the level of satisfaction she'd always associated with finding *real* love. The thought that she'd ever find "the one" out there somewhere started to fade from her mind. None of her previous encounters amazed her.

Her longest relationship, which had ended two years prior, lasted for a year. It ended when her ex, Louis, told her that he was in love with her and could see them having a long life together. Unfortunately, she couldn't say the same and, after while, it caused a strain on the relationship. She had a great time with him; however, as things between them progressed, she realized her feelings had not and she was back at square one. Even her sex life was lacking. She hadn't been intimate in seven months and, even then, it was a huge mistake!

One night, she and Louis ran into each other while they were both out with friends. The groups ended up merging and partying the night away. After quite a few drinks, she and Louis went home together. The next morning, he assumed they were reconciling, but Alana hadn't received that memo. In fact, it only made her realize that their breakup was the right thing to do; there was no *real* chemistry. The revelation jump-started her involuntary celibacy streak, which was still going. Sadly, her most consistent "relationship" with a man had been her *friendship* with Simeon.

"Well, if you've never been in love, I'd love to be the one to change that," he said, gazing at her intensely. "Maybe that dress wasn't the only thing made for you." Alana could feel something stirring inside her. She started to say something to the overly confident stranger, when Donnie suddenly appeared with the records.

"Sorry, love. I got a call," Donnie said.

She smiled and grabbed the records, flipping through them with excitement. Billie Holiday, Big Maybelle, Little Jimmy Scott and James Moody were all in the midst of the small pile Donnie had saved for her. Her excitement almost made her forget the handsome stranger was there…*almost*! Once again, he spoke to her, sending chills up her spine.

"I see you like old things," he said.

"I like young things, too!" she said with sass. "And I wouldn't call these old. I'd call them educational. You can understand the present better if you take a glimpse into the past."

"So, you're looking for someone to teach something?" he asked flirtatiously as he grabbed one of the records. "I can teach you a thing or two. You think you know music, huh?"

"More than you'd be willing to give me credit for."

"Something tells me you could talk me into giving you anything," he fired back.

Alana couldn't believe the feeling of nervousness that took over her. *"I don't get nervous,"* she thought to herself. But, she was. In fact, he gave her a feeling she'd never experienced before. From the corner of her eye, she could see the stranger looking her up and down as if he was hungry and she was his last meal. He asked Donnie for a pen and wrote on the back of a receipt he'd pulled from his pocket. As Donnie rang up the records one by one, the stranger wrote quickly, in hopes of finishing before Donnie was done. Once Donnie gave Alana the total, the stranger handed back the pen and folded the small piece of paper, handed it to Alana and walked out of the store. The door chime persuaded her to take one last look at the stranger as he exited. She looked behind her and saw that he was sneaking one more look, as well.

"Handsome guy, eh?" Donnie asked while ringing her up.

"He's okay," she answered with a cracking voice.

She thanked him for the newest additions to her collection and told Donnie to call her if anymore came in. Once outside, she hurried to her car as small drops of rain fell onto her skin. She hustled as quickly as her stiletto ankle boots and skin-tight jeans would allow, hoping not to get drenched. She closed the car door just in time enough to avoid the sudden downpour that soon pounded her car. After putting the bag in the passenger seat, she rushed to open the small piece of paper. In addition to his phone number, he had written her a small note, which read:

I admire your fascination with the old ,but call me when you want something new to captivate you. Besides, we already have two things in common. One, we're both music lovers! When you call me later, I'll tell you what the second thing is. Hope to hear from you, Al.

Alana could still smell the scent of his cologne dancing in her nostrils. "Perhaps this could be the start of something new," she thought to herself as she drove off into the autumn storm.

The week moved along swiftly, but it wasn't until Alana received a text from Sheree, her hairdresser, asking if she was still coming for her appointment, that she'd even realized it. *"Had Friday really come that quickly?"* she asked herself. Sheree was so accustomed to Alana arriving fifteen minutes early that, when she read 1:45 p.m. on the clock, she wanted to make sure everything was okay. Alana's mind had become overwhelmed over the past few days, which seemed to have no shortage of life-changing events. She hurried to get dressed after telling her talented beautician she would be there within ten minutes. Alana couldn't believe she had completely forgotten about her appointment.

Simeon's big announcement, which would have been the only thing on her mind any other time, fell in line behind what was *really* consuming her thoughts. It was in fact the run-in she'd had with the sexy, manly marvel. The memory of his voice and the thought of his face kept her mind in a constant state of cloudiness. Although she wanted so badly to call him, she had yet to do so because she had no idea what to say. Usually, men asked for her number. She had never made the first call, and it was throwing her off her game.

After rushing through the doors of Hollywood Hair Salon, she realized her timing was perfect as Sheree's last client proceeded to get out of the chair. A few moments later, she was leaning her head back into the shampoo bowl, enjoying the lather of the soapy suds being massaged into her hair and scalp. Her eyes closed as Sheree's fingertips made circles throughout her wet mane, and the two women discussed the beautician's two-month-old daughter. Sheree had only been back to work a couple of weeks, and Alana wondered if she missed being at home with her baby girl. Sheree expressed how great her husband was with the baby and how she really appreciated the thoughtful man that he was. But, make no mistake about it, her appreciation for her husband and love for her new role as a mother didn't come without some drawbacks.

"Girl, I *needed* to get out of the house," Sheree said. "My husband doesn't want to go anywhere and doesn't want to leave the baby with anyone--not even his own mama!"

"I hear ya! I've been all work and no play myself lately," Alana responded.

"Well, I'll tell you what. The two of you are coming out with me tonight!" interjected Jackie, the owner of the salon. "My old man and his jazz quartet are playing at

Smooth Grooves tonight and I have some extra tickets. You tell your husband he's watching the baby tonight and you...I know you have no excuse!" she said, playfully pointing at Alana.

The two women didn't have to give it much thought. One short phone call and a couple of hours later, the ladies were arranging where and when they'd meet up for ladies' night out.

At 8:45 p.m., they met at the door of Smooth Grooves, dressed to the nines. They barely made it on time due to the heavy traffic, which was no surprise for a Friday night downtown. When they walked in, heads turned as what looked like a walking ice cream sundae, equipped with French vanilla, caramel and chocolate-colored skin tones strutted through the crowd with confidence. Jackie's boyfriend, a handsome man named Henry, who was in his mid-forties, had reserved a table up front for her. It would have been a real treat had Alana not found his set to be so awful. As somewhat of a jazz aficionado, she knew good delivery when she heard it. On the contrary, she cringed with disappointment when she didn't. She remained grateful for the free ticket she received which, in her opinion, was well worth its price.

Once it was time for the band to take a short intermission, Jackie asked Alana to go with her outside so that she could talk to Henry, who she knew would be taking a smoke break. Sheree volunteered to stay behind and watch over their drinks, which also gave her the opportunity to make a quick call to her husband to check on him and the baby. Outside, the ladies ran into Henry, who was furiously puffing on a cigarette. He was concerned that his trumpet player sounded *off* during the set. Both women complimented him on how well everything was going, in an attempt to reassure him of himself, even though Alana secretly agreed with him.

Jackie took a joint out of her purse and lit it. She inhaled deeply and gave Henry a long kiss as she exhaled the smoke into his mouth, hoping to relax him. The two giggled as he kissed her on the forehead and rushed back in. Jackie took one more puff of the herbal refreshment before asking Alana if she was ready to return inside. Alana told her that she would be in after she finished checking her voicemail. She listened intently at the message Simeon had left her, asking if she was at home bored and for her to call him if she wanted some company. She sipped some scotch from the glass she had snuck out of the club and laughed, rolling her eyes at his assumption that she was sitting at home with nothing to do. A quick message from Gigi followed, who inquired about why she hadn't heard from Alana all day.

She giggled at the threatening voicemail before honing in on the deep, and somewhat familiar, voice behind her. She hung up the phone and turned around to confirm the identity of the mystery man who stood talking with two other gentlemen. Lo and behold, it was the man from Donnie's Basement, Al! Her eyes looked him up and down as she stared in a satisfied silence. He was definitely wearing the hell out of his suit, as she scanned him like she was a price gun and he was for sell. She gave him a twice over before her eyes unwittingly stopped at his crotch.

"You sure you can handle something that stiff?"

"Excuse me?!"

"The scotch. Are you sure you can handle something that stiff?"

"Oh! Wow…yes…I uh…I'm definitely sure."

"Are you alright, Alana?"

"Yes I'm f,f,f—"

"Fine? I can't argue with that," he said.

There he was again, for the second time in one week, and sneaking up on her as usual. He looked scrumptious as he stood there in a crisp white shirt, black suit with a satin lapel, and a dark red handkerchief, which had been folded into a three stairs fold. Ironically enough, it matched her dress perfectly. A group of women who walked in between them to go inside nearly caught a case of whiplash trying to check him out.

"What are you doing here, besides starting a fan club?" she asked.

"I'm guessing the same as you, young lady. I came to hear some good music."

"You might be disappointed then!" she blurted out. "Oops! Did I just say that out loud?"

"Yes, you did," he answered, laughing.

"Sorry. I've been told I can be a little too blunt sometimes."

"Please don't apologize. I love a woman that gets straight to the point. Beating around the bush is for gardeners."

"I guess I was just expecting something…*different*. And I definitely wasn't expecting to see you here."

"Obviously, tonight's the night for the unexpected to happen."

"Wait a minute. How did you know my name? I never told you."

"I asked your friend, the one you left at the table. I saw you when you first walked in. She told me flat out, 'That's Alana! She's 31, successful and single!'"

"Wow! She certainly was subtle," Alana said. "And that would make you…"

"Al. I'm 35, mildly successful and single, as well."

"Ha! And you're calling me a *young* lady? Because this single gray hair makes you old, huh?" she said, rubbing her hand over his hair. She quickly realized how touchy feely the scotch had made her, causing her to quickly snatch her hand away and apologize. She nervously fiddled with the belt of her long black pea coat as he smiled at her in amusement. He tried to ward off her embarrassment by offering his version of a comforting word.

"Don't be embarrassed. You can rub on me anytime," he joked.

The two laughed and stood trading looks for a few moments before two gentlemen came outside, searching for Al. He introduced his comrades to Alana before she excused herself. She hoped to return to a new and improved sound, instead of the awful music that was playing when she'd left. With her back to him, she smiled and clutched the glass tightly before he called out to her once more.

"Hey! You never called to see what the second thing is that we have in common."

Alana turned around and walked up to him. She stood closely as she stared into his eyes for a moment, causing him to look completely caught off guard, but intrigued. She moved to his side and leaned in as if she were about to whisper something into his ear. She inhaled the enchanting smell of his cologne and let the words spill from her lips.

"I still have time to call you. If you believe there is something else we have in common, it will always be there, whether I call you today or tomorrow, right?"

Alana pulled away as they both smiled. She walked back to the door and held on to the handle as he winked at her. Once back inside, the girls immediately questioned Alana non-stop about the handsome man that had been so eager to meet her. She held it together, but secretly, she couldn't wait to get home and put the number he'd previously given her to use. Thirty minutes passed before Alana decided she couldn't take one more note. The band was butchering one of her favorite tunes and she decided it was time to politely make her exit. She thanked Jackie for the invite, and told the ladies she was exhausted and would catch up with them the next time. As she made her way to the door, she looked toward the bar to find Al staring at her, just as he had in the store. His friend was babbling to him uncontrollably, but he was more engaged with the non-verbal communication between him and Alana. He waved goodbye, using his thumb and pinkie to mimic a phone. He mouthed the words, "Call me" as Alana waved back, knowing that once she got home, she was surely going to reach out to him.

After taking off her clothes and makeup, she was all too excited to find out a little more about Al, who seemed to be popping up everywhere. She threw on her satin robe, curled up on the couch with a bowl of ice cream, and thought long and hard about what she would say. His unnerving ability to remain cool at all times caused her to be even more nervous. She didn't want to seem too eager, but she didn't want to come off as uninterested either. After about an hour of thinking of an opening line, which was rare for the normally confident word-smith, she decided to text him something simple.

Alana: Hi Al. It's Alana. Still up?

Al: Hello beautiful! I am now.

Alana: Sorry to text so late.

Al: Trust me, I couldn't wait to hear from you, no matter the time. I've been thinking about you since you left the club.

Alana: Is that right? And what were you thinking?

Al: I was thinking that I'd love to take you to a place where there is no doubt you would enjoy the music. And maybe even my company as well.

Alana: Both sound great, but my schedule is crazy right now. Can I let you know next week?

Al: Of course. I'm not going anywhere ;)

Alana: Well, goodnight Al. It was nice to see you again.

Al: Goodnight Alana. The pleasure was ALL mine!

Alana put the phone down and smiled, wondering how long she could manage *not* to text him again. Desperation was not good for her complexion! But, she had to admit, the manly, milk chocolate, mystery man had truly piqued her interest, and she yearned to see him again.

Chapter | 3

"I met someone," Alana said, right before she took a sip of her morning coffee. Gigi was so shocked by the announcement that she almost broke her cup as she sat it down on the small matching saucer. She stammered to find her words as she shifted in her seat, prepared to grill her best friend, who was way too calm in her opinion about her new mystery man.

"What! Who, where, how, when?"

"Okay, okay! Well, the first time—"

"Wait a minute! This is a mini-series?" Gigi joked.

"Yup, so get comfortable and grab some popcorn. The first time was the other day at Donnie's Basement, and then again last night at Smooth Grooves. I seem to keep running into this guy."

"Sounds cosmic. So, what does he look like?" Gigi asked, lifting her brow.

"Girl! Tall, fit, handsome. And his skin?! Girl, it's so smooth and chocolate that it has to taste as sweet as it looks!"

"I'm getting a cavity just hearing about it!"

The ladies giggled before Alana continued. Gigi listened intently and watched how Alana's face lit up as she spoke about Al and the nervous feeling she had during their interactions. It had been a long time since Gigi saw such a look of excitement in Alana's eyes about meeting someone new. And, as far back as she could remember, no one had ever caused Alana to become tongue tied. It wasn't long before the conversation was interrupted by the sound of heavy feet crossing the wooden floor, the same as they did every morning. The echo was always so loud due to the absence of customers and music that they would wait for him to sit before continuing. The girls sipped and smiled as Simeon sat down between them. He grabbed Alana's coffee from her hand and drank the rest of it, just to annoy her.

She slapped his arm as he smiled and said, "Happy Saturday, ladies! So, what are you talking about that's got you all quiet all of a sudden?"

They looked at each other, scrambling for an answer. Alana was always hesitant to tell Simeon about anyone new. No matter who it was, he found something wrong with them, whether it be the way they met or the way the person looked. She decided she had already been doing enough of that on her own. She didn't need his unrequested assistance.

"We were just discussing—"

"Chocolate! We were just discussing chocolate," Alana answered, interrupting Gigi.

As Simeon began giving his blow by blow of his wild events from the previous night, Alana tuned him out while wondering if she and Al would ever have any X-rated moments to brag about. The old friends soon wrapped up their coffee-filled conversation and proceeded to start their day. Gigi whispered to Alana that they would finish talking later just as a text message came through on Alana's phone; it was from Al. Alana sat back down in her seat by the window, excited as a kid in a candy store as she opened it.

It read: *I saw the sunrise this morning and I thought of you because of how beautiful it was. Even still, it does not compare to how stunningly beautiful you are. I hope you have a great day gorgeous!* Alana was beaming. *"Where did this handsome, Shakespearean come from?"* she thought to herself. She texted him back: *Thank you for thinking of me and for the well wishes. I hope your day is great as well handsome.* Alana put the phone on the table and laughed at the notion that she was becoming incurably infatuated with someone she barely knew. She spent the rest of the weekend plotting how she should tell Al that it was finally time to take him up on that offer. She decided she would contact him at some point during the week to see if they could make some music of their own.

Once the weekend passed, time seemed to fly by as Alana looked at the calendar on her phone. It was already Thursday, and the time had finally come to meet Diego's friend. Apparently, he'd just moved back to town and had put two very good offers on hold for the chance that he might get to work with his old pal again. Knowing that her most reliable employee wouldn't recommend anyone less than extraordinary, Alana agreed to meet with him. But she hoped that he would come well prepared, as she was not the type to be easily impressed. Besides, after dealing with Simeon's big announcement, and her back-to-back run-ins with Al, she was looking forward to focusing her thoughts on something other than those two.

The lunch rush was just starting to die down as she sat at one of the tables to have a short meeting with her "eyes and ears" of the restaurant: Simeon, Elizabeth and Damien. Elizabeth was the day manager. The married, proud mother of two was smart, sweet and very business-savvy. She saw everything as either a loss or gain, and had really helped promote the business when it first opened. Damien, the night manager, was the man everyone wanted to know. He was only twenty-two, but had already established a huge network of connections.

He also played a very intricate part in The Cocoa Marra's success with his monthly showcases. He invited jazz quartets to perform, spoken word artists to recite poetry, and even held a mix-and-mingle for young professionals. Last, but not least, of course, was her best friend, Simeon. Over the years, word had spread around town about his soon-to-be legendary culinary skills. On top of his success at the restaurant, he had recently persuaded Alana to expand the perimeters of the business and start high-end catering. With Diego's help, he took the initiative to bring in three interns solely for its purpose. They took on everything: anniversary parties, corporate meetings and even birthday extravaganzas for members of high society. Simeon proposed that they add items exclusively for catering customers only. Within three months, profits had tripled, and Alana renegotiated each of their contracts to make sure they were being well-compensated for their hard work and dedication. Now that things were transitioning, she was also hoping to negotiate a partnership with Simeon that would ensure an expansion of the business upon his return from Le Cordon Bleu.

At the end of their short meeting, she was joined by Greg, her financial advisor. He wanted to go over some numbers, seeing as it had been a good quarter for her and a few of her stocks were way up. She gleamed at the news of her ongoing success as customers chatted away and dined on their exquisite cuisine. Mellow music, the smell of food, and the rich scent of cocoa beans floated through the air.

It was almost 2 o'clock when she checked the time. The crowd was mostly businessmen and women who were grabbing a late lunch. At a table nearby, she could hear two men arguing over who would pick up the tab. At another table, a young woman was advising her co-worker to buy his wife some of the infamous strawberries for her birthday. Someone in the kitchen dropped some dishes and Alana jumped, wondering how much money that had just cost her. A couple of regulars waved goodbye as they were leaving, and one even stopped to say his hellos and compliment her on the dress she was wearing. It was the same guy she'd overheard discussing his wife's special day.

Offering up a charming smile and a hand shake, she let him know how pleased she was that he kept coming back. She also added that if he wanted to purchase the burgundy dress that he admired so, that it was sold at the boutique across the street. Inside, she laughed at the shameful plug she'd just done for her friend's business. But, she knew she'd do the same for her. Greg nodded at the gentleman as he spoke to him, as well. After the faithful patron left, they continued with their small meeting, which was soon interrupted again by an incoming call on Greg's cell phone. He asked Alana if it would be alright for him to take it, to which she had no objections.

She looked over her statements silently as he put up his index finger, indicating that he needed to step outside for a minute. Upon his return, he informed her that the caller was someone very important to them both.

"Mom said hi, and she'll see you next Thursday for lunch," he said.

"And how is Georgia?"

"She couldn't be happier that I'm getting married. Well, unless of course you were."

"Me? I have to have some prospects first."

"Are you actually trying? I know you can be pretty hard on the fellas."

"Gosh, you're starting to sound like Gigi!"

"No, no! I'm not gonna give you a hard time. I just can't believe you've never been in love."

"Well, I've had the puppy love thing. I've definitely had the lust thing. Just never the *real* thing."

"Just keep doing things the way you're doing them now; it will come. You're right not to look for it; let love find you. That's usually when it shows up."

"Are you sure you're Georgia's son? She thinks I should be out there with a heat-seeking missile, trying to find the hottest love affair possible," she said sarcastically.

"Look, mom just wants you to be happy. We all do."

"Let me ask you a serious question. How do you know it will work? You know, the love thing?" she asked him.

"You don't. You have to approach love the same way you do your investments. Even if I give you a prospectus, there's no guarantee it will pay off in the end. You just have to take a risk. Who knows, your big 'payout' might be waiting for you to invest yourself into him as we speak."

"If it's that simple, why doesn't 'Mr. Wonderful' just walk through that door right now?" They both looked at the door as Alana pointed and laughed hysterically as an elderly man in his seventies came walking in on his cane.

"Well, they say women want security. So, there you go! Social security!"

As with most of her associates, she and Greg had a relationship that was both business and personal. Not only did he provide her with sound financial advice, but he was also the son of Georgia Kinsley, her grandmother's best friend. Georgia became Alana's mentor after her grandmother died, and for good reason. She was one of the most high-powered corporate attorneys in the city, representing one of the largest companies in the Midwest. She had also become Alana's legal counsel after she went into business for herself.

Her love and influence meant just as much to her as her grandmother's had. She pushed Alana to complete college when her grandmother died suddenly during her freshman year. She was also the one to give her the loan to renovate her building and pursue her dreams. After paying Georgia back, Alana thought it would be smart to try some of the same investment practices. So, she sought out Greg for his expertise. Their conversation about love was about to go even deeper, until Greg's fiancée called to inform him that he was late for their appointment with the planner. The two quickly wrapped things up so he could join his bride-to-be.

Alana motioned for one of the servers to get her a drink. But, as her hand went in the air, her eyes wandered over to the end of the bar closest to the door. She couldn't believe who she saw standing there; it was Al! Al, the man who had made quite a first impression. The man who'd wrote her the alluring note. The man who looked so damn good in a suit that she would gladly finance his own personal line of fashion. The man she hadn't been able to stop thinking about! Alana had been so busy that she hadn't had time to do as she'd planned and take him up on his offer. Completely blindsided by the sight of him, she reminded herself not to appear too eager. She tried her best to focus on saying her goodbyes to Greg.

"Damn!" she thought to herself, as her inability to look away took her by surprise. She watched him talk to Mark, the bartender, who was usually the one with women staring at him due to his ice blue eyes, tattooed forearms and slicked back ash blond hair. His features gave him a sort of sexy, bad boy appeal. But it was Al whom she

couldn't stop looking at. Her heart raced, and her thighs tightened as she crossed her legs in an attempt to stop the warm sensation she felt between them. She and Gigi had always had an inside joke that if women give men "wood," then men must give women "river." For certain, she was experiencing some serious white water rafting!

Alana thought he might be looking to be seated since the hostess was missing from the podium. He sat the messenger-style bag he was carrying on one of the bar stools and took a seat. She couldn't help but wonder if she'd just jinxed herself. Had fate brought him in? Greg grabbed her arm and told her she had zoned out for a moment. After giving his sincerest apologies for having to leave so abruptly, she simply smiled and let him know that they could continue at another time.

Just as she was standing to see him out, Mark and her newfound friend started approaching her. It felt as if she was seeing him walk in slow motion. The song "Heaven Must Be Like This" by The Ohio Players rang in her ears. She didn't know if the song was actually playing, or if it was just in her mind. When the two men reached her, Mark introduced them officially.

"Hey, boss lady. This is Alex Wright, Diego's friend. He's here for an interview," he said before returning to the bar.

"Shit! This is not happening!" she thought to herself. The excitement she felt suddenly drained from her body. Undeniably, the attraction was still there. But, Alana had a strict code about dating employees…or, in his case, a potential one. She didn't believe in letting things get in the way of business. Perhaps she should have explained that to her mouth because she was tongue tied. When she finally gained her composure, she kindly introduced herself as if they'd never met.

"Hello, Alex. I'm Alana Jones. It's so very nice to meet you."

"Hello, Alana. Alex Wright and the pleasure is all mine!"

He was noticeably as stunned as she was, but realized just as she did that it would be better to appear not to know one another. His words almost escaped him when he extended his hand to shake hers. Their hands and eyes remained locked in an almost trance-like state. She was relieved when Simeon walked up behind her and introduced himself. Alex finally let go of her hand to shake his and, after a brief conversation, she suggested they go into the kitchen and reconvene in the office to conduct the interview.

Diego's face glistened with excitement once he saw Alex, but he remained professional and only offered up a hearty handshake. Alana, Elizabeth and Simeon sat behind the desk, like they were on a panel. They looked through copies of his resume and references, which were provided to each of them. They asked questions, one after the other, to get a better feel of his personality and ability to act quickly on his feet.

Alana struggled to concentrate, often finding herself staring at his mouth as he spoke. She wondered what those lips felt like. She wondered if he was a good kisser. She wondered if he was packing. She wondered if he liked to eat pussy! When she wasn't daydreaming, or fidgeting with her pearls, she was stumbling over her words. At one point, Simeon leaned over while Elizabeth continued the interview to make sure that

Alana was okay. He told her that she looked flushed and that he could handle the interview without her if she wanted. But she was determined to snap out of whatever ridiculous school-girl behavior she was succumbing to.

After what seemed like forever, the interview finally came to an end. Alana was still in a frazzled state when she shook Alex's hand and rushed out to the dining room, where Gigi was waiting at the bar for her afternoon espresso. Alana greeted her friend as calmly as she could, but gave her reason for concern due to her noticeably flustered state. Gigi really got concerned after hearing Alana order a glass of wine in the middle of the day. As she sipped from her coffee cup and waited for Alana to say something, it became apparent that she would have to be the one to break the silence.

"Everything okay?" Gigi asked.

"Of course," Alana answered, trying to loosen her collar.

"You sure? Because you seem a little wound up."

"Yeah...well...I just finished conducting an interview."

"You interviewed someone else, yet *you're* the one who's nervous?" she asked, confused.

Alana shrugged her shoulders and inquired about Gigi's day, hoping to distract her. Her friend began by thanking her for the business she had sent her way earlier in the day. She then told her that the gentleman not only bought the dress he'd been so taken with, but that her top sales girl, Lexa, had talked him into buying two of her original pieces. Lexa wasn't a regular at the restaurant, but she occasionally found her way through the door, hoping to catch a glimpse of Simeon.

The beautiful young Dominican girl with waist length black hair wasn't very good at hiding her crush. Her infatuation with him was known to some, but when it came to Simeon, he was either oblivious to it or didn't share the same feelings. Alana listened to what sounded like a lucrative day for the talented designer when, out of nowhere, Gigi smiled and turned her attention elsewhere. Simeon was walking Alex to the door when they stopped to speak to the ladies and offer an introduction. Alex was both charming and suave as he carried on the conversation.

"It was a pleasure to meet you, Ms. Campbell," Alex said. "And I hope to hear from you soon Ms. Jones."

Alana smiled and said goodbye as the men proceeded to the door. The warm cup of espresso rested comfortably in Gigi's hands as she giggled and blew into her drink to cool it down. She seemed all too pleased with herself, which spurred Alana's curiosity.

"What's so funny?" she asked.

"Well, I see why you're so worked up. Girl, you got river, didn't you?" she asked, giggling.

"What? Why would you ask me that?"

"Girl! That man is fine!"

"Fine? Is he? I hadn't noticed," Alana snapped.

"Please! It looks like somebody went to Build-a-Brotha and made that man! And what the hell is going on with you?" Gigi asked.

Alana grabbed her by the wrist and pulled her all the way back to the office in the kitchen. Gigi closed the door behind them, trying not to let on that she was concerned. Alana sat down behind the desk and put her fingertips to her temples. Gigi stood quietly waiting for her to tell her what bug seemed to have gotten up her butt.

"That was him!"

"That was who?"

"Remember the chocolate we told Simeon we were talking about? Alex is the chocolate!"

"Wait a minute. How did you not know this?" Gigi whispered aggressively.

"Girl, I know him as Al. And we hadn't exactly gotten around to what we did for a living!"

"Well, it's okay. Calm down. You can still see him. Girl, if he gives you river--"

"No! I won't—"

"What are you two ladies talking about?" Simeon interjected as he flung open the door out of nowhere.

"Field and Stream magazine. You know, camping, rivers--" Gigi said sarcastically before being kicked under the desk.

After rubbing her shin and making up something, she headed back to work, with Simeon walking out behind her to run his kitchen. Alana stared at his resume a little more thoroughly. His accomplishments were quite impressive. They stood out even more than his good looks. He'd previously worked at some very well-known places and had been mentored by one of the best. With every line that spelled out his life, her mind reverted back to his face, his voice and that body! She soon realized that she had been sitting there, daydreaming for twenty minutes, before snapping back into reality. She put down the resume and looked at the names of two other individuals who were recommended to her.

Her mind was made up; she would not be hiring Alex. She didn't know what the unnerving feeling was that he gave her, and she decided she didn't want to find out. She moved his manila folder to the bottom of the pile and looked over the other two resumes, preparing specific questions for each candidate. She wanted to have both interviews set up before the end of the week. That evening, as she returned home after quite an eventful day, her cell phone chimed. Without unlocking her screen, she noticed the words '*New Message*' at the top of her screen.

Al: Hi. I was wondering if you wanted to talk about today.

Alana: Why didn't you tell me your name was Alex?

Al: I mostly go by Al. I would have told you eventually.

Alana: Didn't it dawn on you when you found out my name was Alana that you were about to interview with someone by the same name?

Al: Diego told me that I would be interviewing with a woman named Elizabeth and the head chef, Simeon. He never said your name. Does this mean our date is off the table?

Alana hesitated before answering. It was true; they had met beforehand. It was true that he hadn't misled her in any way. It was true that she still wanted him! But she stuck to her guns, as she always did, and tried her best to let him down easily.

Alana: It was great interviewing you today. We will notify you soon to let you know whether or not you got the job. Goodnight Alex. She put the phone on the nightstand and stared at the ceiling, wishing things were different.

Chapter | 4

The next day, Alana found that she was still consumed with thoughts of Alex. She couldn't help but resent the dumb luck she had. Why did it have to be him? She pondered the thought as she put petty cash into the safe in the office. Like clockwork, she heard Diego greeting Simeon, and it wasn't long before he barged in all too excited. She braced herself for whatever it was he was going to say. The last time he rushed in this pleased with himself was when he delivered his big news. She sipped her coffee with one hand and used the other to make a circular motion, urging him to spit it out.

"Forget the other two interviews. Alana, you've got to hire him!"

"What? Why?" she asked, shocked.

"This guy is almost as amazing as me!"

And with that, Simeon told Alana all that he knew. He had been concerned about how *his* kitchen would be run in his absence, so he decided to do some digging on Alex. It wasn't that he didn't trust Diego, but he knew that friends would do and say just about anything to help each other out. In this case, it turned out that Diego had undercompensated his friend's achievements. Alex had graduated at the top of his class. A few phone calls revealed that he came highly recommended by every one of his former employers.

But what truly impressed Simeon was when Alex made headlines after being invited to cook for a dignitary. The high-ranking official had read about Alex in the newspaper the day after he and his buddy were arrested for feeding the homeless or, as the paper stated, "technically trespassing." He was contacted and personally congratulated for helping his community, before immediately being offered a job. That one job presented many opportunities to cater to others in high offices, some of whom were still waiting for his decision as he'd put them on hold to interview with Alana. But, on a more personal note for Simeon, the two men connected when they realized they had something else besides cooking in common.

Alex also spoke a little French because of his creole grandmother. According to Simeon, he was slightly rusty, but still good. Alana listened to her best friend go on and on about someone other than himself, which was truly out of his character. It was bad enough that she had been struggling all night to stop picturing Alex and hearing the soothing sound of his deep voice. But now, here was Simeon bragging about him first thing in the morning.

"Come on, Lana. I've got a good feeling about this guy. Have I ever steered you wrong?"

"I'll think about it," she said nonchalantly.

The handsome head chef turned back into the kitchen, baffled. She could tell by the look on his face that he was wondering why she didn't seem as impressed as he was. She closed the door and pulled out the other two resumes she had received along with Alex's. Alana looked over them carefully, one after the other. He really was the most qualified.

She considered how ridiculous she was being. How could she believe it was fair to consider passing over someone so incredible just to avoid interaction with him? She had never allowed her personal feelings to affect business decisions before, and she wasn't about to start now. It was already mid-September and she wanted to have someone start training A.S.A.P. Why not go with the best? She took a deep breath and called Simeon back into the office, after determining her feelings would just have to take a back seat. Besides, what harm could there possibly be in seeing a face like Alex's more often? With nine words, she gave in to her friend's persuasive request. "Call him up," she said. "See if he can start tomorrow."

Alana wasn't sure what she should prepare for, but she knew things were about to change. The next morning, Alana found herself up and at 'em even earlier than usual. *"What are you doing?"* Alana asked herself as she looked in the mirror. She realized that she'd been taking an unreasonable amount of time to get ready. *Coincidentally*, it just so happened to be Alex's first day. She tried to convince herself that he wasn't the reason, but surely, she wasn't putting in the extra effort for her lunch date with Georgia.

Technically, she didn't *need* to be there to greet her new employee. That was why she hired managers. But, she'd always made it a point to welcome new hires on their first day. One of the perks of living above her business, aside from someone making her morning coffee, was the fact that she could pop in at any time. She knew this kept the employees on their toes and performing their best. Excellent service produced happy customers, which meant there were fewer problems.

Today was going to be busy for her. She had an appointment with her accountant during the morning, lunch with Georgia in the afternoon, and a meeting in the evening with a potential client, who was interested in holding a fundraiser at the restaurant. Events like those brought in huge revenue and free additional advertisement for The Cocoa Marra. Her itinerary for the day would cause her to be in and out, and she realized she would barely see Alex. But Alana seemed hell bent on making sure their short interaction would be a memorable one. She rubbed her thighs to smooth the dark orange sweater dress clinging to her body, while reminding herself that he was an employee— nothing more. The calendar on her cell phone chimed, alerting her that it was time to get a move on.

After bypassing the elevator and taking the stairs as usual, Alana rushed through the back door while putting on her lip gloss, in hopes of grabbing her morning coffee from Diego. However, she found Alex there instead. She was excited by the sight of him. He stopped chopping just long enough for their eyes to lock. She rubbed her lips together to smooth on the gloss, but broke their hypnosis when she finally mustered up a quick,

"Good morning." Alex returned the greeting and, as she proceeded to walk past him, he suddenly called out to her.

"Alana, I have something that I think you want."

"What?!" she asked, whipping around with a surprised look on her face. It was as if he'd read her mind and was standing there, holding his dick in his hand.

"Here. Your morning coffee. Three creams, two sugars, piping hot. Is that right?"

"Oh…yes. Thank you, Alex."

"What did you think I was talking about?"

"Nothing!" she answered quickly. "I just thought Diego hadn't gotten around to it yet."

"He went up front to let in your friend, so I figured I'd help him out."

"You made this?" she asked.

"Yes. I made it my mission to find out just how you like it," he said, leaning onto the counter and glaring at her. Alana felt chills go up the back of her neck. She took note that her feelings were already clouded concerning him, so she didn't know whether he was flirting or not. Whatever the case, she felt she'd better address it.

"So, you didn't really answer me last night," he whispered. "Us going to listen to music, is it—"

"Yes, it's off the table. Things are different now," she said.

Alex nodded to let her know that he understood as he turned to resume his work. Alana walked toward the main room, but quickly caught his reflection in the window on the door. His eyes were glued to her ass, which seemed to have an extra switch in it suddenly. She stopped and turned to say something, but found herself speechless as he continued staring with no qualms about it.

"I can still look though, right?" he asked in the most alluring tone. "That's one of the best things about working here."

Alana turned back around and continued to the main room before he could see the smile forming on her face. Diego passed her and offered up his usual long drawn out, "Good morning, boss," followed by a little salute. The moment she sat down, Gigi immediately began talking about how cute Alex looked in his chef jacket. Alana casually laughed it off and told her that she'd already decided not to pursue things with him. Gigi voiced her disappointment as fantasies of Alex swirled in Alana's mind.

She innocently tuned her best friend out while daydreaming about him chopping those very same vegetables, shirtless. His broad muscular chest and arms tightened every time the chop of the knife came down. Gigi continued talking, not realizing that Alana hadn't heard a word. She imagined him placing the knife on the counter and wiping his hands with the towel that was hanging over his shoulder. She envisioned him throwing the towel and rushing toward her, pinning her to the wall. His hands slid down her body before firmly grabbing her…

"Alana!" Gigi yelled.

"I'm sorry girl. What?" she answered, snapping back into reality.

"I said Simeon's new car is nice, right?"

Alana nodded affirmatively as the two women listened to the engine of his new Porsche revving into the back parking lot. The shiny, black attention getter was a present from his father to congratulate him on his acceptance to Le Cordon Bleu. Simeon's father, Mr. Ito, was very wealthy. He had a master's degree in International Business, and he worked in import and export. He could more than afford the lavish gift for his son. He had a huge influence on Simeon and his younger brother, and was probably to blame for most of Simeon's cocky behavior since he very rarely denied him.

It wasn't long before the ladies heard him putting on his best 'tough chef' routine for Alex. Diego was used to him running a tight ship and was always amused to see the surprised look on a new person's face at how quickly Simeon wanted everything done. But Alex had an extensive background as a sous chef and was taking it like a pro. After about an hour of drilling him and the other kitchen staff, Simeon finally came to speak to the ladies. Alana could see Alex peeking out curiously at Simeon, who had kissed both women on their temple.

His curiosity flattered her as the friends went on discussing the new car, the new hire and the new day set before them. The morning went well. Alana spent an hour with her accountant, before leaving him to go run errands. Shortly after 1 p.m., she came rushing through the door of The Cocoa Marra. She had always been on time for her lunch dates with Georgia, and she didn't want to keep her waiting. She knew that, not only was her time precious, but *expensive*. She looked over at the tables by the window and found her sipping a cappuccino, ignoring the younger men attempting to flirt with her.

"My darling!" she exclaimed, standing to hug Alana.

"Georgia, beautiful as always. And not without a shortage of admirers, I see."

Georgia Kinsley was the type of woman every girl aspired to grow into. She was in her late fifties, but one would never know it. Her strict regimen of kale smoothies, spa treatments and workout sessions with a very high-profile trainer kept her appearance youthful looking and her attitude quite vivacious. Her clothes, hair and makeup were always flawless and, in addition to her beauty, she had brains. Not many topics crossed her path that she didn't have some level of knowledge on. She read excessively and soaked it all in like a sponge. And the word 'late' had never been introduced into any category of her life. She had a playful, sometimes sarcastic way about her that made Alana laugh because, over the years, she found herself picking up those same habits.

"So, have you found love since the last time we spoke?" she asked, as always.

"Oh, mother," as Alana jokingly called her, "When will you stop asking me that question?"

"Oh, dear. No use in questioning something you have absolutely no control over."

"Well, then. To answer your question, yes. I found a Sauvignon Blanc that I absolutely love."

Ignoring her protégé's smart mouth approach, Georgia soon changed the topic to that of Greg and Shelby's engagement. Instead of complaining about how long it had taken him, like Alana thought she would, she told her she was just grateful she had lived long enough to meet the woman he'd chosen to journey through life with, which Alana knew was still her cleverly veiled way of complaining. She noted that Alana would always be like the daughter she never had but, at least with Shelby, she'd get a wedding and some grandchildren. The ladies continued catching up on everything else that had happened since the last time they'd seen one another when Simeon made his way to the table.

"Young man, if I were a few years younger!" Georgia said as they embraced.

"Younger? Woman, I want you just as you are. With all that experience!" he responded flirtatiously. He poured them both a glass of wine before heading over to a table that wanted to offer their compliments to the chef.

"My darling--" Georgia said, as if she had a question.

"Yes?" Alana answered sweetly.

"Are you blind or dumb? Because it has got to be one."

"If you keep complimenting me like this, my head will swell. But, for argument's sake, why do you ask?" she replied, unmoved by the insult.

"That fine, scrumptious man has been under your nose for how long, and you haven't found anything to do with him? I've got some Kama Sutra books at home that you can borrow if you need some pointers!"

Alana couldn't help but laugh as Georgia continued to inquire about both hers and Simeon's love life. Unbeknownst to her, back in the kitchen, a nosey Alex began a line of questioning of his own. After peering out the window at them for a moment, he decided to rack Diego's brain. First, he started with casual questions about Alana, then Georgia. As Diego carried on, Alex felt a little intimidated, unable to believe how accomplished Alana was at such a young age.

Diego told him that, over the years, she had become one of his closest friends and was like an unofficial godmother to his youngest son. But he soon realized there was a different relationship his old friend was *really* curious about. Alex looked out the door, watching Simeon as he joined Alana and Georgia at their table. He watched how they interacted with each other, how the ladies laughed at what he said, how he would occasionally squeeze Alana's arm, and how she patted his hand in return. When Simeon returned to the kitchen, he nodded at Diego and Alex before going into the office and closing the door. Soon, Alex started in on what it was he *really* wanted to know.

"Since it's my first day and all, bring me up to speed on something. What's up with pretty boy and the boss?" he asked.

"Well, they're best friends," Diego answered.

"Oh, okay then. So, she's free?"

"And you're asking because?"

"No reason. I just think she's amazing, that's all."

Diego chuckled as he cooked, forcing Alex to question what amused him so. After badgering him to spill the beans, Diego motioned for him to step outside for a moment so they could speak privately. Sid, the line cook and Benny, the fry cook, agreed to look out for the two so they could speak outside the back door. Diego thought he would give a little advice to his old friend, in case he was thinking of going after Alana. He started by saying that, as a grown man, he didn't usually gossip. He merely wanted to warn him to avoid pursuing her at all cost. It wasn't just that she had never fraternized with the employees. But, most importantly, he felt it wouldn't be in his best interest to piss off Simeon.

Alex didn't understand why someone would be so worried about their "friend's" love life. Diego revealed to Alex that, in *his* opinion, Simeon was secretly in love with her. He may have appeared to be a free-spirited player, but their past still lingered with him more than Alana realized. The comment sparked even more curiosity within Alex. He wanted to know exactly what Diego meant by their "past." After begging persistently for answers, Diego began to tell the tale of two friends, according to what he'd heard from Gigi.

It was already well known that the two had met in college when Alana sought out a French tutor. But, what everyone else in the restaurant didn't know was that, back then, the two had a *friends with benefits* relationship. Simeon had developed a reputation for being a ladies' man. But, when he met Alana, he noticed a shift in power. It could have been due to the fact that, unlike the other girls he encountered, she charmed *him*, instead of the other way around. Her bold, blunt personality had him completely intrigued by her. After a few months of tutoring and secretly lusting after her, one night, he decided to make a move. He invited her to stay behind and hang out after one of their late-night study sessions. He never expected that Alana would in turn make a move on him. But after a night of clubbing, smoking pot and listening to music at his place, that's exactly what she did. Simeon even admitted to Diego that, even now, he smiles every time he hears "Magic Man" by Heart, as it was playing on the radio the first time she kissed him. By the end of the night, they had slept together, and he was smitten.

Unfortunately for him, it didn't happen again for a while. One night during her tutoring, French lessons soon turned into French kissing. The two somehow ended up doing shots of tequila, followed by her asking him to translate dirty words and sexual phrases for her. After a few overly suggestive sentences back and forth, the two ended up having yet another night of passion. Before they knew it, they had become friends with benefits, and apparently, she drove him crazy! He became a better lover. His confidence skyrocketed, and even the way he spoke to women changed. He became a lot smoother. Four months into it, Simeon realized he had fallen in love with Alana and was all set to tell her.

However, the day he arrived at her apartment to confess his love, she introduced him to her best friend, Gigi, as him being her "close friend." Alana was oblivious to the look of disappointment on his face. But Gigi, even having just met him, noticed right away. When Alana left the room, she suggested that he tell her what he was obviously feeling. But, when the moment came, he chickened out. After that weekend, the three began hanging out religiously and the sexual aspect of their relationship tapered off slowly. One day, he realized it had stopped completely. They had become closer, however. Before he knew it, he woke up a couple of months later and realized that he had been demoted from lover to friend...best friend! He never brought it up and neither did Gigi, although she always wondered if he was still harboring feelings for her.

"So why didn't he just tell Alana anyway?" Alex asked.

"Maybe he thought it was better to have something than to risk having nothing."

"Risk equals reward."

"You just met her. You willing to risk your job?" Diego asked.

"Shit, for a woman like that, I'm willing to risk it all!"

The two men laughed as they headed back in and returned to a screaming Simeon, who was unhappy about their short absence. Both men apologized and began working diligently as they traded looks back and forth. Diego mouthed the words, "Don't piss him off" to Alex, who tried his best not to laugh. On the outside, he seemed to be taking heed to his friend's warning. But inside, he'd already decided that he wanted Alana, and he didn't care who he had to piss off to get to her.

At 9 p.m., Alana approached the entrance to her building, worn out by the events of the day. As she headed up the stairs, Gigi called her to let her know that a package had come to the boutique for her and that she'd used her spare key to leave it on her dining room table. Alana had no idea what it could be or from whom the package came. She switched on the lights in her loft and found a long white box with red satin ribbons tied around it. She smiled and opened it with excitement, thinking Gigi had just made up a story and was really responsible for the fabulous gift.

When she opened the box, she couldn't believe it! It was the navy blue and white dress from Donnie's Basement. A long-stemmed red rose was placed across it with a note attached. It read: *Some things are just meant for each other.* Although there was no name signed, Alana knew exactly who it came from. She hurried to her bedroom and sat on the bed, wondering what she should do. She was going to call, but after her speech in the kitchen that morning, she opted to text him instead.

Alana: Thank you for the dress. I don't think I should accept it.

Alex: Of course you should. I only got it because I hoped to see you in it some day.

Alana: I told you, I don't date people that work for me.

Alex: So don't date me then. Just use me!

Alana: I already am-as a chef in my kitchen!

Alex: Yeah, but you have a lot of other rooms. I'd love for you to put me to work in some of those ;)

Alana: Unfortunately for you, I don't need a handyman in my utility room or a plumber in my bathroom.

Alex: Yeah, but what about a lover in your bedroom?

Alana: Goodnight Alex!

Alex: LOL. Goodnight beautiful.

Alana laid back on the bed and stared at the ceiling. She couldn't stop her thoughts of him. She closed her eyes and pictured his face. It wasn't long before she reached into her nightstand and pulled out her vibrator. As she pulled off her dress, wishing that it was him undressing her and him sliding himself inside her, she knew without a doubt that he was going to be trouble.

Chapter | 5

S imeon knew how much Alana hated exercising first thing in the morning. Yet, every Friday since the beginning of summer, he had forced her to join him for his morning workout. At 7 a.m., she struggled to drag herself out of bed and throw on some exercise gear, before heading downstairs to meet him in the parking lot. After getting into his car and peering at him over her designer shades, she couldn't help but pose the same question she asked every single time.

"Do we have to do this so early? I mean, I know you like to get it out of the way, but seriously? And why are we working out so hard anyway? We still look good," she added.

"Yeah, but we're over thirty now, babe. We gotta work hard to stay looking good."

She rolled her eyes and slumped down into the seat while he laughed at how annoyed she was. He turned the radio up full blast as they made their way to the gym. Alana's eyes were closed, but sleep wasn't on her mind. Alex was. He had been working at the restaurant for two weeks now, and her lust for him wasn't letting up. It had become much stronger. He always remained professional in the presence of others. But whenever they were alone, he found some excuse to brush up against her, which he always labeled as a "mistake." He never thought twice about watching her pass by him. They even started texting each other more frequently, which she kept telling herself was a no-no. She always tried her best to keep it friendly. But with Alex, there was no mistaking his intentions. He continuously asked her out and complimented her on how well she looked. He always texted her to say goodnight, or simply to let her know he was thinking of her.

Sometimes she responded and, other times, she didn't. But since she hadn't told him to stop, he assumed she liked it. And she did! Her daydreams and fantasies were at an all-time high, and he was always the lead character. A call came through on the Bluetooth of Simeon's car, both surprising him and distracting her from her thoughts. Alana assumed it was one of his many lady friends. As usual, she was right.

"Hey, sexy!" the woman said with a sizzling seductive voice.

"Selene, how are you gorgeous?"

"Well, I'm horny. Can you come fix that for me?"

Simeon quickly took the call off hands-free as Alana looked at him with amusement. *"His women are bold, if they weren't anything else,"* Alana thought to herself. He quickly ended the call, which was immediately followed by another. He was relieved to see that it was Gigi this time, saving him from further embarrassment.

"I know y'all are headed to the gym," she boasted.

"Then why are you calling?" Alana asked, sarcastically.

"Look, witch! Don't get smart! We all know you hate getting up early to exercise, but get smart with the person sitting next to you!"

"You joining us, my chocolate treasure?" Simeon chimed in.

"Oh no, baby! Not this morning. I'm counting on a round of good sex to burn off my calories."

"You should have told me that's how you wanted to work out. The three of us could have exercised at my place."

"Ha! Pervert!" she responded. "Well, anyway. I'll let y'all get to it."

"Hey, G. Before you hang up, I wanna run something by you two," Alana said. "Do you believe in love at first sight, or is it just instant sexual attraction?"

"Alana, 90% of the women I date claim to fall in love with me the first time they see me, and 100% of them want to fuck me," Simeon joked.

"Don't pay attention to him, LaLa. Love, not so much. Interest maybe. And as far as instant sexual attraction, hell yeah! I knew right away that I wanted Brian's cream in my coffee!"

Gigi laughed, and Alana smacked her lips and shook her head as they ended the call. They finally arrived at the gym and Simeon grabbed their bags as they headed in. The two parted ways and jumped right into their workout routines. But, as Simeon did his pull ups, Alana's question swirled in his mind. Had she met someone and wasn't ready to tell them? Was he ready to see her with someone else?

It had been so long since Alana had been in a relationship that he had gotten used to being the main man in her life. He decided to let it go, trusting that if there was anything to tell, she wouldn't be able to keep it to herself for long. On the other side of the gym, Alana blankly stared at muscular calves and flexing biceps. She listened to power lifters grunt while she daydreamed about Alex's physique. His body seemed so firm. She wondered how often he worked out, how he worked out, and with whom he worked out, more importantly. If he didn't already have an exercise buddy, she wouldn't mind at all if one day they tried some stretching and bending together. Surely a few sessions together would loosen her right up and tone muscles on parts of her body she hadn't used in a while. About an hour into their workout, Simeon approached her, thinking it was a good time to ask her about something else he'd been curious about.

"So, I hear you've got a date tonight?"

"Do you and Gigi talk about anything other than me?"

"Of course! But since you never tell me the juicy stuff, I have to get it from her."

"It's nothing. Some guy she and Brian convinced me to go out with invited me to happy hour."

"Oh well, I know not to make plans to meet him!" he said, laughing hysterically.

"What do you mean?" she asked, a bit offended.

"Lana, those two never hook you up with anyone that you actually end up liking. It's safe to say tomorrow will be no different. And who can overlook the fact that he takes a first date to happy hour instead of a nice dinner? One of my power play moves, babe."

He walked toward the bench press, looking cocky and leaving Alana annoyed at how much pride he took in his knowledge of everything, including her pickiness. Soon, she began to question herself. *Was she just that hard to please, or was every guy she'd dated so far simply wrong for her?* Then, she thought of Alex. *Could he be a good fit for her? Was he "Mr. Right"?* The two old friends put in another half hour of exercise before going back to Alana's. In no time, Simeon whipped into the back parking lot. Just as they were getting out of the car, Diego and Alex were entering the door.

Alana couldn't be sure, but she thought she saw a flash of jealousy in Alex's eyes when Simeon told Diego he was running up to her place to shower and that he'd be back down soon. Once they were in her loft, she made a few business calls and grabbed an apple from the fridge while waiting for her turn in the bathroom. After some time, she finally heard the water turn off in the shower. She couldn't wait to get in and wash off the sweat. She pulled off her headband and hung up the phone, having checked all of her messages. When she turned around, she found a wet, naked Simeon standing in front of her. She hadn't even heard the bathroom door open. The water cascaded down his muscle-ridden body; the sight alone made her jealous of the drops. She had forgotten just how good he looked naked, but was shocked at the sight all the same. The apple fell from her hand, making a thumping sound as it hit the floor. Her mouth stayed gaped with surprise, even after the loud thud made her snap out of her trance. She felt as though she'd stopped breathing for moment before he blurted out, "You moved the towels."

"Um...sorry...I...uh...they're in the dryer."

"What's wrong?" he asked, as if he didn't know.

"Um, you're naked," she said, smiling. Simeon leaned onto the island in the kitchen, causing the muscles in his arms to flex.

"You've seen me naked before. Quite a few times, in fact," he stated before walking to the dryer.

It had been years since Simeon was so overly flirtatious with her. She also didn't recall him being such an exhibitionist. But she had to admit, not only was he right, but he still had it! For a brief moment, she remembered why she was so attracted to him back in school. She shook her head and picked up the apple as he returned to the bathroom. Alana retreated to her bedroom and sat on the bed to remove her shoes. She found herself smiling like she had just seen a naked man for the first time. She giggled at how shocked she was, listening to Simeon's heavy feet crossing the room.

"I'm headed downstairs. I'll make your coffee."

"Okay," she said. "You do that." All the while, she thought about how he had just mind fucked her.

Simeon entered the back door with a huge smile on his face. He patted Diego on the shoulders before putting on his chef jacket. Quickly, he began helping with the prep before ordering Alex to make a huge pot of coffee for Alana.

"She's exhausted!" he said, raising his eyebrow before going into the dining room. Alex glared at him, unimpressed, before Diego took notice. It was at that moment that Simeon realized just how much Alex liked Alana. Initially, he thought maybe it was merely a momentary infatuation. But he was taking things a lot more personal than an innocent crush would. Diego urged him to lose the ever-growing attitude, but Alex didn't take kindly to Simeon's blatant insinuation.

"I hate it when he does that," he said.

"Does what?" Diego asked.

"When he tries to suggest—"

"Oh, come on, Alex. He's not suggesting anything. Everyone here knows they work out every Saturday morning together. He meant she's exhausted from exercising—"

"We both know what he meant for it to sound like," he said, chopping ferociously.

Simeon quickly returned to the kitchen and began shouting orders again. The interns hustled as Diego and Alex continued at their stations. In the midst of his tyranny, he sensed Alex's attitude. In true Simeon fashion, he questioned his work. But Alex knew better than to let him get a rise out of him. He laid into him heavily, but was soon interrupted by Alana coming in for her coffee. Both men seemed to calm down once she entered. She heard some of the commotion before coming in and was quite surprised that Simeon even bothered to play nice for her. She looked over at Alex to see how he was holding up, but he seemed to be taking it all in stride. After a brief check-in with Elizabeth, she headed off to go shopping, hoping not only to avoid the storm that was supposed to be coming, but to avoid the one brewing in the kitchen.

The afternoon rain poured with no mercy. At times, it was so heavy that Alana had to pull over on the side of the road because she couldn't see. It was extremely windy, and, at times, wet leaves were sent whipping through the air before landing on her windshield. She noticed the lunch crowd was very light due to the storm as she returned home and pulled into the back parking lot. A patron had parked in her spot, which was designated for tenants only, causing her to have to park farther away. She dreaded the thought of running back and forth with the bags of groceries she'd just bought. So, she sat in the car for a moment, trying to build up the courage to brave the cold rain that was sure to soak her clothes. Alex was standing by the back door on his cell phone, but got off quickly when he saw her watching him. He yelled out to her to wait as he disappeared inside.

Soon after, he returned with a huge umbrella and opened her car door. He walked her to the back seat, where she took out a few bags and handed him a couple, hoping to only make one trip. The two ran for the door, but a gust of wind caught the umbrella right as they reached it. It was almost ripped right out of Alex's hand before he began to wrestle with it. Cold rain crashed down on them both as he struggled to get control of the umbrella again. Alana fumbled with the keys as the bags weighed down her hands and wrist, making it harder to gain entry. Once inside, the two looked at each other and began laughing. They were drenched! Alana's hair dripped and water poured down Alex's face as they made their way to the elevator.

"Kind of reminds me of the first time we met," he said.

"How so?"

"The rain. It started raining hard the moment I left the store that day."

Alana thought it was kind of cute that he remembered that little detail. They rode the elevator in silence as she thought about just how badly she wanted to pull the emergency brake and ravage him with no mercy. His hand brushed against hers for a moment before she felt his finger rubbing the side of her hand. They arrived at the top floor and Alex grabbed all the bags, while Alana opened the cage doors of the elevator and grabbed the umbrella. In front of them was a huge antique-style door, and to the left of them was a window, which led to the fire escape. Alex looked to the right and smiled at Alana's bike, which leaned against the wall of the long, narrow hallway made of bleached wood.

She unlocked the door, which led them straight into the coat room made of dark, shiny hardwood. It was a nice sized room with brass hooks going all around it. Straight ahead from the front door were three steps that led up to the actual living space. Alex looked around at the absolutely stunning home and wondered if he was out of his league.

"Look around. I'll be right back," she said as she ran off to grab them some towels.

Once at the top of the stairs, he had a chance to really take the whole place in, which took up the entire fourth floor. He turned to face the door and saw that, behind him, it appeared to be long brick walls on each side of the banister, both with special edition paintings on them. At the end of each wall was an opening that led to a bedroom. Alex turned back around to admire the spacious loft with tigerwood floors, thick wooden doorways and walls made of exposed brick. Outside the opening to her bedroom, found to the far left of the front entrance, was a seating area with two chairs, a round glass coffee table with magazines spread on it, and a small bookcase under the window.

Further out into the loft sat the kitchen, which was also on the left of the room. It was huge, with an island and breakfast bar, stainless steel appliances, large cabinets built back into the wall, a deep double sink with a black and silver backsplash, and granite countertops. Straight ahead from the entrance were huge windows, which offered a view of the other businesses on the block. By the windows was a long dining room table, which sat on a one-step platform. There were three chairs on each side and a chair at each end. A beautiful centerpiece, equipped with long-stem yellow roses, sat in the middle of the table. The table was complemented by the natural light shining through clear cathedral-style windows.

To the far right was a hallway. In the hall, there were storage closets. At the end of it was a stacked washer and dryer. The left wall of the hall was where the two large double doors to her closet were. On the other side was the bathroom. It was painted baby blue and had a bowl sink beneath a vanity mirror, and an antique dresser, which served as a towel and toiletry storage unit. Next to the toilet was an old-fashioned bathtub with silver hot and cold handles, and silver legs in the shape of bear claws. There was even a small shower that stood separately from the tub.

As he walked back out in the loft, the wall to the left of the bathroom was where the entertainment center sat. There were two tall wooden pillars on each side of the television stand. The shelves of the pillars held decorative accents and sculptures. On the stand was a large flat screen television that she really only used when she had company. With Alana being an avid music lover, she mostly took advantage of the surround sound she had installed throughout the loft. In the middle of the room was a long, red suede couch with a huge coffee table in front of it. At each end were brown loveseats that faced each other. Decorative pillows littered each seating area and, on each lamp table by the couches, were pictures of her grandmother, Georgia, Gigi and Simeon. Hanging on two brick pillars behind the red couch were framed newspaper clippings: one of the grand opening of Cloth, and the other being a piece written about Simeon, which read: *'Young, hot, Chef on the rise'*

"You and your friends are really tight, huh?"

"Extremely!" she yelled from the other room. "Sad to say, but they're all I've got. My mom's dead, my grandmother's dead, no siblings. I have an aunt and two cousins down south, but we barely keep up with each other. Those people you're looking at are my family."

Alex's stubborn mind began to realize that if he really wanted to get close to Alana, at some point, he'd have to be involved with Simeon. He continued admiring her place and putting the bags on her kitchen counter when her phone rang. He could hear her telling the unknown caller how Alex had seen her struggling in the rain with her groceries and came out to help her. She entered the room and handed him a towel, drying her hair and thanking him for his help.

"That was your boss," she joked. "I told him you'll be down in a minute." Alex smiled a little, knowing inside that Simeon probably wasn't too happy with someone other than him coming to her rescue. He tried his best not to stare at her, but her wet hair and skin, along with the chill in the air, caused her nipples to harden and press through her white tank top. Alana grabbed a remote and turned on her stereo, while Alex complimented her on how beautiful her place was. Nat King Cole sang "Autumn Leaves" as she put away her groceries. For the first time since they'd met, they were completely alone.

"I know I must look a mess," she said, as she tugged at the wet blue jeans clinging to her legs.

"Alana, you couldn't look bad if you tried. Nice collection, by the way," he said, tilting his head toward the huge wall of records. "I'm still wondering when I will get to hear one."

"You're hearing one now, if you listen."

"I guess holding my tongue isn't my strong suit. So, why do you love music so much?" he asked, drying himself off.

"Well, it always makes me feel good. We all have something like that. Don't you?"

"Yes...*you*. You make me feel good. In fact, just the pleasure of looking at you makes me feel great," he said.

"So, I guess it wouldn't feel great to hear that *that* pleasure will belong to my dinner date this evening?"

"It would only be good to hear if it's me on the other side of the dinner table!"

As usual, he held his gaze with no hesitation. His eyes caressed every curve of her body. She felt out of her element as her breathing deepened and her heartbeat became more rapid. The attraction in the air was more than evident. The space between them was filled with unspoken words and desires that they wanted to act on, but both chose to suppress. Alex took a step toward her, and Alana knew at that moment what would happen if he took another.

"Un Un! Don't!" she said.

"Don't what?"

"Don't come over here."

"Why not?"

"Because I'm afraid of what will happen if you do."

"I'm afraid of what will happen if I *don't*," he countered.

Alex rushed toward her and held her face in his hands. He pushed her wet hair back and kissed her sensually. Her hands rested on his strong arms while his mouth rested on her lips. After a brief moment, his lips took hold of her bottom lip before he bit it gently. Suddenly, the sound of thunder crashed loudly, frightening them both. Lightning illuminated the room. Her eyes popped open and locked with his as he began to speak to her, still holding her cheeks.

"I like you, Alana, and I think that you like me, too. Maybe you should consider us as a possibility. Please!" he whispered in her ear.

Alex stared at her chest for a moment before looking back into her eyes. Her mouth remained open, her thoughts suspended in time. Alana had no idea what to say or what she should do; she only knew what she *wanted* to do. She could feel him getting hard right before he let go of her and backed away. He walked to the door, adjusting his pants and trying to shake off his arousal. Before he disappeared through the door, he looked at her one last time.

"I said please. You don't want me to beg hard!" he warned.

Alana stood there, both turned on and relieved, as she watched the door close behind him. She looked up at the ceiling and let out a long, deep breath. Her hands rested on her neck and chest, as if she'd just caught her breath.

"Oh, thank God for thunder!" she exclaimed.

Chapter | 6

At 10:30 p.m., Alana arrived back at The Cocoa Marra from her date. It was the earliest she'd ended a date in years and the fastest she'd ever been on one—having only lasted a little over an hour. Needless to say, things didn't go the way she hoped they would with Dan, an associate of Brian's. According to Gigi, they'd actually met once before at one of Brian's Super Bowl parties. But it had been so long ago that she didn't remember him. Something told her not to listen to those two as they went on and on about how she needed to go out with him because they were bound to hit it off. But, after a night of inconceivable incompatibility, she was starting to wonder if her friends even liked her!

It stung her like a bee to admit it, but Simeon was right. Gigi and Brian never got it right when it came to hookups. The date was awful! So awful, in fact, that Alana was downright baffled at how surprised he appeared to be that he didn't receive an invite to her place. The only way he could have been a worse match for her would have been if Gigi made a list of all the things that turned Alana off and put out a personal ad with that very description.

His first strike of the night was when he arrived almost 20 minutes late to pick her up, without calling. Even though she was a stickler when it came to being on time, she was seriously considering giving him a break. After all, she'd put time into her makeup, effort into her hair, and almost all of her energy just to get into the dress she was wearing. He rushed out of the car with a single, long-stem rose and apologized for his tardiness. The look on his face showed how stunned he was at her beauty. She accepted the flower, apology and compliment with grace and proceeded to his vehicle, where strike two was lying in wait.

As they put on their seatbelts and raced to the dinner reservations that they were now late for, Alana's hound-like senses picked up on a hint of perfume in the air and alcohol on his breath. This suggested to her that perhaps he was late because he'd already attended happy hour with someone else. With Simeon as her best friend, it made it easy to spot things like that. But she figured they could at least enjoy a meal together before she opted out of calling him again. Besides, she thought that maybe he'd surprise her over dinner. There was always that possibility, right? But, she was so wrong!

The entire dining experience consisted of strikes three and four. When he wasn't talking about money or himself, he was talking about money or himself! It felt like she was a third wheel on a date with him and his ego. She was pretty sure he only asked her one question about herself, and it had to do with how much money she made. And if his self-absorbed attitude wasn't enough to make her throw up, his rude treatment of the waiter did the trick. The young man was being incredibly patient and polite.

As a restaurateur, and because she understood his position, she made sure that she was just as kind as Dan was callous. She remembered Brian mentioning that his extremely successful, but demanding, job made him a bit of a firecracker at times.

However, he was acting more like a stick of dynamite! He blew up over a simple water stain on his butter knife, causing the young man to turn beet red from embarrassment, and Alana wasn't too far behind. She was so put off by his behavior that, not only did she call him on it, she suggested that instead of having dinner, they have a few quick drinks instead and save dinner for another evening--an evening she knew would never come!

After a couple drinks each and more empty, one-sided conversation, Dan excused himself to the men's room looking pleased, as if he'd just made some great impression. Alana immediately apologized to the waiter for her dinner companion's ignorance before sliding a twenty-dollar bill into his pocket, followed by a wink. He smiled at her before turning to leave, but he was so moved by her kindness that he confirmed her earlier suspicions, hammering the nail in Dan's coffin. The waiter insisted that she was too good of a woman to be wasting her time on such a douche bag. He told her that Dan and two other gentlemen were at the bar earlier with a couple of women having drinks. The fifth and final strike!

"Thanks kid!" she said as she slid the young man another twenty. She gulped down her drink and, immediately upon Dan's return, told him that she'd had a little too much to drink and that she was ready to go. He must have thought she was inviting him over; luckily, she hadn't told him where she lived. So, he assumed he was merely taking her back to her place of business to retrieve her car.

The restaurant had been closed for half an hour, but Donny, the youngest member of the staff, was just now stacking up the orange valet cones in front. He looked surprised to see her back so soon as he opened her door and helped her out. Alana said her goodnights to 'Disappointing Dan' who continued yelling out of the open door that he hoped to hear from her soon. She smiled politely and waved goodbye one last time before he pulled off, barely missing her eye roll. She stood on the sidewalk, holding her coat closed. She waited for Donny to finish gathering the cones as they engaged in small talk.

"So, boss lady. Back so soon?" Donny said with a smile.

"Not soon enough, kid!"

"Chef Simeon said that you might be coming back early, but I didn't think it would be this early."

"Oh, he did, did he?" she asked with a smirk. "I could just choke him for jinxing me. Anyway, what are you doing here so late? I'm sure your parents are worried sick by now, Mr. Senior in high school!"

"I called to let them know one of the waitresses got sick and had to leave, so I offered to help clean up. They were actually proud of my work ethic," he said, straightening his bow tie in a mocking manner.

"Aww, how cute. Who else is still here?"

"Mark is wiping down the bar. Lisa just finished cleaning the bathrooms, and Diego and Alex are finishing up the kitchen. Simeon took off, though."

"Of course, he did, honey! It's Friday night. He has a date every Friday night."

They entered the door just as Mark was counting his tips, which came easily thanks to his good looks and pleasant personality. He pushed his sleeves up and put his money away before offering Alana one last call.

"Can I get you something before I leave, Alana?"

"A tall glass of anything red."

"Rough date, huh?"

"No, that would be putting it mildly. Refereed wrestling matches are rough; this was the street fight of blind dates. I could have had a V8!"

Alana made a funny face, as if she was disgusted, causing them both to erupt into laughter. He emerged from behind the bar and took two of the chairs off a nearby table. He finished pouring her Cabernet as she sat in one of the seats and propped her feet up in the other. She thanked him, and told him and Donny to take off as she sipped the fine wine and leaned her head back. Diego burst through the doors so he could lock up and was surprised to find her sitting there.

"Hey, I was just about to head home to my old lady. You okay?" he asked.

"Just peachy," she answered, dryly.

"Uh oh! Date turned out to be a bust, eh? You've got that look."

"Well D, it was definitely *something*."

Diego grabbed a chair from one of the other tables as she began to protest. She knew that it had been a long day for him and that he wanted to get home to his family. But Diego wouldn't be Diego if he didn't lend an ear or a shoulder if he thought it was needed. He insisted that a few minutes of his time to a listen to a friend's troubles was no trouble at all. Alana tilted her head and smirked at the thought that her dates may not always be the best, but her friends sure were. She sipped some more wine before sitting straight up in the chair with perfect posture, as if she were about to have a business meeting and wanted to present all of the facts accurately.

"He was late."

"Okay, so we know he's selfish. He thinks his time is important, but yours isn't. Next!"

"He was wildly rude to the waiter."

"Apparently he didn't care if your food tasted like spit. Next!"

"He talked about money the entire night. How much his car cost, how much his suit cost, how much he spends to go on vacation--"

"So, instead of him being on a date, it seemed more like he was trying to buy one?"

"Exactly! Then, after feeling like his accountant the entire time, and seriously trying to figure out if he could write some of that stuff off on his taxes, he actually, *actually*, thought I would be interested in a night cap."

"Ouch! What an asshole! You want me to jack him up?" he asked, mashing his fist into his hand.

"No, but thank you Diego. You have a family to think about. And trust me, he isn't worth it. Then, the next girl he dates will have to hear about how much he spent on medical bills!" They shared a chuckle before Diego patted her hand, followed by a quick, "Any time." He locked the front door and shut off all but the bar lights. Alana told him that she would lock up the rest after she finished her wine and chilled out for a moment.

"Look at the bright side: at least you never have to see him again."

"I know, D. But when am I going to meet that guy that I crave to see again?"

"Soon, boss. Soon! I've got a good feeling about this," he said as he pointed to his heart. They said one last goodnight before he made his way to the back door. It barely had a chance to close behind him before the rain started to fall. Luckily, it wasn't a downpour like earlier in the day. Alana actually found it soothing, the way it lightly tapped the window pane.

She grabbed her cell phone and put on some music as she walked over to the bar to grab the bottle Mark left for her. As she returned to her seat and refilled her glass, the smooth sound of Randy Crawford's "Give Me The Night Chill Version" soothed her senses. She slipped off her shoes and placed her feet back onto the chair in front of her, as she wrestled with her dress that was beginning to travel up to her thighs. She ran her hands over her legs and joked to herself that, even though there had been a snag in the evening, at least there wasn't one in her stockings.

She took off her earrings and necklace, and placed them on the table, followed by running her fingers through her hair and massaging her scalp. An incredibly relaxing feeling came over her, prompting her to let out a small moan. She felt herself unwinding, but it was short-lived. As she opened her eyes, she was quickly plucked from her peaceful place as Alex unintentionally startled her. She'd forgotten anyone else was there, so she was surprised to find him standing in the doorway of the kitchen, staring at her. Even when he wasn't trying to, he looked sexy!

It was obvious that he was ready for a late-night workout, having changed out of his work attire into gym shoes, black basketball shorts and a thin white t-shirt. She could see the outline of every toned muscle that his arms, chest and stomach had to offer. And when her eyes traveled further south, there was another very noticeable outline on the front of his shorts--a rather *large* outline! His hands were shoved into his pockets as the light from the kitchen shined behind him, making him look like a gift straight from heaven. He dropped his gym bag and walked toward her, causing her heart to race and her palms to sweat.

He made her feel the complete opposite of what she'd felt on her date. Earlier, she was assertive, clear-minded and fearless to say what was on her mind; she usually always was. Yet, Alex's presence, at times, made her feel timid, scatterbrained and afraid. Not afraid *of* him, but afraid that she would be too weak to keep the wild woman inside of her, the one that wanted him, at bay.

"I'm sorry I scared you. I just heard some moaning and wanted to know what the commotion was all about," he said with a tantalizing smile.

"I'm…uh…fine…you know, I um…I just forgot about you, that's all," she said, still clutching her chest and trying to figure out why the hell she was stammering over her words.

"Guess I need to work on my kisses then," he said, rubbing his hand over his thin, scruffy beard.

"I meant I forgot that you were here."

"Ah! So my kisses *don't* need work then!"

Alana waved him off as he reached for the chair in front of her. Without warning, he lifted her feet and sat down, placing them back down onto his lap and nearly taking Alana's breath away as he massaged them. He stared at her toes for a moment before leaning his head to the side and checking her out while he licked his lips. She sat across from him, dazed and confused. She didn't know whether she should stop him, or let him continue giving her one of the best foot massages she'd ever received. With every twist of his hands and every deep rub with his thumb down the middle of her foot, she could feel her body melting like butter in a frying pan. He noticed Alana staring at him and abruptly stopped.

"Sorry! Is this okay?" he asked, lifting her foot.

"Now you ask? Look, usually I'd stop you because it is rather intimate. But I've had too crappy of a night to say no now."

"Well, I need to run into you after terrible dates more often. No telling what I could get you to say yes to." He smiled and continued rubbing while the music played and Alana sipped her wine. The dim lights above the bar accentuated their skin, as if it were setting a sultry, sensual stage, with temptation as the leading role. His strong brown hands seemed to have a golden glow as she watched them move up and down her feet slowly, foretelling every feeling they would cause her to have if they ever found their way to the rest of her body. Her face appeared all too perfect as he watched the light illuminate the gloss on her lips and the shadows contour her bone structure. Pretty soon, the sight of his solid body and her tempting cleavage were enough to make them both enticed. Alex decided to add sound to the silence by discussing Alana's 'less than hot' night out on the town.

"You know, I heard what you said about your date. He should have known money wouldn't impress a woman like you. It's apparent you've got money. You need something else. Something big. Something you'll want given to you aggressively and gently. Something that can be hard to hold and even harder to take. Do you know what I'm talking about?" he asked, staring into her eyes intensely.

Alana felt flushed as she looked away and hoped to God she wasn't slobbering like a Saint Bernard as her mouth watered. In her mind, she answered, *"Yes, baby. I know what you're talking about. Your dick!"* But what actually came out audibly in her cracking voice was, "No, what is it that you're talking about?"

"Love, baby. A woman like you needs and deserves the real thing. I'm talking flowers for no reason, candlelight dinners, introducing you to mama, taking vacations,

Sunday morning service, fuck you until you're weak, think about each other all day, put a ring on it love."

Alana was both speechless and turned on. She used every ounce of will power she had not to straddle him in his chair and ride him until the wood snapped under pressure. She shook her head to loosen the grip he had on her dirty mind and swallowed the last of her wine. Alex could tell she was a little rattled. But, instead of completely shaking her cages, he decided to lighten things up a bit. Besides, he didn't want to go too far without knowing if she was feeling him as much as he was feeling her. The moment the music stopped, he took a break from rubbing her feet and whipped out his cell phone. He scrolled for a while before stopping and placing the phone down on the table.

"Are you in a rush to get home?" he asked.

"Not really. Why are you asking?"

"Just wondering if a so-called music connoisseur would be up for a little music challenge?"

"Oh, you don't want to do that to yourself!" Alana said confidently. "I may be a jazz collector, but I listen to everything. I don't think you're ready for me." She sat up and put her shoes on as she grabbed her phone. Alex stated the rules. Each of them would play a song, any song from any genre, on their phone and give their opponent two minutes to name the title and artist. Whoever was the first with three strikes was the loser. She accepted the challenge with a handshake, followed by her rubbing her index finger under both eyes and telling him she'd just put on her war paint. Alex laughed as he picked up his phone and let the games begin--but not before being asked to clarify what the stakes were.

"So, what are we playing for?"

"Oh, come now, Alana! If I win, I want what every man wants…"

"And what would that be?" she asked as she watched his eyes move up and down her body.

"A day off with pay!" he said.

"Oh, I can cover that--especially since you won't be winning!"

"Okay, hot shot. So, what do you want if you win?" he asked.

"A feast fit for a queen."

"No problem! And, for the record, I'll cook for you any time you want me to. You don't have to get spanked in a competition just to get it."

Getting spanked by Alex? Now there was a thought! Alana got up and refilled her glass as he played his first selection, which she guessed in seconds. He was shocked by the quick response as she lifted the bottle to offer him a glass. He nodded affirmatively as he listened closely to the tune she played, and he answered just as quickly as she had. His knowledge of music was equally impressive, so it didn't take long to realize they were in for a long night. He tried his best to think of songs that would leave her completely stumped but, time after time, he was unsuccessful. Within a couple of hours, they'd each chosen songs from every genre: rock, rap, R&B, jazz and alternative. But Alex had two strikes to Alana's one. Panic set in as he feared that a loss was just around the corner. Hoping to throw her for a loop, he presented a challenge within a challenge, confident that she would lose.

"I'll tell you what. So that this doesn't go on forever, if you can name the song that was playing at Donnie's Basement the day we met, I'll concede," he said, arrogantly.

Alana gulped down her wine, frowning her brow, as if she couldn't remember. Their eyes locked as the time counted down on the stop watch on Alex's phone. The seconds ticked away as they held their gaze, both trying to wear down the other. Twenty seconds were left on the clock when Alana blurted out, "Beast of Burden by the Rolling Stones."

Alex's smile melted into a puddle of defeat, causing her to laugh uncontrollably. He put his hands up and bowed to her, exclaiming that she was indeed the queen of music. After happily accepting her accolades, she looked at the time and realized it was a little past 12:30 a.m. Alana told him that they both needed to be heading home, as she grabbed the wine bottle and glasses, carrying them into the kitchen. Alex apologized for keeping her out so late and offered to walk her home so he could sleep soundly, knowing she was safe.

Alana giggled at his offer to take the long journey a few feet from the back door! She grabbed her purse, coat and keys, and headed to the back exit. They shut off the lights in the kitchen and, as she locked the door, Alex stood with his hand against the building, hovering over her. His nose brushed her hair and Alana immediately noticed he shut his eyes tightly. He hoped that if he concentrated hard enough, his memory would hold onto the sweet smell of her. They walked a few feet down to the back door entrance of the lofts and stood in silence, both confused about what to say next. Alana couldn't believe that he was standing there with no coat on while she, on the other hand, shivered like crazy.

"You don't need a jacket on or something? You aren't cold?"

"I'm actually hot, *real* hot! You wanna feel me?" he asked.

Her pulse raced as he began to rub her arms softly to warm them. It was hard to ignore the wet sensation between her legs, as the tireless twinkle in his beautiful brown eyes sucked her in. He smiled a sly smile before kissing her cheek in a spot not far from her lips.

"Tonight was fun. The most fun I've had since I've been back. Thanks for that," he said. He turned to walk toward his car, but Alana felt the need to say something. Her attraction to him was put on hold just long enough to get a sentence out. She yelled out to him, stopping him in his tracks to make sure that they were on the same page.

"Hey! You know this wasn't a date, right?"

"Of course! You don't date employees," he said, smiling and looking over his shoulder.

Alana smirked as if she weren't amused. But once she was on the other side of the door, she couldn't help but laugh at his smart mouth, which was saturated with confidence. She undressed on the way to her room, as if she couldn't take being contained by her clothes any longer. Her hand reached into the nightstand for the second time since they'd met, thanks to him.

"Oh boy, is he trouble!" she said before turning on the turbo speed and taking off.

Chapter | 7

I t was a quiet, early Saturday afternoon for Alana—that was until Gigi called to question her about her date with Dan. She told her how her supposed match made in heaven turned out to be the date from hell. Gigi was both shocked and disappointed in his behavior. She offered to call him straightaway for a good old-fashioned cursing out, but Alana told her it was no big deal. She did, however, make Gigi promise to stop playing matchmaker, which she swore she would. Alana wanted so badly to tell her about her impromptu jam session with Alex, which more than made up for her terrible evening. But, she kept it to herself, partly because she didn't want Gigi getting too excited. But mainly, she felt that having a little secret was kind of exciting.

Gigi felt bad about the date flop and told Alana that she should accompany her and Brian to visit her parents. She figured her mother's home cooking could cure anything, even men problems. It had been some time since Alana had seen the Campbells, so she happily accepted the offer. She was also getting a kick out of pretending to be more disappointed than she actually was. Hanging out with Alex had more than made up for the night and, although she knew it was probably a bad idea, she wanted to spend some time alone with him again. The happy couple picked her up and soon, they were headed out to the suburbs.

A few times a week, her bestie made it a point to visit her parents since her father suffered a stroke the year before. Gigi's mother, along with the help of a live-in nurse, now cared for him full-time. Gigi had always been a daddy's girl, so it hit her pretty hard to see her father in such a vulnerable state. When they were children, he was the father that all the boys in the neighborhood feared. He was a tall, brown, large man with massive hands and a mean look about him. But once you got to know him, you realized he was just an oversized teddy bear who melted whenever his daughter was around.

Brian went with her majority of the time. He was the one boyfriend that Mr. Campbell actually liked. Aside from being successful and supportive, Brian was quite the handsome and charming guy, which also made him a shoo-in with Mrs. Campbell. Like Simeon, he was very much into fitness and it showed. His light, caramel complexion and his big, brown puppy dog eyes were always enough to make Gigi melt. With the exception of the weekend, he was always in a suit. Even when he wasn't, he somehow still looked professional, hardly ever wearing jeans.

His thin, black mustache and dark hair never went ungroomed, and the cologne he wore would make the poorest female on earth open a bank account at his branch just to get a whiff. If one couldn't tell from his appearance that he was a well put-together man, they would certainly realize it after he spoke. The business graduate was very articulate and intelligent; one never had to wonder why Gigi was so smitten.

On days that her father was having a "bad day," Brian would often have to comfort Gigi on the ride home because she always took it hard. Not that he minded. Right before

Mr. Campbell first returned from the hospital, it was Brian who paid to have everything in the house made handicap-accessible. His love for Gigi was more than apparent, and her parents couldn't be happier that they had found one another. At around two in the afternoon, they entered the house, and the smell of pork chops frying was detected at the door.

Her father sat in a recliner, watching T.D. Jakes give a sermon. But soon, his eyes lit up when he saw his baby girl. The small wrinkles in the corners of his eyes tightened the bigger his smile grew. Alana looked slightly concerned about the few pounds he had lost, but she hid it well. His hair seemed as if it began to gray overnight. The left side of his body was now paralyzed, and he had just really begun to speak clearly.

His mouth twisted when he spoke. But as long as he spoke slowly, you could understand every word. She rushed to him and playfully pecked his forehead over and over, like she was a chicken. He spoke slowly and murmured the words, "My baby" as he looked on lovingly. She hugged the nurse, a thick blond girl named Amy, who rode a hog and didn't take any mess—which was what her father needed. Mr. Campbell was very old-school and had always been the king of the household, so he wasn't used to taking orders from a woman. It took some adjusting on his part to realize that even men need help sometimes. Gigi retreated to the kitchen to hug her mom, while Brian stayed behind. He grabbed Mr. Campbell's hand, holding it up for him so that he could shake it. Again, her father spoke, pointing his eyes in the direction his daughter had just gone in.

"How is she?" he asked Brian slowly.

"Very well, sir. I'd love to say I'm taking great care of her. But, as you know, you raised her to do quite well on her own."

"Good man," he said.

Soon Alana stepped up to greet him, as well. He smirked at her while she kissed his cheek and lightly squeezed his shoulders. "Hey, Pop!" she said, sitting on the arm of his chair.

"Brian," he struggled. "You're a lucky man to hang out with such beauties."

"Don't I know it, sir," he answered as they all laughed.

Alana leaned back a little and saw Gigi sneaking money into her mother's purse, and a little something extra into Amy's inside jacket pocket, which was hanging on a hook by the small staircase. She'd most likely call them later on to tell them it was there. She always did things like that. Mrs. Campbell never wanted to take money from her daughter because she felt she was already doing enough by paying the nurse. But Gigi didn't mind any of it. She was an only child and had been spoiled all her life. Her father had given her and her mother everything they ever wanted, so she always felt it was the least she could do. After giving them a few more moments of privacy, Alana finally went into the kitchen to say her hellos.

"I swear you two don't eat!" Mrs. Campbell said, hugging her. "I never thought I'd have such a skinny daughter." She smacked Gigi on her butt. Her mom was a short, busty woman with wide hips and chubby cheeks. She was the sweetest woman you could ever meet, not to mention she could be quite comical. She had been a homemaker all of Gigi's life, so she was no stranger to caring for her family. Only now, the care was a lot more extensive. She waved the girls toward the back door so they could go outside. Mrs. Campbell wanted to show off her garden in the backyard, and she had every right. It was quite a sight. She had rows of vegetables, a lemon tree smack dab in the middle, and sunflowers, which were her favorite, lining the back fence.

"Wow, mom! It looks great!" Gigi exclaimed. "I can't believe you did all this yourself."

"Amy was nice enough to help me. I'm too old to do all this alone, honey. Besides, that's a strong bitch in there!" she said, pointing at the door.

The best friends laughed hysterically while Gigi shook her head at her mother's bluntness. But Alana realized those smiles would soon turn to frustration as she watched Mrs. Campbell take a pack of cigarettes and a lighter out of her housecoat. Her mother hadn't smoked in years, something Gigi never liked in the first place, something she knew her mother only did when she was overwhelmed or stressed.

"Mom! When did you start smoking again?" she asked, snatching the cigarette from her lips and throwing it to the ground.

"Shhhh! You want your father to hear?"

"If you have to hide it, then maybe you shouldn't be doing it!" Gigi snapped.

"Ha! Words to live by. Does your father know you're having sex before marriage?"

"Mother!" Gigi exclaimed. "I never said that." She put on her best innocent face.

"You don't have to say it, sweet pea. If that fine ass man were mine, you'd need gorilla glue to keep my knees together!" Alana laughed hysterically before getting the evil eye from her friend. Mrs. Campbell employed her to tell Gigi that she was a grown woman, but Alana didn't dare! Her friend was downright upset about her smoking again. Alana was relieved when her phone alerted her that she had a new text message.

She went back into the kitchen and grabbed a fork to turn the pork chops over. She looked at the screen and Alex's name appeared. The message read: *Good day Ms. Jones. It completely slipped my mind last night, but I'm having a dinner party tonight. I know it's last minute, but if you're available, would you please come?* At that moment, Gigi and her mother entered the kitchen, obviously having made up as they were discussing what she would do about the garden when winter came. Mrs. Campbell patted Alana's back to let her know she could take the cooking back over, and Gigi went out into the living room to check on her dad and Brian. Alana stood in the corner of the kitchen, pondering whether or not she should accept the invitation.

"That's a damn good man she has out there!" Mrs. Campbell stated, peeking at her daughter in the other room. "I know you'll get one just as good when you finally decide to open that stubborn heart of yours." She pecked Alana on the cheek and joined the others.

Alana leaned against the doorway, watching Gigi with Brian and watching how much Mrs. Campbell loved and cared for her husband. She watched her kiss him and help him drink water, while Amy came in to prepare their plates. Alana wondered what it must feel like to love someone so much. For the first time, she took into consideration that, perhaps, she was passing a good man by and maybe she should ease up a bit. Besides, a party wasn't a date.

Perhaps it would give her an opportunity to see a side of him that would persuade her to change her rules. She whipped out the phone and texted him back. *What time is the party?* Alana was nervous and excited. Nervous as he texted the address, and excited as she plotted on what she should wear.

It was around 8 p.m. when she pulled up to the address in Indian Village. He told her the party was starting around 8:30, but she wanted to get there early so they could get some things straight. There were no other cars in sight when she arrived, so she figured she was right on time. She shut off the engine and reminded herself of her cardinal rule: do not get sexually involved with employees. She walked up to the brick home with ivory columns and a white wooden swing bench on the porch. She smirked with a hint of confusion in her brow as she thought to herself, *"This place doesn't match his demeanor."* It seemed more like a family home than a bachelor's pad, like it belonged to someone of a much more mature age.

She rang the bell, straightened her jacket and smoothed down her hair, which the wind had blown out of place. "What are you doing?" she asked herself. "This is not a date!" She peered into the long, skinny glass windows, which were on each side of the front door. She saw Alex lightly jogging to the door, wiping his hands with a towel.

"Hi!" he said excitedly.

"Hello, Alex."

"You look beautiful! Royal blue is your color. I don't think I've ever seen you in it before."

"Maybe you just didn't notice it."

"I pay attention to everything you do. Trust me. I would have noticed."

Alana tried not to seem flattered as she smiled and rolled her eyes. Her four-inch heels tapped the floors lightly before she stepped out of the doorway and onto the Persian rug in the front hall. The chandelier hanging above her head was dimly lit, but provided enough light for her to check out the layout of his home. Her curiosity led her to the doorways on both sides of her. First, she poked her head inside the room to her left.

The fireplace was burning in the cozy looking living room, and she could hear Chris Botti playing "A Thousand Kisses Deep" throughout the house. Even standing as far back as she was, she could feel the heat on her face. The burning wood made a crackling sound as her eyes scanned the room. Photographs of his family rested on the mantle amidst light gray walls. The black baby grand piano by the large picture window had a family portrait on it in a shiny silver frame. It appeared to be him with his parents and siblings. A dark brown, leather Chesterfield couch sat against the wall facing the fireplace, and photography books littered the long, wooden coffee table in front of it.

She did an about-face to find Alex waiting to take her coat. He looked dashing in his crisp personalized chef jacket and black slacks. She paid him a compliment as he took her jacket off slowly. He admired the skin-tight calf length dress, which looked like it would have to be peeled off. Alex bit his lip in approval and nearly walked into a wall as he went to hang up her garment. Next, she continued to the right side of the hall, where she found the dining room. It had a beautiful antique table with matching chairs. It was covered with a crisp, white table cloth and. In the middle of the table was a silver candelabrum with several long candles burning. Against the wall was a wooden buffet with a built-in wine rack. Hanging over it was a large LED marquee that spelled out "EAT." He walked over to one of the chairs and pulled it out so she could be seated, then placed her purse in the chair next to her. She felt silly that it wasn't until that moment she realized there was no dinner party.

"There's no one else coming, is there?" she asked.

"No, I don't believe there is," he said, smiling and placing a napkin across her lap. "Why would I invite anyone else to the queen's feast?" he asked, referring to their wager.

"Cute! And how did you know that I'd come alone?"

"I didn't, but I hoped with everything in me that you would."

"And what if I hadn't?"

"I made enough for three. I would have simply pointed out that I had forgotten to tell you that it was cancelled, but that you and Gigi were welcome to stay because I know that's who you would have brought!"

"You think you know everything, don't you?"

"Not really. I don't know what it takes to win you over. I'm hoping to change that tonight."

Alex walked back into the kitchen to retrieve a corkscrew for the bottle of Merlot sitting in between them. It was the only room that seemed bright as the others were dimly lit, obviously for romance purposes. Placed directly in front of her plate was a small vase filled with African violets, one of her favorite flowers. She smiled, thinking that either it was a hell of a coincidence, or he had obviously done his research. Deep down, she knew the answer. Alex rushed back in, presenting her with a long rectangular plate that held three small servings of different dishes.

"For you," he said, opening the wine.

Alana grabbed her fork, but stopped to pray over her food--and for the strength to keep her hands to herself. She opened her eyes to find Alex gazing at her. She quickly turned her attention to the exquisite meal, hoping to take her mind off of how nervous she was. Everything looked so good that she didn't know where to start. He smiled for a moment before pointing to the item in the middle, requesting that she start there.

Her first tastes were of the seafood dish, made with lightly breaded garlic shrimp, bacon- wrapped asparagus and Gouda melted on top of a lightly toasted, thin slice of artisan bread. The second dish was a wine-soaked sirloin with chives, inside of an Asian-style potsticker drizzled with teriyaki sauce. Last, was a fiery based soup with pork, peppers and onions. Alana closed her eyes, savoring every sensation his culinary creations brought her. If she ever had any doubts about his level of expertise in the kitchen, they were suddenly shattered.

"You are an excellent cook! What made you want to be a chef anyway? Is your mom a good cook?" she inquired. Alex laughed hard, putting his hand to his mouth so that his food wouldn't show. After he finished chewing and gained his composure, he explained why the question was so side-splittingly funny.

"I wish my family could have heard that," he said. "To answer your question, my mom is an *awful* cook. She could sell her dinner rolls to the local police station as a part of their riot gear."

"You're awful!" she said, laughing.

"I'm serious. If it wasn't for my dad and my grandma, there would have been no survivors."

The conversation flowed like wine as the two chatted back and forth about their lives. Alex was the youngest of four children. His brother Eric, who was the oldest, was a firefighter, who also happened to be one of his neighbors as he lived just a few blocks over. His twin sisters, Sherri and Sheila, lived two hours away, where they owned and operated their own daycare. His parents were both dentists who'd recently decided to relocate to Atlanta. The home he was in had in fact been theirs. He joked that they had given him the family discount. Alana enjoyed hearing about his family and how close everyone was. It was a far cry from what she had.

Unlike the disciplined young woman Alana had been, her mother was a bit more rebellious. She was incredibly book smart, which led her to believe she knew everything else there was to know. She met a young man her senior year in high school who Grandma Marra didn't much approve of. Not only was he in college, but he didn't seem to share the same values as she'd been raised to uphold. Much to Grandma Marra's disappointment, Alana's mother ran away after being convinced by her older boyfriend that he would take care of her and that they'd be together forever.

After no contact with her family for almost a year, Alana's mother showed up one day on her mother's doorstep, worn down and pregnant. It turned out that the young man she thought she knew better than anyone was living a complete lie. He wasn't a struggling college student at all. He was, in fact, a dropout who didn't feel the need to complete school since his family had an overabundance of wealth. The man she had been so in love with left her the moment he found out she was pregnant. He ended up marrying the girl that his family thought better suited him and their status. She never spoke much about him once she returned home, and Grandma Marra never pressed the issue. She was just glad to have her daughter home.

Grandma Marra could tell that her daughter felt foolish for letting "love" take her so far off the successful track that she was on. However, she always tried to reassure her that, one day, she would know *real* love. After months of rebuilding her life and her relationship with her mother, it was devastating for Grandma Marra when Alana's mother died a few weeks after Alana was born due to complications from her hard labor. According to Grandma Marra, her last words as she looked at her baby girl were, "You were right, mom. Now I know what real love is." But Alana's life hadn't been all sad. Her grandmother was a blast when she was growing up, and she lavished her with nothing but love.

It was heartbreaking for Alana when Grandma Marra died her freshman year of college. But, right on cue, another strong woman filled her shoes as a motherly figure: Grandma Marra's best friend, former colleague and Alana's godmother, Georgia. After two and a half hours of eating, drinking wine and having in-depth conversations about life, the two finally arrived at the topic of love.

"So, why have you never been in love? You obviously date, so what's the problem?"

"I don't know. I've just never felt that spark. What about you? Ever been madly in love?"

"Yes, I have," he said seriously, before walking out of the room to retrieve dessert. It was evident that someone in his past had hurt him. He soon returned with a cocoa-flavored cake with chocolate liquor-based icing. He also brought a bottle of dessert wine to pair with it. He sat down and cut the cake while Alana decided to pick up where they had left off.

"So, who was she? College sweetheart?" she asked.

"Kinda. We met at a college party, became friends, then fell in some time after."

"And then what?"

"And then, she broke my heart," he answered. "But it hasn't stopped me. I'm hoping to fall again, real soon. This time, I can tell it'll be the real thing."

Alana smiled before digging into her dessert, which was absolutely incredible. After chatting a little more, Alex suggested that maybe she take her wine and sit by the fire while he cleaned the kitchen. But, Alana wouldn't have it. She figured since he prepared such a breath-taking meal for her, the least she could do was help with the dishes. She cleared the table as he washed the dishes and, before long, they were both drying and putting them away. As she stood on the footstool to reach some of the high shelving, it began to slip from under her. Alex turned around just in time to catch her. Her arm flung around his neck, grateful that she hadn't hit the floor. His muscular arm held her tightly, while his other arm decided to join it around her waist.

"I'm sorry!" she exclaimed. "I lost my footing."

"I know the feeling."

"What do you mean?" she asked.

"You knock me off of my feet, too."

Alex leaned down and kissed her. Alana kissed him back as the two embraced, but she pulled away abruptly and headed back into the dining room. He followed behind her, stopping her as she reached the table. She stood there, her mind racing while her fingertips made circles on the tablecloth. Alex stood behind her, his hands sliding around her waist and his tongue finding its way to her ear. She felt him slowly drop to his knees behind her.

His large, warm hands slid up her legs, starting from her ankles. He slowly moved over her calves, which were tightening from her stilettos. Soon, his hands were at her thighs, then on to her hips, where he gently slid the lace thong she was wearing off. He stood and turned her around so they were facing each other. His hands grabbed her waist, pulling her in closely to him as he whispered onto her lips, "Now for *my* dessert!" he said, before slowly pushing her onto the large wooden table so that she was seated. He pulled up a chair, seating himself directly in front of her.

As she sat on the table, she thought to herself that she should stop him. This was wrong! She was going to have to see him at her place of business, and it was sure to be awkward. Employers should not socialize, at least not sexually, with employees. She put her hands on his shoulders and pushed him back in the chair. He sat back, prepared to accept rejection. But, to both his surprise and hers, Alana scooted back on the table and spread her legs. He looked at her for confirmation, which he received as she uttered the words, "Bon appetite!"

Chapter | 8

Alex's touch remained gentle as he took his time sliding her dress up to her hips. One by one, he placed her legs onto his shoulders. Suddenly, she could feel his tongue, which was more than determined to make her cum, circling around her clitoris. His lips kissed her clit, followed by his tongue licking it. His mouth moved in unison with her hips, as if he and her heavenly spot were tongue kissing each other. Her right hand grabbed the back of his head while her left stayed planted on the table, struggling to hold her up. His hands rubbed her breast, then her stomach, then her hips.

His arms wrapped around her thighs as he pulled her in closer. Her arm, which had given her support, quickly gave out. She lay back on the table as Alex's tongue unleashed all of the desire he had been feeling up until that moment onto her. She stared at the chandelier above her, the crystal ornaments twinkling like stars in her eyes as his mouth began to suck her senseless. She grabbed handfuls of the tablecloth that lay beneath her and soon, her moans drowned out the music still playing quietly in the background. As she let herself go, she came harder than she ever remembered doing before.

She laid there for a moment to catch her breath. After gaining enough energy, she sat up, unable to believe what had just taken place. She didn't know what to say as he sat in the chair, as cool as ice cubes, wiping his mouth with the dinner napkin on the table. He stood up and rubbed her hair back into place.

"I think I liked you much better than the meal," he said before pecking her cheek. Alana panicked and slid off the table.

"I have to go!" she said, frantically grabbing her purse and heading to the hallway to retrieve her jacket. Alex smirked as he stood in the doorway of the dining room, leaning against the wall. She hoped he wouldn't say a word as she hurried to the door.

"You're always running from me," he said. She attempted to say something, but stopped. All she could come up with was "Thank you for dinner." She felt like an idiot as she walked to the door, unable to say anything else. As she turned the knob, Alex called out to her once more. "Hey Alana, thanks for *coming*!" he said seductively. She didn't know if the pun was intended, but she knew she had to get out of there.

The next morning, she woke up early with a slight headache. She couldn't figure out if it was from all the wine she drank at dinner, or from all of the thinking she'd done once she made it home. Last night seemed surreal and had it not felt so good, she probably wouldn't have believed it happened. Flashbacks plagued her throughout her morning routine. As she brushed her teeth, she thought of kissing Alex. As she ate her cereal, she thought of the meal he'd prepared in her honor. As she put on her underwear, she thought of him taking them off.

Around 9 a.m., Gigi called to see if she wanted to surprise Simeon and Diego by inviting themselves on their trip to the farmer's market, a street market they often frequented on Sunday mornings to stock up on fresh fruit, vegetables and rare spices for the restaurant. Since the business was closed on Sundays, Gigi knew that Alana would most likely be at home resting. She also knew that Diego usually stopped by the restaurant around 10 a.m. to get money from petty cash and the pouch for the receipts. She figured they could catch a ride with the boys and go look at some of the trinkets and knick-knacks the vendors sold there.

The call couldn't have come at a better time. Alana knew it was just what she needed to take her mind off things. After accepting the offer, she hurriedly got ready and waited for both Gigi and Diego's arrival. She went down to the restaurant and sat on a stool in the kitchen. While she waited, Alex sent her a text. Just the sight of his name caused a stir in her. She smiled as she read the message: *Good morning gorgeous. Can we talk about last night?* Alana didn't answer right away. Because she had made such a fool of herself the previous night by being unable to form a sentence, she wanted to say just the right thing. She began typing, but both Gigi and Diego entered the back door of the restaurant. She put away the phone and gave them a smile.

"So, I hear you two will be joining us today?" Diego asked.

"That's right, buddy, and don't you dare try to warn Simeon either! I know him. He'll make up some excuse to try and cancel because he thinks we'll have him out there all day," she insisted.

As he grabbed the petty cash, the two ladies made their way to his van. He laughed at them as he locked up the restaurant and listened to them argue over the front seat. On the way to Simeon's place, Alex texted her again: *Are you playing hard to get? Because I can play hard to resist.* Alana rolled her eyes and looked out the window. She wondered where, if anywhere, all of this would lead. By the time they reached Simeon's, it was 10:30 a.m. To no one's surprise, he was still entertaining company from the previous night. The three of them stood outside his door, listening intently as his spirited companion yelled and screamed during the throes of passion. Her excitement seemed somewhere between pleasure and pain as she said his name loudly and moaned in ecstasy. She apparently had no shame in expressing her gratitude for the enjoyment.

"Oh, God!" she yelled out. Gigi couldn't resist poking fun at the phrase. "No wonder your business is doing so well. God is cooking the food," she said. Both Diego and Alana muffled their laughter while Gigi continued her shenanigans. She bit the tip of her leather gloves and shook her head back and forth, like a wild dog.

"Is that how you used to be?" she asked Alana, referring to her and Simeon's "friends with benefits" relationship in college. Diego's eyes widened with humor as Gigi caught an elbow for the overly personal question. The show had just ended when Alana began to pound on the door obnoxiously. The group heard the two scrambling on the other side of the door before Simeon yelled out, "Just a minute." He and his guest whispered back and forth about who was at the door. The young woman was suddenly curious as to whether or not he thought they had heard them. Simeon ushered his guest off to the bathroom as he shuffled to the door and yelled out to what he thought was only Diego. The look on his face said it all once he opened the door.

"D-man you are—"

"Right on time!" Gigi said as the door flung open.

"Whoa! Hey…um…ladies. I didn't uh…I didn't know you were joining us today," he said, shocked to see them.

"Obviously," Alana answered as she smiled and patted his chest lightly.

The two women barged their way in as Diego followed behind, hunching his shoulders up at Simeon as if to say, "What did you want me to do?" Like Alana's loft, his place was quite spectacular. The two-floor high rise condominium fit him perfectly; it was the perfect bachelor's pad. The first level had an open kitchen with a large island and chopping station. It also had a huge living room and a large storage closet for the washer and dryer. There was a quaint guest bathroom that sat in the small hallway off the dining room, which he turned into a billiard room. The area was perfect for entertaining, as it was equipped with a full bar and hanging flat screen.

On the second level was a full bath, a small bedroom, which he had converted into a walk-in closet, and a huge master's suite. The restaurant's success, paired with his father's occasional "gift giving," helped support his expensive taste and lavish lifestyle. Simeon stood there, holding a towel closed over the bottom half of his body. Diego covered his eyes and begged him to please put some clothes on. The four friends chatted until a small voice coming from behind Simeon interrupted them. Somehow, they'd forgotten all about his companion, who emerged from the bathroom, having straightened her clothes and hair as best as she could with the small amount of time that she had.

"Everyone, this is Cree," he said. The young lady smiled and waved, but quickly added that she needed to get going. Simeon walked her to the door, kissed her on the cheek, and told her that he would call her later. Not a moment after the door closed behind her did his three buddies start screaming and moaning ridiculously loud at him. Gigi bounced up and down on the couch on her knees, yelling, "Oh, God!" Diego started banging his fist on the coffee table while repeating, "Whose is it?" over and over again in Spanish. Alana slapped him with couch pillows and moaned loudly as they all continued with their production of "Simeon's Sexcapades."

Knowing that she had most likely heard them mimicking her, Simeon pretended to be mad. But, he couldn't help but laugh as he jogged up the stairs to shower. "Assholes! All three of you!" he shouted. As they waited for him to get ready, Alana received yet another text message from Alex.

Alex: Did I move too fast? Do you not want to talk to me?

Alana: No, that's not it at all. I'm just headed to the farmer's market with the crew. Of course we can talk about last night. In fact, we need to. When are you available?

Alana continued with her conversation, but was soon puzzled by the response he sent. After a long pause, Alex came back with: *Sorry, my best friend just popped up unexpectedly and we're about to step out. I'll text you in a minute.* Alana responded with a simple *Ok*, feeling nervous about the conversation to come. Simeon finally appeared showered, dressed and ready to go. But, before the group headed out to see what the market had to offer them, Alana offered up a half-hearted apology to her best friend.

"Sorry we made fun of your girl," she said, covering her smirk.

"Shut up," he said. Simeon draped his arm over her shoulder and looked down at her with a small smile of his own. "You're my girl," he said as they all exited.

They arrived at the farmer's market and prepared to make their way through the sea of people. Potential buyers sniffed fruit, hoping to inhale its freshness. Some were caught squeezing melons to check their ripeness, while other shoppers looked through piles of green, leafy vegetables, making sure they weren't wilted or turning brown. As they continued through the market, they came upon a vendor with mountains of fabrics. Every color and pattern imaginable was there, as well as a few handmade pieces of jewelry, which Gigi couldn't resist. They stopped at the table and admired the beautiful pieces, but they were soon distracted by a woman trying to comfort her crying baby.

"He's precious!" Gigi said right as the baby calmed down.

"Thank you so much!"

"How old is he?" Alana asked.

"He's five months today," the woman answered. "And he's getting a bit hungry. Hey, Al. Come over here with the baby's bag please."

Alana felt her stomach drop as she saw Alex, who was at another booth, turn around and look at her with surprise. She was all too confused at the fact that he actually looked happy to see her. Simeon and Diego walked up just in time for Diego to hug the pretty woman, who he obviously recognized. Alana felt betrayed! Sure, they weren't in a relationship. But after all they'd discussed the night before, including family, ironically a baby never came up. Simeon shook Alex's hand and, just as Alana felt the urge to grab him and storm off, he began making conversation.

"Hey man! I didn't know you had a kid," Simeon said inquisitively.

"Oh, I don't!" he insisted. "Everyone, this is my best friend and older sister, Sherri. And this is my nephew, Noah. They popped up on me this morning."

"You look great, Sherri. It's been a long time," Diego said, grabbing the baby.

"Sherri, this is Gigi. You know Diego, Simeon, the head chef at the restaurant I work at. And this is Alana, the owner and boss," he said, introducing everyone.

"It's nice to meet you all," she said. "I like to pop up on him every now and then to make sure he's staying out of trouble. Although it looks like he's in more trouble than I thought," she said, after looking at Alana, then back at her brother.

"No trouble these days. I'm keeping him in line," Diego said, assuming she was talking about the two of them working together again. They continued making small talk for a while before Sherri hinted that it was time to get the baby home for a nap. As they parted ways and continued throughout the market, Alana felt embarrassed that she hadn't recognized Sherri from the family portrait on Alex's piano. She laughed at herself, wondering what her face must have looked like when he introduced them. It wasn't long before he texted her, insisting that they meet up later in the day.

Alex: *I want to see you later. We need to be alone...to talk that is. Can you meet me at Margaret's Apple Orchard?*

Alana: *I don't know Alex...*

Alex: *Why not? Are you afraid that being surrounded by the forbidden fruit will remind you of how I tasted yours?*

Alana: *Lol. I'll meet you there at 3 p.m.*

Alex: *Cool. By the way, you're kind of cute when you're jealous* ☺

Alana smacked her lips and smiled as she put the cell phone into her pocket. Half an hour later, she and Gigi bought some hot chocolate while the guys loaded up the van. They all returned to the restaurant, where they quickly restocked, and Gigi took off so she could go meet Brian. Alana had enough time to spruce herself up and head to the apple orchard, which was about forty-five minutes outside of the city. She was looking forward to setting things straight. What was happening between them wasn't responsible or the most appropriate. Logic told her that last night would be better off remaining an isolated incident. But, deep down, she was starting to like what they had going.

Alana arrived at Margaret's Apple Orchard and found Alex leaning against his car, waiting for her. He stepped up to her car and opened the door for her, followed by a kiss on the cheek. He complimented her on how stunning she looked as she stepped out in her red and black cape coat, tan leather driving gloves, black skinny jeans and knee-high riding boots. She didn't know if this was a date or not, but she knew the jean and sweatshirt look from earlier wouldn't do. They walked over the gravel parking lot and met up with one of the attendants to go over the rules, prices and closing time. Afterwards, Alex grabbed their baskets so they could begin their stroll through the orchard. For the first ten minutes, the two would sneak looks at each other, but quickly look away if they found the other looking back. Finally, Alex decided to stare at her relentlessly, until she broke down and spoke to him.

"Has anyone ever told you that your stare can be quite intense?"

"Well, my father once told me, 'Son, if you find what you want in life, gaze upon it with such intensity that it would never be able to escape your grasp.'"

"So, you use this approach often, do you?" she asked.

"I wouldn't say often. But that's what I did when I wanted to become a chef, and that's what I did when I wanted to become your man."

"Oh, you're cute!" she said sarcastically. You're not my man—"

"Not yet anyway. I'll give you a few weeks to get used to the idea."

"You're a bit of a conundrum."

"How so?" he questioned curiously.

"I mean the cocky part is expected. I've never known a chef, especially a talented one that wasn't. But a philosophical cook?"

"I think they go hand in hand."

"What does?"

"Food for the body and food for thought. They both feed the soul."

"Oh, you're so deep today! Laying it on thick, aren't you?" she said jokingly.

He laughed as Alana continued putting apples into the basket. They stopped in a spot where the sun was beaming down and enjoyed the warmth on their faces. He put the basket down and picked a leaf from one of the branches, twirling it nervously and hoping not to say or do anything that would cause her to run off again.

"Anyway, you're one to talk about conundrums. Science fiction movies are your favorite? Really?"

"Why is that so hard to believe?"

"I'm sorry, beautiful. But one doesn't look at you and think *The Matrix* must be her favorite movie."

"Oh yeah? Then what would your judging eyes have told you?"

"*The Devil Wears Prada.*"

"That would be Gigi," she said.

"Or *Breakfast at Tiffany's.*"

"That would be Diego!"

"Well, I'm glad you surprised me. I think science and philosophy are a good match up, don't you?"

"I don't know yet," she said with a small frown.

The chill in the air increased, making their words look like smoke as they left their lips. They were walking and talking for some time before they finally approached the cider mill and grabbed some warm drinks. They saw a log nearby and decided to sit for a moment. Alana continued to pick his brain, appreciating his willingness to tell the truth, no matter how bluntly.

"Be honest. You like picking apples?"

"Hell no! My back is killing me from carrying that basket and it's kinda cold."

Alana thought about it for a moment, but before her mind could talk her out of it, she leaned over and kissed him. He dropped his empty cup and put his hand to her cheek, kissing her
deeply. Her fingertips caressed his jawline before she stopped suddenly and stared into his eyes. He pulled away and leaned up so that his elbows were resting on his knees. She smiled once she realized he was hiding his hard on.

"It's getting warmer though," he joked. Alana laughed as she put her arm through his and they continued talking.

"So, what do you look for in a man, Ms. Jones?"

"It's hard to say. Every man I've ever dated has been different from the last."

"Yeah, but there has to be something specific that you start with," he insisted.

"Okay, I guess you're right. He has to have a career."

"Wouldn't you know it. I just happen to have a career!"

"I'd like him to be handsome, if possible."

"Take a long look at me woman!" he said, putting his hand to his chin and posing.

"He has to have his own life and interests. I don't want to be his everything and only thing."

"Girl, I'm not trying to be up under you all the time," he joked, snatching away.

"He has to believe in God."

"I thank Him for letting me meet you every day."

"He has to be realistic when it comes to relationships."

"Meaning?"

"Meaning, it's a possibility that I won't feel the same way about him that he feels about me. I don't exactly have the best track record."

"Ah, you mean the love thing, right?"

Alex took that into consideration. Since first meeting Alana, he hadn't been able to think of anything else except getting close to her. And now, here she was telling him something that could potentially push him away. Her inability to fully connect with someone in the past had often caused men to resent her. Alex decided to weigh in on what he wanted more: the possibility of being with her, or the possibility that he'd be broken by her. Diego's warning also popped into his head. Did Simeon really long for her, or was it just speculation? And with him being so close to Alana, would he be able to pursue her quietly and avoid workplace drama? The questions were certainly there. But rather than throw caution to the wind, he decided to adopt a different philosophy, one that his brother often repeated to him whenever something major was on the line: no guts, no glory!

"Alana, I don't know what you could possibly feel for me one day, nor do I care at this point. All I know at this moment is that I can't settle for last night being the only time I ever get to taste your skin or wrap my arms around your body. We can keep it as quiet as you want, for as long as you want. Just give me a chance, a chance to get to know you inside and out."

Alex picked up their baskets so they could make their way toward the exit. Alana thought about it as she gave him her best poker face. He thought his speech had been all for naught, when she began to present her terms.

"We have to be careful and keep things quiet for now. I don't want anyone at work knowing, especially not while things are so casual."

"We can do that."

"If things don't work out, we'll remain professional and part ways as friends."

"I can do that. Anything else?"

"Next weekend, if you're free, we should be alone again. Maybe I can abuse my power and take advantage of you."

"You can definitely do that!" he said before kissing her once more. He paid for their apples and put them in her car as they called it a day. Alana had butterflies in her stomach the entire ride home. It had been such a nice date. In fact, it was blowing her mind that she could even admit it was a date! Once she made it home and plopped down on her couch, Alex sent her one last message to end their day on an even more positive note. *Next weekend can't get here fast enough. Be sure you get lots of rest before you come over here again and for your own sake...stretch! Your muscles might get a workout.*

Alana blushed as she relaxed for the first time all day. Thoughts of her budding, secret relationship thrilled her.

Chapter | 9

"Terrible Tuesday" was suddenly becoming a regular thing. For some reason, the most difficult customers found their way into the restaurant on that day, and all but Alex and Alana seemed to notice. Both remained on cloud nine since their day together at the orchard, and it was spilling over into their daily lives. People close to Alana kept commenting on her "happy glow," and Alex's positive attitude and non-stop work ethic showed his co-workers that he was indeed the best man for the job. The day before, he even managed to beat Diego to work, which was virtually unheard of.

However, there was one person who noticed something else going on with Alex: Simeon. He couldn't help but notice his inability to look at anything other than Alana when she walked by. Numerous times, he caught Alex gazing at her with a longing in his eyes that seemed all too familiar. At times, an almost territorial feeling manifested within Simeon. He knew that he was in no position to confront him over someone that didn't belong to him, but he also didn't take too kindly to his eyes watching her ass move through their workspace.

Simeon wondered if he was just imagining things. Alana was a beautiful woman and, surely, Alex wasn't the only male member of the staff who noticed. But Alex's eyes indicated interest, and Simeon had no room for competition—not that he felt Alex had a dying chance. Alana was way out of his league, in Simeon's eyes. But, just for kicks, he decided to see if a little harmless flirting could gauge his true intentions.

Alana had just finished having lunch with one of the organizers of the cancer fundraiser, which was going to be held at the restaurant. She went into the office to drop off the contract they'd just signed. Before she could exit the kitchen, she was stopped by Simeon.

"Hey Alana, Diego, you guys want to come over tomorrow night around 10? It's been a while since we had a game night. I'll tell the other members of our circle. It will be fun," he said in a persuasive tone.

"I don't know, Simeon," she said. "You know Gigi and I are getting up early to leave—"

"Oh, come on. Starting tonight, you're on vacation. I won't keep you out too late, I promise. Not unless you want me to, that is!"

"Fine!" she said with a fake attitude. "I've really got to learn to say no to you."

"No, you don't. I love it when you give in to me," he said.

"Well, you guys can definitely count me and Carla in. I'm going to call our babysitter right now!" Diego exclaimed.

As the two dispersed, Simeon looked over to find Alex still working, but noticeably agitated. His jaw was tense, as if he was mashing concrete between his teeth. His eyes had narrowed and a frown was upon his brow. But, through it all, he still maintained his professionalism. He jerked his head to crack his neck, relieving some of the tension building up inside of him. Simeon smiled to himself, now realizing that Alex might in fact have a crush on Alana.

"Something wrong, new blood?" he asked the newest member of the team. Diego returned just in time to notice something brewing between the two, so he took it upon himself to inject some calm into the atmosphere. He looked at Alex and flexed his arms, which was their code for "toughen up." Alex realized at that moment that Simeon was trying to bait him, but he wouldn't fall for it so easily.

"Wrong? Not at all," Alex responded with a small smirk. "Where's boss lady off to tomorrow?"

"Every year, she and Gigi take a trip a few hours up north and hit every winery in town. They always end up coming back with more bottles than either of them can carry."

"Alana certainly does know her wines," Diego added.

"She's not too bad at French either," Alex interjected.

"Of course, she's good at French. I taught her. I taught her *all* things French: speaking, cooking and *kissing*," Simeon added before winking and walking toward the door. He looked around to make sure he'd said it low enough for only the three of them to hear. Diego rolled his eyes, knowing that he was just showing off. But Alex wouldn't let him get the last word. Before he could proceed through the door, he added his own tidbit of information.

"You certainly did a wonderful job, chef. And I'm sure there is someone somewhere who is regularly reaping the benefits of your hard work."

Simeon couldn't believe the audacity of Alex to return the dig he'd just thrown his way. It had indeed backfired and he wasn't happy about it. He turned around and stared at Alex for a moment before heading his way, causing Diego to shake his head and whisper to himself, "Here we go." He stood at Alex's station as he continued chopping and acted as if he hadn't even noticed Simeon standing there. Alex looked up, pretending to be startled before Simeon spoke, exuding every ounce of annoyance he was feeling.

"You care to elaborate on that?" he asked. Diego stood at the station behind him, shaking his head negatively, as if he needed help answering. Alex didn't want to expose his budding romance with Alana; putting a woman's private business on display wasn't his style. He also didn't want to disregard the fact that Diego had gone out on a limb and vouched for him so he could get the job. To top it all off, Simeon was soon to be Alana's full-fledged business partner. Alex decided to be the bigger man. He would humble himself and let Simeon's arrogance prevail this time…*this time*!

"No, chef. Nothing to elaborate on."

Simeon marched out of the kitchen just in time enough for Diego to throw a towel at Alex, hitting him in the face. He looked at him, shocked, before they both started laughing.

"Bro, what the hell was that?" Diego asked.

"Hey, he started it! Did you hear that bullshit?"

"Trust me, I didn't like it either and I'm going to say something to him about it later. She's our friend and boss, for that matter. But chill out! Your little crush is gonna get you crushed."

"As long as you can promise she'll be the one crushing me. I'd die happy under that pile of flesh!"

Diego laughed and, even though he seemed okay, Alex apologized and told him that he would never want to let him down after he was cool enough to refer him. He promised that, from now on, he would check himself so that no more problems would threaten their work environment. In his mind, he couldn't wait to put Simeon's great *teachings* to use in his own time.

The following evening, 10 p.m. crept up quickly and game night at Simeon's was just about to begin. Homemade pizzas baked in the oven as shrimp cocktail chilled in the refrigerator. Rarely did he have more than a couple of guests over to his bachelor pad. But when he did, it was always the same few: his brother Jirou and his girlfriend Shawny, Diego and his wife Carla, Alana, Gigi and Brian. Since he had the day off, he had more than enough time to clean up his place and prepare the light feast. He even lit a few Voluspa Crisp Champagne Candles to add to the ambiance.

Alana put on some music and opened a bottle of wine, while Gigi and Carla danced in front of the couch. Carla demonstrated some of the moves from her Zumba class, which helped her shed her baby weight. Diego had just shown up from work and, with Simeon's blessing, excused himself for a quick shower and change of clothes. In the billiard room, Jirou and Brian played a friendly game of pool, while Shawny pulled out Guesstures and Uno. Alana brought bowls of chips to the table and, after cutting up the gourmet pizzas, Simeon emerged from the kitchen with two platters and eight small serving plates. He placed everything onto the oversized coffee table in front of the long suede sectional. The group sat around the table on pillows and almost immediately began to dig into each other's business before game time.

Simeon stuffed his face and grilled his little brother about how medical school was going. Jirou explained how intense his courses were and, in turn, asked his big brother when he was going to settle down with someone already. The two were extremely close, so he was well aware of his affection for Alana.

"I mean, who knows? Mrs. Right could be right under your nose," he said. Gigi told the group that she knew for a fact Lexa, the salesgirl from her boutique, had a huge crush on Simeon and that maybe he should ask her out. But Simeon noted that she was a little too young for him and quickly changed the subject. Alana asked Carla about the kids as she went to grab another bottle of wine. Carla began telling a funny story about them, while Simeon silently threatened his brother to cut it out. Once they had all indulged themselves with food, good conversation, and a couple more glasses of wine, the games were in full swing.

Jirou suggested that they play two couples to a team. He knew that Simeon and Alana had no choice but to join up, and he found it amusing that he could use it to taunt his older brother. In retaliation, Simeon suggested that his team join up with Diego and Carla. He figured since his brother wanted to be funny, he would make sure the joke was on him by beating him a few times. As usual, the men took the game way more seriously than the women. Even long after the games were over, the guys made up their own games just so they could continue to compete.

A little after 1 a.m., Jirou complained about the time and insisted that he and his lady needed to be going. In big brother fashion, Simeon teased that perhaps he was just tired of losing. Brian followed suit shortly after, but Diego was willing to stay. After all, he had a babysitter and was off the next day. But Carla insisted that they go home and have some "private time" while the kids were asleep. Simeon walked everyone to the door while Alana took the dishes into the kitchen. The brothers hugged goodbye, followed by Jirou giving him a small punch in the arm as he mouthed the words, "Say something to her." Alana scrapped the plates into the trash and ran some dish water. Before Simeon joined her, he put on some more music, hoping to calm his nerves.

"Lately it seems that I'm becoming an expert at helping men do dishes."

"Oh, yeah? Who else had the honor?"

Alana quickly realized that she was about to open Pandora's Box when she made something up about helping one of the workers at the restaurant. He thought nothing of it as he put the corks back into the empty bottles littering the island. The two cleaned for a moment before Alana homed in on the music that was playing. She nodded her head and moved to the beat as she sang the chorus to "I Want You" by Common. She laughed at her friend as she began to tease him.

"What do you know about that?"

"I can relate to the lyrics."

"Oh yeah? How so?"

"A real man recognizes when he let a great woman slip through his fingers," he said sincerely.

Alana looked up to find Simeon looking back at her with lust in his eyes, a look she hadn't seen since the last time they'd fooled around. Nervously, she broke eye contact and commented on how good the wine tasted as she gulped down what was left in her glass. Submerging her hands back into the warm, soapy water, she scrubbed the pan and tried hopelessly to move on to something else. Simeon stood next to her, rinsing the plates and placing them in the dish rack.

They stood in silence, allowing the music to drown out the awkwardness in the air. One of the wine bottles had a few swallows left in it. So, Alana poured it into her glass and took a sip, before Simeon took the glass from her and finished it off. After letting the water out, she flicked some suds at him and turned to rinse out her glass. But Simeon grabbed her wrist. There was so much he wanted to say to her, things he had wanted to confess for years.

He whispered her name, but nothing followed. *"This always happens,"* he thought to himself. He was so confident in other areas of his life, even with other women. But when it came to Alana, he always reverted to the same semi-shy guy he was in college. The silence became more than he could bear, when his hands found their way to her face. He held her cheeks gently, looking over every beauty mark, every eyelash, before placing his lips onto hers.

He pecked her once. Then again. Then again. His lips took hold of her bottom lip, sucking it gently before sliding his tongue into her mouth. Alana was caught completely off guard, but could not pull away! She held firmly onto the glass with one hand while the other moved to the back of his head, without thinking. It was as if she was on autopilot, as if her body were reacting based on memory. They kissed passionately, then wildly before his lips made way to her neck and back to her lips again. Their heads twisted from side to side as they kissed like there was no tomorrow. Her red lipstick smeared across her mouth, leaving a trail of desire that Simeon was happy to follow. His hands slid down to her ass and began to squeeze, surprising her. She was jolted out of the moment when she dropped her glass. The sound of it crashing to the floor startled her.

"I'm sorry," she said. She backed away from him and began to pick up the shards of glass. But he pulled her up, wanting to continue.

"Alana, its okay. Leave it."

"I, um. I think I better go."

"But why?"

"I don't think we should get carried away."

"I like it when we get carried away!"

"Yeah, but—"

And with that, Simeon didn't want to hear or say another word. He rushed toward her, crushing the glass under his shoe. His mouth smashed into hers while his arms scooped her into the air, placing her onto the island. Empty wine bottles crashed to the floor as he ripped open her blouse, sending buttons flying in various directions. She struggled to pull his shirt over his head, but her fingertips caressed his six-pack with ease.

He pressed his nose in between her breasts for a moment and inhaled the smell of her skin, a smell that he'd longed for, but seemed to elude him over time. It didn't matter how much time had passed. The scent was still the same: sweet, like sugar on a rose. His hands dug into her hips as his tongue trailed from between her breasts back up to her neck. She was even more intoxicating than he remembered and, like a fine wine, she'd only gotten better with age. Her legs wrapped around his waist as they kissed with no hesitation.

Just as Simeon began to kiss her collarbone and slide her bra straps off her shoulders, his buzzer rang. His eyes popped open, wild with disbelief. This could not be happening! Who the hell was ringing this late and unannounced? He begged Alana not to move as she sat both confused and exhilarated. She smiled and continued to hold the air sarcastically, like he was still standing between her legs. He smiled at her as he walked backwards to the door, not wanting to miss anything. He was so hard that he couldn't think straight. He stumbled over his words before he was able to form a complete sentence. Secretly, he hoped the unwanted caller had the wrong apartment.

"Who the fuck is it?" he asked, frustrated but laughing.

"It's Lisa, asshole. We're supposed to be going to the after hour, remember?"

And, like a flash of lightening, the moment was gone. Alana hopped down off the island, as if the sound of the woman's voice snapped her back into reality. Simeon tried his best to get rid of his guest while Alana put on her now buttonless top and tied it in a knot. The young lady continued to argue with Simeon over the speaker as Alana grabbed her purse and headed to the door. He leaned against the door, apologizing for the interruption and begging her to stay.

"Please don't go, Alana. I swear Lisa is just a friend," he explained. Desperation took over his eyes and she knew that he did indeed want her to stay. But at what cost to their friendship? She kissed him on his cheek and responded as kindly and sincerely as she could.

"So am I, Simeon. I'm just your friend, too. Let's not mess that up, okay?" she said, holding his cheek. Alana walked out and headed toward the elevator. She could hear his fist hit the door as he yelled out, "Shit!" on the other side of it.

What had she done? Had she hurt him? Was he angry? And what was going on with her sense of self-control? Before tonight, Alex consumed her thoughts. She anticipated his calls and melted from his text messages. She couldn't wait until their dinner date on Saturday. So, what happened? Why did she want Simeon so badly in that moment? And an even better question was why was it so easy to turn off? Alana got into her car, grateful for the interruption that possibly saved her friendship. She decided to go home and sleep it off. Even after what had just happened, she still found herself thinking of Alex.

The next morning, Alana couldn't get out of town fast enough. She only slept a few hours and was up at the crack of dawn so she and Gigi could start their three-and-a-half-hour drive. She was feeling out of place after her encounter with Simeon, and she was concerned that she may have hurt him, which was weighing heavily on her. To make matters worse, she received a text message from Alex right before she pulled off: *Be careful, have fun, return to me soon.* When she pulled up to Brian's place to pick up Gigi, the two were at the curb kissing as if she'd be gone a week. It was beyond Alana's understanding how Brian could be in the cold autumn air with only a thin, white t-shirt and blue plaid pajama pants, and not be freezing.

Gigi's thick, dark curly hair blew in the wind as he slid his arms inside of her coat and wrapped them around her tiny waist. In turn, she wrapped her long, black pea coat around him as best as she could to shield him from the teeth-chattering cold. They both smiled as their lips pressed into each other's. Brian pulled back his head and stared deeply into the irises of her eyes to confess his love.

"I love you baby."

"Oh yeah? How much?"

"Give me ten minutes, and I'll show you, again!"

Gigi giggled as she tore herself from his arms before she became more turned on. Brian opened the passenger door for her and placed her bag in the back of the Range Rover. He poked his head through the window for one last kiss and told Alana to return his queen in one piece. The two entrepreneurs proceeded on their way for a well-deserved break from work and plenty of time to talk.

"You two look like you had fun this morning," Alana observed.

"Girl, that man right there! I'm telling you, I'm gonna get diabetes sucking on all that sweet stuff!" she exclaimed.

The two friends laughed. They stopped to grab some coffee and fill up the gas tank before hitting the highway. The further they got out of the city, the more Alana got to admire the clusters of trees along the roadside. She enjoyed seeing the array of colors all clumped together. Some were bright orange like pumpkins, filling large trees entirely until they seemed as though they were suspended pumpkin patches. Others had turned lime green, fiery crimson and amber. She found herself more partial to the rare plum-colored leaves. Their deep, rich purple tones were scarcely seen, but were a sublime treat when they were.

Two hours into their trip, it had become normal to come upon a pasture with horses trotting around their enclosed area. The girls got a kick out of how funny the cows looked as they chewed wildly on their cud. The sky was gray and gloomy, but sunrays cut through some of the clouds like swords. Groups of birds flew in formation, sometimes flying back and forth as if they were doing a coordinated dance. The peaceful ride calmed her mind, which was heavy with thoughts. Alana finally began to feel some shred of relief.

Gigi opened a bag of popcorn and flipped through fashion magazines while she spoke non-stop about Brian, the boutique and the upcoming holidays. Alana tried her best to stay engaged in the conversation, but still felt slightly out of sorts. Images flashed in her mind of kissing both Simeon and Alex. She thought about how strong Alex's arms felt around her waist when he caught her. She thought about how strong Simeon's arms were as he lifted her onto the counter and tore open her shirt. She thought about how gently Alex's hand had held her cheek before sliding down to her throat. She thought about how aggressively Simeon had pulled her hair, like he wanted her more than anything. Gigi chatted for a while before she noticed how silent her travel companion was being.

"What's wrong with you? And why is 'Uh huh' your answer to everything?" she inquired. When Alana struggled to answer that as well, her best friend decided to ask her something a little simpler. She asked about Alex.

Gigi said she couldn't help but notice him always checking her out and that maybe she'd made a mistake by not pursuing things. The memories switched back and forth at warp speed: Simeon, Alex, Simeon, Alex! After pondering what she would say, the words finally burst out of her, like a water pipe that could no longer contain the pressure.

"I kissed him!"

Chapter | 10

Gigi turned down the radio, unable to believe what she'd just heard. She figured maybe it would be a good idea to put it on a volume that would allow her to hear clearly what she *thought* she heard.

"Did you just say you kissed Alex?" she asked.

"Oh, yeah. Him, too."

"Him too?! Wait! Who were you talking about in the first place?"

"Simeon!" Alana answered, squinting and bracing herself for a hit.

"Okay, wait a minute. You mean to tell me we've been on the road for two hours, and you're just now telling me this?" Gigi asked, slapping her arm. "Oh, you know I've got so many questions for your sneaky ass! So, where did Simeon kiss you, slut?"

"In his kitchen last night."

"Oh, boy! The pussy bandit strikes again! We'll never be able to shut him up now!"

"No, no! No pussy bandit! He was more of a lip looter. Nothing happened!"

"Okay, if you say so. Where did Alex kiss you? Anywhere interesting?"

"Yes, on his dining room table, on my lips….both sets!"

"Girl, shut up! Well, was he any good at it?"

"Good? The tongue was so good, I'm afraid of what his dick has in store!"

"Oh, so the brother was passing out orgasms left and right, huh?"

"Like spoons at a soup kitchen!"

The girls couldn't stop laughing for at least half a mile. Alana told her everything: about their late-night texting, the dinner with Alex, the moment with Simeon, and how she may have possibly ruined a perfectly good friendship. Gigi stared at her in disbelief, continuing to shove hands full of popcorn into her mouth. She couldn't believe all of this had been taking place right under her nose, but she could tell that the situation with Simeon was really bothering Alana.

She wanted so badly to tell her that her friendship with Simeon was in no danger of ending, and that she knew for a fact he'd secretly been waiting for that moment for a long time. But, Gigi knew it wasn't her truth to tell. If Alana was ever going to find out how he really felt deep down in his heart, it needed to come from his lips, in his words, in his time. Besides, the way she lit up when she spoke of Alex was something she could see was worth seeing through. But as usual, on cue, Alana went from full blown excitement to full blown panic.

"Seriously, tell me what you think? You think I made a mistake? This is stupid, isn't it? It's unprofessional. It's irresponsible. I haven't known him long. You're right. I should just—"

"Stop! Breathe! Go with the flow! I mean, sure, you took employee appreciation to a whole other level. But Alana, you should see your face when you talk about him."

"I know! I can't explain it. But when I'm around him, I feel like I can't get enough of him."

"I see! I've never seen you like this before. And who cares how long you've known him? Whether it's five months, five weeks or five days, if there is something there, it doesn't matter."

"What about Simeon? You think—"

"I think he'll be fine! Look, keep it quiet like you've been doing. See what happens. Let it flow naturally. Keep that open-minded attitude. Don't let your stubborn heart get in the way." After their heartfelt talk, the ladies arrived at their hotel. They were ready to get out, go wine tasting, and to hopefully end up somewhere doing drunk karaoke.

Saturday afternoon, they returned home, ready to face all that awaited them: their businesses, their bills and their boys! After dropping Gigi off, Alana entered her building to take her small suitcase upstairs, but stopped once she noticed an envelope sticking out of her mailbox. There was no return address on it but, once she opened it, she knew right away who it was from. Inside was a folded piece of paper that had a key in the center of it. The handwriting matched that of a note she had previously received. This one read: *Welcome back! A little early for keys, I know! But I want you to get the full experience of coming home to me. I hope you're ready to eat because I've been preparing something special for you all day. See you at 8 p.m. Al.*

With all of the drama going on, she had almost forgotten about the date she made with Alex...*almost!* Excitement overtook her as she got into the elevator with plans to pick out an outfit for dinner that could stop a truck! After checking her messages, going through her mail, and putting her tenants' rent checks to the side, she decided to go down and pop into the restaurant. She spoke to Diego and Simeon before rushing into the office, where she found Damien, the evening manager, on the phone. He nodded at her as he continued going over an order they'd just received. Once he was finished, they spoke for a while about how things had gone the past couple of days. Fortunately, there was nothing major to report to the overly anal-retentive business owner. So, Damien made his way to the bar, where a young lady was waiting for him. Alana proceeded to add some money to the safe when Simeon stepped in and closed the door behind him. She was actually grateful that Alex had the day off so that she didn't have to face them both right away.

"You haven't been returning my texts," he said quietly.

"I know. I am so sorry. You know how crazy Gigi and I get when we're out of town. I didn't answer anyone, to be honest."

"It's cool. I just wanted to make sure we're okay. Are we gonna address what happened the other night?"

"Oh, um, sure. I guess we do need to do that. But do we have to do it here?" she asked with a little smile to lighten the mood.

"Of course not. You're absolutely right. I'll let you get settled back in."

As Simeon exited the office, Alana's heart felt heavy again. She knew that she couldn't keep dodging him. He was obviously just as disturbed by what happened as she was. He was one of her best friends in the whole world, and she hoped with everything in her that she hadn't ruined that. She cared about him and his feelings, but she had to admit that her focus was somewhere else. Besides, she had no way of explaining what happened that night or why. She could only guess that they were caught up in the moment and fell prey to the effects of the wine.

Her interest in Alex, however, had become something more than momentary. Their silent courtship, filled with flirty text messages, the private dinner where she became his dessert, and a couple of instances of phone sex, had progressed over the past few weeks. She found herself connecting with him in a way that she never had with anyone before. Her well-kept secret was becoming something she liked, *someone* she really liked! That was what she wanted to deal with at the moment and, hopefully, Simeon could put off what happened until she figured out how to approach it.

Alana arrived at Alex's, dressed to kill. Her hair was pinned over to one side with small curls cascading down. Her black knee-length dress with cap sleeves showed just enough cleavage to make Alex's mouth water, and her makeup made her look like she was ready for the cover of *Ebony*. She held her white wool cape closed as she nervously approached his door for the second time. Immediately, she started to second guess whether or not she should go through with the date.

On the skinny glass window was a sticky note that had been taped in place. It read: *You made it this far, don't chicken out on me now!* Alana laughed at his arrogance. *"He thinks he knows me!"* she thought to herself. She snatched the note down, crumbling it and putting it in her purse while retrieving the key he had left for her. Once she entered, she was pleased to find red rose petals everywhere. Some led from the door to the living room, while others led to the dining room. She stuck her head into the living room and found a small fire burning again. But, this time, the photography books that filled the coffee table had been replaced with a shiny silver tray equipped with white wine and strawberries.

"Alex!" she called out.

"Hey, beautiful!" he yelled out from the kitchen. "Have a seat in the living room. I'll be in there to take your coat in a second."

"That's okay. I remember where it goes."

"Oh yeah, how could I forget. Last time you grabbed your coat and shot out of here like a bat out of hell!"

After hanging it up, she returned to the living room and took a sip from one of the wine glasses. She walked over to the piano and rubbed her fingers over the keys. Alex snuck up behind her and wrapped his arms around her waist before planting a kiss on her neck.

"You play?" she asked.

"One song," he said with a chuckle. "You want to hear it?"

"Sure!"

Alana took a seat on the couch and gave him her undivided attention. He proceeded to play a rather child-like rendition of "Chopsticks" as she held in her laugh, trying to take his feelings into account. Once he finished, he turned to find her obviously amused, but pretending not to be. She rubbed her lips together as if she were fixing her lip gloss, but a small laugh soon emerged.

"Are you laughing at me?"

"No, that was great," she said with a small clap.

"I suppose you think you can do better?"

"Oh, baby! I *know* I can!"

"I believe you. And I like it when you call me baby," he said, getting up from the bench. He walked over to Alana and pecked her on the lips before challenging her. "But you still have to prove it to me, though."

She got up from the couch and removed her heels before sitting down at the piano and staring at the keys. It had been a long time since she'd played. Grandma Marra made her take lessons from the time she was six up until she was fifteen. During her formative years, she had unwillingly become both Marra's and Georgia's pupil. When she wasn't at the museum with Marra, she was at the opera with Georgia. When she wasn't with the both of them at a fancy dinner, she was accompanying them to a play.

Alana thought she had to be the only teenager in her school who knew the work of Gustav Klimt or the music of Kathleen Battle. In her youth, she often wondered if their lessons were to make sure she didn't follow the same path as her mother, if maybe her grandmother felt she had failed in some way. But whatever the reason, Alana grew to appreciate it. It didn't hurt to be well-versed in music and art, and her exposure to different cultures had made her opportunities seem boundless. She closed her eyes and let her fingers play what they remembered. Alex listened as she played Chopin's "Nocturne Op. 9, No. 2" perfectly! When she finished, she turned to find Alex staring at her, astonished.

"What are you thinking about?" she asked.

"How awesome our kids are going to be."

"Ha! Kids? We have to get married or at least have sex first!" she joked.

"Is that a proposal and a proposition?"

"Depends. Which are you most interested in?"

"Either one. But if we're talking tonight, I'm damn sure picking the proposition."

The two smiled at one another and, after she slipped back on her shoes, Alex grabbed her hand and led her to the dining room. The meal looked like it had been plucked from the pages of a Martha Stewart magazine. She couldn't imagine how long it had taken him to prepare it.

"You know you didn't have to do all of this, right? A cheeseburger would have sufficed."

"I guess I'm still trying to impress you."

"Oh, I'm impressed!" she said, looking him up and down as if he were the meal.

She took a seat and let the aroma engulf her. Everything smelled as good as it looked, including him! Whenever she wasn't receiving whiffs of sautéed vegetables or slow-roasted meat, she was treated to a hint of his Gucci Guilty cologne. Alex poured them both another glass of wine as they stared into each other's eyes, waiting for the other to look away. But it had become apparent that neither would be backing down tonight.

"Music?" he asked.

"Absolutely."

He grabbed a remote and continued to satisfy her senses. Luke James' "Make Love to Me" played on the surround sound as her host winked at her and prepared to dig into his food—and hopefully her. Alana's ears perked up, and so did other parts of her body, as she realized her dinner music was more like a sexual appetizer. She drank her wine down to the bottom of the glass and placed it next to her plate. Resistance was no longer an option as she stood up from the table and made an announcement.

"I've had enough to eat. How about you?" she said, removing the pins from her hair and placing them on the napkin. Alex dropped his fork and stood from his chair, as well. He licked his lips as he realized the dinner portion of the evening was about to be postponed.

"But you haven't touched your food," he responded, unbuttoning his shirt.

"Well, I'll leave it up to you. Would you rather eat *me* right now, or this food?" Alana slowly unzipped the hidden zipper on the side of her dress. She stopped halfway down and held the dress closed, before rubbing her fingertip across the dollop of whipped cream on the sliver of cake in front of her. She licked it off and waited for his response.

"Now that you mention it, I just remembered I have a microwave. The food can wait."

The handsome host walked over to her and grabbed the zipper on her dress, finishing what she had started. He slid his cold hand onto her warm waist and snatched her close to him. Before he went any further, he wanted to make sure she knew they were about to cross a huge line—again."You sure about this?" he asked her.

Alana let the dress fall to the floor as she grabbed another strawberry from the table and headed toward the staircase. Alex watched her strut in her heels, wearing only a black bra, black thong and black garter stockings. She leaned on the banister and popped the garter against her thigh before saying, "Lead the way." Alex rushed to her, his hands slowly caressing her body. He lifted her in the air, holding her thighs as she wrapped her legs around his waist and her arms around his neck.

She pushed the unbuttoned shirt off his shoulders and kissed his collarbone before arriving at his neck. After carrying her up the stairs like she was a feather, he held her up against the wall as he moaned and kissed her with excitement. Alana could feel him getting harder and harder, until it felt as though he would rip through his pants. He continued down the hallway until he reached the bedroom. The room was dark, with only the light of the streetlamp casting through the thin curtains.

Alex put Alana down gently onto the bed. The cold touch of the bedspread sent chills all over her body. There was just enough light for her to admire his physique as he finally removed the crisp white shirt off his chocolate skin. His six-pack looked like it could break walnuts as easily as it could hearts. She stared at him, as he often did her, while watching his pants and underwear drop to the floor. Alana grinned a little as she thought to herself, *"Just the right size."* She crossed her legs and began to remove her shoes, when Alex stopped her.

"Oh, you don't have to take those off," he said as he hovered above her. "They'll be in the air pretty soon anyway." They both smiled as Alana crawled backward toward the pillows, with Alex hot on her trail. He kissed her thighs, then her stomach before making his way up to her rib cage and breasts. He grabbed her bra with his teeth and pulled it down until she was totally exposed. His tongue circled her nipple before taking it into his mouth. He used one hand to hold her wrist over her head, while the other slid between her legs. His fingers slowly moved back and forth as she grabbed his head, smashing his mouth further onto her breast. The sweet smell of her body drove him wild as he ripped his head away and stared into her eyes.

Alex kissed her, making her cum instantly. He reached into the nightstand and grabbed a condom before ripping the lace thong off her with ease. Slowly, he pushed himself inside her. Alana's nails dug into his shoulders as he plunged deeper and deeper. Her legs tightened around him as she nibbled on his earlobe. Alex's eyes shut tightly as he squeezed her hips and kissed her again. His hands slowly caressed her flesh before gripping her shoulders and pulling her down onto him until he could go no further. He moved inside her as if he were searching for her most hidden treasure. Alex rolled over, pulling Alana on top of him. She sat up, staring down at him and dominating him with her eyes. Her hips moved back and forth slowly, then in a circular motion. He stared up at her, unable to believe how incredibly sexy she was in that moment.

She rubbed her finger over his lips, which he grabbed and began to suck. She slid her other hand behind his head and pulled him to her so that they were face to face. She wrapped her legs around his waist once more. She removed her bra and leaned back so that he could see her. She continued thrusting onto him, leaning her head back as she enjoyed the ride. After what seemed liked forever of Alex trying his hardest not to cum, finally, he couldn't take it anymore. He grabbed her, thrusting his pelvis upward, further diving into her as her arms closed around his neck.

"Damn, Alana!" he exclaimed as his body shook. They remained in their embrace for a moment before she rubbed the tip of her nose against his and fell onto the bed. Alex fell back next to her and moved his hand along his forehead, pretending to fling his sweat. They both laughed a little. After a few minutes of cooling down, he started to stare at her with a look of confusion.

"What?!" she asked.

"A beautiful woman, who seems to be fun, smart, successful. Loves Sci-Fi and boxing. Plays the piano, and wears shit like *this*?" he said, pulling at her garter.

"Yeah, so?"

"I'm sorry, Alana, but I think I'm dreaming. I don't think you're real," he joked, lightly pinching her skin.

"If this were a dream, we would go downstairs, pig out and drink some more of that delicious wine before returning to this room for round two," she said, rolling over on top of him.

"A dream girl indeed!"

Alex kissed Alana deeply. After getting themselves together in the bathroom, the two raced downstairs in their underwear and sat down for dinner, the same as they would have with clothes on. Once they finished eating, Alex grabbed a bottle of wine and their glasses, suggesting that Alana follow him back upstairs.

"Prepare for me to take over your pleasure palate tonight," he said. Alana's cell phone rang, interrupting yet another moment filled with sexual tension.

He told her to answer it while she was still able to talk. He headed to the bedroom to light some candles while she took the call. Alana grabbed the phone from her purse to find Simeon's name flashing across the screen. After rejecting the call, she sent him a quick text that would hopefully hold him over until the next day: *Hey Simeon, kinda busy. I promise we will talk tomorrow. Promise!* she wrote before turning off her ringer. Alana hurried up the stairs to find the room lit by large scented candles, which smelled like hot chocolate. Alex handed her a glass of wine and suggested they make a toast.

"Here's to second-hand stores and all the one-of-a-kind treasures they've given us." Their glasses clinked together as they sipped in honor of their meeting place. Alana pecked him before pushing him back onto the bed, ready to ravage him once more.

Chapter | 11

"What time is it?!" Alex exclaimed as he jumped up wildly from his sleep. "I don't know...morning," Alana moaned. "Come back to bed." "Alana, I have to go to work. You of all people should know that," he stated, slapping her on the butt. He rushed into the bathroom and turned on the shower. Alana could hear him brushing his teeth vigorously, hoping to speed up the slow start to his morning. "Simeon is gonna rip me a new one!" he said illegibly as he brushed his tongue. Alana laughed at the fact that she'd actually understood him. She sat up in the bed, pushed her hair out of her face, and noticed her clothes folded neatly in a pile on his dresser. He must have done it when he got up in the middle of the night to put away the food. He had even lined up their shoes side by side next to the bed and placed her purse on the nightstand.

"I see I'm not the only neat freak I know," she murmured. She grabbed a piece of gum from her bag, hoping to combat the morning breath that Alex was lucky enough to have gotten rid of. After a quick shower, he bolted into the room and tried to get dressed as fast as humanly possible. He grabbed the neatly pressed chef jacket that hung from the doorknob of his closet, but not before he put on his pants faster than Alana had ever seen anyone do before. Alex sat on the edge of the bed to put his socks and shoes on while simultaneously staring at Alana's reflection in the mirror in front of him. They both smiled deviously as she started to crawl up behind him with the thick, white sheet wrapped around her body. Her arms wrapped around him as she started to kiss the back of his neck. Her hand grabbed his chin, tilting his head back as she manipulated his ear with her tongue. Alex's eyes closed tightly as he bit his lip in angst and tried his best to resist her.

"Whoa...Alana...do you know what you're doing to me?"

"Yes, I have a good feeling," she said as she slid her hands onto his lap and grabbed his morning wood.

"Okay, maybe a better question would have been why are you doing this to me? Come on, baby. You know I can't afford to be late. I'm still on probation!"

Alex dug deep down into his source of will power and peeled Alana off him. After a few deep breaths, and a couple of false starts to the doorway, he finally pecked her on the lips and ran toward the door like his life depended on it.

"Hey!" she yelled, causing him to turn around just in time to see her throw the sheet off her naked body. He gripped the door frame and bit his fist as she teased him. She laid on her stomach and swung her legs back and forth in the air as she beckoned him with her index finger.

"Last chance for breakfast!"

"I can't believe you're doing this to me!" he whined. He ran out of the door as Alana lay across his bed, laughing at his sexual frustration. She relaxed for a few minutes, but decided she'd better get a move on, as well. As she stood in the mirror flipping her hair around in an effort to see if the curls could be salvaged, a smile came across her face with just the thought of the night before: the food, the wine and the *sex*! The sex was unlike anything she'd ever experienced before. Alex was so aggressive, yet so sensual. He continually kept her guessing, and she couldn't wait until the next guessing game.

She started to pin her hair up, but her overactive imagination made her clumsy. Soon, she found herself fishing out bobby pins from his wastebasket. When she stooped down, she noticed a crumbled-up piece of paper and envelope right on top of the trash heap. It didn't take long for curiosity to take hold of her and, before she knew it, she was pulling out the pretty discarded stationery. The return address was for an N. Davis, and the letter was dated around the time Alex told her he'd moved back. It wasn't a long letter, but the words were that of a person who had come to realize the mistake she'd made in losing him. It read:

> *Dear Lex,*
>
> *I'm sure I'm the last person you want to hear from. But, after all we've been through together, I figured I had nothing to lose by taking a chance. I stopped by the other day, hoping to say all of this to you face to face, but you weren't home. That's when I decided to write you this letter. Sorry doesn't begin to express the way I feel. I never meant to hurt you, contrary to my behavior! I still love you and, after my job relocated me to the same place you moved back to, I couldn't help but think that perhaps it was fate. I'm not foolish enough to think we can pick up where we left off before things got so crazy. In fact, I don't want to. But I would love to start over, to try and be the lover and friend that you were to me (even when I didn't deserve it). My cell is the same. Call me once you've thought about it. I hope to hear from you soon.*
>
> *Love always, Nat*

Alana stopped to think about the deeply passionate letter. This must be the great love that Alex told her about the first time they had dinner together, the one who'd broken his heart. She wanted to think only of the passion she felt for him and the connection that had been obvious from the moment they met. But after reading those words, she wondered if it was fair to let Alex gamble on the hopes that one day she'd love him, when he already had someone who did. Her tendency to overthink everything was just getting started when she looked down at her cell phone and Alex's name appeared.

"I guess I should have asked if you feel comfortable locking up for me?"

"I suppose. I could use the key that was given to me far too early. Habit of yours?" she joked.

"Ha ha! Once before, my first love had a key. And since I'm going to be your first love, I guess it makes sense."

"You sound mighty sure of yourself!" she answered with a giggle. "And thanks for being honest, about your ex I mean. You could have lied to make yourself look good."

"Alana, if we're going to do this thing, secretly or eventually out in the open, we have to be straight up with each other. We're already lying to everybody else. Deal?"

"Deal!" she said, pleasantly surprised by his sincerity.

"Anyway, I hope I don't have to tell you how incredible last night was," he said.

"You don't. I was there."

"Can I see you again tonight?"

"Well…I think I can arrange that. Have a good day dear! And check your left pants pocket, by the way." While Alex put her on hold to rummage through the deep pocket, Alana placed the letter and envelope back in the trash, where she'd found it. She wanted to tell him that she read it and ask him if he had feelings for "Nat" in return. But she decided to let nature take its course. After a few moments of silence, he finally returned to the conversation just long enough to issue Alana a warning about the little gift she'd left for him.

"Woman, I'm gonna tear your ass up later!" he said before hanging up.

Alana laughed as she thought of how shocked he must have looked as he pulled out her black lace thong. Although it wasn't her style to walk around a-la-nude, she figured she could manage the ride home. Unfortunately for her, a cool breeze on her bare bottom wasn't the only thing on her mind. She now had to juggle thoughts of things to come later and the mystery woman that wanted Alex back. She really did like him, but she also knew she had no right to be jealous; they had just started seeing each other. For now, she'd just have to roll with the punches and hope that nobody got knocked out in the process.

After arriving at The Cocoa Marra late, Alex tried his best to sneak in the back door unnoticed, but his efforts failed miserably. A couple of the employees tapped each other and pointed at him, signaling that they knew something was coming his way. He expected that soon he'd hear the yells of Chef Simeon, demanding an explanation as to why he was "ruining the essence of excellence," as chef often said of people being late. Instead, he was met by an equally demanding Diego, who threw up his hands and pointed to the clock on the wall. Alex thought he was lucky as he realized Simeon was absent, but Diego was in no mood or position to show favoritism. He scolded his old friend the same as he would any other employee.

"Really, Alex? Don't start with the late shit! Just because Chef Simeon is out today doesn't mean it's play time! I don't hate a lot of things, but there is one thing I hate more than anything. What do I hate staff?" Diego asked loudly.

"Tardiness!" the kitchen staff yelled in unison.

"I'm sorry, Chef D. It won't happen again, I swear!" Alex said.

"It better not. I'm letting you off easy. You don't want the big boss riding you!" he said before walking away.

"*Trust me*," Alex mumbled to himself, "*She was trying to!*"

Alex made his way to his station and began working like a machine to make up for disappointing his friend yet again. After about an hour, Diego had calmed down enough to accept Alex's apology and make small talk. The guys went over the previous night's football game, which Diego couldn't believe Alex had missed. He followed up by telling Alex he should thank his lucky stars that Simeon and Alana were scheduled to check out a possible location for the second restaurant--or else he would have been toast! Shortly after their discussion, Alana came through the door, glowing in a crisp white button-up and dark brown form-fitting slacks.

Her hair, which she didn't really have time to comb, had been stuffed under an ivory beanie with brown feathers along the side of it. She tightened the belt on her trench coat and asked Diego if she could get two espressos to go. Alex peeked at her as Diego handed them over and reminded her of her appointment. She inhaled the beans for a quick pick-me-up before heading across the street to have her morning chat with Gigi. As she passed Alex, he offered up a quick, "Good morning," as if he hadn't already given her one. Alana spoke back and informed him that his left pocket was hanging out. She smiled at his embarrassment before continuing through the main room and out of the front door.

When she arrived at Cloth, Lexa let her in and pointed toward the indigo ottomans by the dressing rooms, where Gigi was sitting. Gigi turned around and smirked at Alana as she sat down the items she was putting together on a couple of mannequins. After grabbing the warm beverage with gratitude, she was prepared to grill her bestie on the events of last night. She straightened her brown and white Aztec poncho, as if she was getting serious.

"Hey, Lexa. Bring me a towel!" Gigi shouted.

"Why? What happened?" she asked, concerned.

"Nothing yet, but I have a feeling Alana is about to spill the beans!"

"Oh, you're starting out on a roll this morning!" Alana said sarcastically.

"Speaking of rolls, did you roll, in the hay, that is? Not that I need to ask with that glow you're sporting this morning."

"Me? Glowing? Perhaps it's from all of the heat I was exposed to last night."

"And I take it you didn't visit a sauna! Oh, yes! Let's get right to the good stuff! So, did he make a *big* first impression or a small one?" she asked, bending her pinkie.

"It was perfect."

"Thank goodness! You don't want it so small that it barely touches your walls. But you don't want it too big, either."

"Too big? Is there such a thing?" Alana asked, skeptical.

"Hell yeah!" Gigi leaned in and whispered, "One time, I saw one so big, I thought there was finally proof that the Loch Ness Monster existed."

"I can't with you!" Alana said, laughing hysterically.

"Girl, I couldn't with *him*! You think I'm playing? I had nightmares about that thing. I dreamt it was going to come up out of my bath water and snatch me under until I drowned!"

The ladies shared a gut-busting laugh and continued gossiping for a while, before Lexa came rushing to the back with the phone. But instead of handing it to Gigi, the caller had asked for Alana. Diego explained that he'd been trying to reach her on her cell, but she wasn't picking up. Alana looked down and panicked once she realized she had four missed calls, two of which were from Simeon.

"Alana, Simeon just called. What are you still doing over there? Appointment, expansion. Remember?!"

She had completely forgotten that her phone was still on silent so that last night's rendezvous could go uninterrupted. She rushed out of the door, but not before handing the phone to Gigi, leaving her to listen to Diego mumble about everyone being off their "A" game today. Alana called Simeon back to let her partner know that she was en route. She drove in silence, quietly questioning if she was now becoming careless in more than one aspect of her life.

Her tires screeched as she arrived at the address Simeon had given her. She rushed through the doors about fifteen minutes late, thanks to her flooring it. But, to her, she may as well have been an hour late. She struggled with her purse and jacket, which were falling off her shoulder due to her darting out of the car in such a hurry. Simeon walked around the space, flirting with the pretty real estate agent every chance he got. As they examined the large room, Alana smirked at how his hand always conveniently found its way to the middle of her back, causing the young woman to gaze up at him. She recognized the facial expressions he was making, which she'd seen him do so many times before.

Simeon would use any part of his body to gain a woman's undivided attention. But the way he used his eyes and lips to soften them up for the kill usually got the job done all on their own. It always amazed Alana that, after watching him interact with so many women, whenever she looked upon his face, she was always met by the same shy eyes and soft-spoken lips she knew in college. Even so, she had to admit that when he wasn't terrorizing the staff, asking her or Gigi to lie to women for him, or being an arrogant prick, he was pretty sexy! As Alana approached them, he removed his hand from the young woman and rubbed it over his short, wavy hair, which he normally would have cut by now. She was just catching her breath when she noticed that his latest victim seemed almost disappointed for the interruption.

"Gina, this is my best friend and business partner, Alana, who is usually never late. So, I can only assume something went terribly wrong this morning."

"Yes, please forgive my tardiness I—"

"Oh, it was no problem at all. Mr. Ito was able to keep me entertained," Gina responded, looking at him with 'do me' eyes.

Alana smiled, but inside, she almost pitied the poor thing because of how smitten she looked. Gina handed her a copy of the building's layout, as well as an explanation of the bank's terms and conditions. She offered Alana a step-by-step tour, which Simeon sweetly requested he be able to give. Gina blushed and gave in before excusing herself to take a call outside. He stepped behind Alana and playfully pretended to choke her for her tardiness. She laughed and apologized once more before the two checked out the space. They both admired the various skylights spread throughout the open area. Like the original restaurant, it also had two levels, but was slightly larger. The look had a certain "je ne sais quoi" to it, giving her a feeling of deja vu. She recognized an indescribable charm, which spoke to her and had only spoken to her once before. It was the same charm she saw the first time she walked through the doors of The Cocoa Marra.

"Simeon, this place is perfect! I'm sorry I ever doubted you."

"C'mon, you know I'd never let you down. Trust me, partner," he said.

And why *wouldn't* she trust him? Since her business had opened, Simeon often received offers from other big-name restaurants, some of which she was sure made offers that were hard for him to refuse. But he always made it clear that The Cocoa Marra was his home, and that he couldn't bring himself to leave the crown jewel that carried her grandmother's name. He grabbed her by the hand and dragged her into the kitchen. He went over every inch of the place, showing her how he wanted to have things set up.

He talked non-stop about how he would communicate with both her and Diego so that his vision could be set up by the time he returned. He also wanted to revamp the menu upon his return to reflect what he was going to learn in Paris. Alana had no objections to either proposal, as she realized fresh ideas were always in higher demand. Simeon continued until he had run out of things to say. He stood with his hands in his pockets, rocking back and forth on his heels, as Alana looked at the ceilings and nervously fiddled with her purse strap. They looked at each other for a moment with kind smiles and loud silence, knowing that the talk they'd been avoiding was about to take place.

"Look, Alana, about the other night. It was—"

"I know. It was so irresponsible!"

"What?" he asked, as the small smile slowly melted from his face.

"I can't believe we got caught up in the moment like that. Look, I don't ever want to lose your friendship. You mean so much to me, Simeon."

"And you to me. More than you know."

"So, what do you say? Do you forgive me?"

"There's nothing to forgive," he said.

Alana moved in closer to him, hugging him tightly. Simeon buried his face in her neck as his heart plummeted to his feet. He had hoped she would say her feelings were a mirror image of his. He had hoped the kiss sparked a fire in her that would burn alongside the blaze he'd been struggling to douse for so long. But, just as she'd unknowingly done before, his hopes were burned to a crisp without warning. He continued to play it cool, smiling once they released each other. He told her how glad he was that they talked. Gina returned from her business call and asked how they liked the place. The partners gave their approval and, for the first time since the contract was drawn up, Alana left Simeon to handle things on his own as a small show of confidence.

Simeon watched Gina's lips moving, but he didn't hear a word she was saying. The man who everyone believed was the epitome of confidence always felt like a lamb in wolves' paws when dealing with Alana. In an instant, he was fragile and at her mercy. He shook himself out of his disappointed state and managed to make a date with the awestruck young woman, who seemed to perk up after Alana's exit. He smiled and flirted with her, offering up his arm for her to hold onto as he escorted her back to her car. He made more small talk, just as he had earlier to keep her busy while waiting for Alana. When she asked why he seemed as though his mind was in two different places at once, he told her that the stress of starting a new business had him a little preoccupied. But that wasn't the truth at all! Secretly, he was thinking that the time would soon come where he would have to lay all of his cards on the table or forever forfeit his hand. He had to tell Alana the truth!

Chapter | 12

It had been weeks since Alana had her usual Wednesday lunch date with Georgia. She was in the midst of a huge litigation and her free time had become sparse. Although Alana understood, so much had been going on in her life that she was eager for their next meeting so she could share it all with Georgia. If there was one thing about Georgia that Alana could count on, it was that their conversations always remained between the two of them. She and Alex had been seeing each other on a regular basis. Whether it was cooking for each other, surprising each other with small gifts, watching some of their favorite programs on the couch, or merely slow dancing by the fireplace, things had really taken off. However, she felt like a bit of a hypocrite while planning to tell Georgia about it, especially since she made Alex swear to keep their involvement a secret. But surely, it was okay to share the news with her mother figure. Besides, how could she tell Gigi, and not Georgia?

Lunch still wasn't feasible due to Georgia's hectic schedule, but she promised Alana that she would meet her at her place for a late dinner. Georgia asked if it was alright for her to bring her best friend, Ronald, a flamboyant wine expert who never had a dull moment. Alana happily welcomed the extra guest, in addition to inviting Gigi over to even things out. Instead of a big fancy dinner, she employed Simeon to set up a small wine tasting for the foursome. She pulled out her fancy silver platters and crystal wine glasses for the rare, but special, occasion. She lit candles to invoke relaxation, put on some music to set the mood, and even decorated the two large tree plants she'd purchased the day before with pale blue string lights for a little dazzle.

At 8 p.m. sharp, Georgia and Ronald arrived, followed by Gigi a few moments later. Alana embraced her mentor as if they hadn't seen each other in ages. After hanging up their coats, the group sat at the long dining room table, admiring the spread that Simeon set out for them. He was even kind enough to provide small spit buckets for the wines that didn't meet their standards. The Cannonball Adderley Quintet played "Mercy, Mercy" on her old record player while the small group dined on their choice of grapes, cheeses, ceviche and beef-wrapped asparagus.

They sipped and swished the heavenly liquid around in their mouths, sometimes spitting it out, while discussing all that had been going on in their lives. Gigi talked about Brian and how she loved going to his family's house around the holidays because his mom and sister were a hoot. Georgia complained about how difficult her client was being and how she wished they would've been able to reach a settlement by now. Ronald started to tell Alana that she should jump on the bandwagon with him and Georgia to take advantage of the online wine auctions at Sotheby's, when he was suddenly silenced by the sound of the buzzer being pressed by someone downstairs at the door.

"Are we expecting someone else?" Gigi asked as she walked to the intercom.

"Not that I know of. Simeon maybe, but he's pretty slammed. Plus, he has a key."

"He has a key?" Georgia asked, raising her brow.

"Yes, but only for emergencies. So does Gigi."

"You have that sexy man using that key for the wrong reasons, baby girl. He should be letting himself in *to let himself in*!"

"Oh, Georgia! You have no shame!" Ronald exclaimed. As Gigi reached the intercom, everyone sat in silence in order to identify the voice of the unexpected guest.

"Who is it?"

"Hi. It's Alex. Chef Simeon ordered me to bring up some more wine. He's kind of tied up at the moment."

Gigi smiled deviously as she buzzed him in. She hadn't been around the two of them together since finding out about their low-key relationship. She had a feeling the interaction was about to be quite entertaining. Alana could feel her heart beating out of her chest. She was going to tell Georgia about him anyway, but she felt a rush of excitement and anxiety just knowing the two of them were about to be in the same room.

Suddenly, her secret lover didn't seem so easy to reveal. In order to relax herself, she daydreamed that her guests weren't there, and that she and Alex went from room to room, making love throughout her loft. She pictured them in the kitchen against the refrigerator, kissing each other with an overwhelming amount of passion. She envisioned them in the seating area on her couch, her straddling him while holding the back of his head as her body moved up and down on top of his. She fantasized that they were on the dining room table. But instead of her being the dessert, this time, they feasted on each other.

The thought of them in her bedroom was enough to make her explode. She knew on her big, spacious bed, they could spread out and really get wild. She thought about how good he looked without clothes on, how his beautiful, brown six-pack tasted just as good as it looked. Without warning, Georgia lightly shook her arm, bringing her back to reality. She and Ronald had been trading looks back and forth as they heard the elevator arrive at Alana's floor. They wondered who exactly the gentleman caller was.

"Who is Alex, dear?" Georgia asked softly.

"Oh, he's the new sous chef," Alana answered, swallowing a large gulp of wine to calm her nerves.

Gigi opened the door, greeting Alex and leading him to the dining room while she twirled her hair playfully at her friend and skipped toward the table. He looked around, as if he'd never been there before, commenting on how beautiful her home was. Alana rolled her eyes with a smile, knowing that he was obviously trying to be funny since they'd shared their first kiss in the very spot he was walking on. Alex placed the bottles on the kitchen counter and approached the table, at Alana's request, so she could introduce him.

"Good evening, everyone. My apologies for not being dressed for the occasion," he joked, tugging at his chef jacket and rubbing his low-cut, scruffy beard.

"Georgia, Ronald, this is Alex."

"Damn!" Georgia exclaimed. "Is it a requirement that you be incredibly attractive in order to cook here?"

"Mother!"

"It's alright," he said with a smile. "I don't believe so. But I see by looking at you, that it must be a requirement in order to eat here."

"Oh, he's got game!" Ronald quipped.

Alex stood next to Alana with his arms behind his back, looking down at her and trying to control his need to touch her. He tried to keep his flirtation to a minimum, only complimenting his *boss* on how nice she looked. Unfortunately, his words said one thing while his face said something totally different. The gaze in his eyes and the manner in which he licked his lips showed that he wanted to have a tasting of his own. Alex also daydreamed, only his daydreams were memories of the night before. Alana had phoned him in the dead of night, asking if she could come over to his place.

When she arrived, they were so overcome with desire for each other that they couldn't make it all the way upstairs to his bedroom or even get fully undressed. He bit his bottom lip as he thought about how they ripped off each other's shirts, which fell to the floor at the top of the staircase. They had the type of sex that left one satisfied for days. He could still see his fingers with strands of her hair wrapped around them, her skirt around her waist, and her underwear ripped on the floor as they gave a whole new meaning to the term doggy style! Her butt accidentally pressed the volume button on the remote to the surround sound as Alex thrusted inside her over and over. The music turned up loudly and stayed that way until they were finished. Alex wasn't surprised when he received a nice note from one of the neighbors the next morning, which said: *Although we too enjoy his music, we prefer <u>not</u> to hear Bruno Mars singing 'Gorilla' in the middle of the night.*

He snapped out of it and asked if there was anything he could do for the group. Georgia and Ronald once again traded looks, communicating with subtle gestures that could only be understood by two people who had been friends for a very long time. They didn't know who Alex or Alana thought they were fooling, but with all of their life experience, they surely couldn't believe it was them.

"So, Alex. I don't know if anyone told you, but I'm having a Halloween party this weekend. The entire staff is coming. I'd love for you to attend, as well," Gigi said, breaking the spell that Alana had obviously cast on him.

"Gigi, I'm sure he—"

"He'd love to," Alex replied. "Can I bring anything?"

"Just yourself," Gigi answered.

"And a twin brother," Georgia added jokingly.

Alex laughed and noted that he would do his best, before he finally excused himself for the evening. Everyone's eyes followed him as he made his way to the door. When it closed behind him, the sound came down like a judge's gavel as all eyes at the table immediately turned to Alana. She sipped her wine and smiled nervously, waiting for Georgia to pounce on the question she knew was lurking in her mind.

"Shall I, or will you?" Georgia asked Ronald.

"I think it's more appropriate coming from you," he answered.

"Okay, fine. My darling, is there something you want to tell me?"

Gigi was no help. She laughed into her glass, knowing that if there was anyone who knew Alana better than her or Simeon, it was the tough-as-nails attorney. Georgia looked at her with an expression clear out of the mother's handbook, a look that let Alana know she had better start talking, *quickly*!

"Oh. Um, yes there is. Funny story. Alex and I are kind of...well, you know. Sort of...I mean technically—"

"Spit it out, dear."

"We're secretly seeing each other...just a little bit," Alana said, squinting her eyes and putting her index finger and thumb together, as if she was measuring the relationship. She braced herself, wondering what Georgia was about to say about her cooking up something more than food with the handsome chef.

"Well, cheers to that! I thought we were going to be forced to tie ropes to your ankles and pull with all of our might to get you to open your legs again!"

"That, or a crowbar!" Gigi said.

The three dinner guests dinged their glasses together and began talking about Alana, as if she wasn't still sitting there. She stared at them in disbelief as they talked about how uptight she'd been since her last break-up and how it was probably because she needed to get laid. Georgia dramatically reenacted how Alana often stated her "dating rules." Gigi mocked and mimicked her as well, while Ronald laughed on, giving high fives to them both. Alana quickly interrupted what she called 'their little fun time,' causing Georgia to feel guilty about the ribbing. Georgia got up and kissed Alana on the cheek, patting her hand sweetly and telling her how happy she was for her.

Alana smiled and pulled her shawl tightly around her shoulders as her mentor inquired about all that had been transpiring between the two. She blushed as she talked about Alex. She told them about his family, about the in-depth conversations they had late at night on the phone, and about their decision to keep things quiet, making his company that much more enjoyable since there weren't a ton of nosey people in their business to ruin it all.

"So, have you found love since the last time we spoke?" Georgia asked excitedly.

"Yes. He made me this cocoa-flavored cake with chocolate icing that I absolutely loved!"

"Okay, I get it. In denial, eh?

"Denial? Hardly! This is not love. You act like I said we're engaged or we're moving in together. We're in a secret relationship. How in love could I actually be?"

"Yet, you made an exception to your rule for him, a pointless rule might I add. But still a rule," Georgia noted, as the others laughed.

Alana explained that her rules, no matter how pointless they seemed to others, had always been in place for good reasons: business and pleasure don't mix well. She assured them that the only reason she'd made an exception for Alex was because they met before he worked at The Cocoa Marra. But Georgia, being the constant attorney, found just the right opening to an argument she'd been waiting to have with Alana for years.

"You and Simeon met before he worked here. Yet, you've never given him a chance, at least not outside the bedroom."

"Simeon? What does he have to do with anything?"

"I've always thought you two would make a lovely couple."

"A couple of what?"

"You are familiar with the term *couple*! Generally defined as two people in a committed relationship that love each other."

"First of all, Simeon is my best friend, just like you and Ronald—"

"Ronald and I have never had sex, darling."

"Okay, one difference! But we love each other the same as you two do, as friends."

"Have you ever actually asked him that? You obviously don't pay attention to the way he's always gawking at you and—"

"And more importantly, how can one ever consider being in a relationship with someone who has such a huge fear of commitment?" Alana fired.

Georgia stopped for a moment as Alana got up from her seat and started to clear away the plates and bottles. She could tell that her protégé felt empowered, having believed that she'd made a compelling argument. But, little did she know, her victory would be short-lived. Everyone watched her as she walked back and forth from the table several times, in hopes that the subject had been changed. She poured herself another glass of wine and returned to the table, where Ronald and Gigi quietly wondered how, after all these years, she truly believed Georgia could be defeated in any argument. Almost immediately, the litigator unleashed a line of questioning that Alana was not prepared for.

"Are we talking about Simeon's fear of commitment or yours?" Georgia's question caused Gigi to choke on her wine, as the question caught her off guard as much as it had Alana.

"Excuse me?! You think I have a fear of commitment?" Alana asked.

"Oh, don't be silly, sweetheart. I don't think that. I *know* that!"

"I've been in relationships before," Alana said.

"Yes, let's talk about these short-lived relationships of yours, shall we? These pitiful little instances that always seem to end the moment you find *something* wrong with them, usually their ability, paired with your inability, to say the words 'I love you.' You would rather commit to a good bottle of wine, a box of chocolates and a night of passion than to a long-term relationship."

"Ouch!" Gigi whispered.

"Well, if that's your theory, there's no need to ever pursue things with Simeon anyway."

"I didn't say that. I actually think he's the one man you wouldn't run away from," Georgia said.

"Oh, trust and believe, she runs from him plenty! The soles of her feet tremble at the mention of his name. I don't know whether to call her Alana or Jackie Joyner-Kersee," Gigi joked.

"Why are we even talking about him? Because of a little fling in college? Come on, Georgia. We both moved on from that."

Gigi sat in silence, knowing that her assumption wasn't entirely true. But her lips stayed sealed. Alana reassured them that Simeon had more than enough women to warm his bed and that she was far from being on his radar. Their friendship was what they valued, and no one could convince her otherwise. The two women went back and forth for a while, especially after Alana pointed out that Georgia could have at least pretended to be happy for her and Alex for more than a couple of minutes. She wondered where this need to push Simeon onto her was coming from suddenly. Did Georgia not approve of Alex? Had Simeon said something to her in confidence? And, more importantly, why couldn't everyone simply see that there was nothing there to pursue? A few horny slip-ups was hardly evidence of some predestined love as *they* would have it.

"It just wasn't meant to be!" Alana exclaimed. "Love isn't a choice—"

"You may not be able to choose when love comes for you, but you can choose *who* you let love you and how you will love them in return. You're just afraid of doing the work, honey! But when it's real, it won't seem like you're doing much work at all," Georgia said, looking into Alana's eyes with seriousness.

For the first time in her life, Alana saw Georgia get teary-eyed. She realized all of this talk about love had caused her to think about her lost love: Greg Senior. The year after Alana's grandmother died from breast cancer, Mr. Kinsley died suddenly after suffering a massive heart attack. She always spoke of him with such admiration. But it hadn't dawned on Alana until that moment that he was truly the love of Georgia's life and how much she still missed him. She patted Georgia's hand in an attempt to comfort her. Ronald handed her his handkerchief while she apologized for being a silly old woman.

Once Georgia regained her composure, she explained to Alana that when she first met Greg, she was a lot like her: stubborn, career-driven and, whether or not she wanted to admit it, lonely. Before Greg, Georgia had very few relationships and even fewer friendships—until one day, Greg introduced himself to her and introduced her to a whole new world. She said he had given her the one thing that no one else had ever offered before.

"What did he give you?" Alana asked.

"Love. And I don't mean fleeting, superficial love. I'm talking real, deep-rooted, undeniable, unbreakable love. Before him, I didn't think men loved that deeply. I'm just glad I *chose* to give him a chance to prove it to me."

And with that, Georgia began to tell the story of the most beautiful love she'd ever experienced. She told her how it was Greg that believed in her and told her she didn't have to settle for being a paralegal, that she should become an attorney, if she really wanted to. It was Greg's idea that she learn how to invest on her own so she wouldn't be at the mercy of anyone, including him, when it came to her finances. He told her that he wanted her to be with him because she wanted to be, not because she *needed* to. She told Alana that what they shared was always so special to her, which was why she was so adamant about her finding love.

She assured her that, although she was sad at that moment because of his absence, she was still thankful to God that she was allowed to be his wife. She was privileged to have given him all the love in her heart because he had certainly given her his. The possibility of love crossed Alana's mind. After all, it was surrounding her: Gigi and Brian, Diego and Carla, Mr. and Mrs. Campbell, and now Georgia and the late Greg Senior! They all loved each other so deeply. But, with that love came a level of vulnerability that she'd never fully subjected herself to. She couldn't figure out what she feared more: never being able to love someone to that degree, or loving them so much she'd be unable to live without them.

"Now, I know I'm always teasing you about Simeon. But I think he would love you the right way. But if you think there is something there with Alex, see how it plays out. The choice is yours. What do I know? Maybe he'll surprise you—if he hasn't already."

Gigi softened the mood by bringing out the Scrabble board and threatening to "whoop on" everyone. The others were happy to accept the challenge. After a few rounds, and a few more glasses of wine, the gang all decided it was time to retire for the evening. Alana saw her guests out and plopped down on her couch, thinking about all that had been said during dinner. She loved Simeon, just not in *that* way. And, as for Alex, she felt something for him alright…and couldn't wait to show him.

She decided to take Georgia's advice and see how things would play out. And boy, did she have the perfect game for them to play! The mere thought of them heating things up with a few rolls of her "Spicy Dice" was enough to put tonight's discussion on the back burner and dial him in the dead of the night. As the phone rang, she put away the Scrabble board and pulled out the dice. She rolled the dice and let them fall onto the coffee table. One suggested a sexual act, another a body part, and the other a location inside the house. The results would hopefully be carried out sooner than later: lick, lips, bedroom. She curled up with her phone and hoped he would be game for some company.

"Hey, babe. How was dinner?" he asked in a raspy voice.

"Hey, you. It could have been better; it could have been with *you*. Do you miss me?"

"Only when I'm awake."

"Well, in that case, can I come over and put you to sleep so that you'll have some relief?"

"You don't have to ask. Just come. I'm always waiting for you to come...home that is."

Alana smiled from ear to ear before hanging up and grabbing a small overnight bag to take her morning must-haves. As she drove to his house on the empty streets, she delighted in the fact that he was just as eager to see her as she was him. Things between them couldn't be better and, for the first time in her adult life, her mentor's opinion of what she needed didn't matter. She knew what she wanted, and *Alex* was it.

Chapter | 13

Gigi was as happy as a kid in a candy store as she prepared for her themed Halloween party, which she was calling, "Time Machine Halloween." Perhaps it was her love of fashion that could be attributed to her eagerness to dress up in costume. Every year, she threw a huge Halloween party at the rental hall her parents owned. As a child, her father always went above and beyond for Halloween. Not only did he throw a party every year for his friends, co-workers and family, but he made their house the most outrageous and also the most popular on the block. Due to his recent health challenges, Gigi was now in charge of renting out the hall she'd spent so much time in growing up and keeping it up to code, which is why Alana always thought she was crazy to only charge five dollars for tickets. Her parties had become everybody's must-attend event of the year due to their crazy themes and overblown costumes and decorations. They ranged from beach bums, with everyone in swimwear sipping tropical drinks, to sports themes with everyone wearing the uniforms of their favorite sport.

The year before, the theme "Hippie's Paradise" had been the most memorable. The guests adorned themselves in hip-huggers, caftans, fringed vests and rope necklaces with peace signs. Hookahs, lava lamps and bean bag chairs transformed the hall into a thing of the past. But what made it most memorable was when Jay, one of the valets, mistakenly ate one too many "special" brownies. By the end of the night, he was stark naked and singing Jimi Hendrix's "All Along the Watchtower" in the parking lot. This year's theme was slightly reminiscent of the previous one. It gave the guests the opportunity to pick the time they found the most interesting or appealing.

The room was decorated to look like some sort of machine, with the front door appearing to be the entrance from which the guests would arrive via the time portal. Gigi knew she would get a real kick out of seeing all the different costumes. To add to the ongoing theme, she instructed the deejay to play music that represented various time periods. A few of her friends had come early to help set up, which of course included Alana. But to everyone's surprise, Alex had also shown up to help prepare for the festivities. Gigi hadn't told Brian about Alex's and Alana's secret relationship, but she was starting to wonder if she would soon have to. He found it awfully suspicious when he showed up early to help set up on his day off. Brian commented that no one was that hell bent on impressing their boss. However, he kept his questions to a minimum, opting instead to save them for Simeon.

The small group of helpers sipped punch and worked together quickly to make sure the room met Gigi's approval—and to give themselves enough time to go home and change into their costumes. Alana stood on a chair to frame the doorway with lights. When she looked over her shoulder, she found Alex winking at her before his eyes went straight to her behind. She laughed before her nose was overpowered by the smell of his cooking. He set up the buffet table with large chafing dishes full of hot wings, garlic potatoes, cheese sticks, homemade salsa for the chips and dip, veggie and fruit trays, and a chocolate fountain. Alana walked over to the table and let some of the chocolate drip onto her fingers. But before she could taste it, Alex grabbed her wrist and sucked it off.

"Tastes good," he said. She didn't know whether she should be horny or nervous as she looked around to see if anyone had noticed.

"Control yourself, heathen!" she whispered as she walked away with a smile. An hour into making sure every detail was right, the time finally came for everyone to go home and get ready. Gigi and Brian decided to change at the hall. That way, they could light the food warmers, help the deejay set up and greet the guests as they arrived.

Alex was the first to leave, saying that he needed to get dressed and pick up his "date," which drew an evil look from Alana. Brian was going to walk him out, in an attempt to be sly and pick his brain. But Gigi beat him to the punch, knowing good and well what he was up to. Shortly after, everyone began to disburse, including Alana, who decided to stop by the restaurant and give the okay to close up early. When she arrived, Simeon had already beat her to the punch and was heading out, which she found weird because they usually rode together. But she didn't want to question him about it, especially since things were just getting back to normal between them. Once she was back in her loft, she received a text message from Alex, which read: *Will you dance with me tonight?* As usual, she played hard to get and answered with a playful, *Maybe.*

For her costume, she decided to wear the 50's style dress he'd given her. She liked how feminine and delicate it made her look. Even her wig paid homage to the hairstyles that most women wore back then. As she finished her makeup, Georgia called to let her know she could ride with her and Ronald. They had a car for the evening since they would be drinking well into the night. She happily accepted the offer and, by the time they arrived, the party was in full swing. People laughed, danced, ate and drank as Alana admired how amazing the guests looked.

It really was amusing to see so many different styles of dress in one place. Gigi and Brian decided to go with the 80's theme, rocking stonewashed jeans and bright neon colors. Her hair looked like something off a rock band's album cover, and she had enough hairspray in it to choke a horse. Simeon chose the roaring 20's. His dapper, pinstriped suit, equipped with a plastic tommy gun, went well with his date's flapper costume. But, leave it up to Georgia and Ronald to outdo everyone. They journeyed all the way back to the 1700's. Georgia's costume was fitting. She looked like a lady of high society with her tall white wig, pale powder makeup and corset-style dress. Ronald looked equally convincing, as if he were a Marquis de Sade impersonator.

After talking to some of the guests, and having a couple of shots from the 'ghost bar' that jokingly read, "We serve spirits," Alana danced around to Usher's "She Came to Give It to You." She lifted her arms, feeling the music as her body moved to the beat, unaware that she was being watched from the door. She turned to find Alex entering with a large, handsome man she recognized from the family pictures in his living room. His "date" was his older brother, Eric. The equally handsome siblings were both dressed in popular 90's attire: blue jean overalls with one strap hanging down, graphic t-shirts and Reebok Pump Up gym shoes. Even in outdated attire, he was a vision.

She watched as women's eyes followed them both across the room, where he introduced Eric to Gigi and Brian. Simeon and his date soon joined the group, forcing Alana to do another introduction. He smiled at her, but nothing that was too obvious. They were both becoming experts on hiding how elated they always were to see each other. She looked just as perfect in the dress as he thought she would the first time he saw her holding it. He quickly introduced her to his brother. She could tell by the look on his face that he already knew exactly who she was.

"Hey, boss lady. You're just in time. Alana, this is my brother, Eric."

"How any man can work for you and stay focused is beyond me," Eric said before kissing her hand.

"Smooth talker!" she said, patting his hand. "I see good looks run in the family."

"Okay now, I'm sure you're making Alex feel uncomfortable," Simeon interjected.

"Oh, I feel just fine. A compliment from Alana is something I'm willing to receive with both hands open."

"And you watch it, as well. She's still your boss," Simeon instructed.

"And who are you? Her bodyguard?" Eric asked sarcastically.

"Hardly. I'm her partner and head chef at The Cocoa Marra," he announced in an as-a-matter-of-fact tone.

"Well, since we're all here to party and not work, they're simply two adults talking at a party. Maybe you should be more concerned with introducing your date. She's looking a little irritated," Eric said, defending his brother, who couldn't stop smirking.

Apparently, cockiness ran in the family also. Simeon was noticeably agitated, but quickly recovered by introducing his date, Veronica, whom everyone already recognized from billboards around town. She was the lead dancer at Bad Billy's Burlesque Show, a popular bar in town, and Simeon's showpiece of the evening. All of the men at the party struggled not to stare at the blond bombshell, all but Alex, whose eyes were glued to Alana's face. She gazed at him, as well, but it was quickly interrupted by Gigi, who couldn't resist whispering that she didn't know why Simeon even bothered to introduce his dates anymore. Everyone knew it would most likely be the last time they would see them. Lexa, Gigi's right hand at the boutique, came from across the room, hoping to gain some of Simeon's attention as she spoke to everyone.

Her eyes had every look of "puppy love" within them. But, as usual, he seemed not to notice. Gigi gave her a light nudge, knowing that she wasn't used to men not melting at the sight of her. Simeon quickly whisked Veronica away to the dance floor, where he showcased why he could be so cocky. He was good at everything! Simeon was an excellent dancer, and by the look of surprise on his date's face, it was going to get him lucky by the end of the night. The group watched him grand stand for a moment before they resumed with their small talk. As they drank, Georgia joined in on the conversation with the intent of thanking Alex for granting her request.

"This must be the new chef's brother. Not a twin, but he'll do," she said.

"I'm Eric, gorgeous. And you are?"

"Well, young man, I'm Georgia, like the state. Tell me, have you ever been down south? Care to take a trip?"

"Mother!" Alana exclaimed, covering her face.

"Only if it's first class!" he jabbed back.

"Oh, and he's just as charming as his brother! What do you do for a living darling?"

"I'm a firefighter."

"Well, you may have to hose me down pretty soon because it's getting hot in here!"

"Ronald, please get her!" Alana begged.

"You're on your own, sweetheart. My specialty is wine. If I had an inkling on how to tame Georgia, I'd be getting job offers from every lion trainer in the country." He quickly grabbed her arm and whispered, "Speaking of animals, I hope you've gotten yourself some cowboy boots for that stallion!"

"You two are hopeless!" she said as Georgia joined their whispers.

"Oh, we have hope, high hopes for you, sweetie! I'm wondering how high those hopes go…7, maybe 8 inches into the air?" she asked, squinting and looking at the zipper on Alex's overalls.

"You dirty old woman!"

Alana kissed her on the cheek and headed over to the food table, barely escaping the inquisition that was about to start. She couldn't help but give Georgia's spunk some thought. She balanced being professional and perverted so well. Alana dined on some finger food as she took stock of the raging party. People sat at their tables, trying to out drink each other. Some challenged their friends to dance-offs, and there were endless flashes of guests taking selfies. As she swayed side to side, listening to Idris Elba's "Private Garden," Alex slid up beside her, desiring a dance.

"So, your brother knows?" she asked, lifting her brow.

"Yes, and it's not like Georgia and Gigi don't. Come on, Alana. He's my older brother, he would never—"

"I know. I trust you."

The admission caught them both off guard. Alana was starting to open up more and she wasn't sure how she felt about that. But Alex was secretly excited. His trust and affection for her seemed to grow by the minute, but he always suppressed his urge to say anything out of fear that it would scare her away. He was so excited by her vulnerability that instead of asking for a dance, he presented her with an opportunity to sneak outside with him at some point so that they could make out in his car like teenagers.

Alana pretended to mull it over before she countered with an offer to go to his house after the party so they could make love like adults, an offer he happily accepted! Just as their conversation was heading from flirtatious to downright freaky, Diego and Carla, who were late thanks to their babysitter, interrupted them. They were so excited that they hadn't missed the party that they talked non-stop for 15 minutes before Alana could break away. She searched for Alex, who'd made his great escape. But, she was soon swept onto the dance floor by a man in a zoot suit. She had no problem tearing up the floor with him as the music blared in her eardrums.

The night continued on without a hiccup and the vibe mellowed. People cuddled up next to their dates and some randomly took embarrassing pictures of the more 'plastered' guests. By this time, Alana and Simeon had joined Gigi and Brian on the old brown couch next to the deejay's table, where they could feel the music vibrating in their chests. They all stared blankly at the crowd in front of them as Simeon's date, Veronica, chatted it up with a girl named Karen, who he'd previously gone out with a couple of times. She too was a very pretty, very skinny girl, who came off as a little ditzy at times. But, the two seemed to be hitting it off. Simeon ignored them both as he played with Alana's fingers for a moment, causing her to look over at him curiously. The overly intoxicated best friends laughed uncontrollably, which in turn made Brian and Gigi join in as if it were contagious.

In the midst of their amusement, Alana found Alex leaning against a wall talking to his brother, yet at the same time staring at her with an unwavering glare. His eyes drew her in momentarily, as they always did. She became so captivated by them that she was startled as Gigi jumped up from the couch and grabbed her hands.

"Come dance with me," she said.

As she struggled to get up from the couch, Simeon decided to lend a hand by pushing her in the butt with his foot and laughing at her as she straightened her wig. Brian stared at the girls, who were resting their heads on each other's shoulders, seemingly exhausted. They danced around in a lazy circle to "A Whiter Shade of Pale" as he and Simeon threw balled up napkins at them for entertainment. Suddenly, Brian looked over at Simeon, as if he wanted to say something. But he shook his head, indicating that he'd changed his mind. When Simeon questioned him about it, Brian suggested he forget it. But Simeon wouldn't let it go.

"What's up, man?" Simeon asked.

"So, when are you going to tell her you love her?"

"Who? Veronica?!" Simeon asked, flabbergasted.

"No, dummy! Alana. When are you going to tell Alana that you're in love with her?"

"I don't—"

"Come on, Simeon," Brian said. "I've been with Gigi two years now, so I've been coming around for a little while. I see the way you look at her. It's the same way I look at my princess over there."

"If it's so obvious, why does everyone notice but her, huh?" he asked with a light slur.

"You mean besides the fact that she sees you running through women like you're a track and field star?"

"Man, c'mon. They don't mean anything to—"

"She doesn't know that. And do you really think it would make it any better if she did? Anyway, a simpler answer to your question is that sometimes the thing in front of us is the hardest to see. It's been there so long, it disappears into the background. So, *tell her*!"

"Too much time has passed. It's too late," he said before taking another swig of his beer.

He told Brian how Alana was the reason he was so wild and that he was actually shy when they met. He confessed that he'd never been with a woman like that who was so confident! It indeed forced him to break out of his shell. Back when they first started fooling around, she made him tutor her in French while they made love. After they stopped seeing each other, it took him six months to be able to speak French to his mother without blushing or thinking about Alana's naked body. Brian listened intently before offering some sound advice.

"I don't know much, but I know you. If you have something to say, you better say it while you can because that dude won't hesitate if the chance ever comes his way," he said, nodding his head in Alex's direction. Simeon looked at his alleged competition, who was now talking to his brother and Veronica. Alex caught him glaring and raised his beer in acknowledgement of being watched.

"Pssh! I'm not worried about him!" Simeon said confidently.

"The ones that we don't worry about are the ones that we should."

"Alana wouldn't go for a peon."

"Simeon, you know what I've always found interesting since I've been in the banking business?" Brian asked.

"I'm listening," he said as he continued to watch Alex, who was staring at Alana.

"A lot of times, it's the smaller banks taking all of our customers. They find them more trustworthy and dependable."

"And what's your point?"

"My point is you should never underestimate the little guy. Even peons prosper, my brotha. The feeling of security is key."

As the guys continued talking, Gigi stumbled over to the couch and tried with as much subtlety as she could to hint to Brian that she wanted to go fool around. But she wasn't as incognito as she thought. Her wink was overly suggestive and her whisper of, "Come with me so you can *cum* with me," was actually in her normal speaking voice, just closer to his ear. Simeon shook his head in amusement as Brian rubbed his ear, which was now ringing. He informed him that there was some business he needed to take care of and suggested that Simeon take care of his, as well. As the two lovebirds left him to his thoughts, he burned with envy as Alex asked Alana to dance. To make matters worse, it was to Raheem Devaughn's song, "Love Connection." He wished more than anything that *he* could in fact make one with Alana.

"Hey, sexy! Ready to go?" Veronica asked.

"Oh, you ready to go already?" Simeon responded.

"Not just me; *we're* ready to go," she said as she put her arm around Karen's waist and licked her lips at him.

"I'm more than ready!" he said, jumping up and allowing each lady to grab an arm.

On his way out the door, he looked over his shoulder one last time to see Alana dancing it up, as if she was having the time of her life. He decided that once they were at work, he would see just where Alex's head was regarding Alana, or if he was just conjuring up things out of jealousy. A short while later, Alex also left so he could drop off his brother and head home to prepare for his late-night guest. At the end of the party, Alana wanted to say goodbye to Gigi. But her and Brian's quickie turned into a complete disappearing act, which she understood perfectly since she couldn't wait to get to Alex's. Since they were already in the know, she had Georgia drop her off at his house, where she and Ronald continued embarrassing her by rooting her on from the car. They pulled off, leaving a tipsy Alana to be surprised by a naked Alex opening the door.

"Get in here, woman. And take off everything, except for those heels and that God-awful wig!" he joked. Alana burst into laughter as he swept her up in his arms and kissed her giggling lips. She couldn't get undressed fast enough as Alex prepared to love her down until she begged for mercy.

Chapter | 14

Alana walked into the living room, with Alex right on her heels. She swung her dress over her head like a lasso, teasing him before throwing it onto the piano. She got onto the couch on her knees, her hands on the wall, waiting for him to join her, which didn't take long. Soon, she could feel him behind her, shielding her back from the heat of the freshly lit fireplace, which warmed her skin. One hand caressed her breast while the other held her chin. He sucked on her neck and kissed her shoulders before stopping at the nape of her neck. He nibbled on it as she reached behind her and rubbed her hand down the back of his neck with approval.

She turned her head to kiss him as he pushed himself inside of her and moaned with pleasure. Their bodies moved in unison, and Alana could feel herself wanting to erupt onto him with every stroke. Soon their breathing seemed to synchronize as Alex glided in and out of her faster and faster with each passing moment. She yearned to touch him, but when she reached her hand back to grab his leg, he took hold of her wrist and delivered a thigh quaking thrust. Alana screeched with excitement as her body shook violently from the overwhelming orgasm.

He continued to run his hands over her soft, silky skin as he let out every ounce of passion he'd been holding in over the course of the evening. He slid his hand between her legs and made small, swift circles until she felt as if her legs were melting beneath her. The more Alana moaned the more excited he became, until he, too, could take no more. He squeezed her tightly as he came vigorously before falling onto the couch next to her. He smiled before pulling off her wig and throwing it on the floor.

"Even that thing can't touch your beauty," he said. They both laughed before Alana lay on top of him, surrounded by the care and strength of his arms. She kissed his lips, then his earlobes, then his chest. Alex held on tight before realizing she was continuing downward.

"Uh, what are you doing, woman?"

"Trying to see if you have a trick or a treat! You didn't think you were done for the night, did you?"

"Well, considering what just happened, I may need a few moments to recharge-"

Alex was silenced by the feeling of Alana's tongue swirling around the tip of his dick. He amazed even himself as he immediately 'sprung' back into action. His hands dug into the couch as her mouth ran up and down her own personal Fudgsicle. Suddenly she stopped, sitting up on the couch, as if nothing had just happened.

"You said you need a minute, right?" she asked sarcastically. Alex stared at her for a moment before picking her up and throwing her over his shoulders. He headed up the stairs, but not before smacking her on the butt and offering a loving warning.

"Your Halloween is about to get much happier!"

It seemed like they'd been making love for hours before Alex finally came a second time. The heat radiating off their skin saturated the sheets with sweat as Alana tried to catch her breath. They both lay on their backs staring at the ceiling, as if mercy itself would fall down from it. After their hearts stopped racing and found a steady rhythm, they looked over at each other and laughed at how they'd worn themselves out. Alana gathered enough energy to slide over just enough to rest her head on his chest. He bent up slightly to kiss her forehead as he played with her hair and massaged her scalp.

"That feels great. Don't you dare stop," she said, fighting her desire to doze off.

"Well damn, woman! Do I ever stop working for you?" he said with a chuckle.

"Hey, during your interview, you said you weren't afraid of hard work. Guess you spoke too soon," she joked. "So, hypothetically, if you could pick the circumstances under which we met, would you change anything?"

"Definitely!"

"Why?"

"Because I would have made it more romantic, more impressionable. I would have made sure I amazed you."

The words caused an exhausted Alana to wake right up. She looked as though she'd seen a ghost. Alex immediately noticed and asked if everything was alright. Her mind went back to the conversation she and Gigi had shortly before she met him. She remembered telling Gigi that she was waiting for the man that could amaze her. She assured Alex that she was fine and asked him to tell her in detail how their fantasy meeting would have taken place had it been in his control. As they lay in bed sharing a glass of wine, she listened as Alex set the scene.

Alex painted a picture of them on a tropical island, both alone and enjoying some quiet time. He described how he'd be sitting on a beach, sipping a Mai Tai, when a beautiful woman, Alana of course, walks toward him. She is wearing a sunhat, shades, a swimsuit and a colorful sarong wrapped around her waist. He watches her strut with the sun glistening off her shiny, tanning skin until she is finally standing over him. He looks up as she asks if the fold out chair next to him is taken. Alex looked Alana in her eyes and told her that his response would be, "Yes, it is. I've been saving it for you!" He told her that after she smiled with delight from the compliment he had just given her, that they would have talked until sunset as a small handheld radio blared in the background and, that by midnight, as the stars shined brightly, they would have fallen in love.

Alana listened with amazement. She wondered how he could speak the words as if they had really happened. "So, sweet cheeks, what would you have changed?" he asked. Alana hovered over him before reaching down and kissing him with a gentleness that she never had before. Alex couldn't help but feel the difference. He could feel the soft, mushy, vulnerable side of her finding its way onto his lips. It both surprised and invigorated him as she stopped and stared into his eyes, she gave him an answer that was as perfect to him as she was.

"Nothing," she said. "I wouldn't change a thing."

Over at Simeon's place, he and his two companions couldn't get out of the car fast enough. They burst through the door of his apartment after what seemed like a lifetime of him struggling to get it unlocked. It wasn't easy with Veronica's tongue in one ear and Karen's tongue in the other. The ladies worked as a team to get his clothes off of him, as well as themselves. Brian's words rang in his ear: *"Why would Alana know how you feel when she sees you running through women like a track and field star?"* He tried to shake it off as he kissed Veronica wildly while enjoying the feeling of Karen's mouth on his muscular back.

The girls ran up the stairs, giggling as Simeon smiled at his luck. He walked toward them and again, his conversation with Brian popped into his head. *"That dude won't hesitate if the chance ever comes his way."* He shook his head, as if it would shake the words loose and send them tumbling out of his mind. He finally reached the doorway of his bedroom, where he found Veronica's head hanging off the bed, and Karen's head between Veronica's legs.

He dimmed the lights before going over to the bed, where both women immediately pulled him down. The two women wrapped themselves around his body, like snakes on a staff, as they aroused him in every way possible. Suddenly, he moaned loudly, "Oh, Alana!" Both women stopped, reminding him that neither one of them went by that name. Simeon jumped up from the bed and paced, wondering what he could possibly say to make nice of the completely awkward situation he'd just created. He apologized and told the ladies that his mind was somewhere else, as if they hadn't figured that out already. He stood by his bedroom door, telling them that he completely understood if they wanted to leave and that, perhaps, it wasn't such a bad idea.

"I've got to start making some changes," he said.

Both women looked at each other and laughed. Neither of them could care less, as they were there for the one thing they knew he was capable of giving: a good time! Karen got up from the bed and went to him. She dropped to her knees and began to pleasure him, while Veronica sat at the end of the bed and spread her legs. She slowly rubbed between them before asking, "Are you sure about that?" Simeon closed his eyes, unable to resist such an enticing offer. "Yes, I'm sure. And I will get on that first thing tomorrow!" he insisted. The ladies laughed as he joined them back in bed and decided to put Alana out of his mind for the evening. He vowed that the morning would bring about new things; most importantly, him turning over a new leaf. Alana would soon see the new and improved Simeon.

Despite being up all Friday night, and well into Saturday with Alana, Alex was actually early for work. He happily chopped alongside Diego, who was nursing the worst hangover he'd had in a while. As the radio blared "Coffee" by Miguel, he couldn't stop thinking of how beautiful Alana looked when he woke her to enjoy the coffee and bagel he made her for an early morning breakfast. Under the small baby blue cup, which sat on its matching saucer, was a folded note for her to find once she lifted it to drink. It read: *Babe. Hope you enjoy this as much as I enjoyed you.* He felt like no matter what happened at this point, nothing could cause him to have a bad day. But he quickly found out that he may have been jumping the gun.

Simeon was in a foul mood and, by the time the rest of the staff arrived, it seemed to have only gotten worse. Inside, he was feeling kind of "salty" because of Brian's observation at the party. It left a bad taste in his mouth. He should have been overjoyed, especially with the way his night ended. It wasn't often that he stumbled upon a threesome with two carefree spirits like Veronica and Karen. But once he was back in his element, he was also back in his feelings. Alex was really starting to irritate him. When he wasn't getting basketball tickets for the busboys, walking the waitresses to their cars at night, or helping elderly customers with their bags, he was just being himself, which everyone else seemed to love. He found it all so…annoying!

When Alana sashayed in for her usual morning coffee with Gigi, Alex offered to bring it to her so that she could catch up on anything she may have missed after she left the party. As she smiled and proceeded through the kitchen in a fiery red dress, a fired-up Simeon instantly started in on Alex, who started preparing her cup of Joe the way he usually made it at his home.

"Who is that for?" Simeon barked.

"Boss lady."

"She doesn't take her coffee like that," Simeon insisted.

"I thought maybe she'd like to try something new," Alex said, continuing to stir. Simeon grabbed another cup and prepared the coffee the way Alana *usually* took it. Alex was in no mood to argue, so he stopped and let Simeon carry on with his shenanigans.

"New is good, but Alana is very particular about how her coffee is served to her; a certain amount of cream and a whole lot of sugar! It has to be stirred a certain type of way for her to really enjoy it. I've served it to her many times before. Allow me to show you," he said sarcastically.

They stared each other down before Simeon finally stopped stirring the hot beverage and clinked the spoon against the cup, as if making an announcement, his pun being intended! He dropped the spoon on the counter and smirked as he walked toward the dining room to deliver it personally.

"What's with your boy?" Alex asked Diego in a not so pleasant tone.

"I don't know, but please don't engage him. I thought after what happened last night, he'd be levitating today," he answered.

"What happened?"

Diego proceeded to tell him about Simeon's "triple delight," which left Alex even more confused. If he had so many extracurricular activities going on in his sex life, why was he so concerned with Alana's? Alex thought about what he was really getting himself in the middle of, when Simeon suddenly returned to the kitchen. He remained as cool as cucumbers, but that didn't stop Simeon from starting what was about to become their first showdown. They both worked in silence, until Simeon caught a glimpse of Alex looking at the door, most likely at Alana. He smiled devilishly to himself before instigating an inescapable argument. With the other staff moving about and seemingly paying no attention to them, he pounced, knowing that Diego had little control over the situation that was about to unfold.

"You know you're a real funny guy, not too slick though."

"You say that to say what?" Alex asked.

"I see you watching her, lusting after her like a bitch in heat. It's sort of sad really, that you believe a woman like that falls for the help!" Simeon said viciously.

Alex smiled, knowing that he had finally done what Simeon had been doing to him for quite some time. He had finally gotten to him. Normally, being called out of his name would warrant an explosive response. But today, he reveled in Simeon's anger. Where Simeon used being cocky as a weapon, Alex decided his weapon of choice would be cleverness. They both continued chopping, like they were in a race. They stared at each other as their knives came down at top speeds.

Neither man flinched or backed down as they stood inches in front of each other. Alex thought carefully about what he would say. He still kept Alana's privacy in mind. After all, he'd come to care for her very much and nothing Simeon could say or do would cause him to throw away what they were building together, even if they hadn't openly acknowledged it yet. But Alex felt it was, however, time to let Simeon know that he was still dealing with a grown ass man, not some little boy.

"I can respect that. She's a beautiful, successful woman who has unlimited choices. But um, speaking of help, you work *for* her, too, right?"

"I work *with* her, not for her. In case you haven't heard, I'm her partner now. And—"

"And are you for sure that I'm the bitch? A real bitch would be running around here sniffing for a scent of hope that some long-standing case of puppy love can one day be fulfilled," Alex fired off.

"What are you implying?"

"I'm stating out right! Even a blind man can see that I'm not the only one wishful thinking, partner! At least I can fess up to that."

"Maybe it would be better for you if you saved your confessions for church!"

"Better for me or better for you? Maybe she doesn't want me, but she doesn't want you either. Can't you tell?!"

Suddenly Simeon nicked his finger. Perhaps it was the possibility that those words could be true that cut into him even more than the cold steel. He slammed the knife on the metal countertop and made his way around to Alex, causing Diego to jump in between them. He pushed both men apart with his hands in their chests, trying his best not to choose sides. Ever the constant professional, he reminded Alex that Simeon was still his boss, and he reminded Simeon that disrespecting staff was not how they operated their business. Testosterone filled the air as he told them both to walk away and let cooler heads prevail. Simeon smiled deviously as he put pressure on his finger to stop the bleeding. As some of the staff entered the kitchen, Simeon made sure to keep his voice low.

"Oh, I'm cool, D! It's technically your kitchen now anyway. Besides, I only need to draw blood once today."

As each of them turned to leave the huddle they appeared to be in, Alana came bursting through the kitchen doors with a radiant smile that quickly turned to a look of concern. Simeon wrapped a small towel around his hand, but she immediately grabbed it and held it under some running water. She leaned over to examine it, before ordering one of the dishwashers to bring her the first aid kit. She wanted to at least apply a bandage before grabbing him a pair of plastic gloves to wear for the remainder of the day. He looked over at Alex and winked at him as she doctored on his hand. But Alex's confidence was at an all-time high, especially since he knew later that night she would be at his house, in his bed, in his arms, where she belonged. Once Simeon was all patched up and his defenses were down, Alex decided to give the two old friends something to really talk about. And, thanks to Diego, he knew just what it should be.

"So, chef, I heard you hit a double last night! Playa! Playa!" Alex exclaimed.

"Where did you hear that?!" Simeon asked, completely caught off guard.

"Oh, a little birdie told me. You must be slicker than a rabbit in an oil spill!"

"So, let me get this straight. You not only left with your date, but the two of you added someone to the party? Well, at least I never have to worry about you being alone," Alana said.

"Yeah, well you may have to soon. I'm thinking of taking a little hiatus from serial dating."

"Really? Why? Things seem to be going so well for you in that department."

"I just think it's time for something more, something with substance. Gigi and Brian have the right idea."

"Yeah they do. I'm proud of you," she said, smiling.

Alana left for the day to handle some business, leaving Simeon to get one last glare. Alex returned the look, knowing full well who Simeon had in mind to settle down with. With his need for confrontation, his surveillance at the party, and his past admissions to Diego, there was no doubt that he wanted Alana to be that "substance." But Alex felt he was in no danger of losing her to him, especially with his harem of women who were just as recent as last night. He thought to himself that if this was the type of man she'd dated before, there was no wonder she was single. If there was one thing he'd taken away from his many talks with Alana about the opposite sex, it was that she had no patience for dogs!

Both men maintained their composure throughout the rest of the day as they worked closely together. But inside, they wanted to be as far away from each other as possible. They pretended to be unaffected by the turmoil between them, while both secretly plotting on how they would win Alana over and relish in the other's defeat. By the time 7 p.m. rolled around, Diego decided that Alex had taken enough abuse for the day and let him leave early. The three of them had been working overtime non-stop so everything would be set after Simeon's departure. But Diego could tell Alex was almost burnt out. That, and he wanted to speak to Simeon alone about the way he was exposing Alana's personal business, past or not. Alex accepted the small blessing and headed home for some relaxation.

As he sat in the driveway of his home, he texted Alana, begging her to come over for what the two of them had secretly deemed The Triple F: fun, food and fucking. She sent back a smiley face with assurance she'd be there within the hour. He walked toward the door, smiling at the thought of her walking around his house naked. Suddenly, he was startled by an unexpected voice coming up behind him.

"Hey, Lex," she said. His eyes focused on the slim figure emerging from the darkness, but he knew who it was the moment he heard her voice. He turned toward her, looking unaffected, as he greeted the uninvited guest.

"Hello, Natalie."

Chapter | 15

"Wow! I'm Natalie now? What ever happened to Nat?" she asked.
"That's a great question; one that only you can answer! But don't feel bad. I could never answer that question for my family either. You know, after your sudden and unexplained departure," he answered coldly.

"I deserve that," she admitted. "So, I ran into your brother. He told me you're a sous chef at one of the most popular restaurants in the city, but he wouldn't tell me which one."

"Well, that's because he can't stand you, Natalie. Oh, I'm sorry, *Nat*."

The beautiful young woman stood in silence for a moment as he unlocked the front door and gathered his mail. She figured she'd better not give him a chance to decline a request to come in, so she stepped in behind him quickly and waited for permission to step out of the foyer. Alex went through the envelopes one by one as he gave her a lazy wave, signaling that she could step into the front hallway. But still, he paid her no attention. *What had he done to deserve back-to-back confrontations with Simeon and now Nat?* he wondered. Unfortunately for him, not only was he unable to come up with an answer, but after looking up from his bills, he quickly realized that if he didn't make things short and sweet, he was going to be paying for a lot more than gas and electricity. Natalie was just as beautiful as she was when they were together and, if anyone was a pro at getting to him, it was her!

Ironically, his sarcasm hadn't been in vain. As he looked at her, he wondered what happened to Nat. She was different. Her long hair was now cut into a short pixie style, something she said she would never do. Her previously thickly framed body was whittled down into a more slender figure. Even her makeup was different! She went from a barely there natural approach, to a contoured look that said, "I'm too painted and pretty to touch." This new and improved version was someone he didn't know.

The two had been in a committed relationship for three years. He met her while visiting his cousin Lewis at college. One night, his gracious host suggested that they go to a food and wine pairing event offered by the culinary students because, according to him, that was where all of the fine women on campus would be. Natalie approached Alex that night and inquired about some of the tattoos on his arm. At first, there weren't any sparks. He thought she was just an incredibly cool girl who he could see himself being friends with. But after talking all night, partying all weekend, corresponding via email, and visiting each other over the course of three months, it grew into much more.

After those three months, he uprooted his life and practically started over in a place where the only two people he knew were her and his cousin--all just to be with her. His friends, all of whom couldn't stand her, told him that Natalie was a mistake from the start. They were polar opposites of each other, which was probably one of the things that made them so crazy about one another. His family barely knew her, not even his sister, which was a huge red flag. Although his parents weren't her biggest fans, they tried to support him since they were living together.

He didn't really become alarmed about the relationship until his brother came to visit. Eric, who was known for his ability to remain silent when it came to people's personal lives, told him she wasn't the one for him. He'd flown out to visit them once and, the moment Natalie left the apartment to grab dinner, he laid it on Alex hard! He told him she was self-absorbed and flighty, and that she could never commit on the level that Alex could. In his opinion, it seemed more like infatuation than love. But Alex was brainwashed, or pussy-whipped, for lack of a better term.

Although Natalie seemed like the innocent one in the relationship due to Alex's rugged exterior, she was the epitome of a wolf in sheep's clothing. There was a very aggressive and adventurous side to her, which introduced Alex to a whole other kind of sex life: costumes, cuffs, blindfolds, riding crops, chaps, and his personal favorite, a sex swing. She had him doing things he didn't even realize he was interested in. As far as he was concerned, he was in it for the long haul. Time, however, would end up being so cruel as to prove just how right his brother was.

While working on her degree, Natalie suddenly began to drop hints that they should think about getting engaged. Apparently, her parents were nagging her about them "playing house" by living together unwed, and it was starting to take a toll on her. Alex didn't feel they were ready. He thought maybe in time they would be, but he wouldn't get the chance to find out. Right after graduation, she became distant. Once she graduated with a double master's degree in Business and Non-Profit Management, it seemed that being with a chef, not even one that was on the rise, was not substantial enough for her to compete with her peers. They were getting engaged to doctors, lawyers and COO's of Fortune 500 companies, an issue that was unknown to Alex.

In his mind, he thought she might be getting antsy about the fact that he hadn't popped the question, even after the insistence of her parents. He still wasn't ready for marriage, but he found himself willing to bite the bullet if it was the only way to hold on to her. His brother told him he was crazy to let someone twist his arm into making such a big decision, but he'd made up his mind. Even after months of arguing, distant behavior and constant turmoil, he arrived home one night with an arm full of roses, a box of chocolates and all of the ingredients needed to prepare her favorite meal. That morning, he'd left a present for her, hoping she would stumble upon it as she got ready for work. He assumed that by the time they made it home, a night of romance would be the icing on the cake.

Instead, when he entered their apartment, it looked noticeably different. Most of her things that were usually left lying about were gone. He rushed to their bedroom to check the closet for her belongings, but he knew he would find nothing there once he saw the envelope taped to the door. When he ripped it open, he was disgusted to find a note that exhibited just how right Eric had been. It read: *I'm sorry. I tried, but what can I say. I want more.*

He tried calling her cell phone, but the number had been disconnected. None of her friends could tell him where she was and, after calling around like a maniac for two days straight, he finally decided to quit. Unfortunately, his cousin blindsided him with the news that one of their mutual friends revealed the truth of her whereabouts to him. Apparently, after months of working closely together, she and one of her clients, a very wealthy man with multiple businesses along the Eastern Seaboard, fell in love, sparking her to move in with him just days after leaving Alex. In the end, he didn't know what made him angrier: the way she left, or the fact that he was going to propose marriage to someone he wasn't even sure he wanted to marry, just because it seemed like the right thing to do.

That was almost a year and a half ago. He tried staying there at first, hoping she would change her mind and return, especially after hearing through the grapevine that the relationship fizzled out quickly. But eventually, he began to make a name for himself in the food world and, after time, his hopes were no longer for her, but for a life of success in pleasuring palates. Thanks to Lewis introducing him around town, he even made a few friends. But they were nothing like his friends back home.

His loved ones kept after him with consistent pleas, and sometimes failed bribery attempts, to get him to move back—until one day, he decided on his own that it was time he did. Unbeknownst to him, at the same time, Natalie's job offered her the position she'd always wanted. Whether it was a test, fate or a cruel trick from the cosmos, it meant she had to relocate to the very place Alex had moved to in order to escape her. When he received her letter in the mail, her handwriting alone was enough to make his skin crawl, admittedly in both a good and bad way. Regardless of whether or not he hated it or loved it, the fact remained that Natalie looked damn good and he was still surprisingly attracted to her, even after all the pain she'd put him through.

Luckily for him, there were three very important things that were kind enough to keep his dick under control. The first was that he wanted Alana and had no intention of messing that up. Sure, they didn't have an official title, but she made him feel like no one ever had before, not even Natalie who, up until that point, had been the Mount Everest of his great loves. The second was that, in an hour, Alana would be there, filling his hands with more sexy, supple, flesh than he could stand. And the third was that he could never forget how Nat left him. No one could, for that matter! He sat on the bottom step as they stared at each other awkwardly. She began to walk toward him, when he raised his hand for her to stop.

"Whatever you have to say, you can say from there," he said dryly.

"Did you get my letter?"

"Yeah. So?"

"Is that really all you have to say to me?"

"What more is there?" he asked.

"I mean, Lex. Come on. We were—"

"Yeah, we were!" he said, cutting her off coldly.

"So does that mean you can't at least tell me what you thought when you read it?"

"Honestly? I thought it was a bunch of bullshit in pretty handwriting!"

"That's not fair!"

"You wanna talk about fair, Natalie?! To me of all people?!"

Natalie knew immediately that she was in no position to make demands of him or expect any preferential treatment because of their past. She had ruined their past, and he seemed uninterested in any future. Even so, there had to be some love left in his heart for her, right? She needed to know, despite his anger. But as she decided in her mind to show him what he was missing, her eyes veered to the right of her, where she saw Alana's Hermes scarf draped over one of the dining room chairs.

"You're seeing someone?" she asked, as if wounded.

"Yes."

"Are you two exclusive?"

"Yes."

"Is it serious?"

"For me? Yes. And why do you even care? Last I heard, from one of our friends no less, you want someone with influence, someone with a title! Is that right?"

Natalie stopped for a moment. She had one more question, but she wasn't sure if she wanted the answer. She'd come there to win her man back, but he was different. It was time to turn on the charm, fast and hard! She began to unbutton her shirt and walk toward him in a way that screamed, "I'm trying way too hard to be sexy." If Alex wasn't so irritated by her unscheduled visit, he would have laughed uncontrollably at how ridiculous she looked. He remained sitting on the step, looking at her, but there was no reaction on his face. She found it strange considering she could see that he was still getting a little hard. After reaching the last button, she let the powder pink blouse fall open as she got on her knees in front of him so that their faces were inches apart.

"Okay, so it's serious. But do you love her? Do you love her like you loved me?" she asked. She put her hands to his cheeks and closed her eyes to move in for a kiss.

"More," he whispered. "Only this time, I knew it the first time I saw her. She didn't have to fuck me six ways from sundown before I figured it out."

It was the first time he'd admitted it out loud, and his only regret was that it was to her, not Alana. Natalie's eyes popped open, as if she'd just been hit in the chest with a defibrillator. She jumped up and closed her shirt, now feeling awkward and embarrassed. She put one arm across her chest while the other wrapped around her waist, like she was shielding herself from the pain. One by one, she began to redo her buttons. But much to his surprise, instead of accepting the realization that he was over her, she responded in an almost "Simeon-esque" style of arrogance.

"I don't believe you. You don't really love her. You're just saying that to hurt me. I get it."

"Obviously, you don't," he said, laughing at her. "It isn't about you anymore."

"So, this new girl of yours. Knowing you, she's beautiful, smart and successful. But I know you! The way to your heart is through your stomach. So, does she do it for you in the kitchen?"

"She does *it* for me in every room of this house. You want to believe something, believe that!" he said with a quick wink.

Natalie smirked as she grabbed her purse from the mail table and replaced it with a small velvet jewelry box she'd taken out of it. She walked slowly to the door and, with her back to him, let out a small, sinister laugh. As she reached the foyer, she pivoted on her toes and delivered one last blow that she was sure would get to him, whether he loved someone else or not.

"Well, I guess I'll be leaving you…again, that is!"

Alex got up from the step and approached her with fury in his eyes. Natalie was sure he was going to hit her, but deep down, she knew he was too much of a gentleman to do so. Instead, he grabbed her arm and rushed her out, before slamming the door behind her.

"Well, you won't mind if I help you leave this time!" he shouted from inside.

It was official: Natalie was no longer the woman he knew. Nat would have never thrown something she'd done wrong in his face so nonchalantly, as if it were a joke. Yet, he was grateful for her callous behavior because it showed him how one-sided their relationship had truly been. True, he and Alana had a long way to go. But at least they both respected and appreciated each other equally. Now that he'd admitted out loud that he in fact loved her, he thought maybe it was time to find out exactly where her head and heart were; but, not tonight. He'd already decided that the moment she walked through the door, he wanted to entangle himself within the peace that Alana's arms often provided.

After about forty-five minutes of waiting and thinking, he perked up as he saw the headlights of her car turning into the driveway. He stood at the door to open it for her. When she finally found her way through it, she did so with both hands full of bags. Alex took some from her, curious as to why she looked as though she was hiding from the paparazzi. Her calf-length coat, large tan floppy hat and dark black shades looked more like a disguise than an outfit.

"Um, gorgeous, what's with the Inspector Gadget look?" he said jokingly.

"I'll tell you as soon as you empty those bags onto the table. Small bag first, then large, then medium."

He smiled, wondering what she had up her sleeves as he carried the bags into the dining room and sat them on the table. He turned up the dimly lit light so he could see what was in store for the evening. The first item he took out was a nature CD entitled, "The Sound of the Ocean." Alana immediately grabbed it and hurried to load it into his stereo. The second item was a small container filled with seashells.

The third item was a large, tan blanket with a wooden sign on top of it that read, "SAND". Alana grabbed it and headed toward the living room, where she moved the coffee table and spread it out across the floor. She put the sign in the middle of the blanket and spread the seashells around it. The other items were two oversized beach towels: one with the word Jamaica on it, and the other with pictures of tropical fish. She took those towels and rolled them out on both sides of the "SAND" sign. Shortly afterwards, she lit a fire and put a sign over the fireplace, which had a red arrow pointing downward and the words "THE SUN." The last two items were men's Polo swim shorts and a couple of frozen wine coolers.

"Go on, change please," she said, waving him off.

Alex couldn't change fast enough. But, as he entered the hallway, his eyes honed in on the velvet jewelry box sitting on the mail table. He didn't want Alana thinking Natalie's old gift had been purchased for her. He would never re-gift something to her that was meant for someone else. He also didn't want to have to explain how it got there. He very smoothly grabbed it and tucked it under the shorts, before heading upstairs. When he reached his bedroom, he found a quiet little corner in his closet to hide it until he knew what he was going to do with it. After changing and returning downstairs, the frozen wine coolers were waiting in two large cocktail glasses as Alana yelled from the guest bathroom for him to pick a towel. As he lay there in a state of complete happiness, she hit play on her phone, prompting Bob Marley to sing "Satisfy My Soul."

With the sound of the music, the sound of the ocean coming from his stereo, the heat of the fireplace, and the cool sip of his wine cooler, Alex felt like he was on a private island. His mouth nearly fell open when she walked in the room still wearing her floppy hat, which was now accompanied by a turquoise and neon green bikini, black shades, and a sheer white sarong. Alex was flabbergasted. She had taken his fantasy and made it a reality.

"Is this seat taken?" she asked as she sat down her beach bag.

"Yes," he said, barely able to control his smile. "I've been saving it for you."

Alana took a seat on the towel next to him and took a sip of her drink. The two smiled at each other, like teenagers in love as they "got to know each other." She grabbed a bottle of lotion from her bag and offered to rub it onto his back to protect him from the imaginary sunrays. He removed his t-shirt and rolled onto his stomach to prepare for his rub down. He closed his eyes while Alana massaged the coconut-scented body cream into his skin, making him moan in appreciation.

"Man, babe. You don't know how much I needed this today." he said.

"Oh yeah? Something wrong? You want to talk about it?"

"And ruin this moment? Never!"

Alex thought about what he could possibly say to her that wouldn't put a damper on their night. His two choices of topics were A, telling her that her best friend was being a grade A asshole by flaunting their secret fling from college in his face, which would make *him* look just as petty; or B, telling her that his ex that broke up with him ages ago with no explanation suddenly popped up uninvited to his home and tried to seduce him shortly before she came over, which would make him look crazy! He decided to go with

C: spending a lovely evening with the woman he secretly loved. At that moment, it hit him that despite their bickering, he and Simeon had one very big thing in common: they were both secretly in love with the same person and chose not to tell her out of fear of scaring her away. It didn't matter though. There was no way Alex would walk away from a woman this wonderful without putting up a hell of a fight.

After his deep tissue massage, Alex's muscles felt like butter as he rolled over to stare up at Alana's beautiful face. He rubbed her thighs and smiled, thinking to himself that things couldn't get much better than this.

"So, what do two people on a deserted island do about dinner? We have to survive, you know," she asked, pulling him out of his trance.

"I could survive on you alone. You're my five-course meal; your mind, your spirit and man, oh man, this body!" he said, gripping her butt in the palms of his hands.

"What happened to the other two courses?"

"Have you ever made love on the beach?" he asked.

"That's still only four."

"If you knew what I plan to do to you, you would count it as double!"

"Well, consider dinner served!"

Alex sat up and wrapped his arms around Alana tightly. He kissed her so passionately that it had a ripple effect throughout her entire body. With her legs wrapped around his waist, and her soft hands caressing his short, scruffy beard, she enjoyed every single nibble that he placed upon her neck. She smiled as his fingers found their way up her back and on the string keeping her top in place. As he tugged at it, his mouth prepared itself to be filled with her tropical melons, but she stopped him before he could indulge himself.

"Feed me, then I'll feed you," she said, pushing his head back and getting up.

He chased her into the kitchen, where she quickly grabbed an apron for them both and shooed him over to the opposite side of the counter. There they both stood in swimsuit bottoms and aprons, when Alex came up with the perfect menu for "island night." Alana insisted on not making a huge meal, so he grabbed some thawed poultry from the fridge and decided they would dine on jerk chicken, Caribbean rice and Jamaican rum cake for dessert. He quickly seasoned the meat to perfection, and grabbed some pots and pans to get dinner started. As the food simmered and filled the house with a delicious aroma, Alana leaned against the counter, stirring the cake batter as she watched him dazzle her. Alex took notice and turned the oven on low so he could pick up where he left off. His hands moved slowly all over her body, before he turned her around so he could grip his favorite sweet treat, which he jokingly called his honeybuns. He pulled her closer to him. She could tell by the firmness in his grip that he wanted her badly. She had no doubt that she would give in.

"Have I ever told you I love baking with you?" he asked as he grabbed the silicone spatula from her. He turned her back around and pushed her forward on the counter, as he smeared some of the batter right beneath the bottom of her bikini bottoms.

Alana giggled as he nibbled on her perfect posterior and licked her spine. He picked her up and carried her back to their homemade beach. But just as his toes touched the blanket, the doorbell rang. Alex was so startled by the unexpected interruption that he damn near dropped Alana like a sack of potatoes.

His heart began to beat out of his chest as he prayed to God that Natalie hadn't left the box behind just so she would have an excuse to return. He apologized to Alana as she nervously struggled to put his t-shirt on. The dim lights in the hallway provided enough cover for her to scoot into the guest bathroom undetected if the unannounced guest happened to peer into the windows. The porch light beamed brightly, but whomever it was stood directly in front of the thick wooden door. Alex yelled to the visitor from the hallway, hoping not to hear Natalie's voice in return.

"Who is it?" he yelled.

"It's Diego."

Chapter | 16

Alex felt as though he should add a turnstyle to his front door with the number of uninvited guests choosing to pass through. But instead of wondering why he was so popular all of a sudden, he took a sigh of relief that it wasn't Natalie returning to cause chaos. Meanwhile, Alana was in a panic.

"What the hell?! Did you know he was coming over here?!" she whispered.

"Of course not! Baby, I wouldn't ambush you like that. I have no idea why he's here!"

Alana was cowering in the guest bathroom while Alex answered the door. He tried cracking it, but Diego bombarded his way in with a six pack of beers, some homemade salsa and chips. Still wearing the black jeans and black t-shirt he'd worn under his chef coat, it was obvious he'd come by straight from work. Alex scratched his head and smiled nervously as he put forth his best effort to be hospitable, all the long worrying about Alana.

"What's up, D? I uh, I wasn't expecting you, bro."

"Yeah dude, I can see that," he said, looking confused at Alex's apron and shorts ensemble.

"Look, man. I'm sorry about earlier today. I know I was a little hard on you, but—"

"Hey, no apology necessary!" Alex assured him. "He *is* my boss and so are you. It was stupid anyway."

"I know right! I mean, come on. Him accusing you of plotting to make a move on Alana; ridiculous! Anyway, I figured we could catch the end of the game since we haven't really hung out since you've been back. Quick question though. Why do you smell like a Pina Colada?"

Alex chuckled a little, although his face was filled with apprehension. Diego started to proceed out of the hallway and into the kitchen when he took a quick look around and finally caught on to what he'd just interrupted. The smell of dinner cooking, the blanket sprawled out on the floor by the fireplace, two glasses filled with wine coolers that glowed from the fire as if it were a love potion, and a pair of wedged shoes by the couch indicated that he'd just pressed pause on his friend's romantic evening. In a hushed tone, he began apologizing profusely for not calling first. He figured Alex's mystery date must be somebody very special for him to be so secretive about her, especially with it being so obvious to everyone lately that he'd been seeing someone.

Alex was so happy during the passing weeks that it was almost sickening. Whenever he wasn't texting and smiling at his phone during his break, there was somewhere he always had to rush off to after work. Besides, Diego knew him well. The two had been friends for a long time and he'd seen Alex in his "player" phase, as well as his "settled down" one. His behavior lately, coupled with this overly romantic display, was a telltale sign that he was actually trying to build something with this girl.

"Thought you weren't seeing anyone?!" Diego joked as he punched Alex in the shoulder.

"Well, it's still new so—"

"Yeah, but you're really into her though. Anyone I know?"

"It's a big city. How can I tell you who you know?"

"Alright, smart ass! I guess I'll leave you to it then."

Diego held the six pack to his chest and tilted his head back, sticking his nose in the air as if he'd just been insulted. Alex shook his head and laughed, as he shut the door behind him. Alana emerged from the bathroom, walking across the floor on her tiptoes in full sneak mode. He assured her that the coast was clear before they both let out a deep breath and returned to the kitchen. Alex checked on the food while Alana hopped up onto the counter and put her arms inside of his t-shirt.

She watched his toned body flex as he stirred a pot here and adjusted some heat there. He turned everything down to a low simmer and decided it was time to turn up Alana's flame. As she rambled on about how fast her heart was beating when they were almost busted, Alex went to her and lifted the shirt over her head, before pushing her legs apart so he could stand between them. She quieted immediately as he stared into her eyes, like he often did before kissing her. He placed his right hand over her heart and his left on the bottom of her back, where he applied a little pressure so that her posture was perfect. As her back straightened and her breast pushed into his hand, he couldn't help but gloat about the effects he was having on her body. Her racing heart, her hard nipples, the goosebumps on her skin, the hunger in her eyes all let him know that she was just as ready to pick up where they'd left off.

"Well, I see what you're saying about your heart. It's still beating pretty fast. Maybe I should check your pulse, too," he said.

He grabbed both wrists, as if he was examining her. He let her know that everything felt just fine as she placed her arms around his neck. His hands traveled to her hips and squeezed tightly. It didn't take long for his tongue to play a one-man game of tic-tac-toe on her neck, which instantly made her wet. Her pussy began pulsating like it had its *own* heartbeat, which had suddenly been shocked back to life by the sensual swirls and soft nibbles coming from his mouth. This man was amazing! Within minutes, he'd gone from her sexy island mate to her handsome, mouth-watering chef and now, her doctor feel good!

"Clear!" she whispered.

"What?" he asked, with a small smile.

"Oh nothing. Anyway doc, what about our island?"

"Haven't you heard? Chefs do it best in the kitchen," he moaned.

Alana's fingertips dug into the back of his neck as he lifted her off the counter and lowered her to the floor. He grabbed his shirt from the counter to make her a pillow before laying her down. He stared at her small frame for a moment, biting his lip before rushing to leave a small trail of kisses down her stomach. His lips continued their travels until they arrived at his favorite place. His tongue parted her lips, flicking back and forth on her clitoris, causing her to arch her back and grab the back of his head. Every so often, his low, scruffy beard would tickle her and it drove her crazy. She was trying her best not to smother him!

The kitchen filled with heat in more ways than one, as a pot on the stove began to boil over, as if it were in sync with her body because she was right on the edge of boiling over herself. Just as she was about to cum, they were startled again by someone pounding hard on the front door. Both Alex and Alana were instantly irritated. She was almost "there" and he could feel it, too, which aggravated him even more! They froze in place, like a stone Kama Sutra statue, before he lifted his head and stared into her eyes. Perhaps they thought that if they didn't move, the unwelcomed visitor would leave.

"Hey, Alex! Man, it's Diego again. Open up, bro!"

They couldn't believe it! They thought he was out of their hair for the night. Had he come back, or had he simply *never left*? Alana pushed Alex's head back and swung her leg over him so she could once again get dressed. He jumped up with a full-blown hard on that had turned his apron into a tent. He told her not to panic as he wiped his mouth and pulled the hidden sliding door out of the wall in the kitchen. As he closed it behind him, he hustled toward the commotion Diego was making, which was this time more nervous than the first.

As he opened the door in jest, it was met with a look of worry plastered onto Diego's face. He walked in and looked around again, twisting his wedding ring around his finger anxiously before turning back around to face Alex. He looked down at the floor and stared for a moment, before giving Alex a look that melted his smile away.

"What's up, D. Everything alright?"

"You tell me."

"What do you mean?"

"I mean why is Alana's car parked in front of your garage?"

"Huh?" he said, caught off guard.

"Oh, I'm sorry. I guess that was a difficult question. Let me try something simpler. What is going on, Alex?"

"D, it's not what you think—"

"Oh, it's not? I think I defended you, man. I think I asked you not to pursue her."

"You don't understand. We met before the interview. I just didn't realize it until I got there. Remember the girl I told you about from the store that day?"

"Wait a minute. The "girl of your dreams" was Alana? Why didn't you tell me that?"

"I didn't think it was—"

"No, I didn't think it was a good idea," Alana interjected as she walked up behind Diego, shocking him. He stood with his mouth gaped open as Alana stood there in Alex's gown-like shirt, wondering what she should say next. She reached over and used her fingertips to push his chin upward so that his mouth would finally close. The smell of something burning sent Alex running back into the kitchen momentarily, leaving the two friends there to stand in a silence so loud that Alana could have sworn she heard the kitchen clock ticking. She didn't know where she should start or if Diego was even interested in an explanation. But she figured the least she could do, after all the sneaking around they'd been doing, is offer him the truth.

"I feel like I'm trapped inside of one of my wife's telenovelas!" he said.

"Look, I never thought we would actually start seeing each other after I hired him. And I didn't want it to look like I hired him because of some sort of—"

"Preferential treatment? Look, I get it. I'm just a little caught off guard right now," he said, before letting his signature smile spread across his face. "You and my boy, eh?" he joked as he nudged his fist into her stomach.

Once Alex rejoined them, the secret lovers started from the beginning so that Diego could be brought up to speed. He put them both at ease, promising them that, as their friend, he would not share what he'd learned with anyone. He hugged Alana, who was eager to go put on some clothes. But as she disappeared up the stairs, so did the smile that was on his face. He waved Alex onto the porch where he shed more than the porchlight on him. Suddenly, he was all business as he began to ask about the possible negative effects the relationship could have on them both.

"So, what happens if this ends badly?"

"It won't," Alex assured him.

"And if it does go somewhere? What about the level of discomfort it will create in your work environment?"

"After what you've seen today, not just with Alana, but with Simeon as well, I obviously know how to keep my private affairs private."

"Speaking of Simeon, have you thought about what I told you? What if he finds out? I'm pretty sure he's in love with her!" Diego said.

"Yeah, well so am I! Eventually, he may just have to learn that and accept it. He's just her friend, right? You said it yourself!" he snapped.

Diego looked at him as if stunned by the admission. He figured Alex felt something toward Alana, but love? If love was now a part of the equation, things were sure to get messy at some point, especially with the way Simeon liked to carry on with her. Even so, they were all adults. Diego decided he'd experienced enough revelations for the evening. After standing in silence for a moment, he simply shook Alex's hand and wished him luck.

As he pulled off into the darkness, Alex stood under the porchlight, trying his best to consider all that Diego addressed. He questioned himself about whether or not he was making the right choice, and even if he should set his feelings aside and keep it strictly professional. But Alex couldn't kid himself. He wanted to be with her. As he re-entered the house and watched Alana walk down the stairs in his robe, he knew that their blossoming relationship was indeed the right choice. Besides, he figured, what was the worst that could happen?

"So, now Diego knows? This is becoming the most well-known secret I've ever heard of!" she joked as she put her arms around his neck.

"Well, I'll make you a deal. After we eat, I'll do something to you that will be just between us." As their lips met once again, they returned to the kitchen for their island feast while Alex silently went over the events of the day, and Alana secretly thought about how interesting her next conversation with Gigi would be.

Time seemed to be going by rather fast, as it had been a few days since Alana and Gigi got to get together and shoot the breeze. She hadn't even had a chance to tell her about the debacle with Diego. Their morning chats over coffee had been put on pause due to Brian's move into a well-known, and hard-to-get-into, apartment building in the posh part of town. Most of Gigi's time was consumed with helping him unpack and organize. She was also executing a cleverly veiled plan to make sure the single female tenants were aware that he was in fact taken. But when Alana called her and said they needed to talk, the ever-faithful sister and friend told Brian that they needed a girl's night.

She arrived at Alana's at 6 p.m. with her favorite popcorn and a quart of butter pecan ice cream for Alana. Alana teased the fashionista, whom she wasn't used to seeing dressed down these days, about how casually chic she looked sporting leggings, a hoodie with Brian's alma mater on it, and a big curly ponytail. Gigi waved her off and put on a DVD, knowing that they wouldn't watch it. Alana hadn't been home in a couple of days, so she grabbed them some blankets to shield them from the coolness in the air while she turned up the heat. The heavy wind and rain outside her window blew through the trees like a hurricane as they wrapped up tightly and settled in for the evening. Gigi ate her popcorn while smirking and staring at Alana, waiting for her to reveal what was so urgent. She wasn't the type to be easily surprised, but she wasn't quite prepared to hear what Diego had stumbled upon.

"O-M-G honey! Well, what did he do?" Gigi asked.

"What could he do? He stood there with his mouth open like a Venus fly trap!"

"And what did you do? I know you were nervous, standing there with no damn clothes on!"

"Nervous doesn't even begin to describe what I felt."

"Oh, I bet you could if you tried. We talking 'floozy confessing to a priest' nervous, or 'hearing the theme music to Jaws while you're swimming' nervous?"

"I'm sorry. Is one of those options supposed to be better than the other?" Alana asked, puzzled.

"Well, yeah! At least with one of them, you know there's a chance someone can save you!" The girls giggled as they continued for a while chatting about Alex and bringing each other up to speed when suddenly, they heard the front door unlocking. They looked at each other deviously as they quieted their chatter, knowing it could only be one person. The hefty sound of men's boots traveled heavily across the room before a rather large frame plopped down on the couch, followed by a head in Alana's lap. His hand reached upwards into the bowl of popcorn that she had quickly lifted to make room for her unexpected guest. She handed it back to Gigi, who was finding humor in her slight irritation.

"Simeon, what a surprise," she said dryly.

"What we watching?" he asked as he kicked off his boots. He sat up just enough for Alana to help him out of his jacket.

"Your favorite: Heat," Gigi interjected.

"Ah! See, y'all knew I was coming over. And have I have a special treat for you, as well!" he said, lifting the plastic bag he was carrying. It was full of miniature Snickers and Reese's peanut butter cups for her junk food drawer.

"I noticed you were a little low the last time I was here."

"Oh, she's been getting her fill of chocolate these days!" Gigi said before being hit with a pillow.

Simeon brushed off the comment as he became more interested in the ivory, shawl-collar sweater Alana was wearing. He pulled back the cover to see if she is wearing his pants, as well, but was pleasantly surprised to find only boyshorts and thick ivory socks to match. As she snatched the cover back, he couldn't help but poke fun at her fashion sense.

"No wonder I can never find my clothes. You're always wearing them," he said.

"Well, you always leave them here! Fair game, buddy."

"Anyway! Did you guys eat yet? I can whip up something real quick," he offered.

"Would you?" Alana asked as Gigi clapped excitedly.

With a quick "coming up," Simeon kissed the palm of Alana's hand and rushed off to the kitchen, causing Alana to give Gigi a look of confusion. He'd been overly affectionate lately and his usual sarcastic quips were at an all-time low. She wasn't sure what was going on with him, but she was certainly curious. As she retreated to the bathroom to put on some pants, Gigi joined him in the kitchen, where he began his interrogation.

"So, who's the guy she's seeing?" he whispered inquiring with Gigi.

"I don't know what you're talking about."

"Please! She's been missing a lot lately for no apparent reason. It must be a dude."

"Why can't it be that she's a business woman with a lot on her plate?"

"You're taking sides? I'm your best friend, too, and you're keeping secrets from me now?"

"Oh, you mean like the secret I'm keeping from Alana that you're in love with her?"

"Shh! I told you that in confidence!" he whispered.

"No, you told me that by accident. It's not the same thing!"

"Stop dancing around the—"

"What are you two whispering about?" Alana interjected as she entered the kitchen.

"Uh…dancing! I was thinking we should all go dancing tonight. You game?" Simeon asked.

"Hell yeah! We haven't gone out in a while."

"I'll go call Brian," Gigi said.

As the friends dispersed from the kitchen and sat around waiting for the food to finish cooking, each of their minds swirled with thoughts they couldn't share with one another. Gigi wanted so badly to tell Alana about Simeon's feelings. She realized how happy she was with Alex, but she felt it would be better for them all if the truth was revealed, even if it didn't work out the way Simeon wanted it to. Alana thought about how happy she was with Alex and how close they were becoming. She was also struggling with the fact that she couldn't share her happiness with Simeon because of all the past lectures she'd given him about dating employees.

Simeon obsessed about the mystery guy that he was *sure* Alana was seeing, and he wondered if now would be the best time to reveal his love for her before things got too serious between them. After filling their bellies and sparking up a joint given to Simeon by a beautiful, earthy girl he sometimes dated who went by the name Moon, the friends blasted off on a space odyssey of their own. It only took a few puffs between them before they each decided to get out of their own heads, get dressed to kill, and take their frustrations out on the dance floor.

Chapter | 17

The night seemed to come alive as Alana, Simeon and Gigi followed the searchlights in the sky that led to the velvet ropes lining the outside of the club. Before arriving, Simeon called ahead to ask Rick, the club's owner, about being put on the VIP list for the evening. The two had become chummy over the years after he hired Simeon to cater his first, second and third wedding reception. Even with a fairly new bride at home, hearing that Gigi would be coming made Rick more than happy to oblige. Since first seeing her at one of Simeon's birthday parties, he'd been infatuated with her beauty.

No matter what the topic of conversation was, Rick always found a way to work in asking about her in an amusing way. If they were discussing the ongoing construction at his home, he'd say, "Speaking of brick houses, how's your friend Gigi?" If they were discussing Simeon's cooking, he'd ask, "Speaking of edible cuisine, how's your friend Gigi?"

As they approached the entrance, Rick appeared from behind the rather large bouncer and welcomed them in with open arms. The girls were eternally grateful that they didn't have to stand out in the cold in the tiny dresses they'd chosen to wear. The men talked as Rick waved over toward the bar, causing his staff to spring into action. Immediately, the bartender filled a bucket with ice and one of the shot girls placed a large black bottle inside. The girls were busy being distracted by all of the attention they were getting, some of which had to do with the owner escorting them to their table personally.

Ordinarily, Rick came out for the big-named guests only and he let his staff handle the regular crowd. But, let him tell it, he was secretly Gigi's number one fan. In any case, it didn't matter. Simeon was always sure to let him know politely that she was not available, which was fine by Rick. Just looking was fine by him! Gigi dazzled in a gold backless, mini-dress with long sleeves. As if she weren't tall enough, her matching stilettos made her tower over Alana, leaving her to look like an elbow rest for both her and Simeon, who was donned in a black suit, black button-up shirt and black shoes. His simple approach did nothing less than make the ladies drool.

Although she came up short in the height department, Alana looked equally gorgeous in a sleeveless, hot pink, turtleneck dress, which she paired with tall black heels. The loud music was almost hypnotizing as they took their seats in the private booth he'd reserved for them. A sexy, young waitress wearing a black leather tube top, skin-tight black leather shorts and black leather cuffs on her wrist, which had long black tassels hanging from them, brought over a complimentary bottle of champagne. Alana didn't know whether she was more stunned by the young woman's beauty, or by the fact that Simeon hadn't seemed to notice, even when she was blatantly flirting with him.

"Are you okay?" Alana asked, putting her hand up to his forehead.

"Yeah, why do you ask?"

"That gorgeous woman was basically giving you a free pass to her erotic amusement park and you…"

"And I told you, I want something different now. I want more than sex. Anyway, I should be asking if *you're* alright. I know this isn't really your scene. Surprised you didn't suggest we go to Smooth Grooves."

Just the mention of the place made Alana think of the night she bumped into Alex there. She wondered what he was doing at that moment. *Was he thinking of her? Was he missing her as much as she was missing him?* The questions swirled in her mind, but brought her to an even bigger question. *Was she in danger of falling in love with him?* To take her mind off of him, she badgered Simeon about why he'd been acting so out of character all of a sudden.

"Did you find spiritual enlightenment or something?"

"Yes, that's why I just downed three straight shots of tequila--so that I can ascend higher!"

"Okay, smart ass! I'm just saying. What's gotten you so ready to settle down all of a sudden?"

He stared at her and took a deep breath. The time had finally come to tell Alana exactly what had him ready to turn in his player's card and become a one-woman man. It was her and it had been for a long time. Alana stared back, curiously wondering what he was about to say. Just as his lips parted so that the words could come tumbling out, Gigi insisted that they finish their champagne so that they could do what they came there to do: dance! Simeon downed the splendid taste of bubbly while struggling with whether he should be irritated or relieved that Gigi had interrupted what was about to be an honest moment. But the more he thought about it, he decided the club wasn't really the appropriate place for a revelation of that magnitude.

Once their glasses were empty, Gigi grabbed them both by the hand, pulling them through the sea of people drinking and dancing, until they reached the dance floor. The deejay filled the room with the sound of Kylie Minogue's "Slow" while Simeon found himself sandwiched between his dates, just like they were back in college. But things had changed since then, and it wasn't long before Brian called Gigi, asking her to meet him at the door, leaving Simeon and Alana to grind on their own. Their bodies moved in unison to the sexy beat of the music. Simeon's hands moved slowly up her side, his nose grazing the back of her neck, provoking him to inhale her signature smell of sweetness.

A small brush of his lips tickled her, causing her to turn and face him. The bright lights flashed with the beat of the music as Alana caught a glimpse of Simeon's striking face. He looked at her intensely as he pulled her close and moved from side to side. His hands rested on her hips, as if instructing her to do the same. Alana couldn't help but acknowledge how good his familiar touch felt, but she didn't want to start blurring the lines again after the close call they had recently. They smiled at each other before Simeon playfully kissed the tip of her nose, and Brian and Gigi quickly rejoined them. Simeon silently vowed that tomorrow morning would be the day that he let Alana know exactly who he envisioned as his future partner in business…and in *life*.

"Simeon never looked so sexy!" Alana thought as he stared at her while slowly unbuttoning his shirt. He approached her from across the room and whispered, "My hands were made to touch you," before kissing her earlobe. "Perhaps they should fulfill their purpose," she responded. He cupped her face and began to kiss her passionately, then ferociously. He pushed her up against the wall and pulled her dress over her head. With her spine pressed hard against the drywall, she struggled not to melt from the heat his mouth delivered as it traveled from her lips to her neck, and down to her breast. Simeon dropped to his knees and ripped her panties off before she felt his soft, moist tongue delving into her most delicate place. Alana grabbed the back of his head as she attempted to speak. I-I-I'm cum…

Alana jolted out of her sleep, as if someone had just burst into the room. She sat straight up in her bed, panting and clutching her chest. She closed her eyes and felt her body to see if she was still wearing her dress from last night. Immediately, she panicked once she felt nothing more than a bra and some underwear.

"Please tell me that was a dream," she said as she slowly lifted the covers, peeking with one eye open in hopes of finding only one set of legs. She breathed a sigh of relief when she found no one else. But she was still curious as to how she ended up half naked. She grabbed her head, which was spinning, and searched the drawer of her nightstand for a bottle of aspirin, which she didn't find. After grunting in frustration, she got out of bed to head to the bathroom. She peeked out of her room to see if anyone had crashed on her couch before walking out in her "house bikini" as she called it.

"G, you here?" she called out in a raspy morning voice. But there was no response. Alana proceeded across the loft with a relieved look on her face, which soon turned to shock when she heard a deep, sexy voice echoing behind her.

"Good morning."

She turned, startled, to find Simeon standing at the opening of the brick wall that led to her guest room. His flawless body almost weakened her as he stood there shirtless with his arms behind his back. He was still wearing his pants from the night before, but she could tell he was no longer wearing underwear. His unbuckled belt caused his low-hanging pants to expose the hairy trail leading from his belly button down to his very nice-sized package. This was the second time he'd surprised her after emerging from one of her rooms. But at least this time, he wasn't totally naked!

She let go of her chest and began frantically searching for something to cover herself with, her only options being the decorative pillows on her couch. She grabbed the biggest one she could find and put it in front of her midsection.

"Damn it, Simeon! What are you doing here?" she snapped.

"Do you not remember last night?"

"No. What happened?!" she asked, afraid of the answer.

"Well, somebody had to carry your drunk ass up here. Besides, I wasn't getting in my brand new Porsche with vomit all over me!"

"Oh no! I didn't?!"

"Yeah, you did. Gigi took off your clothes and I washed my shirt out in the sink. After that, I crashed in the guest room."

Alana was embarrassed about her projectile puking performance, but was relieved that nothing else happened. She apologized to Simeon repeatedly and offered to cook him breakfast as a token of her appreciation. He happily accepted as he stood smiling at the fact that she was still holding the pillow, which barely covered her. She rolled her eyes and threw it back on the couch after realizing how silly she looked. But before going into the bathroom, she decided to offer a quick threat to the overly entertained chef.

"Don't tell anyone you saw me in my underwear."

"Trust me. It's our secret. But damn, you look good with your clothes off!" he said, smiling.

She waved him off and closed the door so she could shower and brush her teeth, leaving Simeon to his own devices. He plopped down on the couch and turned on the television. But his obsession with sitcoms was put on hold as Alana's cell phone began to vibrate in the clutch she'd left on the coffee table. Simeon opened it, believing that is was Gigi checking up on them. Instead, the word "Chocolate" flashed across the screen. A look of both amusement and curiosity came across his face as he took the phone out, not knowing whether or not he should answer for her. His finger hovered above the accept button for a moment before he decided to turn it off instead.

It had been a while since they had breakfast together, and he didn't want anyone or anything interrupting them. After hearing the shower stop, he put the phone back and returned the clutch to the table, where he promptly threw his suit jacket over it. He continued flicking through the channels as Alana emerged from the bathroom, feeling as good as new.

She went straight into the kitchen so that she could make them a fresh batch of coffee and get to work on the breakfast she'd promised him. Simeon decided he couldn't let her do all the cooking, so he took the easy route and sat at the island, buttering two pieces of bread to be toasted. She fired up the stove and placed sausage patties into the skillet, before cracking a couple of eggs into a bowl and whisking away. Simeon watched her lovingly and thought to himself how beautiful she looked in the morning. He smiled at her Richard Pryor t-shirt, mismatch ankle socks, and calf-length jogging pants, which was a far cry from the sexy outfit she'd worn just a few hours ago.

It didn't matter though. She was still beautiful, and the mere sight of her made his mouth water even more than the smell of the food. But Simeon wouldn't be Simeon if he didn't put aside his affinity for her and promptly tease her about her upchuck reflex. He insisted that he knew the exact moment when she'd had enough and how he had tried to warn her.

"I knew that if you took that last shot, you would get sick," he boasted.

"You think you know everything!"

"I don't know everything, but I know *you*."

"You think so, huh?"

"Try me. But I'm telling you, Alana, there isn't a thing I don't know about you."

"Let's see then, Mr. Know It All! What's my favorite color?"

"Too easy. Cobalt blue."

"My favorite flower?"

"African violets."

"My favorite food?"

"Your favorite comfort food is grilled cheese. Your favorite food for flavor is Thai."

"Okay. You know a little something! My favorite--"

"Your favorite type of music is jazz. Your favorite song is 'Again Never' by Branford Marsalis. You always tell people your favorite movie is *The Matrix*, but I've seen you watch the 1978 version of *Invasion of the Body Snatchers* more than any other movie you've got in your collection. Your favorite season is fall. Your favorite flavor is chocolate, and your favorite memory from childhood is the first time Marra took you to the zoo."

Alana looked back at Simeon, shocked by his last bit of information. She had no idea he remembered something like that. He stared at her with his best poker face, but she got the feeling that there was so much more he could say, and, for whatever reason, he was holding back. She scrambled the eggs as they both stewed in silence. Alana thought about Alex and how he repeatedly stated that Simeon may have liked her in a capacity other than friendship. She didn't know if it was because she was hung over, but for the first time, his body language, his tone, his demeanor and the way he was looking at her began to make her wonder if he was right.

She began to feel incredibly uncomfortable as she made his plate and poured him a cup of coffee, not knowing what to say or perhaps even ask. Had the moment they had a few weeks back conjured up something she wasn't expecting or ready for? She wanted to get things straight, especially if she was seeing something that wasn't really there. Although she couldn't tell him, she wanted Alex! And, more importantly, she didn't want to lose the comradery she had with Simeon. She turned toward the island to hand him his plate and, at that moment, he stood up as if he were about to make an announcement. Without warning, Alana heard the door unlock as Gigi and Brian came bursting through. Alana let out a sigh of relief for her savior, while Simeon let out a sigh of disappointment toward his cock blocker.

"I hope you made enough for us," Gigi said, grabbing a patty from Simeon's plate.

"Hey guys! I am so sorry if I ruined your night."

"Ha! Not even if you tried, Pukey Patty!" Gigi joked. "We had a hot night, honey! But this morning he cooled me down with all this ice," Gigi said, holding out her hand.

"Oh my God! Oh my God! Is that a--"

"Yes! We got engaged!"

Both women screamed on cue as Alana dropped her fork on the floor and ran around the counter to give her best friend a hug. They jumped up and down, yelling inaudible words, while the guys looked at them like they were crazy. Simeon's frustration quickly melted away as he got up to congratulate the happy couple and grab his shirt. They convened at the dining room table so they could hear the juicy details.

"Why didn't you call me?" Alana yelled.

"I called you a few times. After the first two, it just kept going to voicemail."

Simeon shrugged his shoulders, insinuating he didn't know where her phone was, as he continued eating his breakfast and talking to Brian. As the girls searched for her phone, Gigi quietly told Alana the explicit details of her night and morning. As she whispered further, Brian, who could sometimes be bashful, warned her that she better not be telling their love story in her usual brash demeanor. But he knew it was falling upon deaf ears. As he threatened to spank her if she continued being naughty, she bent over to both tease and provoke him as she continued. She removed Simeon's jacket from the table and handed Alana her clutch. With a sigh of relief, the girls continued in Alana's bedroom so she could recharge her phone and her belief in love by listening to Gigi's romantic tale.

After leaving Alana's the night before, Gigi had been unable to contain her passion for Brian. The moment they were in the car, her mouth was on Brian's neck and her hand was in his pants. Her intoxication had turned her into a wild woman, and he was more than willing to try and tame the beast. During the drive, she turned the radio all the way up. As Ro James belted out "Burn Slow," she released the passion inside of her. The more she turned him on, the faster he drove. By the time they were halfway home, he was doing 90 miles per hour on the freeway, as her mouth did 90 miles per hour on his dick.

After reaching the parking structure of his apartment building, they jumped out of the car and raced to the elevator. They were happy to be the only people in there as they kissed each other passionately and tore at each other's clothes. When they reached Brian's floor, they stumbled out as she struggled to undo his belt and he struggled to unlock the door. Once they were on the other side of the door, they tore through the apartment like a tornado—knocking over chairs, throwing pillows off the couch, and almost ripping down the curtains as they made love against the tall, thick windows overlooking downtown. The next morning after sunrise, Brian kneeled down next to the bed, admiring her beauty, the depths of his love for her, and how she could look so incredibly sexy and peaceful at the same time.

"Stop it, creepy! I know you're watching me sleep," she joked, with her eyes still closed.

"How do you know what I'm doing without even looking at me?"

"Because I know my man. I'm in tune with you." They both smiled before Brian pulled the sheet up over her head and grabbed her hand from underneath it. He put her fingertips to his cheek and quizzed her.

"What am I doing now?"

"You're smiling at me." Pleased with the answer, he slid her fingertips down to his lips and began kissing them.

"What am I doing now?"

"Ooh! I would say turning me on, but I know you'd rather I say kissing me." Again, he slid her fingers down, this time placing her entire hand over his heart, which was racing.

"What am I doing now?"

"You're letting me hold the most precious thing you have." He then removed her hand from his heart and placed it on top of a box that had been sitting next to her face the entire time. Still under the sheet, she felt the box size and assumed there were diamond earrings inside.

"What am I doing now?"

"Spoiling me!" she said, ripping the sheet off her head and playfully extending her leg toward him. He rubbed her smooth skin as she lay on her side and held the sheet over breast, as if she was posing for *Playboy*. He rubbed his hand over her shoulder, down her side, over her hip and down to her calf, where he began to squeeze. She smiled as her beautiful, naked body almost completely distracted him from his original goal. He removed his hand from her smooth, chocolatey skin and gained his composure in order to ask the most important question of his life. He remained on his knee next to the bed as Gigi propped her head up and stared at the box.

"I'm doing much more than spoiling you, baby. I'm proposing to you. Will you marry me?" he asked as he popped open the box, revealing a huge yellow diamond surrounded by smaller white diamonds, which also lined the band. Tears rolled from the corners of her eyes as she grabbed him and pecked him over and over again. With every kiss, she said, "Yes!" so that there was no mistaking her answer. Afterwards, he told her that he'd purchased the ring weeks ago and had even received her father's blessing, but was struggling with how to ask her. He said that when he woke up to make coffee, and looked out at the rising sun, he looked back over at her as she lightly snored with a cute little snort and he knew that it was time.

"Ugh! You two are so stinking cute. I don't know if I want to throw you an engagement party, or murder you both in your sleep," Alana said as she hugged her tightly.

"Aw, boo. That's so sweet! Just make sure we're buried together if you do!"

As she ended her story, Alana started to tell Gigi about the strange vibe she received from Simeon earlier, but her mind was instantly filled with Alex once she saw his text messages. They ranged from, *"Hey lovely. Just thinking of you"* to *"I haven't heard from you in a minute, baby. Should I be worried?"* Alana texted back immediately to let him know that she was okay and thinking of him. She told him about the engagement and how she would tell him all the juicy details later. After receiving his congratulations text to Gigi, she wondered if it would be a mistake to tell him about how the evening ended.

Although nothing happened between her and Simeon, he *did* spend the night and he had seen her in her underwear. It wasn't like the two men were tight; there would be no reason for Simeon to say anything about it to him, right? She figured she would think on it. In the meantime, she would go over the details of when and where the wedding would take place. Immediately, Gigi told her that she would be her maid of honor, which made a sentimental Alana tear up. She chatted with her bestie non-stop, unaware of the drama that would soon ensue in her own love life.

Chapter | 18

"**H**old still!" Alex ordered.

"I can't, babe! It tickles!" Alana answered as the small brush traveled down to her side. She tried her best to be cooperative as she lay on her back on the old tattered quilt Alex had spread over his bedroom floor. He dipped the small paint brush into the cup of red paint and moved it over her rib cage as she wiggled like a worm. The cool touch of the paint, coupled with the long strokes of the brush, tickled her as his wrist moved in a downward motion. Alex had become aware of Alana's love of art since they'd been secretly seeing each other, which he was also starting to enjoy. She was always looking for original pieces from up and coming artists trying to take over the art world, or commenting on the latest exhibits at the museum. Even her home and business were filled with her love of brilliant colored latex paints, complemented by the artistic expression they ultimately delivered onto captivating canvases. He decided to surprise the art fanatic with a night of body painting for two.

After arriving at his place, he immediately requested that she take off all her clothes in the guest bathroom, where a black silk robe was waiting for her. She followed directions before entering the room, finding Alex waiting for her completely naked. The candles that he'd lit safely surrounded the quilt as the sound of Kem's song "Human Touch" played in the background. Alex helped her disrobe before asking her to get comfortable. At one end of the quilt, different color body paints in small containers were lined up alongside each other, with a small pile of long, skinny brushes in front of them. She lay down and rested her head in the palm of one of her hands before asking, "What are you about to do to me, Alex? Should I be worried?"

Amused, he sat next to Alana and dipped one of the brushes into the red paint before responding, "I'm about to paint this curvaceous canvas! You want me to use this paint brush or my own?" he asked. She looked over and laughed as he moved his dick at her, like it was waving. She rolled her eyes at the offer before he kneeled over her and began painting. Helplessly, she giggled as the bristles of the brush tickled her relentlessly. He painted a beautiful red rose on her right breast, with a long green stem traveling down her midsection. She tried her best to stay still so he could finish, but she couldn't take the tickling any more. Alana jumped up and stood in front of the full-length mirror, admiring his creation. She was surprised at how good the painting was since she was expecting it to look like something a child had drawn.

"Great job, Van Gogh! Now, your turn," she said. She pointed to the blanket, urging him to lie down in the spot she'd just gotten up from. Once he complied, Alana straddled him and began painting his chest and stomach. As he lay on his back with his hands behind his head, he couldn't stop smiling at his own personal Picasso. He tilted his pelvis upward and warned her not to sit there naked for too long.

She continued with her masterpiece, but soon started to tease him. As she grinded against him, Alex closed his eyes and tried not to get aroused. He didn't want Alana thinking that he expected sex every time she came over, but she wasn't making it easy. He held himself together long enough to let her finish before he, too, could take it no more. He hopped up to walk over to the mirror.

"Really? Alana's property? That's cute!" he said before returning to the blanket. "Maybe I should write a little note, too!"

Alex turned her over and began painting her derriere. In retaliation, she grabbed her paint brush, sparking a graffiti war between the two. They wrestled each other for containers until they were both covered in different shades of paint. She quickly jumped on top of him and pinned his arms over his head, forcing him to call a truce. Alana stared in his eyes for a while, moved by the happiness his smile was exuding, before she began to kiss him, further weakening his defenses.

She kissed him long and deeply, loosening her grip on his wrist. When he could no longer hold back, he pulled her down onto him, squeezing her naked body out of sheer desire. Their bodies rubbed together, ruining their creations, but making something much more beautiful. They made love! Alex rolled over on top of her and slid inside slowly. Alana moaned at the pleasant surprise that filled her with ease. She squeezed his chocolate treat, contracting the muscles within her walls. Alex thanked her by moaning and, in return, he dived deeper into her ocean.

After an hour of neck nibbling, back scratching, hair pulling, lip biting and reverse cow-girl, Alex came with such force that he struggled to stop his leg from spasming. Alana laughed at him before rolling over, hoping to catch her breath. He looked at her and smiled at the fact that she kept taking his away. After regaining his strength, he got up and retreated to the bathroom. She could hear him striking a match to light the huge candle that sat on his sink.

He turned on the water in the shower, every couple of minutes checking the temperature to make sure it was perfect. He beckoned for Alana to join him so they could wash off the paint and sweat that covered their bodies. She entered the dimly lit bathroom and stepped into the warm, streaming water that was already running over Alex's beautiful brown flesh. The muscles in his arms flexed as he lathered up and stood directly under the shower head so that the water could run over his hair. He reached down to peck Alana before grabbing her closely and playfully rubbing his soapy chest on her.

He took the bar of soap and rubbed it over her skin. Starting with her back, he made small circles, just as he'd done with the paint brush. It didn't take long for him to find his way to her butt, which caused him to suddenly need the use of both hands. He rubbed her body slowly as his long fingers lathered her neck and breast, sliding around with ease before the soap slipped from his hands.

"Whoops! I dropped the soap!" he said before dropping to his knees to get it. He kissed her belly button and thighs as he continued washing her legs.

"I feel like I'm in the movie *Coming to America*! Bathers!" she yelled before clapping her hands loudly.

With a smile, he lathered his hands up with soap and rubbed her lower belly, even reaching for the small strip of hair that covered his favorite place.

"The royal pussy is clean, your highness!" he said, putting his own spin on a quote from the movie, which made them share a huge laugh. Alana snatched the soap from him and told him that it was his turn, which he had no problem taking. With one of his hands on the shower wall, he stood firmly and let the water run over his face as her small hands ran up and down his wide back. She, too, made circles with the soap, as if she were a window washer. He moaned from the relaxing feeling she was giving him.

She rubbed the loving lather across his shoulders and giggled as he turned to kiss the top of her head. Steam filled the bathroom as he faced her and grabbed her chin. He planted a kiss on her lips as they embraced and continued listening to the music in the bedroom. Soon, Alex began to move from side to side, grabbing one of Alana's arms and placing it around his neck, while his hand held the other so that they could slow dance.

"I've never danced with a naked woman," he insisted.

"I've never been naked with an employee!" she countered.

"Well, I'll take this over company stock options any day! So, you wanna dry off, or get wet some more?"

Alana dashed out of the shower, knowing that he had no problems going a few more rounds. He laughed as she begged for mercy, which he was happy to give her because secretly, he was tired, too! Both were exhausted from a long day of working and a long evening of love making, so Alana wanted to pace herself. She wasn't just worried about tiring each other out physically; she didn't want to tire out the relationship with an overabundance of sex. He couldn't miss it unless he was sometimes deprived of it! They toweled off and got dressed for bed, Alex in boxers and Alana in one of his t-shirts. She started to doze off. Just as Alex started to blow out the candles, he remembered something and stopped her.

"Wait! Before you go to sleep, I have something for you," he said. Alana's eyes popped open. She sat up against his headboard and continued to fight her sleep, while Alex disappeared into one of the other bedrooms. It didn't take long for him to return with a covered canvas. Her curiosity piqued as Alex sat the mysterious gift on the dresser, like he was preparing to make a presentation. He cleared his throat and began to speak.

"So, I heard you locked down the second location. Congratulations, by the way, baby. I'm so happy for you! And because I care for you so deeply, I got you this. I thought it might look good behind the new bar since you've got a painting of your grandmother behind the current one."

As he pulled off the cloth, Alana gasped! She was unprepared for the thoughtful and unexpected gift. She covered her mouth and attempted to keep the tears in her eyes at bay, but it wasn't easy. It was apparent that he'd not only paid a pretty penny for it, but that he'd found someone very talented to create it. There on the canvas was a painting of

Alana standing behind her grandmother, with her hands on her shoulders. They were both dressed in white, with a look of pride on their faces.

Alana got up and slowly walked over to the painting. One hand remained over her gaping mouth as she used the other to brush her fingertips across Grandma Marra's face. She marveled over the detail: the lines in her grandmother's hand, the crow's feet she'd started getting before she died, her pretty brown skin with a reddish hue, the slight smile she always had in pictures that let you know she was both sweet and sassy. It was perfect!

"So, you like it then?" he asked.

"Are you crazy?! How could I not?" she answered, wrapping her arms around his neck. Alex rubbed her back, comforting her as the tears flowed out of her eyes. He wiped them away and kissed her on the forehead, telling her that he only wanted to do something nice for her. Alana was blown away by the gift and, as she stammered over her words, she hoped he realized just how much it meant to her. The lovers climbed into bed and pulled up the covers. Alana thought to herself, *"This was the perfect end to a perfect day."*

She laid her head on his chest and snuggled up to him. Just before she fell asleep, she whispered, "Thank you for my gift, baby. I love it!" Alana immediately drifted away into dreamland. As she let out a little snore, signifying the depth of her exhaustion, Alex kissed her hair and whispered, "I know the feeling."

With all the positive happenings going on in Alana's life, she decided to throw an impromptu employee appreciation party for her staff. The city was experiencing a severe case of an Indian Summer, so Alana decided to take advantage and have a barbeque. Everyone was excited as they converged onto a local park not too far from the restaurant. They dined on grilled hot dogs, hamburgers and ribs cooked by none other than Diego, Simeon and Alex. Alana offered to have it catered so they could have a break, but the men insisted that they prepare the meal.

The guys huddled around the huge grill that Alana had rented for the occasion, competing with their culinary skills at every turn. Every now and then, one of them yelled at the other that their meat was better seasoned or cooked to perfection. For the sides, Diego brought his famous Mexican Street corn. Alex supplied the bacon and brown sugar baked beans, while Simeon settled on making the potato salad. Piles of potato chips, and coolers filled with soda and beer, surrounded their area. A huge banner hung from the picnic shed, which read: *The Cocoa Marra proudly presents: Employee Appreciation Day!*

People played frisbee and horseshoes, and even chased each other around with small water guns while "Pumped Up Kicks" by Foster The People played loudly from someone's car stereo. Some of the employees with families watched their little ones play on the nearby playscape or in the bounce house, while a small group enjoyed a good old-fashioned potato sack race. Alana dodged water balloons as she went around passing out gift cards she'd gotten for her awesome crew. A few of the waitresses couldn't help but sneak a peek at Brian as he sat at one of the picnic tables, looking scrumptious in a V-neck t-shirt and jeans. It was no wonder why Gigi was always so happy!

She caught a couple of the glances, and pointed her index and middle fingers at her eyes, before pointing them back at the women to let them know she was watching them. Simeon brought one of his lady friends as usual, a talented and beautiful ballet dancer by the name of Katia. Alex was grateful for his guest, knowing that it would give him and Alana more time to talk. The day progressed without so much as a tiny tiff between the guys, something that was becoming a real rarity recently. Everyone talked and mingled with the crowd, and Alana and Alex flirted in their own subtle way. However, it was nothing that would cause anyone to suspect that they were secretly wild about each other. As the good time flew by, the wonderfully warm afternoon soon turned into night. Those with children headed home, while the singles and a few couples stayed around for a bonfire.

The group of sixteen sipped on beer and talked about everything from social media to politics. It was inevitable that they would eventually stumble upon the topics of love and sex. To make things interesting, Alana tore a piece of paper from her planner and tore it into sixteen strips. She passed around a couple of pens and told each person to write down an anonymous question about either love or sex, and fold it up. She collected each piece of paper and dropped them into one of the gift bags someone had given her with a bottle of wine in it. She then proceeded to shake it up and pull out each strip of paper, one by one.

"Okay, everybody. First question: Do women like sex as much as men do?"

"Ha! Yes. But they still insist on waiting for the man to make the first move," Simeon yelled.

"I disagree with that last part," Alex said. "Some women know exactly what they want, and they take it." Some of the others piggybacked off what the two men said. They gave their own thoughts and opinions on the topic, while the two rivals side-eyed each other, knowing that it was just the beginning of their battle of wits. The first debate lasted longer than expected, so Alana had to take charge and move on to the next question.

"Alright, guys. Next question: Should you try dating a friend?"

"Why not?! Especially if the chemistry is there," Brian said, widening his eyes at Simeon.

"Never! Let your friend be your friend. Because if things don't go right, there is no guarantee that you'll be friends again," one of the waitresses said before rolling her eyes at Simeon. The two had previously engaged in a brief fling that ended horribly. Nevertheless, he ignored the obvious jab and instead focused on delivering a clear-cut message of his own.

"Just because you started out as friends doesn't mean you weren't meant to be more. Maybe the friendship was just a way to understand your future lover better." Alex glared at him with disdain, but kept quiet. Alana noticed his flaring nostrils and was all too glad when one of the busboys brought him over a beer, which helped him loosen up.

"Moving along," she said apprehensively. "Does size really matter?"

"I say no," answered another different waitress. "As long as a man knows how to use what he has to his advantage, he should be good to go."

"Hell yeah, it matters! There's nothing sadder than when a man buys a condom he knows he can't fit. Fellas, stop buying Magnums if you can't fill them. Condoms don't come with suspenders or magic grow," said her archrival, who was also a waitress at the restaurant. The two had become enemies a couple of years ago when they realized they were both messing around with Simeon at the same time.

"So, what do you do then? Treat it like a meal and send it back if it's not the right portion size? Besides, he might know a little something and surprise you."

"It's not a meal if it doesn't fill you up! And I'd prefer he didn't have a *little something* as a surprise. If it looks like his balls are wearing a sweater, and his penis is the tiny button, why waste your time? I bet you're one of those women who fakes orgasms for a guy, too!"

"I've never had that problem," Simeon added.

"If she was faking it, how would you know?" Alex asked.

The guests argued back and forth, prompting some of the spectators to chime in. Others sat back and listened while laughing over both the big and small problems that penis size could cause in the bedroom--and apparently at bonfires.

"Okay, it's getting late and the park is closing. So, let's do two more and get out of here. Can you be in love with more than one person at a time? And if so, can you love them equally?"

"Duh! Of course! It's called polyamory," Katia answered.

"I don't care what it's called. I think you'll always love one person more than the other," Gigi sniped, having decided she didn't like Simeon's date anyway. It irritated her how Katia would repeat the last word of every comment he made just before tossing her hair.

"I agree with G. A man can date as many women as he wants, but one will always be nearest and dearest to his heart," Brian remarked, aiming it at Simeon once again.

"I can only speak to what I know. And, for me, one woman, one *good* woman, is more than enough," Alex stated. Alana felt flushed just hearing his revelation. His veiled attempt to compliment her had just earned him brownie points for later. But leave it to Simeon to ruin her moment.

"Well, we'll have to find you that someone, won't we buddy? You seem to always show up to these functions alone. I was starting to wonder if you needed a few pointers," he said, grabbing Katia's thigh. She smiled at what she thought was his way of showing her off, not realizing the only person he was showing off was himself. But Alex knew exactly what he was doing, and he jumped at the opportunity to brag a little, as well.

"No pointers needed! Just because I don't flaunt it doesn't mean I don't have it. I've got a lady, a wonderful one. Trust me. You wouldn't believe your eyes if you saw her!"

Simeon perked up, ready to question him about this unbelievable girl when Alana insisted they move on. She could feel her heart wanting to beat out of her chest as her pulse raced. She felt like everyone could visualize his thoughts, as if everyone would know. Alex noticed the irritation on her face, but knew that he had no choice but to address it later on. Luckily, her irritation wasn't only reserved for him. Simeon's behavior was really starting to repulse her.

"No need to showboat, Alex. I'm sure your lady is lovely. And Simeon, nice to see you turning over that new leaf you were talking about the other day," she said snidely. Simeon snatched his hand away from Katia's lap and wondered if Alana was paying attention to his mannish ways more that he thought. Alex wondered the same thing, only he was more concerned with why she would care at all about him changing. An air of confusion, annoyance, suspicion and jealousy quietly circulated amongst the three of them. The secrets they'd been keeping were nearing a dangerous intersection, and it seemed that there would only be a matter of time before someone ran the stop sign.

"Okay, last question," she said as the small crowd booed her. "Does sex on the first date ruin any chance of a real relationship? Well, damn! I hope not," she said, answering her own question.

"Why would you hope not? You've never had sex on a first date in your life. Unless…wait a minute! I knew it!" Simeon exclaimed. "You're seeing someone! Is that why you keep getting flowers every other Friday?"

"What? You're crazy!"

The group became curious, wondering if she would reveal the mystery man Simeon was convinced existed. Gigi sipped her beer, hoping the uncomfortable moment would soon pass and take the spotlight off of Alana, whom clearly didn't want to answer the question. But when someone tried to jump in and answer the original question, he was cut off by Simeon's nosiness.

"Come on! Who is he? He must be pretty lame if you're hiding him."

"Or maybe she's hiding him from you because you're lame."

Alex mumbled just loud enough for a few people to hear. Simeon prepared to unleash a verbal assault onto him, but Katia intervened and asked Simeon to take her home. Alana was getting a little tired of their schoolyard feud, so she was happy when Simeon opted not to go back and forth. He grabbed Katia's hand and said goodnight to everyone, but not before giving Alex one last dirty look. Questions were left unanswered as they realized it was time for everyone to pack up and head home. They filled the trash cans around their area as Alex unsuccessfully tried to make small talk with Alana, who was visibly irritated. She tried her best to contain her frustration. But when he asked if something was bothering her, she decided to share what was on her mind.

"You wouldn't believe your eyes if you saw her? Really, Alex?"

"Ah, so it's me you're mad at?"

"Why do you have to do that? Why do you have to let him sucker you in?"

"Look, I'm tired of his smart ass comments! That asshole has called me the help, a bitch, and now you're dating a lame?!" he whispered angrily.

"He doesn't know I'm dating you. And if you have to keep participating in this cock contest, I won't be for much longer."

"Well, you know what, Alana? I won't keep letting him or you treat me like I'm still on the clock—him with his orders and insults, and now you with your reprimands! I don't need this shit!" he said before storming off.

It was their first fight and Alana didn't know how to feel about it. She knew it had to be hard on him. Not only did he have to keep hiding their relationship, but dealing with Simeon's crude behavior simultaneously was surely no picnic. As his tires screeched on the concrete, Gigi and Brian checked on her one last time before leaving, oblivious to what had just taken place. She faked a smile and waved them off as she and a couple of stragglers finished their beers before walking to the parking lot together.

She got into her car and sat in the dark for a moment, wondering if she was overreacting or if he was. But, at that moment, she couldn't be sure. As much as she wanted to call him and smooth things over, she figured a night apart just might do them some good.

Chapter | 19

Alana felt annoyed the moment she woke up, and it wasn't just because Indian Summer had come and gone only to leave behind cold weather. It had been a couple of days since the picnic, and she was still mad at Alex! She found his need to go back and forth with Simeon during the bonfire really immature. The change in the weather oddly enough was doing just what she had been trying to do: cool down! It was also the first time they'd had a disagreement that lasted for more than a few minutes without someone caving in, that person usually being him. She hadn't called him, and he hadn't called her either, which seemed to make her pout even more.

Every time she passed him in the kitchen, and he spoke to her, she wanted to say to him, "So you can say hello, but you can't call and apologize?" But she knew she couldn't do that and she knew she couldn't continue to stew in her spoiled ways nursing her attitude. The big day had finally come for the Wipe Out Childhood Cancer Fundraiser, which was being held at The Cocoa Marra. The day was sure to be a long one. As if the stress of an event of this caliber wasn't enough, she got a late start at the restaurant due to a problem in one of the tenant's lofts. So, by the time she arrived, the staff was running around like mad men.

The contract gave the clients full service and all-day access to ensure everything met their approval. The team devised a strategy that would allow them to keep up with all of the wants and needs of the client. Damien was in charge of coordinating with security retained for the evening, as well as valet. Simeon and Diego were in charge of the kitchen, of course, as well as instructing the wait staff on the table settings. Elizabeth and Alana were to work directly with the event coordinator, Ms. Davis, on last-minute requests, which Elizabeth was handling until Alana arrived.

The young woman, who was also the committee's chair, wanted to go over every detail with a fine-tooth comb: the guest lists, VIP's, security, gift bags, table settings, red carpet for the sidewalk, extra valet attendants, and even the strategic placing of the banner that would hang out front. Extra tables had to be brought up from the basement and taken to the second level of the restaurant. A hidden storage room at the end of the bar by the kitchen had been cleaned out the night before and would serve as the coat check room for the evening.

To raise money, a talent show, made up of former young patients, was scheduled. The acts included a nine-year-old magician, whose former nurse volunteered to be his assistant; an eleven-year-old girl, who made up one half of the duo that currently held first place in the youth division of the state-wide salsa competition; a seven-year-old comedian, who started performing for the other patients during his chemo and continued to do so at hospitals all over the city after he became well; and a thirteen-year-old opera prodigy, who was taking the country by storm. A small stage was brought in and placed by the long windows to give the tiny stars the spotlight they deserved. White drape panels, with yellow and lavender string lights embedded within them, were positioned right behind to give it extra flair.

Alana was the first to admit that she was looking forward to the kids' performances more than anything. Around noon, she finally showed up to take over for Elizabeth, who was still working with the overly obsessive coordinator. She appeared to be extremely nervous and wanted to make sure that the event was not only a success, but that it went on without so much as a hiccup. Alana completely understood that kind of passion, having gone through three contractors herself when she was trying to get her place exactly how she wanted it.

Simeon had only come out once to greet the panicked young woman before Alana arrived, but he found her to be so overly dramatic that he hurried back to the kitchen and left her in Elizabeth's hands. Afterwards, he sent Alana a text message, urging her to get to the restaurant as quickly as she could, joking that she should take a Valium beforehand. As she and Ms. Davis talked non-stop, something caught the young woman's attention as they walked past the kitchen door, causing her to stop midsentence. She even did a double take, as if she couldn't believe what she was seeing.

"Oh my God!" she said. "Can we stop in the kitchen for a moment? I don't want to interrupt them, but I think I see an old friend of mine."

"Of course!" Alana insisted as she led her through the door. The two women smiled at the staff as they worked ferociously. Diego was the first to look up, and his expression was that of someone who'd just seen a ghost.

"Hey guys," Alana said.

"Hey…hey…hey," Diego repeated over and over again, like a broken record. He stared and lightly elbowed Alex repeatedly, who was chuckling and trying to swat him away like he was pestering him.

"What are you doing? Stop playing around!" Alex said. But as he turned and faced the ladies, he soon realized why Diego was letting his elbow do all the talking. He couldn't believe who was standing there. He couldn't believe who the client was: Nat!

"Hey, Lex," Natalie said. He tried his best not to look stunned, but he wasn't doing a very good job. He struggled just to get the word, "Hi" out of his mouth.

"I didn't know you two knew each other. All this time she's been working with Simeon and I. Who would have guessed you two were old friends?" Alana asked, surprised.

"Sort of," he responded.

"Boy!" Natalie said, slapping his arm. "Sort of? We were engaged, once upon a time. I don't think your boss will mind. It's too late to cause a conflict of interest. When I stopped by the other night, you should have told me you worked here."

"Alex! How'd you let a gorgeous creature like this get away from you?" Simeon asked.

Engaged? Stopped by the other night! Alana couldn't believe what she was hearing. Alex never mentioned being engaged before! All the time they'd spent together, all of the feelings they'd shared, all of the stories about their past indiscretions and somehow, he neglected to tell her he was almost somebody's husband. *And stopped by the other night?* He damn sure neglected to reveal that tidbit of information!

Why was he hiding things from her? She thought they always agreed to be open and honest with each other. Alana's face bore a look that Alex couldn't quite put his finger on, but he knew it wasn't good. Even with her containing her emotions, the look resembled that of a love child made from surprise, anger and confusion. They were already on rocky ground because of what happened the night before, and now this! It was the first time since he'd met her that he wasn't looking forward to being alone with her. He didn't know what she would say when they got a chance to talk, but he knew there would be some curse words thrown in there somewhere! He could only hope that unlike her favorite season, which seemed to be on its way out, that he wasn't on his way out, as well. Alana did an about-face and exited the kitchen, with Nat hot on her trail.

"We have so much in common. We're both successful, both well-respected in our fields, and now we even know the same people!" Natalie exclaimed.

"I'm sure we have even more in common. Perhaps more than either of us realizes," Alana said in return.

"You're lucky to have Lex with you. He's a hard worker and a good man. I wish I had the sense to see that when we were together. The grass or, in our case, 'the lettuce,' was definitely wilted on the other side!"

Natalie smiled a little, but excused herself quickly as her eyes began to water. Watching her walk away, Alana realized maybe he hadn't told her about the engagement because of the embarrassing way it ended. The comment she'd made obviously meant she'd left him for another man and things didn't turn out so well for her in the end. Whatever the case, Alex still had some explaining to do. As she signed for a few deliveries, Alex went to the bathroom and began texting her.

"Baby, I know it looks bad, but BELIEVE me when I tell you things are not what they seem. She popped up at my house unannounced and I made her leave! I told her that I had someone and that my feelings for her were long gone. I know you are upset with me, but please give me a chance to explain everything later. You're the only woman I want, Alana, and I care for you more than you realize."

Alana read his words with an open mind and a conflicted heart. Her feelings had become stronger than she ever anticipated. He had amazed her unlike any other man ever had. When he wasn't cooking her favorite foods, he was buying her favorite wine. When he wasn't sticking flirty notes in her purse, he was sending her well wishes via text. When he wasn't sending her flowers, he was sending her to the spa for a well-deserved massage. When he wasn't making her cry with thoughtful gifts, he was making her smile by constructing their own private drive-in movie theater in his backyard by using an old projector and his garage. When he wasn't waking her up with a trail of kisses on her face, he was putting her to sleep with a trail of kisses all over her body. Recently, she thought that maybe they should move forward in their relationship. But with all that was happening at the moment, she wondered if it was best that she'd kept the suggestion to herself. However, Alex had been nothing but good to her, so she wanted to give him a chance to explain himself.

After mulling it over for a bit, she responded, letting him know that they would talk later. She wanted her main focus of the day to be business, not pleasure. Alana got her head back in the game and, before she knew it, a couple of hours went by as if it were a couple of minutes. The preparations were complete, and everyone began leaving in shifts so they could freshen up and get dressed for the evening. Simeon wanted the chef jackets to be crisp and the wait staff uniforms to be pristine. He also insisted that everyone wear the small button pins in the shape of yellow ribbons they'd been given. He wanted to show their unified support of the cause and their appreciation for the business.

At 7 p.m., guests began to arrive. Luxury cars pulled up curbside as guests handed their keys to the young valets. Security checked handbags at the door and monitored the premises for any suspicious activity. There were quite a few wealthy guests attending, so everyone stayed on their P's and Q's. Tunes like "Lil Darlin" and "Dark Morning" by Count Basie warmed up the crowd as the air filled with the smell of expensive perfume, designer cologne, and the scent of fresh-cut yellow roses, which sat on each table. The kitchen staff, however, was taking in a different wave of smells: filet mignon, lobster tails, strawberry torte and, of course, their infamous chocolate-covered strawberries. Although Simeon was being the perfect example of a tyrant, Alex still found moments to peek out of the window every now and then, hoping to get a glimpse of Alana when she entered. He also hoped that she wasn't having girl talk with Natalie. She surprised him, and everyone else in the kitchen, when she entered the back door, looking more stunning than ever.

Alex's jaw almost hit the floor as he stared at her in a black ankle-length cocktail dress with lace sleeves. Her bob had been freshly cut, and her makeup looked so perfect that she could have passed for a doll. Simeon grabbed her hand and twirled her around.

"Tu es belle!"

Alex cut his eyes a little before offering up a compliment of his own. "Boss, that dress is saying so many wonderful things," he said with a small wink.

"What kinds of things would it being saying to you?" Simeon asked.

"They definitely can't be repeated in the presence of small children."

Alana smiled and thanked both men for their sweet words before proceeding through the kitchen, hoping to avoid any back and forth that might take place again. Luckily, they were too busy to argue. Alex took one last look and hoped like hell that they would make up soon! As she entered the dining room, she was given a friendly nod from Natalie, which she kindly returned. She went to the second floor and looked down on the growing crowd for a while. She kept a watchful eye on the staff, making sure they kept the champagne and wine glasses full, their attitudes friendly and the guests happy. By 8:30 p.m., the party was in full swing and the talent show was just beginning. Max, the magician, was up first. His charismatic personality dazzled the crowd as he incorporated his experiences with treatment into his act.

"And now, ladies and gentlemen, time for a little payback. I'm sorry, I mean a little *magic*," he joked as he prepared to saw his former nurse in half. The crowd laughed as he pretended to hook her up to an IV.

"You might need this!" he told her. Alana laughed alongside Elizabeth and Damien, who were standing on each side of her, surveying the party as well. One of the men from security came up and whispered something in Damien's ear, prompting him to leave the ladies to speak amongst themselves.

"These kids are so talented!" Elizabeth said.

"Yeah. And to think of how much they've been through. It just makes you love them even more."

"Do you want children, Alana?" Elizabeth asked after noticing the sentimental look in her eyes as she watched the performances.

"Yeah, eventually."

"Any husbands on the horizon to make that happen?"

Just as she posed the question, Alex emerged from the kitchen and headed up the staircase to fix a problem with the dumbwaiter elevator. Both Alana's and Elizabeth's eyes followed him all the way to the small corridor. He looked scrumptious in his monogrammed jacket, neatly lined up hair and low scruffy beard.

"Could you picture being married to that?" Elizabeth asked with spunk. The ladies watched the muscles in his arms flex as he struggled to get the dumbwaiter back on track. Alana knew all about those muscles and how each one felt. She bit her lip as he pound his fist against the wood until it was back on track. After completing his handywork, he headed back downstairs and gave the ladies a little wave, as their eyes followed him all the way back down.

"Could I *picture* it, or could I *fantasize* about it? Fantasies are so much more fun," Alana asked.

"Girl, take your pick. As long as you can visualize him naked, what does it matter?"

The two ladies laughed and high-fived before Elizabeth excused herself to address a problem she'd noticed. As Alana stood alone, she realized that although she was upset with Alex, she still desired him…a lot! Suddenly, she wanted to make up. She wanted to put it all behind them and simply move on. She wanted to go home with him and put on one of his t-shirts as they cuddled up and watched a movie or listened to some music. She wanted to wake up with him in the morning and have breakfast, as they so often did. For him to lie at the opposite end of the bed with her foot on his chest so he could play with her toes, as she read the newspaper or did a word search puzzle.

She wanted him to hold her and tell her that everything would be okay, that nothing else mattered but their feelings for each other. But there were some serious topics that needed to be discussed, and she could only hope that afterward, one of those scenarios would be the end result. After the second act concluded, dinner was served. As the guests dined on their gourmet cuisine, Natalie made a small speech where she thanked the sponsors, the donors, the restaurant and, most importantly, the children. She gave a very impassioned speech on the importance of children's health, cancer research, and how saving a child's life meant saving the future. Two other speakers followed, and, by the end of the presentation, Alana was so impressed that she decided to make a generous donation on behalf of the restaurant. As dessert was served, the last two acts of the talent show graced the stage, with the young comedian going first, and the final act being the young opera singer. The young man had the crowd in stitches, followed by the young girl leaving them in tears. Her voice was astounding for someone so young, and it was one of the most moving performances Alana had ever seen.

As the spectacular evening drew to a close, in her closing remarks, Natalie asked Alana and Simeon to come up on stage. She thanked the partners for a job well done and presented them both with a small thank you gift. Alana was completely caught off guard by the thoughtful gestures, but even more so when she was asked to say a few words. In true Alana fashion, she took the spotlight off of herself and instead directed the accolades toward her staff. She asked Elizabeth, Damien, Diego and Alex to join her up on stage, but not before thanking each and every member of her wait staff, kitchen staff and valets. Once her main players joined her on stage, she in turn presented Natalie with a donation on behalf of her and her staff.

The guests stood to their feet and applauded a job well done by all parties. After concluding the evening, guests rushed to get their coats, stood at the curb for their cars, and some even lingered around conversing until the crowd died down. The staff began cleaning up what they could and getting as much back to normal as possible. Once there was barely anyone left, Alana hoped to go up to her loft and unwind when Simeon suddenly burst through the kitchen doors and lifted her in the air. He spun her around while kissing her cheek, causing both curiosity and shock to fill her face. The rest of the kitchen staff came out, as well, like a small stampede as Simeon grabbed a chair and stood in it to make an announcement.

"Well, everybody, we did it!" he yelled, followed by cheers from the crowd. "I just wanted to compliment everyone on the amazing job you guys did tonight. I couldn't ask for a better team. And let's give it up for this brilliant woman who made it all possible."

He put his arm around her and kissed her temple, liked he'd done for years. Only this time, he had Alex glaring at him with jealousy. Alana put her arm around his waist, unaware that their affection for one another was adding to an already sensitive topic in her growing relationship. Everyone clapped before disbursing. Elizabeth and Damien both said their goodnights before leaving Simeon and Alana to converse alone.

"Do you know how much business we're going to get because of this? I'm actually second guessing whether or not I should be leaving right now."

"What? You can't be serious! I thought you wanted that more than anything," she said.

"I mean, I do want it…but not more than anything," he answered.

Alana couldn't help but wonder exactly what he was talking about as he stared into her eyes, sipping bubbly. She sipped, as well, while butterflies formed in her stomach. Her mind went back to the morning Gigi announced her engagement. There was something he wanted to tell her that he never got a chance to reveal, and she was wondering if this *thing* he wanted was it.

"The business will be here. Go chase your dream," she said.

He smiled at her sweetly, but Alex's frown could be felt a mile away. The heat from his stare burned the side of her face before it was interrupted by none other than Natalie. Everyone thought she'd left, but she emerged from the ladies' room and headed straight toward Alex. He and Alana tried their best to carry on in their conversations without looking jealous, but that was exactly what they both were feeling. Alana sat on one of the bar stools and looked past Simeon as he talked, while Alex looked over Natalie's shoulder at her. Every now and then, their eyes locked and it wasn't long before Natalie noticed that he seemed more interested in what his *boss* was discussing than what she was saying to him. She tried not to sound condescending, but she couldn't help but address it.

"Uh, is that conversation something you need to be a part of?" Natalie inquired.

"What are you talking about?" Alex asked.

"I've been standing here talking to you, and you can't seem to focus. Unless you're focusing on her!"

"Excuse me?"

"Alana! You can't stop looking past me to stare at her. Don't tell me she's the one you're seeing!"

"What? You're crazy!" he said, rubbing his hand over his hair and beard.

"That's your tell! You always do that when you're lying. You rub your hair, then your beard. C'mon, Lex. I know you."

"Like I said—"

"Right! I'm crazy!" she said.

The two stood there for a moment in silence, unsure of what to say. He hated to admit it, but Natalie was right. She *did* know him, and there was no point in trying to lie about something she could obviously see. It wasn't her wish to out either of them, but she wanted to offer up a small bit of advice. Although their relationship didn't end on good terms, nor their last conversation, Natalie completely shocked him with what she said next.

"She's great, Alex. Seriously, I get it." Natalie stared down at her hands for a moment to give herself a second to fight back tears before continuing on with her heartfelt apology and genuine support.

"Look, I know I was kind of a bitch before I left your house the other day and I'm sorry. I'm sorry for a lot of things. And, believe it or not, I really do want you to be happy. Just make sure it's not always on her terms. Trust me. I know what I'm talking about."

Natalie leaned in and kissed Alex on the cheek before heading toward the exit. As she passed Simeon and Alana, she shook both of their hands and said her goodbyes. Simeon returned to the kitchen and, right as she was letting go of Alana's hand, she looked her square in the eye and said something no one was prepared for.

"Take care of him, will ya?"

Alana could see in her eyes that her hand was not the only thing she was letting go of. She stood at the front door of The Cocoa Marra and watched Natalie to her car. Once Natalie pulled off, a text came through on Alana's phone. It was from Alex, who was only a few feet away. *"Baby would you please come home to me tonight?"* Too tired to argue and too eager to refuse, she simply responded, *"Meet you there."*

Chapter | 20

After grabbing an overnight bag, and talking briefly with Gigi about the success of the event, Alana arrived at Alex's house. The temperature, which had dropped dramatically, made her feel like she was freezing as she struggled to get the key into his door. After hearing the click of the lock, she rushed in and rubbed her hands together for some warmth. She hung her coat on one of the hooks and noticed that the house smelled like baked apples and cinnamon. Alex beckoned for her from up the stairs, causing Alana to take a deep breath to relieve some tension. The extremely busy day had wiped her out and she really just wanted to pass out. But her need to get the entire story about his failed engagement outweighed her desire for sleep.

She slowly climbed the stairs and walked into his bedroom, where she heard the bathtub faucet shutting off. The soothing sound of Nina Simone singing "Sugar in My Bowl" played from a distance as she entered the bathroom. There she found Alex sitting on the side of the tub. He'd changed out of his work clothes into a t-shirt and jogging pants, which showed the outline of his dick, which seemed to be growing at the sight of her. He stood and hugged her before vigorously rubbing his hands over her arms to try and warm her skin. His lips found their way to her neck, where he kissed her softly and inhaled the smell of her fancy perfume.

He looked her in the eyes and smiled before placing his forehead against hers. Slowly, they swayed from side to side, as if they were rocking themselves to sleep. Alana had to stop so that she didn't accidentally doze off to the soothing feeling. He asked her to get into the warm, sweet smelling water, which she did happily--but not before he helped her get undressed. He turned her around and unzipped her dress at a snail's pace. When he found no bra or underwear, he took a swig of the cognac he'd left sitting on the sink to calm his nerves. He flicked the lights off to reveal the glow in the dark bubble bath in the water.

She smiled and stepped out of the dress, which had fallen around her ankles, first testing the water with her toes before getting in. The flame from the large apple cinnamon candle that sat in the sink flickered as her hard-bodied beau got on his knees besides the tub and began washing her back. He handed her his glass of cognac. As she sipped from it, he offered a heartfelt apology.

"I'm sorry about today, sweetheart. I don't want you to think I'm keeping things from you," he said calmly.

"But aren't you? I just don't understand why you didn't tell me you were engaged."

"Actually, we never officially got engaged, and I don't even like to think about her. You have no idea how embarrassing our break-up was."

"I would if you told me. Why was it so embarrassing? People break up all the time."

"Yeah, but I almost made the biggest mistake of my life trying to please her and her parents, even after everyone told me she was wrong for me."

"Well, people do crazy things when they're crazy about someone."

"Yeah, but I was about to propose marriage! And not because I felt I was ready, but because someone else thought we were."

"You also did it because you loved her. It's okay to admit that, even if you were unsure about the engagement. I guess I'm just wondering if the real reason you didn't tell me about her is that maybe you *still* do."

Alex looked offended by the statement. He squeezed the washcloth he'd lathered up and let the suds run down her back. He placed the towel on the edge of the tub and gently grabbed her chin, turning her attention toward him so their eyes could meet. He wanted her to see the truth for herself.

"Alana, I may have been unsure of things back then. But my head is clear now. There's no fire to my feet, making me jump into things I'm not ready for. Now I know how you're supposed to feel when you can truly see yourself with someone for the rest of your life."

She had no idea what to say. She didn't know if he was stressing his point or making a first-time admission. But if he was, was she ready to say it back? They sat quietly for a moment, with only the sound of droplets hitting the water each time he wrung out the towel. She gazed upon his handsome face and, at that moment, she found her answer. She wanted to say it, too. But, for some reason, she didn't. Instead, she kissed him and pulled at his arms, hinting for him to join her in the bath.

Alex undressed as she turned on the hot water to heat it back up. He hopped in behind her, pulling her back onto him so that she could use his chest as a resting place. She laid the back of her head onto his wet skin and completely relaxed for the first time all day. His long legs stuck up out of the water, while his arms wrapped around her and rested on her breasts. She pecked his hand before rolling over to face him, causing him to smile at her bottom bobbing up and down in the water like a buoy.

"With all that you went through, tell me the truth, do you ever regret being with her?"

"No. A wise man once told me never regret a break-up, especially if it taught you something."

"What lesson did it teach you?"

"It taught me to go after something because I really want it and to make a better effort at finding out what a woman really wants. But, enough about that! Let's talk about what you've taught me thus far."

"Ooh! Well, you have my undivided attention," she said.

"Hopefully what I wrote you says it all. I figured I'd better come with something good after seeing the look on your face earlier. Since you're a fan of poetry, I did my best to come up with a little something."

He pulled an envelope from under the large folded up towel sitting on the wicker basket next to them. Alana sat up straight, eager to read his words. She wondered if his usually playful demeanor had spilled onto the pages, or if she was about to read a "roses are red, violets are blue" type of thing. But it wasn't! Alex had tapped deep within himself and wrote her something truly beautiful. She opened the envelope and unfolded the paper, which held the words of his heart. She squinted as she read it aloud by candlelight. And, as Alex held her, he listened to the sound of her soothing voice with ease.

They don't see it, but we know it is there,
in the bend of your eyelash, in the curl of your hair.
A connection, a feeling, something that you can't explain;
two souls converging with one common goal: to be one and the same.
A familiarity in each other's eyes; oh, yes I have seen you before.
Perhaps not in this world, but in my dreams...and now at my door.
The music of our hearts keeps us in tune with each other,
an unexpected friend you've become, as well as my lover.
The cracks of my broken heart are sealed every time I see you,
dazzled by your wit and captivated by your smile, I have come to need you.
For me, your face is my black beauty and your hips are my heavenly hills;
your eyes are pure eclipses, your hands like genies with fantasies fulfilled.
Let me lie on your breasts, which are bountiful blessings, and hang on your brilliant notions.
Let me gaze upon your body, which is a fleshly poem, with lips like love potions.
My body becomes weakened by my memories of you alone,
the softness of your skin, the luster in its tone.
I now know I searched for you in her, and that is why it failed,
Because my destiny lies in the fortress of your arms, my lover, my friend, my fairytale.
                                    Sincerely, The Philosophical Cook

"Did you like it?" he asked her quietly.
"Like it?" she asked with teary eyes. "That's an understatement."
"So now you know, I only want you."
"Well, let's dry off so you can show me just how much."
The two raced to get out of the water. They toweled off before Alex lifted Alana in the air and rushed into the room. She wrapped her legs around his waist and kissed him wildly before they fell onto the bed and began making love. They took turns licking and sucking each other. Alana came hard on his lips, before being flipped over and taken from behind. He penetrated her deeply before she pulled away, attempting to return the favor as she placed her lips around his thick, chocolate stick. But Alex pulled back, not wanting to cum just yet. He lay back on top of her and rubbed her hair, kissing her softly

with every stroke. As he sped up, she gripped his shoulders and took every blow his dick delivered. He held on until after she came before finally tapping out himself. Basking in her euphoria, she knew that things were getting serious. For the first time in her life, she didn't mind at all.

"Time flies when you're having fun," Alana thought to herself after realizing it was two days before Thanksgiving. It had crept up on her, and everyone at work was talking about their plans for the holiday, except her. Usually, she spent Thanksgiving with Georgia. This year, she would be out of town on business, so Alana didn't have any solid plans. Even Alex had already made the decision to make the two-hour drive to enjoy dinner with the twins and their families, which they weren't prepared to do as a couple yet. So, she was more than willing to take Simeon up on his offer to join him and his family for a Thanksgiving meal. Besides, it was the last holiday they would get to spend together for a while.

Simeon was set to leave for Le Cordon Bleu two days before Christmas so he could get settled into the city, as well as the spare room being set up for him at his uncle's place in Paris. Since neither he nor Alana had a whole lot of extra time lately to hang out, she figured this would be the perfect time to spend with her best friend.

On Thanksgiving morning, she tried to sleep in. But, for someone with no previous plans, she sure was getting a lot of calls. At 8:30 a.m., she got her first call, which was from Alex. He invited her over for breakfast, which was immediately followed by love making. They snuggled in bed for a while and, before they knew it, it was noon. Her second call came from Gigi, who was in a panic. Apparently, the dish she was planning on taking to her future mother-in-law's house was not going well. Alana kissed her sweetheart goodbye before rushing off to the rescue. Alex patted her on the butt and thanked her for joining him for breakfast. He told her that he didn't plan on hitting the road until 2 p.m. so he could arrive just before dinner was about to be served. He promised her that he would text her once he got up from his catnap and onto the road. He also joked that her "date" for the evening had better not get too "handsy."

When Alana arrived at Gigi's, Brian answered the door and shook his head, signaling that it was not looking good. She tried her best not to laugh at Gigi as she walked into the kitchen, only to find her with flour smeared across her face like war paint.

"Help!" she screeched as Alana went over and hugged her. She took the bowl and spatula from her, sat her down on a stool, handed her a glass of wine, and started everything from scratch. As she prepared the quiche on her friend's behalf, she smiled at the happy couple as Brian got up from the couch and came in to hold her, as if she'd been defeated.

"It just wasn't working," she whined.

"I know, baby. It's okay. You have other talents: designing clothes, decorating and uh-," he said before whispering something into her ear. She laughed and slapped his chest before calling him a dirty dog. Gigi excused herself to the bathroom, giving Brian some time to sneak in a good word for his good buddy Simeon before she returned.

"So, I hear you're going to the head chef's house for dinner?"

"Yup! Gonna spend some Q.T. with my bestie. It will be cool. I haven't seen his parents in a while."

"That's great. Yeah, that Simeon. He's a great guy," Brian boasted.

"He has his moments," she said, wondering where the conversation was going.

"Yeah he does. And I know he *really* cares about you."

"You think so?" she asked.

"I know so! In fact, he told me he I—"

"Brian, can I see you in my room for a minute," Gigi interjected.

Brian looked as though he was in trouble. Alana wondered what he'd said that caused a problem. But she let the newly engaged couple continue with their whispering, as her third call of the day came in. It was Simeon. He offered to pick her up and reminded her that dinner started at 5 p.m. sharp. She passed on the chauffeuring offer, but promised that she would be there at 4 p.m. so she could talk with his brother and parents. After ending her call and saying goodbye to her favorite couple, who was still carrying on a secret conversation, she went home and lounged around for an hour before she started to get ready. The fact that Alex hadn't called her yet was strange, but she figured he may have gotten busy himself.

Clothes began flying through the air like a tornado as she went through outfit after outfit. She couldn't decide on what she should wear. But, more importantly, she couldn't figure out why she was making such a big deal out of it, considering how she and Simeon were always so casual about things. As she applied her makeup, she thought about the first Thanksgiving they spent together. They dined on cold turkey sandwiches that led to more of a food fight than an actual dinner. They made out a couple of times that night. But mostly, they just listened to music, played cards and practiced her French. He was the first man she ever truly cared about. But she knew she shouldn't be thinking about that, especially since Alex was becoming a first of another sort.

Once she was dressed, she checked her phone. Still no word from Alex. She was starting to worry but, with so much going on, she decided to give him a couple of hours before she started texting him. At 4:30 p.m., she arrived at the Itos' mansion on Long Lake Road. She rang the bell and stood at the front door, moving her legs back and forth to produce some heat. She held onto the homemade pound cake she'd baked and waited patiently until Mai, the Itos' long-time maid, came to the door.

Alana hugged her tightly and kissed her on the cheek. It had been ages since she'd seen her. But she still looked pretty much the same, only slightly older. Mai was about five feet even with caramel-colored skin, long black and gray hair, which was always pulled back neatly into a bun, and tiny wrinkles around her eyes. What she lacked in height, she made up for in personality. Simeon always said that when he was growing up, when it came to getting in trouble, he feared Mai—even more than his own mother!

She took Alana's coat and told her how good it was to see her, before leading her to the large, fancy dining room. As they entered, Alana could hear various languages being spoken by the wide array of guests that were already there. Mr. Ito sipped scotch with a business associate while Mrs. Ito entertained family and friends. As soon as Simeon saw her, his face lit up. He looked handsome, as always, in a navy blue sweater, khaki pants and a big, bright smile. He rushed to her for a hug and attempted to escape with her to another room, but his mother put a stop to his plan. She approached the two and kissed Alana on both cheeks before introducing
her to the room.

"Everyone, this is Simeon's friend and business partner, Alana Jones, whom unfortunately, I haven't seen in how long?" she asked her.

"Too long, Mrs. Ito. But you look fabulous, as always. Hello everyone," Alana said, nervously.

The ladies chatted for a while with a few of Simeon's cousins, who all looked like towering goddesses. It only confirmed that their bloodline had no shortage of tall, beautiful people. They couldn't get over the fact that Simeon had actually brought someone to family dinner, something he'd never done before. There were a few times in college when Alana and Gigi joined him and his parents, but she had yet to meet the entire family until now. Mr. Ito came into the room and kissed his wife on her cheek before grabbing Alana's hand.

"Young lady, I certainly hope you've come here to make a husband out of my son. You've certainly had no problems making a man out of him, with the amount of work you have him doing. But I admire it. It keeps him from becoming lazy," he said.

Mr. Ito loved his sons and had no problem doting on them. But he could be very critical about their lives, which sometimes made him look overly judgmental. It was no secret to Alana that he never really wanted Simeon to become a chef. But once his name became well-known and his face appeared in the paper, he suddenly acted as though he'd encouraged his career from the very start. When Jirou and Shawny finally arrived, Mr. Ito informed him that if he wasn't early for dinner, then he was late. But in the very next breath, he bragged about his "soon-to-be-doctor son" to his business partners. But that's the way he was and, for the most part, the two brothers were used to it.

It was finally time for dinner to be served and, luckily for Alana, she was seated in between Simeon and Shawny, giving her some familiar faces to converse with. Mr. Ito stood at the head of the long table, which was covered with beautiful gold and white china, and thanked his guests for attending. He also thanked his son for orchestrating the menu for the evening. Apparently, Simeon was in no mood for a traditional Thanksgiving meal and had chosen instead to go a different route. As the servers came through the doors and placed serving bowls and platters on the table, Alana began to slowly recognize the familiar sight. It was the exact same meal he cooked her on the night he graduated from culinary school. Instead of turkey, there was stuffed quail. Instead of dressing, they had wild rice. In place of green beans, they had spinach with garlic cloves and, instead of potato salad, they dined on pureed candied yams with brown sugar and bourbon-glazed marshmallows.

She looked over to find Simeon smirking at her, wondering if she'd caught on to the heartfelt flashback. Everyone commented on how good everything looked as they began to pile food onto their plates. Alana smiled and elbowed him playfully to let him know that she was well aware of the significance of the meal. A comforting feeling came over her. He had an uncanny way of making her feel at ease, like she'd returned home from a foreign place. She chatted away with both he and Shawny, until it was time for the dessert portion of the meal.

Simeon grabbed her hand, urging her to follow him to his old room. On the way up the stairs, she checked her phone. Still no text from Alex. She sent him a text message, asking if everything was alright, as she followed Simeon down the long hallway to his room. It still looked exactly the same as it did in college. There were various posters of rap and rock groups on the walls, a small basketball rim suction-cupped to the back of his door, and pictures of him and his buddies on a large corkboard over his desk, including one of him, Gigi and Alana.

She rushed over to the photo and laughed, having forgotten all about it. It gave her a nostalgic feeling, thinking of how their lives were then and how things were beginning to change now. With Gigi being newly engaged, and Alana dangerously dangling on the edge of love, she wondered if finding someone special was even a priority to Simeon. Surely, work couldn't be the only thing he loved.

"So Sim, I'm curious. Out of all of your lady friends, is there one you find a little more special than the others?"

"Why? Did anyone say anything to you?"

"No. Just curious. You seem to like them all the same. I guess I was just wondering if there was one that stood out from the rest."

"Well, there is this one girl. But we're not seeing each other. In fact, she doesn't even know I like her. But every time I see her, the feeling is unlike anything I've ever known."

"Really?! So, what's up? Don't tell me you're too shy to tell her. You're a long way from that guy," she said, pointing to the picture of them on the corkboard.

"Nope, definitely not shy anymore. But I am afraid."

"You? Afraid to say something to a woman? Please! You've never been anyone's coward. No need to start now."

Alana walked over to his desk and started flipping through the small photo album that sat there. She felt butterflies in her stomach when she realized it contained mostly pictures of her or their trio. He walked up behind her and put his warm hands on her shoulders. He looked at the pictures with her, laughing at some of the faces they made and some of the clothing they wore. About fifty pictures into the album, she closed it and turned around, sensing that he was about to say something.

"You're right about one thing: I'm not a coward," he said. "I should do and say more of what I feel and stop letting fear hold me back. And there's no time better than the present."

Without warning, Simeon grabbed Alana and kissed her.

Chapter | 21

Simeon's hands held firmly onto her face as he pressed his lips against hers. Completely caught off guard, she wasn't able to pull back so quickly. She couldn't be sure if it had to do with being in shock, or if it was because Simeon's kisses had a way of drawing her in. Just as her eyes were about to close, and her lips were about to lock with his, Alex popped into her mind, causing her to snatch away. But before either of them could utter a word, Jirou knocked on the bedroom door.

"Dude, Dad's looking for you," he said.

"Thank goodness! Look, I gotta go!" Alana said, grabbing her purse.

"You sure you don't wanna stay for dessert, Alana?" Jirou asked. "Plus, there is so much food left downstairs. You sure you don't want anymore?"

"Yeah, you sure you've had enough? There's a lot more of what you like," Simeon said with a look so intense it could have melted her clothes right off of her body and onto the floor.

But Alana rushed out of the door while she still had the strength and good sense to. Thoughts swirled in her mind as Simeon followed behind her. She felt guilty, confused, somewhat flattered and, oddly enough, turned on. Even in his arrogance, he was so damn sexy! But other than his good looks and an occasional attraction, there was nothing else there, right? Her mind was going haywire as she tried to get her vagina on the same page as her heart. Jirou apologized to his brother for possibly interrupting something, but Simeon assured him that he didn't.

When Alana reached the bottom of the staircase, her phone alerted her that she had one new message. It was from Alex. She focused on clearing her mind of what had just taken place, as if Alex would be able to see her thoughts when she opened his message. She really was happy to see that he finally had a moment to text her. But her joy soon turned to panic. He apologized for not texting her, but told her that he was at the hospital with Eric, his older brother. It turned out that as Alex was preparing to get on the road, he received a call from his brother's lieutenant, letting him know that Eric had been injured in a fire. Alex was listed as his emergency contact and, of course, rushed to his brother's side. He'd been at the hospital all day and was getting non-stop calls from his parents and sisters, who were all concerned about Eric. Mrs. Ito rushed to Alana after seeing the look of worry on her face, followed by her equally concerned and love-struck son.

"Is everything alright sweetie?" Mrs. Ito asked.

"Yes. I'm sorry, but I have to be going."

As Mai went to retrieve her coat, Alana said her goodbyes to everyone. Mrs. Ito also asked Mai to pack her some dessert to go, giving Simeon a chance to pull her into the pantry so he could see exactly what was going on.

"Look, Alana. You don't have to leave. I know I keep screwing up. I know I keep kissing you and I'm sorry. No, I'm not sorry. I mean I had something I wanted to say and now I'm just—"

"Simeon, calm down. I'm not leaving because of that. I promise I'll tell you later, but it's an emergency and I really need to go. Thank you for the dinner."

Alana kissed him on the cheek and rushed out of the pantry. Mai helped her with her coat before handing her a plate with a slice of pound cake, a slice of red velvet cake, and a slice of cheesecake on it. She hugged Mai and ran to her car, leaving Simeon to explain the hasty exit to his mother. Mrs. Ito pulled him to the side so they could speak in private as she inquired about more than Alana leaving.

"So, son, did you tell her?" she asked.

"Not yet, but it's coming."

A few days earlier, Simeon had revealed to his mother that he was in fact head over heels in love with his best friend. Mrs. Ito had always been a fan of Alana's, so she encouraged her son to reveal what he was feeling before it was too late. He figured he could find a quiet spot after dinner and let it all out. But, as usual, fate had other plans. He was glad that he'd at least laid the seed. Now, he just needed to make it blossom.

Outside, Alana hustled to her car and called Alex the moment she closed her car door. She sped off, demanding that he tell her what hospital he was at. He insisted that she didn't have to come, but Alana knew there was no other place she needed to be other than by his side. She demanded that he give her the information and, within minutes, she was on her way. During her drive to the hospital, she thought over and over about what had just taken place with Simeon. She had to admit, seeing those old pictures, being in his old room, did trigger some old feelings. Besides, there was already someone on his radar.

Was *she* the mystery girl he was referring to, or did the sight of their old pictures take him back to a place and time where one of those kisses would have been normal? Was it something she'd done? Her lips did lock with his just a little too long. She always prided herself on knowing exactly what she wanted, without second guessing herself. Usually, she went after things with certainty and fearlessness.

But these occurrences with Simeon were confusing her. Georgia always said, "We can all be strong in multiple categories, but we'll always be weak in one." And, speaking of Georgia, she had pointed out Alana's track record when it came to love. Was she in fact afraid of commitment and this was her subconscious way of sabotaging things with Alex before they got any deeper?

Hours earlier, she'd spent the morning cuddling and making love with him. Whenever he wasn't around, she wished that he was. Whenever he touched her, she couldn't imagine being touched by anyone else. Whenever they slept in each other's arms, her slumber couldn't be sweeter. What started out as a casual relationship had turned into an unconventional, yet happy courtship that she couldn't imagine *not* having. Yet, she still let Simeon kiss her. She was so sure she was falling for Alex. So how did she come so close to losing herself with Simeon again?

It wasn't long before she pulled into the parking lot of Beaumont Hospital and immediately focused her mind on Alex. As she hustled to the front entrance, sleet began to fall. The cold wind blew wet leaves onto the sliding doors as she stepped through them, struggling with the feeling of anxiety that was trying to consume her. She hated hospitals! She hated the smell, the temperature and even the scrubs. Scrubs reminded her of being at an evil sleepover.

She hadn't spent time in a hospital since Grandma Marra had become ill, but Alex needed her support. So, everything else would have to take a back seat. Butterflies filled the pit of her stomach as she watched the numbers on the elevator count up. When the doors opened on Eric's floor, Alex's face was the first one she saw. He sat in the family area with three of Eric's co-workers, who were keeping him company. He excused himself so that he could embrace her and speak to her privately down the hallway.

"How is he?" she asked.

"He's still unconscious. He has a concussion, a broken arm, a broken collar bone and three cracked ribs."

"Geez, Al! What happened?"

"A part of the ceiling caved in on him and he got trapped under it. Thank God the guys got him loose when they did."

"Are you okay?" she asked, rubbing his face gently.

"I'm okay. Just worried about my big bro. He's gonna be in a lot of pain when he wakes up. Thanks for coming, babe. You didn't have to."

"Are you kidding me? Of course, I did! We've got each other's back right?"

He grabbed her hand and kissed it as his cell phone rang. Alana could hear his sister questioning him frantically on the other end before she went to the cafeteria to get him some coffee. She arrived in the cold white room and smiled at a few nurses who were on break. She pushed the button on the coffee machine and watched the hot, steamy liquid pour into the Styrofoam cup as her mind tried once again to fill with confusion. She looked over at the window and gazed out of it with a blank stare, watching the sleet hit the glass and quickly melt away. Over the past few weeks, the weather stayed true to the ever-changing Midwestern climate. It had gone from cool to warm, to downright cold, and was now on the verge of snowfall. The passing weeks had also brought about changes in her relationship, having gone from casual to steamy, to intense, and was now on the verge of love. Or *was* it?

Although she was there supporting Alex in his time of need, she asked herself: if she'd just kissed Simeon less than an hour before being by Alex's side, was she ready to be committed? What they were experiencing together would only bring them closer, and that is exactly why she needed to be sure she was truly all in before uttering the words that would change everything. Alex was a good man who had already been through one relationship where his partner said she wanted one thing, but showed him something else. Alana didn't want to do the same. So, she decided that once things were calm, she would have a long talk with Simeon to get some things clear.

When she returned to the family area, she handed over the fresh smelling java and took a seat next to Alex on the couch. He informed her that his sister decided they would head down first thing in the morning to be by Eric's side. They even had a three-way call with their parents to convince them not to leave their Hawaiian vacation early. All three siblings assured them that everything was under control and that coming home wouldn't change anything. After catching her up on everything that had taken place during the day, he laid down and tried to spread out as best as he could, with his long legs hanging off the small couch in the waiting area. He placed his head in her lap and closed his eyes as she massaged his temples and smiled. Suddenly, his eyes popped open and he began inquiring about her Thanksgiving dinner.

"So, how was your date?"

"Date? You mean dinner with my best friend and his family?"

"If that's what we're calling it. Was he a gentleman, or do I have to knock his ass out when I see him?" he asked before laughing.

"He was fine, and please keep your hands to yourself. I think we're a little too old for schoolyard brawls. That would be kinda childish, don't you think?"

"Oh yeah? You don't like playground tactics?" he said, reaching up and lightly pulling her hair.

"And why did you do that?"

"Because I like you. Isn't that what they do on the playground?" he said with a goofy grin.

"Boys are so dumb."

The two laughed at their child-like behavior, but it was just what Alex needed to stay upbeat. They talked for a while and played games on Alana's phone, until one of Eric's buddies emerged from the room with news that he was waking up. Alex jumped up, eager to see his brother awake for the first time all day. He grabbed Alana's hand and dragged her along. As they reached the door, the sound of Eric's groans made Alex noticeably emotional. His brother was in a great deal of pain and there was absolutely nothing he could do about it. He rushed to his bedside and grabbed his hand as the nurse injected pain medication into the IV drip. Eric's eyes quickly darted toward his brother and, just as Alex was about to tell him that everything was going to be alright, Eric's reaction let him know that he was doing better than he thought.

"Oh, God! First, I miss Thanksgiving, then my body gets mangled, and now my only source of comfort is the sight of this ugly mug?" The two brothers looked at each other for a moment before bursting into laughter. Eric hissed at the pain as he tried to chuckle as carefully as possible.

"That's what you get, asshole! You had me worried, bro. Anyway, I'm not your only visitor," he said, waving Alana over. She stood next to the bed and rubbed Eric's hand, causing a small smile to spread across his face as he thanked her for coming.

"Glad I'm waking up to a fairytale," he said.

"Oh yeah? And which one would that be?" she asked.

"Isn't it obvious? Beauty and the Beast."

"Damn, big bro! You are so rude. Calling my lady a beast!"

Alana slapped Alex's arm and kissed Eric on the cheek before leaving the room so they could talk. As she stood in the hallway, Simeon texted her to make sure she was okay. She let him know that she was fine. But inside, she wasn't; she felt conflicted. Simeon and Gigi had been her two best friends for years. She loved them exactly the same, right? Georgia's words rang in her ears, but Alana wasn't so sure she liked the sound. She never considered herself to be the "have our cake and eat it, too" type of girl, but that's exactly what she was behaving like.

She wanted Simeon to be her friend, yet this was the second time in recent months that they'd crossed a line that friends shouldn't. She wanted to carry on with Alex as though he was her boyfriend. Yet, she was reluctant to openly acknowledge them as being together. She realized she couldn't have things both ways with both people and, if she wasn't careful, her flighty behavior was going to cause way more heartache than happiness. The two brothers talked for a while and, before she knew it, it was after midnight.

Alex emerged from the room just in time to see Eric's girlfriend, a pretty stewardess named Gail, running down the hallway. She hugged him before rushing in with Eric and bursting into tears. She was upset that she hadn't been able to switch flights with anyone to get home to him sooner. Once she calmed down and stopped apologizing, she told Alex to go home and get some rest, and that she would stay the night. She promised to call if anything went wrong. Once Eric urged him to go as well, he and Alana headed to his house for some much-needed relaxation.

After a short commute, they pulled into his driveway. As they stood at the door trying to get in, Alana wrapped her arms around him and screeched from the cold. They burst through the door, grateful to no longer be at the mercy of the frosty wind. But, Alex looked worn down. He'd been working like crazy almost every morning, spending time with her almost every night, and now this. She helped him out of his jacket and told him to head up while she fixed him a sandwich. She threw her coat and purse on the dining room table and headed to the kitchen to make him a small Thanksgiving sandwich.

She grabbed a butter knife and smeared spicy mayonnaise onto some deli bread before piling on layers of turkey, cheese, tomato and lettuce. She cut it in half and poured him a tall glass of orange juice to wash it down. The plate of desserts Mai had given her came in
handy as she placed one of the pieces of cake next to the sandwich. She smiled to herself as she considered how "at home" she always felt at his place, especially when they were doing simple things like cooking for each other or drawing one another a bath. It made her feel like they truly appreciated each other and, perhaps, they could make a *real* relationship work. She turned out the lights and headed up with the small meal. But, by the time she made it to his bedroom, he was stretched out over his bed and snoring. She put the plate on the nightstand and began to remove his shoes when he suddenly woke up.

"Thank you, baby. I didn't realize how tired I was."

"I know. You can go back to sleep," she said, removing his shirt and pants.

"Not until I enjoy this fancy meal you prepared," he joked. Once she'd stripped him down to his boxers, she prepared for bed herself. She removed her clothes and proceeded to grab one of his t-shirts out of his top drawer, when he interrupted her.

"No T-shirt tonight. Wear your pajamas."

"I don't have my overnight bag."

"I mean the pajamas I bought you. Look in the closet. You might find some more surprises."

Alana smiled and rushed over to the closet, filled with excitement as Alex finished his dinner. When she flung open the door, there was a huge basket sitting on the floor. On top of it was a long, satin and lace nightgown with a matching robe. She picked it up to see what was underneath and found that the basket had been filled with all of the products she used in the morning and at night, down to the specific brand. There was a toothbrush, toothpaste, deodorant, a comb and brush, makeup removal wipes, a few of her favorite body washes, and even some perfume.

"I thought it would be a good idea for you to have some things here already. You know, so you don't have to keep packing a bag."

Alana rushed over to the bed to lay on top of him. He wrapped his arms around her as she kissed him and thanked him for being so thoughtful. Just as she thought the surprises for the evening had concluded, he reached over into his nightstand and pulled out the key she'd used many times before.

"I don't know why you keep returning this, but you may as well keep it so that you can come and go as you please. You're the only one I'm seeing, secretly or otherwise. So, it's yours if you want it."

Alana nodded in agreement, accepting the key and telling him that she wasn't seeing anyone else either. Alex was more than pleased since she usually seemed so convinced that it was too soon. He figured the past few months had finally begun to wear her down, and he was hoping she had finally caught up to where he was in their relationship. They talked for a short while and concluded that, although it wasn't official to everyone else, they were already exclusive. He kissed her again and placed the key on the nightstand before turning out the lamp.

"Baby?"

"Yes?"

"Thank you for being there for me tonight," he said.

"Thank you for being so great that I would want to be."

Alex pulled her body close to his. As he drifted off to sleep, she ran her hand over his hair and kissed his cheek, grateful for the happy ending to their day. It was barely dawn when Alana heard the sound of metal scrapping on the cement outside. She rolled over to complain to Alex, but found the other side of the bed empty. She peered out the window to find Alex shoveling. Overnight, the sleet had turned into the first snowfall. Alex was already shoveling the fluffy white substance off his porch, the walkway leading up to his door, and the sidewalk that stretched from his end of the driveway to his neighbor's. She leaned her forehead onto the window and grinned, wondering how he always had so much energy. With all that he'd gotten done, it looked like he'd been out there for some time. So, she knew he had to be a little tired at least, especially since they hadn't been asleep very long. She decided to do something nice for him before he headed back in.

She went into the living room and lit a fire, like she'd seen him do dozens of times. Afterward, she hustled into the kitchen, turned the radio on and started breakfast. Coffee was the first thing to go on, as she needed a cup herself. She grabbed some eggs, butter and bacon from the fridge, as well as two plates from the cabinets. The same coffee cups they used every morning sat in the dish rack on the counter, as if they were waiting to be filled.

She filled each cup almost to the brim, but left just enough room for cream and sugar. A hot beverage would be just what he needed when he came in from the cold. The caffeine kick she yearned for couldn't be swallowed fast enough as she scrambled the eggs, turned over the frying bacon, and popped some bread into the toaster, buttering it once it was nice and brown. Even with the radio on, she noticed she no longer heard the shovel scraping the pavement. She rushed to put the piping hot breakfast on a tray and carried it to the coffee table in front of the fireplace. She sat on the couch, hoping the surprise would warm his heart, as well as his body. She smiled as she heard the door open and feet stomping on the old mat to discard the chunks of snow on his shoes.

"Good morning!" she said, turning to find a face she wasn't prepared for.

"Good morning to you, too!" Sherri said in return.

Chapter | 22

Alana jumped up from the couch and pulled her robe tight to shield herself from the cold air that followed his sister in. She tried her best to smile, but only felt embarrassed as Sherri's twin Sheila came in right behind her. They stood in the doorway, kicking the small chunks of snow off of their boots and onto the small, tattered rug Alex put down earlier to accommodate the season. He ran in shortly after them, shivering and with a look of panic spread across his face. Apparently, his sisters had the same idea as him this morning: to get an early jump on things. He hadn't expected them for a couple of hours. So, when they pulled up unexpectedly, he didn't have time to warn Alana, especially since they'd already noticed her car in the driveway.

"Hey, Alana!" Sheila said, as if they'd already met. "You're right, sis. She's gorgeous!"

"Told you! And look, how sweet. She made him breakfast. Maybe he's finally learned his lesson and left selfish women alone."

The twins continued conversing as they went to hang up their coats and make more coffee, leaving Alex and Alana to stand in silence. She had no idea what to say, and neither did he as he wrestled to take off his hat and gloves. It was the second time she'd been caught off guard by one of his visitors and he wasn't sure how she would react. He just hoped she didn't think he was purposely ambushing her. She rushed up the stairs, with Alex following swiftly behind her. After entering the bedroom, he shut the door behind them for some privacy. She didn't even attempt to pretend she wasn't angry. Tension filled the air as Alana began to get dressed and Alex began to undress. He removed the layers of clothing that had protected him from Old Man Winter, while he secretly wished for some type of barrier that could protect him from her attitude, which was as contagious as the black plague! Her irritation seemed to have leapt onto him as he tried his best to apologize for her discomfort.

"Look, I'm sorry. By the time I saw them, they'd already parked and were--"

"So, let me get this straight. Your sisters know. Eric and Gail know. Gigi knows, Georgia knows and Diego knows. Is there anyone that *doesn't* know about us quietly seeing each other?" she snapped.

"Yeah, Simeon!" he snapped back.

"So! Why do you care so much about him knowing anyway?" she asked.

"Seriously?! You haven't noticed a running theme within the few people that *are* aware of our relationship?"

"You mean besides the fact that none of them were supposed to know about us in the first place?"

"Firstly Alana, you broke our rule way before I did. Gigi and Georgia damn sure didn't find out from me! And secondly, my point is that they're all people that are close to us, which puzzles me since he's your best friend and all. Don't best friends usually tell each other everything?" he asked sarcastically.

"What is it you're trying to say?"

"I'm saying I used to think you wanted to take things slowly so that you wouldn't get hurt. But maybe it's because you don't want to hurt *him*."

"What? That's ridiculous!" she snapped.

"Is it?"

"You know what, Alex? I'm tired of you and anyone else that tries to make there be something between me and Simeon."

"Are you sure people are trying to make something out of nothing, or are they simply pointing out what's already there?"

Again, they stood in silence. Alana watched as Alex's nostrils began to flare. Frustration filled them both and, as much as Alana wanted to tell him just how wrong he was, her mind reverted back to the kiss Simeon planted on her after dinner the night before. She wondered if she hadn't left when she did, would there have been something more serious to deny? Her relationship with Alex was going great; she'd even been flirting with the idea of them becoming an official couple. He'd even commented on how they were too grown to have to keep sneaking around. But her point was neither of them had made a move yet to make that happen. So, he was in no position to tell her when and how she should tell anyone!

"I think I better go, Alex, before things get heated. Give Eric my love when you go to see him."

"I'm glad *someone* in this family can get it!"

The comment slapped Alana in the face like the snapping of a wet towel. But, she decided to let it go. She didn't even look at him as she straightened her hair and stormed downstairs. She almost made it out of the door before Sheila stopped her to apologize for their early arrival. The ladies chatted politely for a short while before Alana explained that she needed to be going. She could hear Alex smacking his lips at the top of the stairs as she grabbed her coat and made a run for it. It was obvious that the lovers were quarreling, but Sheila decided to save the real prying for her younger brother.

Alana dashed out into the cold and dusted the snow off of her car. She watched the powdered sugar-like substance fall to the ground as she let out a long deep breath. *This morning isn't turning out the way I planned,* she thought as she climbed into the driver's seat. It seemed as if the car would never get warm as she sat in the driveway, letting it run. She blew into her hands and rubbed them together before sticking them under her thighs. She wondered how she and Alex had gone from such a lovely ending to their night, to such a rotten beginning to their day. She pulled out of his driveway and noticed that, even in his anger, he watched from the window to make sure she was alright. Driving slowly on the slippery streets helped her to calm down and, ultimately, question why she was really mad at him in the first place. Still, she couldn't ignore that things were becoming as messy as the slush she was sliding in.

Her plan was to go home, kick back, relax with a mimosa, check her emails and hopefully smooth things over with Alex later. But then there was the *thing* with Simeon.

She didn't know the best way to address the kiss. But once she pulled into her parking lot, she realized she might have to think of something quickly. Simeon's car was there and, with the restaurant being closed for the day, her apartment was the only other place he could be. She rode the elevator, fully annoyed, and hoped to God that she wouldn't say the wrong thing. The smell of his cooking hit her as soon as she walked in. He smiled at her and continued multitasking between flipping chocolate chip pancakes, playing a game of solitaire on the island, and listening to "Again" by John Legend. The alone time she so desperately yearned for seemed completely out of reach.

"Good morning, gorgeous!" he said cheerfully.

"Correct me if I'm wrong, but didn't you pay a shitload of money to live in that fancy schmancy place of yours?" she asked.

"Yeah, so?"

"So why are you here in *my* house cooking *my* food and playing with *my* cards?"

"Well, damn! Somebody's grumpy this morning! I was just worried about you."

"Why? I told you I was fine."

"Maybe because you ran out on Thanksgiving dinner with an emergency."

"And? I can't have an emergency?" she snapped.

"I guess I was just wondering what could have been so important. It's not like it was because of fa--"

"Family? It's not like I have family, right? That's what you were going to say, isn't it?"

"Look, I wasn't trying to—"

"So, if I don't have any family, what could possibly be more important than you, right?!"

"I didn't say that or even hint to it, and you damn well know it! Maybe I'll leave and come back later when you have a better attitude!"

Simeon flicked the playing card he'd been holding onto the countertop, as if it were a plucked flower petal that landed on "she loves me not." Alana's unprovoked attitude had aggravated him and he was not going to stay and be her whipping board, especially since he'd come over to tell her something important. He proceeded to the couch, where he snatched his jacket from the arm and headed to the door. Alana watched him as he stormed toward the door and, suddenly, she was overtaken by guilt for her awful behavior. She yelled out to him, but he'd already slammed it behind him.

The loud bang echoed in both of their ears, as if the sound of their friendship had come crashing down. They stood on each side of the door, wondering what to do next. As he pressed his forehead against the cold wooden door, the elevator started to come up. The gate slid open and soon he was met by the smiling faces of Gigi and two of her girlfriends, Riya and Annette. Alana flung the door open, hoping to apologize to Simeon. But the ladies rushed in to hug her; all but Gigi, that is. Besides the fact that he'd barely spoken to them, Simeon's face gave her cause for concern. She grabbed his arm before he could get onto the elevator and hoped that it wasn't too serious. But he gently pulled away.

"Hey, everything okay?"

"Ask your friend in there! I don't know who she's mad at, but it ain't me! Maybe it's that dude she's been creeping around with!"

"What dude? She's seeing someone?!" Gigi asked in her best surprised voice.

"Oh please, G! You're way too smart to play dumb. It doesn't even look convincing on you, so give me some credit!"

"What did she say?"

"She doesn't have to *say* anything! You think I don't know her the same as you? She's disappearing all the time. I can barely reach her. She's getting flower deliveries, like she's fucking a florist!"

"Oh come on, Simeon. Let's get serious. Maybe she's seeing the guy that drives the delivery van," she said as she poked him in his side, trying to make him laugh.

"That's not funny! And whomever he is, he must be jealous of what we have. It's like we have a playbook we go by when she gets a man. They get into it over how close we are. She takes it out on me. He gives her an ultimatum, and she chooses me, as usual. I'm just not in the mood to play this game today."

He kissed her on the cheek and apologized for his tone before slamming the gate and descending out of her sight. Gigi turned to find Alana standing behind her, looking pitiful. Gigi started to say something, but Alana let out a hefty sigh and returned to the kitchen to cook the rest of the pancake batter Simeon had left on the counter. After making the mimosas she'd been yearning for, the ladies spent a little time catching up, filling their bellies, and sharing their plans for the day. They figured they'd start off by splurging on a few Thanksgiving Day sales, followed by having a late lunch at the museum.

After the impromptu breakfast, Annette offered to do the dishes so Alana could get dressed and join them. Maybe a girls' day was what she really needed, instead of sitting at home alone sulking. She got into the shower, hoping the warm water would wash away some of the stress, but to no avail. Standing under the showerhead, she put her head back and stared at the ceiling, thinking about the fact that now both Simeon and Alex were mad at her, not that her attitude hadn't been a major contributor. She needed this day of fun to clear her mind, just enough for her to come up with the right words for her apologies.

She grabbed her bottle of Amazing Grace lotion, knowing that it was probably the only grace she'd be receiving thanks to her behavior. She gently massaged it into her skin. She threw on some jeans, a thick oversized sweater with a matching knit hat, and knee-high boots to prepare to go back out into the cold. She emerged from the bathroom, looking as if she didn't have a care in the world. As the group exited the loft, she was determined to enjoy the day, no matter what. The girls loaded up in the car and, after a short while, they arrived at the mall, with every intention to shop until they dropped.

The mall looked like a bargain bin battlefield as waves of women waged war on each other for who would get what. Hangers scraping racks could be heard for miles as the ladies went through countless tops, jackets and dresses. The girls circled clearance sections like sharks, hoping to find the perfect piece for the perfect deal and pounce on it! To make things a little more civil, Riya and Annette, who were both married, decided to give their newly engaged friend some tips on dealing with difficult mother-in-laws. Gigi didn't think she needed it, especially since she and Brian's mother got along quite well. But she let the ladies vent anyway. Even with their lives being so different, the two 'Mrs.' seemed to face some of the same problems.

Riya, a pretty Indian woman with long, thick black hair, which she kept in a braid reaching her waist, had difficulty with her very traditional mother-in-law in the beginning. When she and Gigi became friends in design school, most of their topics of conversation were about her. Her mother-in-law complained about everything from her cooking to her clothing. Her designs, which were praised in the fashion world for being the perfect mixture of traditional Indian clothing with a modern, sassy twist, were not very praiseworthy to her husband's mother. Nothing Riya ever did was good enough, until she gave birth to their son. Suddenly, she was the perfect daughter-in-law.

Annette, a busty brown bombshell with shoulder-length dreadlocks, was one of Gigi's friends from high school. She and Alana had become closer over the years due to their mutual friendship with G, and the fact that she, too, ran her own business as a professional makeup artist. Her brand known as "Face Makers," catered to everyone from brides to pageant beauties, and even local TV anchors. In the beginning of her marriage, she and her mother-in-law got along great, too. That is, until they started planning the wedding. That's when she noticed her special way of *critiquing* things, especially anything concerning her son. His mother always felt that *her* way was best because that's what her son had become accustomed to over the years, as if he couldn't so much as eat a pork chop unless it was cooked with her recipe.

They went from store to store, trading stories like baseball cards. Before any of them had realized it, they'd been walking around for hours. Looking down at the bags that weighed heavily on their wrists, they decided to call it quits and head to the museum for lunch. On their walk to the car, Gigi noticed that even though Alana's bags were full, the smile on her face seemed very empty. She still hadn't had a moment to ask what happened with Simeon and she wanted to make sure she was okay. But, by the time they made their way downtown, parked the car, walked a couple of icy blocks to the museum entrance, and sat down to eat in the café, Annette jumpstarted a different line of questioning.

"So, we hear you might be joining the couple's club soon," Annette announced.

"Yeah, we heard about your secret boyfriend, and that you two are really crazy about each other. Please tell me it's Simeon. You two would have the prettiest babies!" Riya followed.

"Really? Nice, Gigi! Really nice!" Alana said as she scowled at her friend. She couldn't believe that she'd gone so long not realizing how many chatterboxes she had in her life. Until now, she always believed Diego was the biggest gossip she knew.

"Oh, come on! I didn't say who it was."

"Anyway! It's not Simeon. Things with my mystery man are progressing, but we're not *there* yet," Alana informed them.

"Well, if you want to get *there*, the first thing you have to do is stop giving so much access to Simeon's fine ass. Girl, no man wants another man cooking their woman breakfast, especially not one that looks like that!" Annette added.

Alana knew that she was right. Keeping things quiet wasn't the only thing that had gone out of the window; so was keeping it casual. Alex was making it more and more apparent that he wanted the real thing. And as much as she didn't want to admit it, so did she. The problem was it had been so long since she'd been in a relationship that she'd forgotten it required compromise. Still, did finding love mean losing a longstanding friendship? She'd gotten used to doing whatever she wanted and, to her, it was normal for Simeon to be around all the time. She didn't want to be one of those women who dumped their friends the moment they got a man. But if she was serious about making things work with Alex, something was going to have to change. For starters, she'd have to stop kissing other people.

Tuning the others out, she thought about how ironic it was that the two men who opposed each other so much had more in common than either was willing to admit. Aside from being chefs, aside from being bilingual, they also shared a genuine affection for her, which she felt in return, just in different ways. Alex was turning out to be everything she never knew she wanted, and her friendship with Simeon was something she could count on. She snapped out of her daze, just in time for Annette and Riya to excuse themselves to the ladies' room. Gigi leaned over, anxious to see what had Simeon looking so sour and Alana looking so sorry. She prepared for something juicy, but was surprised when she received a playful kick under the table.

"Nice job keeping secrets, heifer!" Alana said.

"Oh, don't pretend to be mad at me. Simeon's the one you're really mad at."

"I'm not even mad at him, to be honest."

"Then why did you two get into it this morning? I know that's what happened."

"I was just frustrated, and he got in the way."

"Why? Is everything okay? What's got you so irritated?"

"I don't know. Alex and I got into an argument. Some of it was about Simeon."

"What brought that on? He didn't find out about the kiss, did he?"

"Hell, which one?" Alana slipped.

"Wait a minute! You and Simeon have kissed more than once since you've been seeing Alex? Well, well, well, little Jezebel!"

"Trust me. I feel bad enough, especially since Alex keeps saying that Simeon has feelings for me. I don't want to believe it, but why else would this keep happening?"

"Well, in his defense, it's only natural for Simeon to always have some sort of love for you. Look at everything you've been to him."

"What do you mean?"

"I mean you're his best friend, you're his boss, and you were his first--"

"Wait, what!? I wasn't his first. Was I?"

Gigi's tongue was suddenly tied. She couldn't seem to answer the question, which didn't matter since her shock pretty much gave it away. She bit her bottom lip, unable to believe she'd just broken her promise to Simeon to never tell Alana. By the look on her face, she seemed unsure whether or not she was messing with her. Gigi had a habit of playing pranks on her. So, she waited for a moment, knowing that she would soon announce that it was a joke; but she never did. The only thing she could hear was Dean Martin on the sound system singing, "Let It Snow." Someone needed to break the silence. But truthfully, it didn't matter what was said for the rest of the day. Those words would be what continued to ring out.

"He told you that? That I was his first?" she asked apprehensively.

"Look, I wasn't supposed to say anything—"

"That's impossible! By the time I met Simeon, he already had a reputation."

"I think he'd know, Alana. Besides, think about it for a minute. In all of the rumors you heard, did anyone actually say they had sex with him?"

"Not exactly, but why didn't he tell me? Why didn't *you* tell me?" she asked Gigi.

"I don't know. Maybe he was embarrassed. And I didn't tell you for the same reason I haven't told him *your* secret about Alex; it's not my place to."

Alana realized Gigi was right. The revelation overwhelmed her, and she suddenly felt more guilty than ever. Guilty because Alex might be right, and guilty because she'd never known just how much she'd impacted Simeon's life. Perhaps it was time that the two old friends had a real conversation with each other.

"Is there anything else I should know about?" she asked. Gigi wanted to tell her, but she didn't. No matter how much Alana wanted to know, she knew she talked a little too much already.

"No, he hasn't told me anything else," she lied.

Alana believed her and decided to move on. Besides, she wasn't so sure she wanted to know anything else. She had enough on her plate and there was no room for any more side dishes of truth. Annette and Riya returned in time enough to ask if they'd missed anything, but the besties smiled and said nothing. The ladies ordered one more round of coffees before heading home. When she finally made it back to her loft, she fell onto the bed and thought about the information she'd been given.

She thought back to the first time she and Simeon had sex. It all made so much sense all of a sudden. It was such a turn-on when he told her to take control that it never dawned on her that maybe it was because he was inexperienced. The way his body moved, the way he touched her, it wasn't just sensual—it was sweet. So sweet that it seemed innocent. It was hard enough keeping one secret from him, and now this? But she didn't want to cause any issues between him and Gigi. So, she vowed to never address it, unless he did.

And then, there was Alex. If he was right about Simeon, what was she to do? She couldn't be with him and keep a secret like that. They seemed to be terrible at keeping secrets anyway! They hadn't texted or spoken to each other all day. She really missed him, but he needed to be with his family. And she needed to think of what to do next.

Chapter | 23

The holiday spirit had fallen heavily upon the staff as they hung Christmas decorations around the restaurant. At a stool in the far corner that often went unoccupied, Eric put up his usual "For Santa" sign with a glass of Sangria and an unlit cigar in front of it. For extra laughs, he got a few Elf on the Shelf dolls and placed them between the bottles of bourbon displayed behind the bar. Everyone seemed to be in such good spirits; *almost* everyone, that is! Alana noticed that some of the vibes weren't so cheery.

A few days had gone by since Gigi spilled Simeon's secret, and she and Alex had argued. Needless to say, things were super awkward. She was barely speaking to either of the guys, unless it was concerning business. And whether she realized it or not, she'd become a master in the art of avoidance. She and Alex texted a few times here and there, but had yet to resolve their issue. His sisters were still in town, so that cut out any chance of them spending time together. And with the influx of meetings with bankers, contractors and interior designers for the new location, it wasn't helping Alex's feelings of jealousy that her *partner* was accompanying her to most of the meetings.

Little did he know, her time with Simeon wasn't exactly candy canes and gingerbread men. Sure, they'd patched things up, courtesy of an apology for her behavior. But getting back to normal meant dealing with the occasional flirt her friend was known to be. For her, it was a big deal now. His usual kissing of her hand with lingering lips would normally go unnoticed. But, thanks to Gigi's bombshell, she was analyzing everything he did. Even their morning interactions were different. Finding out that she was his first became a distraction.

At times, she looked at him and felt incredibly uncomfortable. Her overactive imagination made her feel as if there was a cartoon bubble hovering above his head, displaying a wildly exaggerated triple X recollection of her "stealing" his innocence, which was kind of comical considering his reputation. Other times, she caught him looking at her and quickly looking away before they could make eye contact. If she found herself alone with him, she always came up with the strangest excuses to leave. Simeon soon took notice of her odd behavior and questioned Gigi, but she simply chalked it up as stress.

Deep inside, Alana knew that she couldn't continue carrying on that way. He was still her best friend. Soon, he'd be leaving for months, longer than they'd been apart since they'd known each other. She didn't want him to go without spending any time with him or without them having a serious talk. She wanted to be honest with him about things, mainly Alex, but she wasn't sure if she could. She was sure, however, that she could give him a proper sendoff. He was set to depart in four weeks, which would surely fly by like days. So, Alana and Gigi needed to get things in motion for his going away party, and fast!

Around 4 p.m., the best friends braved the cold winds and small crystal flakes to meet with Ms. Stevens, a party planner that Georgia recommended. Their secret meeting was to take place at a small Mexican restaurant across town. Despite the place not having much curb appeal, they served some of the best authentic Mexican food in the city. Their top-secret meeting would give them two advantages: Gigi would get the rare chance to curb her craving for arroz con pollo, and they could plan in private. Simeon had a tendency to be very nosey and, if Diego was made privy to the information, Simeon would only sucker him into telling him every last detail of the party. Even though Alana had already given him fair warning out of fear that on the night of, he'd be AWOL with one of his scantily clad lady friends, she still wanted there to be *some* surprises in store.

When Ms. Stevens arrived, the young waiter with a thick accent took the bundled-up beauties' orders as they munched on tortilla chips and salsa. While waiting for their food, they traded ideas before being inspired by their appetizer with the perfect theme. Alana went to dunk her chip into the delicious red dip when it hit her: a "salsa sendoff" in honor of Simeon's love for salsa dancing. Gigi delighted in the idea, knowing that with a sexy theme like that, things were sure to get extra hot in the cold city. They decided to use Gigi's rental hall, which Mrs. Stevens assured them would be transformed into a Miami hot spot. With Damien's and Jirou's help, the ladies would put together an invite list full of the who's who in the city, as well as family and friends.

Damien's connections could also guarantee them the hottest deejay in the town. Ms. Stevens suggested that the invites be sent via email and text. That way, they could be downloaded and responded to quickly, giving them a better idea of how many people to expect. She also had the perfect caterer for them to use, one who might even impress the likes of Simeon. After an hour of making sure the major elements were in place, Ms. Stevens took her notes and deposit, leaving the girls to guzzle a few margaritas. It didn't take long for them to land on their usual topic of discussion, which also happened to be their favorite: men.

"How's Brian?"

"Handsome, horny, and happy. And speaking of happy, I'm glad to see you and Simeon made up."

"You know we can't stay mad at each other for long. I just feel so weird around him though."

"Why? It's not like the inner workings of his bedroom were a secret to you."

"That part was! Being somebody's first is a big deal. I didn't know what I meant to him back then."

"Would it have made a difference if you had? Is there something you're not telling me?" Gigi asked.

Alana decided to take a brief trip down memory lane and tell Gigi about the night she never knew existed. Apparently, back in college, after Alana and Simeon had been messing around for a while, she toyed with the idea of them possibly becoming more than "friends with benefits." She was prepared to ask Simeon if he wanted to take things up a notch. But the night she went over to his place to discuss it, she overheard him having a less than encouraging conversation with Jirou about her. He was hounding Simeon for information about the girl he'd been spending so much time with. Simeon told him in what seemed to be a very cold manner that she was no one, just some girl he was tutoring, and that there was nothing special between them.

At that moment, she turned and left, glad that she'd never fully invested in him and decided to let it go. The very next day, she introduced him to Gigi as her friend. Gigi was floored! Simeon had always wondered why she seemed to distance herself overnight, but now it was all making perfect sense. It seemed that, unbeknownst to them both, their friendship had always become victim to the same unforgiving prey: miscommunication! Alana had no way of knowing that he only told his brother what he did, and in the manner he did, because he was irritated with him meddling in his personal affairs. He had no way of knowing she'd turned cold to protect her heart from the "player" he was rumored to be. Neither of them had ever known the truth: that at one point, they both wanted to pursue a relationship with the other.

Gigi didn't know what to do. She thought about how narrowly they missed their opportunity. Had Simeon confessed his love, he may have very well become the first love that Alana was still waiting to have. But it *was* years ago, and now Alex was that possibility. If everything truly happened for a reason, then she and Simeon had become friends for a reason. Still, matters of the heart could be tricky and she wanted to make sure Alana was being honest with herself before things got any deeper with Alex.

"So, you had feelings for Simeon once upon a time. That's understandable. Question is, do you *now*?"

"No. I don't…I mean…I did…I mean, I do. Just not…look, I know how it looks since we—"

"Since you two keep spontaneously swapping spit?"

"Touché! But both times alcohol was involved, so it doesn't count. I guess I just wonder what would have happened if he told me back then. Then again, it probably didn't mean much to him, so I guess nothing." Gigi bit her tongue, but it was a struggle. Of course, it meant something to him. It meant *everything* to him! But why should it fall on her to say it? This time, she stuck to her guns. No secrets would be coming out of her this time.

"Okay, so that brings us back to the present. Alex, you're really feeling him, right?"

"G, I can't even explain what I feel when I'm with him! Happiness, passion, fear, excitement!"

"Okay, I'm sensing there's a *but* coming."

"But I'm tired of arguing over the same thing."

"You two still haven't made up?"

"Not really. I'm working on it."

"Well, the second thing you need to do is ask him what it is he wants from you exactly."

"And the first?" Alana asked.

"Ask yourself what you really want."

As usual, Gigi was right. Just as she had before, Alana questioned whether or not she was looking for something to be wrong with Alex so she could have an easy way out, or if she just wanted to have her cake and eat it, too. It wasn't that he was being unreasonable. He never asked her to end her friendship with Simeon—only that she set up some boundaries and let him know that she was involved with someone. Wouldn't it make sense to leave past behaviors behind and pursue something more meaningful than a few brief moments? Alex was not only helping her to feel differently, he was helping her to *think* differently. Maybe she needed to start seeing in him the same things she saw when she first laid eyes on The Cocoa Marra: what it could really be if she put everything she had into it. She snapped out of her daydream, just long enough to refuse Gigi's offer to pay the tab and head home.

"We better get out of here," she said as the girls looked out into the darkness, which now came earlier with the season change. After they said their goodbyes, Gigi was halfway to the door before she stopped in her tracks and walked back to Alana to offer one last bit of advice. She slid off the long black elbow-length leather gloves she was wearing and popped Alana's hand with them before handing them to her.

"If you wanna make up with Alex tonight, you'll wear these. Only these!"

The two shared a laugh as Alana realized patching things up with Alex was overdue. Dealing with the cold weather was bad enough, but the chill that had been blowing from his direction was becoming too much to bear. Determined not to let another day end with them still in turmoil, she decided Gigi's plan might not be so bad and, hopefully, it would be hot enough to melt even the coldest of hearts. She sent a quick text, nervous that he might be a bit more reluctant to make up than she was. However, she was pleasantly surprised by his quick response. Maybe he was just as eager to wave the white flag.

Alana: Hey. Are you at the hospital?

Alex: No. I just got home. Funny, I was just about to text you.

Alana: How's your brother?

Alex: His spirits are up. He's really happy my sisters are here.

Alana: Do you need anything?

Alex: All I need is your company tonight.

Alana: I don't want to disturb your visitors.

Alex: They decided to stay at Eric's house so that they could clean up for him and keep an eye out for his house. So, if you come home to me tonight, I can get down on my knees and...beg for your forgiveness☺.

Alana: Sounds good! Give me an hour and I'll be there.

She let out a sigh of relief, grateful that the tension between them was finally letting up. Hopefully, after a night of kissing, caressing, love making and cuddling, they could get more than their naked body parts out in the open, including what was next for them. Alana rushed home to spruce herself up. Just the thought of his touch pushed everything else out of her mind. Suddenly, the issues with Simeon didn't seem like issues at all. She rushed into her loft at top speeds and headed straight to the shower.

Afterward, the smell of Warm Vanilla Sugar lotion and body spray blanketed her skin, making her smell good enough to eat. She hit the remote start on her truck, knowing that the car would need to be nice and hot for the outfit she planned to wear to his house. As she put on next to nothing, she laughed to herself while staring in the mirror and thinking of how proud Gigi and Georgia would be that they were finally rubbing off on her. Her coat was the last piece to the puzzle as she ran out of the door to get back onto the slushy roads.

She arrived at his place in record time, unlocked the door, and closed it behind her quietly. Alex paced back and forth in the dining room, talking to his brother on the phone. He turned around and gave her a sexy smile as he listened to Eric babble on and on. Alana kissed him as he whispered to her, "I'm sorry." She offered up an apology of her own just before going into the kitchen and pouring them both a glass of wine. She returned and handed him the glass, while holding a bottle of Hershey's milk chocolate syrup in her hand. He looked puzzled as he offered to take her coat. But soon, no explanation was needed.

She turned on some music, electing John Legend and Brittany Howard singing "Darkness and Light" to help set the mood. She put the cold bottle that she'd taken from the refrigerator down on the large wooden table he'd first devoured her on. With any luck, he'd do it again. She let her black and white trench coat fall to the floor. Alex's jaw dropped as she stood before him, wearing nothing more than a red silk scarf tied like a bow around her neck, black elbow-length leather gloves, black thigh-high fishnet stockings with red satin ribbons that laced up the back of her legs, and black heels. He stuttered and stared as his brother said his name over and over on the other end of the line, trying to gain his attention.

"You up for an early Christmas present?" she asked.

"Oh, I'm up alright! Uh, bro, I have to call you back," he said before dropping the phone to the floor. He rushed to Alana, kissing her passionately. His hands moved frantically over her entire body, as if he didn't know where he wanted to touch her first.

"Al, I'm sorry. I know it's hard dealing with Simeon--"

"I don't give a damn about Simeon!" he said as he moaned and kissed her more.

"Still, thank you for being patient with me. And for that, Santa's coming early this year!"

Alana pushed him away and started to walk slowly up the staircase. Her leather clad fingers motioned for him to follow her, which he had no problem doing. One hand held onto the bottle of Hershey's syrup, while the other slid up the banister. He licked his lips and traced his eyes along the trail of the red ribbons traveling up the back of her legs, leading to her perfectly curved bottom.

"Santa will be the only thing coming early tonight!" he promised.

"Really?" she asked, giggling. "Wait! So if I'm Santa, aren't you supposed to give me some milk and cookies?"

"Looks like you've got a healthy helping of your own. And boy am I hungry!" He smiled and walked slowly behind her as he removed his shirt and unbuckled his jeans. She looked over her shoulder at him, flirting and teasing him, until his eyes became narrow with passion and his hands became eager with lust.

"You're a dirty boy."

"Filthy!" he replied.

Alana reached the bedroom first and sat on the end of his king size mattress, crossed her legs, and patiently awaited his arrival. He walked into the room shortly after and slowly took off the last piece of clothing that stood in between his body and her mouth. He grabbed her wrists and gently pulled the gloves off each of her hands with his teeth. He took her hands and rubbed them over his body before dropping to his knees and softly caressing her thighs. He pushed her back onto the bed and admired her beautiful body before taking the chocolate syrup from her hand and squeezing the bottle.

He watched as the sweet brown substance flowed like a river between her breasts down to her stomach. Alana's eyes shut tightly as he sucked on her neck and whispered, "This is my pussy!" She arched her back as his mouth slid down to her breast. His hand cupped it firmly as he devoured it with his mouth. Alana began to moan, encouraging him to go further. She could feel his teeth softly nibbling on her ribcage and licking the chocolate off her stomach until it was clean. He moved down to her inner thigh, but quickly jolted back up to her ear and continued to whisper every dirty phrase that came to mind, while his middle finger moved in circles on her clit.

She held onto his muscular arm as she rotated her hips in a circular motion, making her orgasm faster. As she exploded onto his fingers, it didn't take long for his heavy chocolate muscles to lie on top of her overly anxious skin. It seemed like they made love for hours as they apologized with every caress and made up with every moan. After simultaneously climaxing, a first for Alana, they lay side by side, trying to catch their breath.

"How do you do that?" she asked with heavy breath.

"Do what?"

"Make me have that feeling every time?"

"What feeling is that?"

"Like nothing on this earth could ever make me feel as good as you do," she said.

"I just try to make sure my body says everything that my mind thinks and my heart feels. Listen, I want to say something to you, babe."

"Okay, what is it?"

"I just wanted to say...I just wanted to say..."

"You just wanted to say..." she urged him along.

"I just wanted to say…I don't want you to feel pressured to tell Simeon or anyone else about us if you're not ready. I don't care if you ever tell him. Just tell me that what we have is all that you want."

"It's more than what I want. It's what I *need*."

Alana grabbed his head and kissed him, assuring him that there was no one else she wanted and there was nowhere else she'd rather be. He stroked her arm gently and rubbed his thumb across her cheek before pulling the sheet up over her naked body. She fought to stay awake, as if she couldn't bear to miss a moment with him. Slowly, her eyes fell before suddenly popping open again. But soon, she was no match for the rhythmic sound of his breathing.

After a well-fought battle, she drifted off as Alex lay next to her, being kept awake by his thoughts. He wondered why he hadn't said what he *really* wanted to say. Had he let the perfect opportunity pass him by, or had he simply chickened out altogether? He knew what he felt. He knew it was real, but it seemed more appropriate to tell her something like that while their clothes were on. He didn't want her to feel like he said it merely because it sounded good after a night of mind-blowing make-up sex. He pulled his arm that she'd fallen asleep on from under her neck and went into the bathroom.

He let the cold water from the faucet run into his hands so he could sip it. He splashed some onto his face and patted it dry as he stared at his reflection in the mirror. The sight of Alana's toiletry basket on the three-tier corner rack behind him made him smile and, suddenly, it hit him. Her two closest friends were getting new beginnings. Gigi was engaged to be married and, whether he liked him or not, even Simeon was moving into an exciting chapter in his life. Perhaps this was the perfect time for a new beginning for him and Alana, as well.

There was a lot on her plate at the moment, especially with the party coming up so soon. But he decided that once the champagne corks had been popped, the food had been served, the goodbyes had been said, and the unwinding had begun, he would tell Alana what it was he'd really intended to say. After the party, he would finally tell her that he loved her.

Chapter | 24

Gigi sat on the floor of Simeon's home, ripping off large strips of tape and strategically laying them on the floor face up. She'd worked out a system to secure the bottom of the boxes that he'd been putting together. Brian and Alana were both running late for the "packing party" due to last-minute meetings. So, the two were made to start the fun on their own. It had been quite some time since just the two of them hung, so they used the opportunity to make some small talk and fill each other in on things they may have missed during morning coffee. He plugged his ears and pretended he couldn't hear her as she went into great detail about her latest role-playing incident with Brian.

Although she and Simeon had always been similar sexually, with the exception that her erotic tales involved the same leading man, while Simeon's co-stars usually rotated, he was acting unusually prudish. Once she'd made him squirm enough, she switched the topic of discussion to his busy schedule for the upcoming year. After listening to him complain about the temporary move to Paris, his full list of courses at Le Cordon Bleu, and his obligation to continue being involved with the business, Gigi suggested that he hire a personal assistant. Though she said it jokingly, he actually found the idea to be brilliant. It would help him tremendously if he had someone to be his eyes and ears at home, while his hands and feet chased his dreams across the globe.

Alana insisted repeatedly that he didn't have to worry about the business and that his position as her partner was secure. But he wanted her to know she could depend on him, no matter what. Not to mention, he wanted his ideas heard, as well. He and Diego had already conspired to Skype at least once a week so he could pass along what he was learning, making it easier for them to slowly introduce new items to the menu. Gigi applauded his dedication, but knew that he'd need some help. She suggested he use a temp service that could immediately pair him with a highly trained assistant to handle his business calls, text messages, emails and anything else he needed. They talked and listened to the radio as Gigi folded the clothes he'd chosen and began labeling the boxes. Simeon loaded a large box she'd marked "shoes" with over a dozen plastic shoe containers, while she loaded piles into boxes marked "shirts" and "pants."

His wardrobe made him look like a real "divo," as she called men with fashion sense. What better place for a divo than one of the fashion capitals of the world? She only hoped that she could persuade Brian into visiting before his return. As she looked around his place, she began to inquire about who would housesit for him while he stayed with his favorite uncle in old Paris. Simeon explained that Jirou's lease would be up a week after his departure, so he volunteered to stay at his brother's place until he returned. With the condo already being paid for, Jirou simply needed to take care of the utilities, which he was glad to do.

In the spirit of brotherly love, Simeon had already started leaving little notes around the place in jest, telling his brother what not to touch. He knew the warning would be ignored. He was just happy that his younger brother couldn't fit his clothes, so whatever he left behind would be safe. Gigi got a good laugh out of their lighthearted sibling rivalry. But as Simeon stepped out of the room to get them some beverages, she was further entertained by a garment she was pretty sure wasn't his. She lifted the pair of red lace panties, which were heavy with perfume, into the air as if she were inspecting them. Her host suddenly reappeared with two beers. In a panic, she hid the underwear behind her back so she could accept the drink.

He sat on the floor in front of her and tapped his bottle against hers, followed by a "Cheers!" They'd been sorting for a while, so a break was just what they needed. It would give them time to pass judgement on the latecomers in good fun. Brian texted that he had just stopped to grab a few pizzas and that he was on his way, followed by Alana, who estimated her arrival to be within the next fifteen minutes. They were ecstatic to hear that food was on the way. After slamming down the first round of beers, Simeon didn't hesitate to head down the stairs to get the second.

Gigi walked over to the window and admired the breathtaking view. Even the eight-degree weather couldn't take away from the magical allure the city lights provided. Simeon joined her, playfully pushing her as she laughed and pulled the underwear she'd found from behind her back, throwing them at him.

"Here! Found one of your dust rags!"

"Hey! I've been looking for those. These aren't dust rags! I'll have you know these were a gift from a very, very gifted woman," he said, smelling them.

"Ew! I bet she was, you perv!"

"I'm kidding, G. Wanna hear something funny?"

"Sure."

"I can't even remember who they belong to," he confessed somberly.

Suddenly, Simeon didn't seem so amused. Something was chipping away at him and, although Gigi couldn't be 100 % sure what it was, she was at least 98% sure that the invisible chisel was Alana. She was right. Out of nowhere, he casually brought up the kiss from Thanksgiving and told her that they may finally be on the same page. But she knew better. Her mind went back to the conversation she'd had with Alana a few days before and she knew that the desire to pursue a serious relationship with Simeon had faded away many moons ago. Something was growing beyond Alana's control with the chocolate-colored cook and, if she didn't recognize what it was yet, Gigi certainly did. She didn't want to see Simeon get hurt and she didn't want to expose Alana's relationship, either.

She decided to try and talk some sense into him by way of reasoning, which would be tricky. Stating the obvious, like the fact that he was leaving the country, and that he and Alana were now business partners and shouldn't mix business with pleasure, wouldn't matter to someone like Simeon. As cynical as he could be, his feelings for Alana always seemed to bring out the optimism in him. Her only option was to point out what he wasn't allowing himself to see.

"Have you ever thought that maybe it's time to let things go?"

"What do you mean?"

"I mean things with Alana."

"How do you let go of what's in your heart? And that's a surprising question coming from you. You're the one always telling me to confess my feelings, so what brought this on?"

"Yes, and you never did. Look, it just seems like all of this back and forth doesn't do anything, but leave her feeling confused afterwards. I'm just wondering if maybe…maybe, the kiss was just a mistake."

"Mistake?! No! Now when you and I kissed, *that* was a mistake."

"Hey, shut up! That was a mix up and you know it!" she said, punching him in the arm and whispering as if someone would hear. "I thought we said we would never mention that, ever!"

"Of course, it was a mix up, and we haven't mentioned it since. It's just so funny when you get mad," he laughed wickedly.

Leave it to Simeon to bring up an uncomfortable accident in order to avoid facing the truth. The year before, the group had gone to a party thrown by Jirou to celebrate his girlfriend Shawny's 25th birthday. All night, Simeon watched Alana, like he usually did when she was all dolled up. In the midst of lusting after her, the party began to grow. As things got a little too loud and crazy, he noticed her slip into his brother's bedroom for a break from the festivities. He attempted to follow her in, hoping to rekindle what they had. But he was momentarily interrupted by a partygoer that was interested in getting to know him better.

As he struggled to get out of the conversation, he failed to notice Gigi go into the room, as well. As she searched for her and Brian's coats, she failed to notice Alana on the balcony since she had closed the curtains behind her, in hopes of gaining a little peace. As Gigi felt around in the dark for the light switch, Simeon snuck into the room behind her and spun her around, kissing her as if she were Alana. The confusion only continued as they kissed passionately because, in turn, Gigi thought she was kissing Brian. It wasn't until his arms wrapped around her waist, and hers onto his shoulders, that they both realized the bodies they were touching weren't ones that they recognized by touch, but perhaps by sight. They stopped mid-kiss, both curious as to whether or not they'd just made a mistake in identity. But it wasn't until Gigi spoke and asked, "Brian? Please tell me that's you?" that their suspicions were confirmed.

Simeon pushed her away and quickly rushed to the light switch. When he flicked it on, he was shocked to find Gigi staring back as him, equally surprised. They tripped over their words before Alana emerged from the balcony, startling them.

"What's up, you two?" she asked curiously.

"Nothing!" they shouted, as she looked at them like they were crazy for yelling at her so aggressively. Once Gigi saw Alana, it all made perfect sense that Simeon would kiss her. And when they finally got a moment to discuss their mishap, they swore to act as if it never happened. Gigi realized Simeon wanted to deflect by bringing up something so meaningless from the past. But that wasn't going to stop her from tackling what was presently relevant.

"As I was saying, maybe she got caught up in the heat of the moment and that it was—"

"Are you trying to sway me because of the guy she's been sneaking off to see?" he asked.

"What guy?"

"Oh, come on! Don't try to play dumb because you're a really shitty actress! Just stick to designing, okay? Now we both know there's a guy. He must be pretty ugly, too, if she's keeping him a secret from us."

"Oh Simeon, stop it!" Gigi snapped. If anyone loved joking and talking about people, it was her. But she was trying to help him as a friend, and he kept trying to avoid it. Simeon recognized her look of aggravation in her cold, hazel eyes and gulped down his beer before slamming the bottle on the window ledge. He crossed his arms in frustration, clearly not wanting to hear whatever it was she had to say. But he knew she would say it anyway.

"Maybe she's not keeping secrets. If there is someone in her life, maybe she just doesn't feel like hearing you rip him apart, like you usually do."

"Oh, so we're all sensitive now? Like you guys don't talk about the women I bring around!"

"Yeah, but that's different—"

"How the hell is it different?" he snapped.

"First of all, we know we'll most likely never see them again. Unless, of course, it's one of the many waitresses at the restaurant who you've fucked! Secondly, maybe we'd show them a little more respect if you did."

"So now it's my fault you two tear down the women I date?"

"Date them?! Don't make me laugh. You bone them, nothing more! And we don't tear them down! We might mimic them or even make a couple of jokes. But we never belittle them like you do the men that come into her life. We poke fun. Your envious ass—"

"Envious?! Envious of those weak ass dudes that can't even hold on to her for more than a few months?!"

"Yeah, well, neither could you! And maybe it's because you have random bitches' panties all over your house! Tell the truth, Simeon. Are you even really in love with Alana, or do you just need another dust rag for your pile?" Gigi gulped down the rest of her beer and slammed her bottle next to his. She hesitated for a moment, wondering if she should continue her tirade. But she figured she'd come this far, so she might as well go for broke. "Look, this is getting really old. For God's sake, if you love her, tell her. And if you don't, make room for someone that does!"

She marched away from the window and returned to the pile of shirts she'd left on the floor. Simeon was seething with anger and was just about to give her a piece of his mind, when they heard the front door open. Alana and Brian had finally arrived, running into each other in the hallway. She used her key and yelled up the stairs, alerting her battling buddies that it was time to retreat to their respective corners and put on their happy faces. Gigi bolted down the stairs first, barely giving Brian enough time to put the pizzas on the counter before she jumped into his cold arms and kissed him deeply. Alana smiled at the sweet sentiment, but decided to heckle them anyway.

"You two make me so sick," she said. Brian tried to say something silly in return, but Gigi's lips wouldn't let up. Simeon came down shortly after a while, still bearing a look of frustration on his face. He went into the kitchen, and grabbed them all some beers and plates so they could pig out—but not before answering Alana's questions.

"What's wrong with you? You tired already?" she asked.

"What can I say? I guess I just don't know when to quit," he answered with veiled contempt.

"Well, maybe you should learn how to recognize when you should. You might save yourself a lot of wasted time," Gigi quipped back.

"If you quit, you never obtain your goals. I'm sure you've heard the term slowly, but surely," he jabbed back.

"Okay, what are we talking about?" Alana asked.

"Beats me! You know Simeon. He never just comes out and says what's really on his mind. He has to take the scenic route first!"

Simeon cut his eyes at the snappy, but truthful, comment as the foursome sat around the table in front of the couch. They lounged around in their t-shirts and sweats while watching television, eating and ignoring the elephant in the room. Brian and Alana threw each other curious looks as they wondered about what may have happened before they arrived that would lead to such a peppery exchange. It was evident that the two old friends were at odds about something. But they both decided to leave it alone and let them resolve the issue on their own. It wasn't the first time they'd been mad at each other, and it wouldn't be the last.

Forever in "boss mode," Alana grabbed the remote and turned off the television. She clapped her hands to round up the troops, demanding that they do what they came to do. For a while, they worked in an awkward silence. Gigi, who was never quiet, packed and pouted while Simeon folded and frowned. It didn't take long for Brian to decide he could no longer bear the uncomfortable silence. So, he cranked the radio all the way up to lighten the mood. "Sing a Song" by Earth, Wind & Fire played loudly as he grabbed a hanger and began to lip-sync. Gigi rolled her eyes at her fiancée's goofy behavior before he threw down his makeshift microphone and grabbed her hand. By forcing her to dance, he was also able to coerce her into smiling. Alana followed his lead by pulling on Simeon's stubborn arm so he could join the impromptu party. They danced around the room with their respective partners, until Brian and Alana pushed the dueling duo into each other.

They tried to stay mad at each other for as long as they could. But, before they knew it, they were both laughing and hugging it out. The rest of the night, they reminisced, drank wine and cherished the time they had together. At the end of the night, the guys stacked the taped-up boxes in a corner by the door and, without warning, the girls felt themselves getting emotional. It was the first time they felt the impact his absence would have on them both. He played so many

different roles in their lives, aside from acting as their personal chef and friend.

For Gigi, he'd been a supporter, a confidant, an advisor, and even a shopping partner. And, for Alana, he'd been a former lover, a shoulder to cry on, a workout buddy, at times, a protector, and now, her business partner. Until his return, their circle wouldn't be complete. Although the boxes held shirts, pants, socks and shoes, they were still pieces of him that signified his departure to France. He knew them both well enough to know that the watering in their eyes was a precursor for their tears. He smiled and wrapped his arms around them both, trying to fight back tears of his own. They held onto his waist before Brian wrapped his arms around the group.

"All of this love amongst so many pretty people," Brian joked, sending them into uncontrollable laughter.

Simeon wiped the girls' faces and kissed their foreheads as he put on his best face, masking what was going on inside of him. He was pretty sure they were saying something, but as he looked at Alana with affectionate eyes and an adoring heart, he felt as though he was under water. He caught a few words here and there, but most of the conversation seemed inaudible. In his mind, he swam through a sea of thoughts. As his eyes caught Gigi's, he gave her a small nod, accepting the fact that she was right.

Her impatience for his procrastination gave him just the push he needed. He decided that he was ready to tell Alana the truth. But he wanted to do it in a more lavish setting, not in a spare bedroom turned walk-in closet. Everyone headed home, leaving Simeon to his own devices. As he heard the door shut behind his friends, it hit him. After the party, once all of the guests had gone home and just the crew was sitting around, like they always did after a big event, he would ask Alana for one final dance. He'd finally tell her what the rest of them already knew: that he was in love with her.

Alana arrived at home to a string of email notifications on her phone. Guests were reserving their spots like crazy, proving that she and Gigi weren't the only ones that wanted to give Simeon a fantastic farewell. She was beyond excited that the turnout may actually be beyond her expectations. But, at the core of her happiness, she was experiencing an unexpected feeling of sorrow. The party planning and the packing made her realize just how much she was going to miss him. For years, they'd seen each other every single morning, hung out a few times a week, been each other's dates to parties and, every now and then, without warning, even each other's make-out partner.

Since being accepted into the prestigious program, his trip always seemed so far away. But now that it was in a couple of weeks, there would be a huge void she wasn't sure she'd be able to fill. Not even Alex's text, expressing how much he had missed her throughout the day, could cure her sudden case of "the sentimentals." She walked over to his framed newspaper clipping on her wall and felt her eyes get misty. She closed them and thought back to the day that the picture was taken. It was hell just to get him to pose alone.

Even though the article was about his talents as a chef and the attention he'd gained for The Cocoa Marra, he was adamant about not wanting to be in any photograph referencing the restaurant without Alana by his side. He told her that he never wanted her to feel that he was taking away from the success brought on by her idea. But she would have known that, even if he hadn't said it. It was things like that which made Simeon so lovable. No matter how arrogant he could get at times, it always ended up being outshined by his modesty. Their bond was dysfunctional, but strong.

As her phone rang and Alex's name popped up on the screen, she decided to ignore it. She knew he would hear the distress in her voice, and she was in no mood to argue about his jealousy over her "feelings" toward Simeon. Instead, she poured herself a glass of wine, pulled out her picture albums, and spent the rest of the night with fond memories and photos of the one man who'd somehow managed to become more than some unmemorable lover from her past. He'd become an irreplaceable friend.

Chapter | 25

The sound of a fist pounding heavily on the front door ripped Alana right out of her wine- induced coma. Her eyes popped open as she put her hands to her head, which was still spinning from all of the cabernet she drank the night before. Since her tenants were usually good about calling if there was a problem with one of their lofts, and being that both Gigi and Simeon could let themselves in, she was quite curious as to who her uninvited visitor could be. She looked like a zombie as she dragged herself to the door, surprised to find Alex on the other side of it, holding a white paper bag and a cup of coffee. She gladly let him in. As he entered with excitement to see her, as well, he couldn't help but examine the specimen that stood before him. He looked her up and down, clearly tickled and surprised by her appearance. She was a wreck! Her hair was wild. Her clothes, which she'd slept in, were crooked and wrinkled. And her bloodshot eyes were smudged with day-old mascara.

"You look radiant, darling!" he said mockingly. "Gigi said I should bring this up. She was concerned when you didn't come down this morning."

"Wait, what time is it?"

"It's 10:30 a.m., which is pretty late by your standards. Usually, you'd be on the go by now."

"Damn it!" she yelled, grabbing her breakfast from him and bolting to the kitchen. He sat in one of the chairs by the island and watched her as she lightly toasted the bagel he'd brought her. She smiled as she felt his eyes piercing into her back, inciting her to walk over and peck him. She asked him to butter her bread while she brushed her teeth and washed her face. Alex happily obliged, and even grabbed a strawberry from the refrigerator so he could carve her a rose garnish. In next to no time, her hair brush, face towel, toothbrush and Visine had completely transformed her. She emerged from the bathroom, fresh faced and ready to entice.

She radiated sexiness in her red satin robe as she leaned onto the island and sipped her coffee. Alex positioned himself behind her. With his arms wrapped around her waist, he casually untied the satin belt, helping to keep her covered. Her cool hips were warmed by his hands as they ran up and down her skin. He kissed the back of her neck and nibbled on her ear, as he tried to talk her into having a quickie.

"So, I don't have to be downstairs for another three minutes."

"Three minutes? Ha! I wouldn't brag about my shortcomings, if I were you."

"Woman, I'll make it feel like the longest three minutes of your life!"

Alex picked her up and carried her over to the couch as she giggled at his overconfident claim. They held onto each other tightly as the sight of his face, the touch of his hand, and the way he could make her laugh with his corny jokes saturated Alana with an overpowering feeling of tenderness. She closed her eyes and let his cologne draw her in. His freshly groomed beard brushed her cheek, awakening whatever senses he hadn't already. In the short time since he'd arrived, he managed to make her feel completely different from the night before.

She could always count on his soothing disposition to calm her many anxieties, even her sudden panic of Simeon's departure. Their connection was stronger than ever and, although it was different from the bond she had with Simeon, it made her realize she wouldn't be as alone as she'd convinced herself she'd be. Alex was in no way a replacement for her relationship with Simeon, but he was just as dependable, just as caring and just as rare. And, like Simeon, he had become someone she didn't want to do without.

It was finally starting to hit her that perhaps Alex was right. Maybe it was time to take things further and make it official. Her heart leapt at the thought as they kissed excitedly. She struggled with the button on his pants as much as she struggled with whether or not to bring up her feelings. And, at the moment she finally got it undone, she braced herself for his thick gift. But instead, she was met with resistance. His eyes had wandered over to the coffee table, which was covered in pictures of some of their friends, but mostly of her and Simeon together.

Her beckoning lips began to go unanswered as his eyes darted from the table to the floor, where he saw the balled-up tissues that had wiped away her tears and the empty wine bottle, which had drowned away her sorrows, still sitting from last night's pity party. He snatched away, appearing irritated and leaving her puzzled as she closed her robe. He rubbed his hand over his hair and low, scruffy beard as he searched for words to express what he was feeling.

"Something wrong?" she asked.

"Um, let me think. Yeah! Yeah there is!"

"Okay…so what's the problem?"

"So, this is why you were ignoring me last night?" he asked, pointing to the table. "A little heartbroken over the head chef, are we?"

"Don't be ridiculous!"

"Am I? Or are you still too drunk from last night to realize just how sensible I'm being?"

"Are we really on this again?" She became even more infuriated.

"You're damn right we are! I'm at home missing you last night and genuinely concerned when I didn't hear from you, and you're over here crying for him?!"

"You know how close we are and he's leaving for a good part of a year. Do you even know what he's been to me?"

"Yeah, I've heard. Let me see if I got the order right: tutor, lover, partner, right?"

Alana was dumbfounded. She felt like she'd gone over the same thing a million times before. How Simeon had been there for her when her grandmother died. How when everyone else thought her building was a waste of space, he helped knock down walls with a sledgehammer during the renovation just so she could see her vision come to life. How he passed on multiple offers from prominent restaurants upon his graduation to head up hers, with no guarantees of success. But Alex was still focusing on the one thing from her past that mattered the least to her. She went from wanting to lay it all on the line to wanting him to get out as quickly as possible. It was the second time they'd had a perfectly romantic morning turn to shit within minutes. She ran out of words, and it wasn't long before she pointed to her wrist, letting him know that he was out of time.

"I think your three minutes are up."

"Maybe I *should* leave. You know Alana, I'm a little tired of always being the one that's wrong."

"Well, you were right about one thing: this *has* been the longest three minutes of my life!"

Alex stormed toward the door, slamming it behind him so hard that it sounded like it might burst into a million splinters. Alana growled out loud, both pissed and puzzled as to what his problem was. Now she wasn't allowed to be sad that her best friend was leaving? She walked over to the table and stared down at the collage. In a fit of rage, she swept the pictures onto the floor as if they had been the cause of her irritation. She only became more infuriated when she realized she would have to pick them all up.

On top of being a late starter, she was now going to have to officially start her day with an attitude, which wasn't easy. Georgia always told her that starting the day with anger only caused one to hurt themselves before the world got a chance to, and she was right. During her morning routine, she hit her knee on the tub, scratched her arm while pulling her shirt over her head, and even broke a toe nail when she kicked over the wine bottle by the couch. The world wouldn't need to beat up on her today since she was already doing a pretty good job of that herself. She texted Gigi, letting her know that they needed to talk ASAP, before heading downstairs to give Elizabeth some petty cash.

Entering the kitchen was the easy part. Trying not to bring attention to the attitude that both she and Alex had toward each other was a tad bit more difficult. They nodded at each other, which Simeon found strange, especially since Alex's greetings were usually followed by smiles and stares. Today, however, he acted completely different. After acknowledging her, he turned around and worked on the station behind him, which then made Diego aware of the odd exchange. His lack of zeal toward her was definitely not normal, but Diego's only hope was that whatever they had going on remained civil. He didn't want to have to tell Alex "I told you so" in the event that it didn't.

Alana went into the office for a short pow wow with Liz and emerged to find a self-absorbed Simeon riddled with questions about his party, which he assumed the ladies were talking about. He took a break from his morning tirade and exchanged it with a curious line of questioning. She indulged him with what little details she was willing to provide. But, unbeknownst to her, it would be a question that *she* asked that would jumpstart a series of dramatic events.

"So, Casanova, who's gonna be your date this time? Another billboard bimbo, or some poor, unsuspecting girl who foolishly thinks she can win your heart with a dance?"

"Actually, it's neither. She's a friend, actually. We've been cool for the past few weeks, and I like hanging out with her."

Alana was surprised by the information. Why hadn't she heard about this new "friend"? He usually told her everything, but she wasn't exactly in any position to throw stones. She'd been seeing Alex for months and hadn't uttered a single word. Yet, she felt slighted by his omission. She played it cool in the moment, but had every intention of grilling Gigi the moment she saw her. If she didn't know what was going on, G had to.

"So, where did you meet her?"

"Here, at the fundraiser."

"Okay, Mr. Bigshot! There were a lot of wealthy women here that night!"

"It's not like that. Seriously, we *really* are just friends. She's like one of the guys, only she looks and smells a whole lot better. Anyway, I told her about it and she promises me she can
really dance!"

"Anyone I would recognize?"

"I hope so since she paid us. It's Natalie."

"Natalie?" Alana and Alex yelled in unison as Alex whipped around from his work station.

As Simeon proceeded to explain how they hit it off after she contacted him to thank him for a job well done, Alex and Alana analyzed each other's reaction to the news. Alex wondered why Alana seemed jealous of the news that he'd been spending time with a female friend that wasn't her. On the flip side, Alana wondered why Alex seemed upset. Was it because his ex was spending time with another man, or was it the fact that the other man was Simeon? If he was truly over her, then although it was uncomfortable, he shouldn't really care, right?

They both thought about the awkward circle of secrets and wondered which one of them made the first move and why? Was it Natalie playing a dangerous game? Simeon playing a childish game? Or a little bit of both? The kitchen staff tried their hardest to work and eavesdrop at the same time, but they weren't very inconspicuous about it. It was no secret that there was a growing rivalry between Alex and Simeon, despite their efforts to hide it. It was rumored that it was good old-fashioned kitchen rivalry due to both of their desire to be the best. But if Simeon's hazing hadn't already taken things too far, spending time with Alex's ex-fiancé was sure to put him right over the edge. Alana was going to leave it alone, but she felt compelled to say something so she didn't appear to agree with Simeon's conduct.

"Do you think that's appropriate?" Alana asked Simeon.

"So, what? I can't be friends with someone because of who they used to be engaged to? That's crazy! Besides, he doesn't mind that we're hanging out, right?" he asked Alex.

"Simeon, I don't think—"

"It's cool, Alana. I don't mind at all, man! Have at her. You two deserve one another."

Beef was in the kitchen, but not the kind that you cooked. A few of the guys were silently siding with Alex. Some were even giving Simeon serious side-eye action, apparently disgusted by his behavior. His motives weren't clear, but the others began to wonder if he would do something so seemingly vicious to them, as well. The sound of water hitting against dishes, food sizzling in skillets, and knives chopping on boards was the only normal action taking place. Alana left out of the front door with nothing more to say, but Diego was just getting started.

"I need to talk to you outside, now!" he said to Simeon angrily.

"Sure thing," he answered, smirking at Alex.

The two disappeared through the back door, leaving Alex to chat with a now divided kitchen staff. One of the dishwashers he often played basketball with expressed his disapproval of what was going on, but Alex assured him that he had already wiped his hands of the entire situation. In the meantime, Diego was wiping his hands on a towel before throwing it at Simeon and folding his arms in frustration. He looked like a father who was preparing to scold his son as Simeon stood across from him, throwing his hands in the air as if to ask what he wanted. Over the years, Simeon had the propensity to be mean, even ruthless at times. But Diego refused to stand by this time and support his wicked games.

"What the hell are you doing, man?" he asked.

"I have no idea what you're talking—"

"Oh, cut the shit, Simeon! Running around town with your sous chef's ex-fiancée?"

"How is that your business?" Simeon asked.

"It's my business when it affects the business!" Diego snapped.

"I'm a partner. You think I don't care about the business? And would we even be having this discussion if he wasn't your friend?"

"Man, please! You're my boy, too. But since we're questioning each other, would you even be hanging with that broad if you didn't think it would get under his skin?"

"She reached out to me!"

"And why do you think that is?! I know you're arrogant, but you can't think you're *that* damn charming, bro! She's trying to start some shit!"

"From what she told me, they were over long before he even knew it. So why does it matter?"

"Says the guy who gets an attitude if Alex even looks at Alana wrong! Stop what you're doing, bro! You keep lighting sticks of dynamite and one of them is gonna blow up in your face!" Diego stormed back into the kitchen, leaving his leader alone and fuming. In a fit of rage, Simeon kicked over the trash can by the door, littering the ground with the cigarette butts from its ashtray top. Snowflakes began to fall and, as Simeon watched them fall on top of the mess Diego made, he caught a glimpse of what everyone was thinking of him: that he was cold and dirty.

Across the street, the ladies were about to have a talk of their own. With Christmas around the corner, the boutique was busier than usual. Lexa greeted her and pointed toward the back, where Gigi worked on her latest creation. She politely pushed past the patrons before reaching her and pulling her into the office. She shut the door and ushered Gigi to her chair behind the desk. She tried sitting, as well, but it wasn't working with all the nervous energy she had coursing through her veins.

At first, she didn't say a word. She only paced back and forth like a mad woman as Gigi tried her best not to sprain her neck following her. Her heels dug into the thick, plush carpet, leaving a trail of tiny circles in her quake. Gigi waited patiently to hear what the source of so much urgency was. But it wasn't until she asked Alana whether or not she liked her coffee and bagel that she started to unload. She gave the blow by blow of everything that had happened since breakfast. The chocolate beauty felt like she was in an episode of "The Bold, The Black, and The Beautiful."

She chewed on Twizzlers as her hazel eyes glowed with excitement, bracing herself for whatever her bestie might say next. With every new detail, Alana got more and more worked up. Hues of pink invaded her cheeks and ears until she was completely flushed. She babbled at top speeds until she was no longer coherent, prompting Gigi to stop her. She got up and grabbed her by the shoulders, forcing her to take a seat before her pacing made them both dizzy. It was the first time in a long time that Gigi was void of advice. She had no shortage of shame however for how entertained she was by all of it. Alana held her hands in the air and slapped them on her thighs, as if it would jumpstart Gigi's brain.

"Well, aren't you going to say something?"

"Okay, okay! So, let me see if I got this right. You're still secretly dating Alex, unbeknownst to Simeon, who is now friends with Natalie, who used to be engaged to Alex, who Alex thinks knows about your relationship, which she isn't telling Simeon?"

"That just about sums it up," Alana said.

"Well, what can I say besides I will not be missing this party! That, and I think somebody is feeling a little intimidated."

"I knew it! Alex *does* care about Simeon and Natalie, doesn't he?"

"If the man says he doesn't, then he doesn't. Besides, I wasn't talking about him. I was talking about you."

"Me? Intimidated?! By who?"

"That's what I'm trying to figure out. You know Simeon would never try to replace you, right? And Alex is *not* thinking about that girl. If he was, he would—"

"You think I'm feeling intimidated by Natalie?"

"Well, aren't you? Be real. Is it because you're afraid that she's taking Simeon away from you, or because you think she still has a grip on Alex?"

Perhaps she was a little jealous that Natalie had decided to latch on to Simeon. But he would do the same thing if the shoe were on the other foot, right? The girls continued to talk about the all-too juicy love square that was forming. Clearly, it was well beyond a love triangle. No one could say for sure that Natalie and Simeon were socializing out of spite. It was quite possible that their personalities really did appeal to each other, encouraging them to form a friendship. Gigi had a hard time believing that, even with their quarreling, he could dislike Alex so much that he would go after his ex in order to ruffle his feathers. But if their rivalry had become that deep, how would Simeon react once he discovered his archrival had infiltrated more than his kitchen?

Gigi also addressed the fact that she knew Alana's feelings for Alex were much deeper than what she was admitting. And as she waited for her to finally confirm it, as if on cue, like he'd heard his name mentioned, he sent her a text.

Alex: Sweetheart, I hate that we fought this morning and I hate this uncomfortable situation we're being put in. Obviously, your best friend doesn't have a problem telling you anything, so I don't understand why you're having such a tough time telling him about us. I'm tired of this! I know we didn't plan to be where we are, but we are here just the same! If we're going to keep doing this, it's time to tell people. I don't want to be your secret anymore. I want to introduce you to my parents. I want a key to your place. I want the key to your heart!

Alana felt a familiar lump in her throat. She usually got it right when things were about to get serious in a relationship. Her usual routine consisted of going over a list of pros and cons, analyzing the relationship as a whole, from start to current day, and determining whether or not she was feeling anything that would make her want to continue things. But this time, she realized the lump was accompanied by something else. Instead of her obsessive need to be in control, for the first time ever, all she wanted to do was completely let go and enjoy whatever life had in store for them—as long as it was together. She was ready to take a chance. She sent him a text as Gigi continued offering suggestions on how to deal with it all and put Alex at ease.

Alana: I hate that we argued, too. And you're right. It's time. All I ask is that you give me until after the party. Then, we'll tell everyone.

The anger she felt when she first walked through the doors of Cloth started to fade away. Now her mind focused on the party, breaking the news to Simeon, and trying to decide if her budding feelings for Alex were in fact the long-awaited L-word. But she still wasn't taking the morning mayhem lightly. Little did she know, it was a just a preview for the drama to come. The sweet flavor of secrecy was taking a sour turn and, after the party, Alana wouldn't be the only one with a bad taste left in her mouth.

Chapter | 26

The weeks leading up to Simeon's last salsa were anything but easy. Tensions were at an all-time high, especially with Natalie stopping by the restaurant twice for unscheduled visits. Both times, she claimed to be in the neighborhood and merely wanted to say hello. But it didn't look good, no matter what the excuse was. Oddly enough, Alex gave the impression that he was unaffected by the possible ruse. At times, he even seemed amused. But everyone didn't find it so funny. Opinions around the previously laid-back work environment had formed. The staff, who all loved Simeon, with the exception of a few scorned waitresses, had turned into what could best be described as the "50/50 Club." Half were against Simeon, believing that his actions were wrong, and they wouldn't blame Alex if he quit or laid him out. The other half remained loyal to the head chef, or at least tried their best to stay neutral.

The atmosphere at home was a little better, but not by much. Things between Alana and Alex were calm enough that they hadn't argued since the morning Simeon revealed his new hanging buddy. But something was slightly off between them. In the back of her mind, Alana couldn't shake the nagging feeling that things were about to go awry. Even with their plan to go public, he seemed unhappy with the status quo. Bottom line was that he was tired of sneaking around!

She wanted to make him happy and had every intention of moving forward with the plan. But nothing made her more nervous than the thought of telling Simeon about them. She thought about the many times she'd made it a point to tell Georgia and Gigi that there was nothing between her and Simeon. But now that she was suddenly faced with telling him there was someone special in her life, the point that *they* had always tried to make to her, hit her like a ton of bricks. He *had* been something like her man, with the exception of sex. Even that wasn't entirely true. They did everything a couple should do, from vacationing and attending events together, to even having keys to each other's homes. Deep down, she knew the news would hurt him, especially with it being Alex. Although she was sure Alex genuinely cared for her, she wanted to make sure his insistent need to come out as a couple had nothing to do with Simeon's socializing with Natalie. Whether or not he would choose to acknowledge it, the timing was awfully interesting.

The day of the party finally arrived, and she was nervous at every turn. When Gigi arrived so they could get ready together, she noticed that Alana seemed a little anxious and poured her a tall glass of vino to help her relax. Annette came by early so she could do the girls' makeup before starting her own. They listened to music and talked about how great the party was sure to be, but even Annette's skilled brushes couldn't paint away the look of worry on Alana's face.

"What's up with you, miss lady? Why are you looking worried, like you missed your period or something?" Annette questioned.

"I'm sorry, girls. I've just had so much on my mind."

"Well tonight, you need to clear the webs of worry right out of the corners of your mind and get ready to let loose! You know when you and Simeon salsa together, you tear up the floor. Annette, get ready for a show!" Gigi added.

"Oh, I'm ready, mama! You'll have to show me some moves to use on my hubby."

Alana lightened up and began to show her a thing or two. They cheered her on as she moved her arms in a loose circular motion and stepped from back to front, demonstrating how graceful and agile she was. Once the ladies' faces were painted to perfection, Annette headed home so she could get ready for the party, leaving the two best friends to lounge around for a bit before getting dolled up in their show-stopping attire. While they were getting dressed, Alex sent Alana a text, letting her know that he was excited for everything the party was to bring, including their future together. She knew that he only wanted to be with her, but she found the mounting pressure a little annoying.

Still, she tried to put herself in his shoes and responded that she was ready for all that the future held for them, as well. She put on her red, backless, halter dress, which was light enough to show off her sexy legs if she were to twirl on the dance floor. Gigi, who wasn't such a bad dancer herself, was ready to show a little skin as well in her beige sequined dress with spaghetti straps that crisscrossed on her back. The asymmetrical hem, with the shorter side coming all the way up to her thigh, would have Brian begging her to dance, even if he didn't want to.

They may have looked hot, but they certainly weren't foolish enough to go out into the cold without putting on their thick matching fur coats to shield them from the cold of winter. Before heading out for an unforgettable night, Gigi suggested they make a toast. She hurried to the kitchen and grabbed two shot glasses from the cabinet, along with the bottle of vodka that was chilling in the refrigerator. She poured them both a hefty shot and handed one over, lifting hers into the air.

"To our best friend Simeon, whom we are very proud of. May he appreciate the great lengths we have gone to in order to pull off the party of the century, and may he enjoy every surprise tonight has in store." Alana lifted her shot and prayed that it would calm her nerves. Brian called to let them know he was waiting downstairs. As they rushed out of the door, Alana doubled back to grab the beautifully wrapped gift box from the dining room table. She shut off the lights and hurried to the car, rolling her eyes as she stumbled upon the newly engaged love birds making out as usual. Just seeing them together, happy and in love, made Alana feel as though she was making the right decision by taking it to the next level with Alex.

"Damn! Can you two make it out of the parking lot without fondling each other?" she asked.

"Nope!" they answered in unison.

After a short drive, they arrived at the rental hall and couldn't believe their eyes. It was nearly unrecognizable. If they had any doubts about Ms. Stevens' abilities, they were immediately laid to rest. She was a miracle worker! The entire building had been draped in string lights and potted palm trees decorated the exterior. Red carpet and velvet rope aligned the sidewalk for the line of guests that stretched out to the parking lot. It appeared that everyone on the invite list showed up with a plus one. There were so many people waiting to get inside that Gigi worried they would break the fire code due to the limited capacity. Security seemed to be running smoothly as two large men stood at the entrance with the guest list. One went through the line checking IDs, and two more surveyed the crowd already inside. Valet for the night was being handled by a couple of Diego's cousins who were college students that needed some extra cash. Alana was impressed that the young men, whom she said could simply wear black shirts and jeans, took it upon themselves to dress up for the evening with burgundy blazers, white button-up shirts, black bow ties and black slacks.

They helped her and Gigi out of the car and, when the girls entered the building, they were stunned by the sight of the inside. It seemed as though by magic they had stepped into a scene from *Havana Nights*. They checked their coats and looked around in disbelief as Ms. Stevens snuck up behind them.

"Is this the vision you were aiming for?" she asked.

"Girl, this is our vision on steroids!" Gigi answered.

The talented party planner waved over a waiter, who gave them the last flutes of champagne from his tray, sparking the ladies to toast to a job well done. She let them continue through the room so they could marvel over every fine detail she'd laid out. It was no mistaking that Simeon's party would be the talk of the town for weeks to come. Professional dancers pulled people onto the dance floor, while the ridiculously good-looking bartenders flipped bottles and glasses in the air while flirting with the patrons for tips. The photographer walked around snapping pictures of ladies in short dresses, fellas in button-ups and slacks, and most importantly, the décor. Each table was decorated simply with a red tablecloth and three-tier candle holders in the shape of margarita glasses. The lighting over the tables had been changed from bright fluorescents to soft pinks, oranges and reds, creating an almost spotlight effect on the dance floor.

The deejay had the party on fire as salsa music flooded the air and couples took turns spinning across the dance floor. Suddenly, Alana realized she recognized a group of girls who were dancing with each other. They were Simeon's gorgeous cousins that she had the pleasure of meeting on Thanksgiving. They danced in a circle as dozens of men stood on the edge of the dance floor, staring and fawning over them. In the midst of the bunch was Simeon, who wasn't supposed to arrive until later. He was showing off his fancy footwork with Lexa, his young crush from Gigi's boutique. Her dark, butt-length hair whipped around, sometimes covering her blushing face, which was turning so pink that it began to look like she had on too much rouge. The girls walked over to greet the man of the hour and, as he turned around, his arms wrapped around, as if he knew they were coming.

"Hello, my lovelies!" he said.

"Simeon, what are you doing here already? You weren't supposed to arrive until later so that you could make a grand entrance."

"Are you kidding me? I didn't want to miss a single moment of tonight! Look at this place! I can't believe this is the same hall! I'm not even going to ask what you guys spent on this party because I'm definitely worth it, so it doesn't matter!" he said, kissing them both on the cheek.

The girls wanted to fuss at him for his premature arrival. But they were interrupted by Mr. Ito, who stopped by the party only for a moment to congratulate his son and give him a bottle of Macallan 25. The two men embraced, inspiring Jirou to join in on the hug. Alana looked around at all of the smiling faces in attendance and noticed that everyone was there--everyone except Alex. She sent him a quick text, asking if he was still coming. She was surprised by his response, which was both comforting and concerning. He let her know that he was already there and that he was trying to enter the building, before he was suddenly pulled aside by Natalie.

Alana's intuition kicked into high gear, telling her that his ex was being shady. She rushed over and grabbed Gigi to ask for her opinion, wanting to hear that she was overreacting. But her bestie agreed that "Nat" was proving to be quite treacherous. The tough twosome agreed that they should retrieve her "behind-the-scenes beau" at once, or at least make Alana's position known. Besides, they wanted to know what was so important that it couldn't be discussed inside. As they reached the entrance, Natalie emerged through the door, looking happy and having appeared to have left all of her modesty at home.

She pulled off her coat and air kissed Alana on both cheeks before tugging at the top of her extra tiny dress to make sure her breast hadn't snuck out. Alana put on her best face, not wanting to appear jealous or judgmental. She spoke kindly to her as she carried on with colorful commentary, like they were old chums. If looks could kill, Gigi would have been booked for murder as she looked her up and down like a target she'd sworn to take out. Natalie picked up on the hint of hostility in the air and was going to ignore it, until she was provoked to do otherwise.

"I think you forgot some of the material for your dress," Gigi said, shocking Alana while simultaneously amusing her.

"Perhaps it's in the same place you left your manners," she fired back.

Gigi stepped forward, prepared to engage in a battle of wits. But Alana stepped in between them. She smirked at Natalie and told her to enjoy the party, to which she responded by flashing a fake smile of her own and moving along to the coat check. She didn't know exactly what Gigi's problem was, but she had a pretty good idea. She seemed like she wanted to avoid anymore awkwardness; yet, she continued doing things that drew attention to herself. After spotting Simeon talking to a small group of people, she very loudly greeted him while Alana very quietly greeted Alex, who had just walked in.

Although he looked a tad bit uneasy, he smiled at the sight of her just the same. She and Gigi wanted to grill him about what Natalie said to him, but the three of them were too busy wondering why she was putting on such a show. Even Simeon looked puzzled by her overzealous greeting, which was complete with her interrupting him mid-conversation and wrapping her arms around his neck, like they hadn't seen each other in ages. The woman that once seemed so confident and driven now only seemed desperate to gain attention. But whose?

"Is that performance for you?" Alana asked Alex.

"I think it's for you, actually."

"Why would she be showing off for me?"

"Well, when we were outside, she told me that she hoped her friendship with Simeon wouldn't cause me not to save her a dance. I told her that all of my dances were saved up for you."

An "unconcerned" Natalie looked over in time enough to catch Alex wink at Alana, which drove her nuts inside. It didn't help matters that she stood there smiling back at him and looking flawless, as he eyed her like the last piece of food on a deserted island. In a huff, Natalie grabbed Simeon's wrist and drug him to the dance floor. Brian collected Gigi and pulled her onto the floor, as well, while Alex and Alana decided to mingle. As much as they wanted to act the way they usually did when no one was around, they knew they weren't good to go just yet.

Alex joined Diego and the line cooks at one of the tables so they could drink and talk about sports, while Alana worked the crowd and personally thanked as many guests as she could for coming. She tried her best to be blasé about the recital taking place on the dance floor. But as she tried not to stare at Simeon and Natalie, she couldn't help but notice how in-tune they were when dancing together. It was the same way he usually appeared with her. She'd never admit it, but the slight sting of jealousy crept in as he whispered something to her that made her laugh, as if it was the funniest thing she'd ever heard. She childishly found comfort in knowing that as good as they looked together out there, it was nothing compared to the way he and Alana captivated the crowd. After a few songs, Simeon took a quick break and joined Gigi, Brian and Georgia.

They sat around listening to him tell the same old stories they'd heard a thousand times, before Alana appeared with the gift box she had gone back for. Simeon was pleasantly surprised. He believed his party was the only gift he'd be receiving, and he was more than happy with that. But leave it to Alana to go above and beyond, adding to all the reasons he wanted to finally confess to her that he loved her. He kissed her on the temple and took a deep breath before opening the box. Inside he found a Casio multifunction watch, which also doubled as a compass. He opened the small envelope taped to the inside of the box and read the short and sweet note, which said: *"Just in case you ever need help finding your way home, this will lead the way. With every tick, know that we are counting the minutes until you return. Love me and G."*

"You like it?"

"You always did have a way with words. Yes, I love it," he said before leaning over and kissing Gigi on the cheek. He turned to kiss Alana on the cheek, as well. But, as she turned toward him, his lips landed dangerously close to hers. He slowly pulled back from the corner of her mouth and grabbed her hand before continuing on about his gift.

"It's a perfect gift. But, rest assured, I'll never need a compass to find my way back to you," he said, staring deeply into her eyes. It was the first time she'd ever noticed the look that Georgia was always talking about. She looked over at her as she raised her brow as if to say, "I told you so." As a nervous Alana tried to say something, anything that would slow her racing heart, Simeon suddenly grabbed her hand and pulled her to the center of the room.

"Come on, partner! You haven't danced with me all night!" he demanded. Marc Anthony's "Nadie Como Ella" played as they danced, with moves so hot they could have burned up the floor boards.

The crowd cheered them on like they were superstars that no one could get enough of, but Alex had certainly had his fill. He could feel the anger boiling on the inside of him, rising like the steam in a pressure cooker, as restaurant employees rooted them on like they were a dynamic duo. Natalie and Gigi could both see the envy in his eyes. But as they both tried to make their way over to him through the crowded room, each with a different purpose, Natalie beat her to the punch. She put her hand on his shoulder and patted his back, as if she was comforting him.

"Well, it looks like she has more than one name on her dance card, sweetheart. You sure you don't want to take me up on that offer? What do you say, just a quick spin?"

"Why don't you just wait for them to finish so you can take your turn with him? Trust me. If you're going to be seeing Simeon, you better get used to doing just that. But don't worry. From what I hear, it'll still be a quick spin!"

"Aww, now don't be salty, sugar! Save that seasoning for your cooking. But speaking of sugar, you may have to wait your turn for yours, as well. From what Simeon tells me, he never has to borrow a cup from the neighbors whenever Alana is around."

"What?! He's a liar!"

"Don't be so sure, darling. Everyone doesn't kiss and tell. You don't!" she said, referring to the fact that she'd stunned him outside by kissing him out of the blue. Although he pulled away, his lips lingered a lot longer than they should have. She winked at him and walked away as his eyes darted back toward the dance floor.

It wasn't long before Gigi stood at his side, having finally made her way through the crowd. She grabbed his arm and squeezed it, trying to grab his attention. But she couldn't hold it for long. The champagne, wine and whiskey had flowed a little too freely by this point of the party. Everyone had had a little too much to drink, which didn't seem to be mixing well with the hidden drama that was brewing underneath the surface. Simeon had apparently been bitten by the same bug as Natalie because, the moment his eyes caught a glimpse of Alex and Gigi watching them from the sidelines, he turned it up a notch. Alana thought he was showing off for the crowd, but little did she know he was deliberately antagonizing his newfound foe.

It wasn't until she was damn near spun off of the dance floor that she noticed the expression on Alex's face and the manner in which he and Gigi were speaking to each other. It dawned on her that some of Simeon's passionate pelvic rolls may have gone too far.

"Your boy is a little touchy feely, ain't he?" Alex asked Gigi.

"I'm sorry. I don't know what's gotten into him tonight."

"Tonight or *every* night?"

"Come on, Alex. He's not doing it on purpose. He doesn't even know about you two."

"You sure about that, G? He knows you two inside and out. What makes you think he doesn't even have an inkling of what's going on?"

"Because he would have said something."

"Oh, trust me, gorgeous. He's saying plenty! Are you looking at the same show that I am? And I don't just mean today. He always puts on a little extra showmanship when I'm around."

"That's just how he is. He's…extra!"

"Look, you'd have to be a man to understand. I'm trying to be adult about this. I don't want to put our relationship on blast and jeopardize either one of our reputations. But he's pushing it. He's pushing me!"

"Well, look. He's about to leave. You two are about to make it official—"

"Wait a minute. Don't tell me we've been waiting for him to leave so we can tell people about us?"

"Well, from what I can tell, you've been telling people plenty! And why does she have to tell the whole world in order for you to know that she loves you?"

"Wait, what? She loves me?" he asked excitedly.

Alana tried her best to gauge whether or not things were calming down between them, but her dance partner was too busy acting out of sorts. The small efforts she made to reel him in a bit failed, as he held her hand above her head and twirled her around on the ball of her foot, like it was second nature. After numerous spins, he stopped her and pulled her close before dipping her back and leaving her draped over his arm. As her hair hung toward the floor, he traced his finger down her chin and neck, onto her chest, mimicking a sexy dance move he'd seen in a competition once. He whipped her back up to conclude their number. But before she knew it, he planted a kiss on her lips.

She didn't even have time to respond as he spun her out so they could take a final bow. She felt nervous and embarrassed as she struggled to keep a smile on her face for the unsuspecting crowd. People clapped and cheered. But as she turned to look at Simeon, her eyes were drained of joy and soon filled with horror as she looked behind him and saw a raging Alex charging toward them. The panicked look on her face caused Simeon to turn around concerned. But before he had time to react, his jaw was met by Alex's fist.

Chapter | 27

Alana gasped, unable to believe what Alex had just done. She couldn't be sure if it was Simeon's sultry salsa, or the unforeseen kiss that did it. Maybe it was both, but Alex had obviously taken more than he could bear. Guests watched in horror as the two men tussled and rolled across the floor, matching each other's punches blow for blow. Members of the staff struggled to tear them apart as neither was willing to concede. For two men claiming to be so vastly different, they certainly were acting quite similar. They were both behaving like little boys fighting over a toy. Chaos and disbelief spread throughout the room as Diego ordered security to escort them both into the kitchen so he could put a stop to the madness.

A couple of the busboys tried to make their way into the kitchen as well so they could get the scoop. But Diego ordered them away, telling security to block the door and only let in the people that Alana gave the okay for. The members of their close-knit crew: Alana, Alex, Simeon, Diego, Carla, Gigi, Brian, Jirou and Shawny all stood around the kitchen. Although she wasn't a part of their circle, Natalie somehow made her way in with the bunch and rushed over to Simeon's side, practically moving Gigi and Brian out of the way. Brian had to grab her arm and reel her in before she could tell her about herself. Carla and Diego calmed Alex as both men nursed their bloody noses and busted up knuckles. Simeon looked at his torn shirt with frustration while Alex glared at him, like there was no one else in the room.

Back at the party, Elizabeth and Damien could be heard on the microphone, doing damage control. They explained to the guests that the fight was a result of a bad mixture of a kitchen rivalry and an open bar. They urged everyone to continue enjoying the party, but even they were curious as to what they'd just swept under the rug. The guests, who were mostly drunk themselves, laughed it off and continued partying. Employees, however, speculated whether it all stemmed from the situation with Natalie. Back in the kitchen, Gigi grabbed a towel and filled it with ice before handing it to Simeon and looking him over. He thanked her as Jirou moved Natalie to the side and began to inspect the cut over his eye where Alex had sucker-punched him.

"You're definitely going to need stitches," he said.

"I'll go get the car," Shawny offered before exiting in a panic.

"Alex, are you crazy?!" Natalie yelled. "Look, I know this thing with me and Simeon is uncomfortable for you, but—"

"Natalie, please shut the hell up! I hope to God you don't think this has anything to do with your messy ass!" he sniped.

"Messy?! Oh, me hanging out with somebody is me trying to be *messy*?"

"Bitch, please!" Gigi snapped. "You know good and damn well you're using Simeon to get back at Alex."

"Well, if this isn't about Natalie, then what the hell is it about, you lunatic?! You know what? It doesn't even matter. Alana, I want his ass out!" Simeon snapped.

"That won't be happening any time soon, bruh," Alex barked back.

"Oh, don't be so sure, slick!"

"You two knock it off!" Alana said as she walked over to Simeon. Her blood boiled like a witch's cauldron. But even as furious as she was with Simeon for kissing her in front of everyone, he was still her friend. Besides, she couldn't help but wonder if her tendency to "dip back into the pot" was the cause of his behavior. She grabbed his chin and tilted his head upward, trying to determine just how deep the cut was, which only added fuel to the fire. Her concern for his well-being only infuriated Alex more. He jumped off the counter and pulled away from Carla and Diego, who were trying to hold him back. He slammed the bag of ice that he'd been handed and began confronting his exasperated lover in front of everyone, while pacing like a mad dog.

"I see you went to check on your boy first!" he sniped.

"You're damn right, I did! Especially since he isn't the asshole who threw the first punch!"

"Oh, I'm the asshole? 'Mr. Grab Ass' is okay to do whatever he likes, but I'm the asshole?"

"Look, I'm sorry about the kiss, which we will definitely discuss later!" she snapped, scowling at Simeon.

"Why are you explaining yourself to him?" Simeon barked.

"And, for the record, he did not grab my ass, Alex. We were dancing. Like we always do, like we've always done, since way before you even came into the picture."

"Listen to what you said, Alana. That was before. This is now!" Alex griped.

"Why do you care about what I am or am not doing with her ass anyway? Why do you care about what I do or don't do with Natalie? Why is any of it your business?" Simeon asked.

"Exactly!" Natalie added. "You're mad about that little kiss they had out there? We're all adults here, Alex, and sometimes people get caught up in the moment. I mean, we just had a moment outside—"

"Wait, you kissed her?!" Alana snapped.

"Hell no! She kissed me!"

"You kissed him?!" Simeon exclaimed.

"Why do you care who she kisses? You two are just friends, right?" Alana fired off.

"He cares because he's been fucking me, just like you've been fucking Alex!" Natalie informed everyone.

"Oh, it's much more than that, sweetheart! I'm in love with her," Alex announced.

"What!" seemed to be the most appropriate reaction as Simeon, Jirou and Brian all yelled in unison, turning to focus on Alana. The room became deafly quiet as they stared at her in disbelief, waiting for an answer. Eyes darted back and forth, from face to face, as everyone searched for what to say and whom to say it to. Simeon could tell by the looks on both Diego's and Gigi's face that the news of them dating was no surprise to them. Suddenly, he felt a level of betrayal that he couldn't even begin to verbalize.

His big plan to reveal his true feelings to her right after the party had just gone out the window. As Carla whispered to Diego that the events of the evening were turning out to be better than any of the telenovelas she'd watched, Shawny pulled the car up to the back service entrance and honked for the guys to come out. Simeon looked wounded as he slowly slid off the counter. He dropped the towel of ice and looked at her in a way that Alana had never seen before. In that moment, she had no idea what he was thinking. She only wanted to salvage the broken pieces of their friendship that now lay scattered across the kitchen floor.

Jirou stood by the door, beckoning for his brother to follow him. But he was temporarily paralyzed by his anger. Natalie decided to excuse herself and return to the party, but it wasn't long before she grabbed her coat to call it a night. Apparently, she was overwhelmed by the drama that her own confessions created. That, and the dirty looks she kept receiving. Everyone else remained stewing while Alex stood there, waiting for Alana to finally confess her feelings for him to Simeon. But if he thought glaring at her would give her the nudge she needed, he was about to be disappointed. As the Paris-bound pretty boy stood frozen in time, she went to him, hoping to console him. But when she rubbed his arm, he snatched away and stood with his back to her.

"So how long has this been going on? You know what? Never mind. I don't wanna know. How could you?" he asked.

"Look, Simeon. I know what I said in the past about getting involved with employees, but—"

"You think I care about those lectures of yours? But since we're on the subject of sleeping with the help, isn't it kinda like you're paying for sex?" Simeon asked spitefully.

"Simeon! Man, come on. You don't have to talk to Alana that way," Diego said.

"It's cool, D. For all we know, he might be well-versed on the topic. As much as he services women, he'd be a fool not to be getting paid for it!" Alana shouted.

"All I'm saying is that maybe you would have figured out how I felt for you if you weren't giving undocumented overtime to the sous chef!" Simeon barked viciously.

"Come on, y'all. Let's not do this now," Gigi suggested.

"No, let's do it!" Alana shouted. "When was I supposed to 'figure out' that you feel something for me? You never said—"

"I didn't think I had to!" he snapped. "Are you dense? I have dropped enough hints over the years to make a damn hiking trail for you!"

"Dense? Okay, park ranger, and which hiking trail of hints was I supposed to follow exactly? The trail of used condom wrappers leading to your doorstep, or the trail of broken hearts I have to step over any time I want to ring your damn doorbell?!"

"Fuck you!" he responded.

"No, fuck you!" she hurled back.

"Okay guys, we're getting way off base here. There's no need to be cruel to one another. We all care about each other. We're family!" Gigi reminded them.

"Wow! Look at that. Someone who actually cares about the way I feel. I guess G's not only a better kisser than you, but a better friend as well!"

Again, "What!" rang out like a choir in perfect harmony as everyone in the room reacted to the news. Simeon and Gigi, kissing? No one could believe what they'd just heard. Jirou closed the door he'd been holding open and sat on a stool close by, as if his legs would no longer hold him up. His mouth fell open, as did everyone else's, as they wondered how they managed to keep such a huge secret from everyone. Alana was both shocked and confused. One thing that she and Gigi never did was ever get involved with a guy that had prior dealings with the other. So, she wondered when it happened and why. But, of all the reactions in the room, Brian's was the one that concerned Gigi most. He looked at her with anger and disbelief before turning his sights to Simeon.

Gigi begged for him to let her explain what happened, but he was unable to control his rage as he hurtled toward Simeon in hopes of knocking his lights out. Had it not been for Diego and his unlikely savior, Alex, holding him back, the two friends would have surely gotten into the second brawl of the night. Brian broke loose from both men and stormed out of the door before Gigi could clear things up. The weight of what he'd just done came crashing down on Simeon, with Gigi's hand in tow. She slapped him as hard as she could, leaving a sting on her palm and his cheek. It felt like he'd been attacked by a swarm of bees, but he knew he deserved it. Blood trickled down his face from the cut above his eye, while he tried to apologize to his very unreceptive friend.

"G, I'm so sorry. I don't know why I said that. You're one of my best friends and I would never want to hurt—"

"Don't say another word to me, Simeon!" she said as she backed away from him slowly. "The sound of your voice…the sound of your voice makes me sick!"

A tear rolled down her cheek before she turned to Alana, assuring her that things were not what they seemed. One look into her best friend's panic-filled, hazel eyes let Alana know all that she needed to. She hugged her and told her to go get her man so they could straighten things out, and not to worry about what was said. Jirou patted his brother on the back and told him they needed to go get his cut looked at. As he ushered him out of the door, things were left unresolved at every angle. Diego and Carla went back out into the party so that Alana and Alex could have some privacy. They even managed to plaster on fake smiles in hopes of creating the illusion that everything was okay. But it was far from it.

Everyone went their separate ways and, for the first time all night, Alex and Alana were alone. She stood across from him, not knowing what to address first: his vicious attack on Simeon, the kiss he shared with Natalie, or his admission that he was in love with her being said in front of everyone for the first time. She felt such a wide range of emotions that her head began to spin. Anger, confusion, embarrassment and shock all coursed through her veins at once. Alex unclenched his fist and hoped that his now calm demeanor would cause her to follow suit.

"Baby, I didn't want that to be the way you first heard me say that I love you, but—"

"That's what you're leading with? What's wrong with you? My reputation, my friendships, all put on the line because you want to have a fuckin' temper tantrum?!"

"Excuse me? Listen, don't speak to me like I'm a child—"

"Then don't act like one!"

Even with all the beauty surrounding them at the party, things took an ugly turn. Insults flew back and forth, like a ball in a tennis match, as Alana continued on with accusations of Alex being a spoiled brat, whose outlook on life had been tainted by his family always giving him what he wanted, when he wanted since he was the youngest in the family. Adding insult to injury, she assured him that he was certainly living up to his role as the baby with his toddler-like outbursts, which only pushed him to become equally unkind.

In his scathing rebuttal, he let her know that maybe the real reason she hadn't found love yet was because the absence of a "real" family in her life caused her to believe she didn't need to make one of her own. The comment burned like the tequila shots flowing on the other side of the door, but she didn't dare show it. Instead, a smug smile spread across her face as she opted to remind him of some things.

"I have a family, whether you choose to recognize them as that or not."

"Some family! A lewd lawyer, a feisty fashionista, a shyster chef, and you, a blind businesswoman! Sounds like a nursery rhyme to me!"

"Wow, the name calling just keeps coming around here. First dense, now blind. And what is it you think I'm blind to?"

"The fact that I'm standing here trying to tell you that I love you just as much as they do, if not more! I don't want to take anyone or anything from you, for that matter. I'm trying to *give* you everything that I have. But you won't let me!"

"Says the person who kissed his ex-fiancé an hour ago!"

"Don't do that. Don't find an excuse to push me away! If you don't love me, then fine. But I didn't ask her to kiss me any more than you asked Simeon. Just decide, Alana. Decide if I'm worth loving or not because I'm not going to do *this* anymore."

Alex exited the kitchen with an unbelievable amount of frustration flowing through him. Elizabeth and Damien caught him before he reached the door and grilled him about what happened. He played it cool and told them that their explanation to the crowd wasn't far off base, that his drinking and Simeon's constant hazing over the weeks had collided, which led to the explosive scene. He apologized to them and asked them to pass it along to everyone else as he excused himself for the evening. Alana peeked out of the door just in time to see him leaving. She grabbed a bottle of champagne from the refrigerator and poured herself a glass. But before she could drink it, sadness overtook her, and she began to weep.

Simeon sat on the gurney calmly as his brother looked over the shoulder of the doctor putting in his stitches. Jirou shook his head at his big brother, who was distracting himself from the pain by flirting with the pretty practitioner. She giggled at him as he joked about her duty to make sure he stayed handsome. She concentrated on the task at hand and, once she was done and he seemed satisfied with the results, she happily programmed her phone number into his cell phone upon his request. After she closed the curtain, the façade he was putting on quickly faded. He sat staring at the picture on his screen: a picture of him, Alana and Gigi at Mardi Gras, and his anger returned.

"I can't believe her!" he snapped. But his pity party was soon interrupted by an irritated Jirou, who seemed to be more shocked at his brother's behavior rather than the source of his anger. He turned his back to him and took a deep breath, after which he asked Shawny to give them a moment alone. Simeon looked confused and wondered what could possibly be so important that he couldn't say it in front of his girlfriend, whom he was virtually inseparable from. Jirou faced his brother, took off his glasses, and squeezed the bridge of his nose in between his eyes in an attempt to relieve pressure. He seemed somewhere in between astounded and appalled.

"It's funny. You can't believe her, and I can't believe *you*!" he said. "When did you become this person? This selfish—"

"Selfish?! Me?!"

"Yeah, you! You just dogged out your best friend for no good reason, and you may have ruined the other one's engagement. And you're sitting here flirting with the nurse?"

"I had good reason. She betrayed me!"

"How, Simeon? You two aren't a couple, and you never told her that you were in love with her. She's a single woman that got involved with a single man. Period!"

"Look, little brother. You don't know what you're—"

"I know exactly what I'm talking about." Jirou quickly calmed himself and sat down next to his brother on the gurney. He closed his eyes, took a deep breath and decided that perhaps it was time for the little brother to give the big brother a good talking to.

"Remember when you first decided to be a chef?" he asked him.

"Of course. I've never seen dad so pissed!" he chuckled.

"He *was* pissed because he wanted you to get a degree in business and finance. But you went after what *you* wanted."

"Yeah, so?"

"And do you remember when you wanted to have your own line of spices in grocery stores? But initially, dad didn't think it would sell well enough?"

"Yeah, and?"

"And you went after your dream anyway. First local, then statewide. And not only did sales exceed your own expectations, but dad was so proud that he started to back you."

"What's your point?" he snapped.

"My point is when you want something, when you *really* want something, big brother, nothing stops you from going after it. How many years have I been telling you to tell Alana how you feel? Why didn't you ever really go after her, if that's who you wanted?"

Simeon stared at his hands, unable to answer the question. He searched for the words. He searched for a reason that made sense, but he found nothing. Soon, his younger, wiser brother offered his own explanation.

"Maybe it's because deep down inside, you knew it would never work. She's afraid of being vulnerable, and you're afraid of commitment."

"That is not true!"

"Simeon, you want to be the only man in Alana's life. But you want all the other women, too. You can't even get stitches without offering a side of dick to go with it."

Simeon laughed, but he understood the point his brother was making. Although he loved Alana, the man that he had once been in his youth, the one that may have been able to be with her and only her, had changed. He wanted to believe that she could be the one to make him settle down. But truthfully, he wasn't sure. And the idea that they could be a power couple was overshadowing that fact. Jirou insisted that either he figure out whether or not he was capable of being in a real relationship, or let Alana move on with the man who'd just confessed his love for her in front of all of her closest friends. Simeon's stubborn personality, and slightly swollen eye, wouldn't allow him to acknowledge any future that had to do with Alex. He grabbed his jacket so his brother could take him home.

During the ride, he thought of Alana, as he often did. But now, she was accompanied by visions of Alex. He thought of him kissing her, touching her, making love to her. And despite his brother's words, it made him more mad than a wild dog. A feeling of guilt also swirled in his mind as he thought of what he'd done to Gigi. She'd been a great friend to him over the years, and he'd thrown her under the bus for no apparent reason other than...Jirou was right: *selfishness*! They arrived at his place and he thanked both Jirou and Shawny for all they had done for him.

As he rode the elevator to his floor, he felt a stinging in his eyes and a burning in his nose. But he would never allow himself to cry. He entered his place and poured himself a tall glass of scotch, hoping to drown out all of the feelings he couldn't shake. But instead of downing it, he sent it flying into a wall. He didn't want to drink. He didn't want to talk. He only wanted to be alone.

Chapter | 28

With all of the drama now surrounding the group—Gigi not speaking to Simeon, Simeon not speaking to Alana, and Alana not speaking to Alex—the girls decided to do brunch and take a full on "daycation" with no interruptions. They endured the long wait with the bubbling church crowd at Favored Flavors, which was well known for its Sunday morning spread. They couldn't wait to fill themselves with savory crepes, warm croissants and sweet cappuccinos. The girls were seated in the middle of the room, surrounded by ladies in beautiful dresses, elegant church hats, and gentlemen in three-piece suits. Gigi brought her bestie up to speed about the kiss she and Simeon shared long ago.

She explained that it was purely a mistake in identity and that he had only kissed her because he believed she was Alana. Although the revelation made Alana feel some relief, she was furious that Simeon would try to create discord amongst them by implying that there was more. They grabbed hands and smiled at each other, reaffirming what they already knew: that nothing could come in between them. Rather than harp on it, they moved on to the crazy men in their lives.

"So that was quite the show last night."

"The dance or the fight?"

"Take your pick. Your bulls certainly were bucking, honey!"

"Speaking of bucking, how's Brian? I thought he was going to kick Simeon's teeth in."

"Well, by the time I ran out after him, he was in the car angrier than any bull I've ever seen."

"He had every right to be. Did he let you explain?"

"Once we got to his place and he calmed down, he let me clarify a bit," she said with a smile.

"So, you two made up then?" Alana asked, pumping her eyebrows up and down.

"We made up. We made out. We made nice, and we made *naughty*!"

Alana listened with ears wide open as Gigi gave a lesson on "Making Up: 101." After she got to Brian in the parking lot, he was sitting in the car, slouching with his hands on his forehead, as if he was in deep thought. His frowning brows met in the middle of his forehead and his jaw was clenched in anger. He didn't say a word as Gigi climbed into the passenger seat slowly and pleaded with him to let her explain. He put his hand up, urging her to be quiet while he calmed down. But she didn't want to run the risk of letting his mind fester.

She took the keys out of the ignition and grabbed his hand. The words flew out of her mouth faster than she could form them as she told him what *really* happened that night. Brian listened to his sweetheart and slowly, but surely, his face became more and more relaxed. When she'd finally finished, he still didn't utter a word as he reached across her and fastened her seatbelt. He took the keys back from her and sped out of the parking lot before turning up the radio. Gigi grabbed his hand and leaned her head onto his shoulder while wiping a tear from her cheek. He kissed her forehead and told her that they were okay. But once they were home, the real making up began.

Once they were through the door, Gigi followed Brian up the stairs to his bedroom. He removed his jacket and cufflinks. But before he could continue undressing, she grabbed his hands and placed them on the straps of her dress. She unbuttoned his shirt and pants, undressing him gently as he followed suit by slowly sliding off her dress and thong. The dim light of the bedside lamp illuminated their naked bodies as they stood at the foot of the bed, holding and kissing each other. He pushed back her thick, black curls and let his hands rest there as if he was framing her face. He looked over her dark chocolate skin and golden brown eyes, which made him give in instantly.

He picked her up and sat down on the bed, with her legs wrapped tightly around him. He quickly found himself in the warmth of her walls as he closed his eyes and allowed her warm, moist flesh to receive him with ease. Gigi sucked on his neck while riding him slowly as their fingers clasped together. Again, they kissed passionately, driving them both wild in their desire for each other. He grabbed her waist and rolled her over onto the bed. She turned to lay on her stomach and grabbed the sheets, as if she was holding on for dear life as Brian sat on the backs of her thighs and enjoyed her from behind. They made love for over an hour, all while whispering words of love, forgiveness and assurance to each other before falling asleep.

Dawn crept up quickly and Gigi barely escaped his grasp to make her spontaneous breakfast date with Alana. As she concluded her recap, she decided to add a little pizazz to her story by picking up a butter knife and sliding it in and out of her croissant, as if Alana hadn't already gotten the gist of her night! She laughed at her as she flipped over the soft, flaky pastry and spanked the back of it, splashing the butter that was melting on top. The couple at the table next to them got an unexpected side of playful, pastry porn with their breakfast as they glanced over and caught Gigi's raunchy reenactment. Her dirty faces and "happy ending," which consisted of melted butter being splattered onto the plate and table, were enough to cause the gentleman to drop his fork, followed by his wife's gasp. The girls straightened up their act and, as Gigi leaned over to apologize to the older couple, they surprised her with a revelation of their own.

"I'm so sorry about that. I hope I didn't offend," she said.

"Young lady, please! The husband and I have had our share of…*melted butter* over the years."

The gentleman grabbed his wife's hand and winked at her before the four of them shared in a good laugh. They finished their breakfast and said goodbye to their dining companions before taking another trip to Coveted, their favorite spa, in hopes of gaining some relaxation and continuing their gossip. Stepping into the luxurious health resort was like stepping out of winter into a brick-bound tropical island. Looking around, one would never know that sleet, slush and snow were on the other side of the door. A lovely young attendant escorted them to their lockers so they could exchange their clothes for terrycloth robes and slippers before being fully submerged into paradise.

Playing throughout the hallways was the sound of Reiki positive energy music to help calm the senses. When they reached their private room, side-by-side massage tables awaited them. The girls were all too eager to lie face-down and let the masseuses work some shiatsu magic on them. Their thirty-minute journey into heaven was only ruined by the fact that it had to end. They wrapped the comfortable robes around their bodies once more so they could retire poolside. Once they received their freshly made pink squirrel cocktails, they got down to the nitty gritty of the juicy drama.

"Simeon's really pissed at me. He hasn't texted. He hasn't called, and he's not answering any of mine," Alana griped.

"Oh, who cares! I'm pissed at him! I still can't believe he would do that to me, and in front of Brian. And anyways, this is his own fault. If he would have just told you like I told him to—"

"Wait, what?"

"Oh, shit! Why do I always have to open my big mouth?" Gigi asked, breaking her vow not to reveal any more secrets.

"Oh, shit is right! You told me there wasn't anything else I needed to know other than me being his first. Why didn't *you* tell me?"

"You know why. You two need to talk to each other more instead of always talking to me."

"You're right. He's right, too. Maybe all of this is my fault. The hints were obviously there—"

"Hints? He got to you with that crap? Please! He can't be mad at you for not being a detective. Who are you, Columbo?" Gigi asked.

"No, but you know. Us kissing, us sleeping together, we've-"

"Alana, expecting you to know how he felt because you two slept together in college is ridiculous!"

"Well…the last time may have been a little more recent than college."

"Wait, what?!" Gigi asked, sitting up on her lounger. "How recent are we talking?"

"Um…well…if I just had to guess…"

"Oh, let's not pretend you don't know, tramp," Gigi joked.

"About a year ago."

"What!" Gigi screamed, disturbing the other clients. A young woman walked over and asked her to keep it down, triggering her apologize to strangers for the second time since breakfast. She demanded that the truth be told and that no detail was left out. It had been kept secret long enough, and Alana was ready to tell her *exactly* what happened the year before when she, Simeon and Gigi had gone to Mardi Gras. After grappling with whether or not she wanted to break up with Lewis, a few nights of partying with her friends helped her decide to end things the moment they returned home. To show their support, and to celebrate since they didn't like him either, Gigi and Simeon took her out for an all-night pre-celebration to her freedom.

Midway through the night, Gigi was well beyond her limit. After throwing up in a trash can and passing out in a cab, they took her back to the hotel to rest peacefully in her "party coma" while they partied out the rest of the night. The twosome made their way back into the streets to hit as many bars as they could. One of them got the bright idea to play a joke on Gigi, so they made a spur of the moment trip to a sex shop. They walked through the aisles, checking out oils, dildos and outfits, which they thought would be funny to buy and place in Gigi's bed. However, when they got back to the room and began dressing her up in a slutty police officer's costume and throwing condoms everywhere, Simeon suggested that they save some of the "goodies" and find more interesting things to do with them in his room.

Good looks, alcohol and sex toys made an all-too tempting concoction, breaking any barriers that stood between them. From the girls' room to his, they kissed madly and clawed at each other's clothes, before bursting through the door of his suite. They gave into their inhibitions and enjoyed a night of wild pleasures. But once the sun was up, so were Alana's defenses. She had snuck back to her room, leaving Simeon to awake to an empty bed. When he finally showed up to their room with breakfast, she hoped he wouldn't make a big deal about what happened. But she could tell by the stars in his eyes that his mind was somewhere else. How could she start anything with him, or anyone else for that matter, when she still had to break the news to Lewis that it was over? She had no interest in spring boarding into a new relationship right away. Once Gigi went into the bathroom to shower, she told Simeon that their night, although magical, should remain just that: a night.

"Well, maybe you two *are* made for each other after all, since you both are just the perfect examples of honesty," Gigi said sarcastically.

"I'm sorry I didn't tell you. I guess. I just figured it wasn't important."

"Ouch, Alana! Not important? Look, I know you're not going to want to hear this. Although I'm in no mood to defend him, I think you owe Simeon an apology."

"An apology? For what exactly?"

"For taking him out of your toy chest whenever you want to play, but then throwing him back in once you've gotten all of the fun out of him."

"Are you saying I've been using Simeon?" Alana chuckled.

"Haven't you? Aren't you doing to him what he does to his lady friends? Unless—"

"Unless what?"

"Unless that's what you're intending to do. Maybe you have feelings for him, too, and these little 'play dates' are a way for you to hold on to him until you're ready to stop playing."

"I think you better put down your drink because you're obviously buzzing. That's crazy!"

"Is it? Then why on earth would you make your best friend your dildo? How could you possibly believe that as close as you two are and with your history, that he wouldn't have the capacity to feel something for you?"

Alana tried her best to defend her actions. She reminded Gigi of the incident in college, when she had gone to confess her feelings to Simeon, feelings that he didn't seem to know or care about, despite their closeness. His obliviousness to her desire to be with him was no different than hers. But her point quickly backfired when Gigi told her Simeon's side of the story. Had it not been for a misunderstanding from her eavesdropping, she would have found out that their feelings had, in fact, been parallel to one another. Apparently, sex and secrets were running and ruining their relationship. But was her relationship with Alex starting out the exact same way?

The girls spent most of their time talking about their buddy. But what about the man that had just declared his love for her in front of their circle? Why weren't they discussing his feelings?

"So, you seem to be very opinionated when it comes to Simeon. What am I supposed to do about Alex?"

"Well that, my friend, is fairly simple. Now that you know how he feels, you gotta figure out if you feel the same. If you don't, you gotta be fair to him. You gotta let him go."

Her advice was sound and spot on. Alana didn't want anyone to think she was selfish or cold because that certainly wasn't who she was. She wanted to get things back on track in her life. So, she figured the first thing she needed to do, if she wanted the atmosphere at work to go back to normal, was to make peace with her partner. Since he wasn't responding to her, she asked Gigi to step in and arrange a meeting between the two. He responded to her text, immediately followed by a very long, detailed apology. Knowing that he owed her, he agreed to meet with Alana later that evening to hopefully put an end to the animosity caused by the awful things they'd said to each other. The ladies laid back on their loungers and enjoyed the rest of their spa day. But inside, Alana was nervous about her meetup with Simeon and unsure of what to say to Alex.

Later that night, Alana paced back and forth nervously in front of the island in her kitchen. It was 10:30 p.m. and Simeon was two hours late, which wasn't like him. Neither she nor Gigi had heard from him and she was beginning to worry. While she waited, Alex had texted her multiple times, trying to get answers of his own. But her anxiety was mounting. She knew she needed to speak to him, but she certainly didn't want to do it while she was in a state of panic.

Worried about Simeon, she patted her palm with her cell phone over and over, like a teacher with a ruler, as various scenarios played in her mind. Had he been in an accident? Was he not ready to talk? Or was he standing her up out of bitterness? She waited another thirty minutes before pouring herself a glass of wine and calling it a night, when she received a call from Gigi. She made Alana promise not to explode before telling her that not only was he okay, but that he'd just posted a picture of himself on Facebook at one of his favorite after-hour spots. Since he hardly ever posted anything on social media that didn't pertain to his cooking, the girls knew he was doing it just to be an asshole.

Alana assured Gigi that she was fine, that she would be the bigger person and let things go. But the moment they hung up, she headed out of the door to where he was, determined to have it out with him. It was almost midnight when she pulled up to The Blue Room. It got its name because of the lights running throughout the inside, which gave the illusion of a blue glow on the skin, making its patrons look like extras in the movie *Avatar*. She looked around as best as she could in the dim, shadowy light, but didn't see him. She only saw the glow of strangers' eyes looking back at her. She walked over to the bar, which was slightly better lit, in hopes that the bartender would know him since Simeon was a regular.

When she inquired about him, the barkeeper, who was wiping down glasses, looked at her suspiciously and said that he knew him, but hadn't seen him. She got the feeling that maybe he thought she was some obsessed ex-girlfriend, so she decided to leave word for him.

"If you happen to see him tonight, please tell him Alana is looking for him."

"Wait, you're Alana?" he asked, surprised.

"Yeah. How do you know me?"

"You've been the topic of a few drunken discussions. I see why the poor guy is so flustered. I'm Tate, by the way," he added, shaking her hand.

"It's nice to meet you, Tate. Well, if you see him…"

"He's in the VIP room in the basement. I'll let security know you're coming. But I feel like I should warn you. He's not alone."

He pointed her to a door in the back hall just past the restrooms. Once she reached it, the bouncer stepped aside and opened it, revealing a black metal staircase leading down to the VIP room. The recessed ceiling lights changed the color of her skin from blue to yellow, and back to blue again, with every few steps she took. A nervous feeling formed in the pit of her stomach as it hit her that she had no idea what she was going to say to him once she got down there. Once she reached the bottom, she looked down the small, dark hallway, which had a huge metal door with music pounding on the other side of it. She could hear "Chains" by Nick Jonas playing as she approached.

She opened the door and, as the rush of loud music flooded her eardrums, she immediately scanned the room. There were about sixteen tables surrounding the glass stage with blue neon lights underneath. The light illuminated the skin of the gorgeous young woman who danced erotically on it. Alana's eyes squinted as she tried to make out the faces at each table. She looked at the small bar that sat in the back corner of the room, but he was not there.

Her eyes went from table to table, until she finally realized he was sitting at the table directly across the stage from her. His date was kissing on his neck and licking on his earlobe as the dancer performed in front of him. The look on his face was empty, as if his mind was somewhere else. Alana went from being angry to feeling guilty. She knew she was the source of his pain. But still, he was treating her unfairly. Didn't he know she would never hurt him intentionally?

As the beautiful performer grabbed the blue fabric hanging from the ceiling and pulled herself into the air for an aerial performance, Simeon's eyes found Alana's. His looked changed from dead to cold, then to calculating in an instant. He smirked at her devilishly before grabbing his date's head and smashing her mouth into his. Alana returned the smirk with one of her own to convey to him just how little she cared about his display. Him lashing out at her with his distasteful behavior was bad enough. But she was just plain disappointed in him when she recognized who his date was. It was Lexa, the sales girl from Cloth! The girl that had been crazy about him for the past year! But rather than fight with him anymore, she turned and walked out of the door, realizing she had made a mistake by going there.

Simeon accidentally knocked over the bottles on his table as he scrambled to follow her. Lexa hadn't even gotten wind of what was happening as he closed the door behind him and caught up to Alana in the hallway. He grabbed her arm, whipping her around, only to find her cold eyes looking back at him as if he were dirt. His words poured onto her with a sort of sharpness, like he'd rather argue than talk.

"What's wrong? Don't like the show?" he asked.

"How could you do that?"

"What do you care?"

"I care because Lexa is a great girl who really, *really* likes you, and you're using her for what? Just to get back at me?!"

"You're checking me about *principles*? Aren't you currently mixing business with pleasure?"

"You know what? I actually came to here to say sorry to you. But since you're being such a little shit, I'm simply going to say goodnight!"

Alana rushed to her car as quickly as she could. She sat there for a moment, with only the falling snow to keep her company. She wanted so badly for the nightmare to be over. She wanted her friendship with Simeon to get back on track, for them to focus on his trip, for them to restore their partnership. She wanted her relationship with Alex to continue and for everyone else to mind their business. She wanted them to figure things out on their own, but she knew it couldn't go back to the way it is was. As the large flakes melted on her warm windshield, the only thing left for her to do was cry.

Chapter | 29

For days, not only did Alana avoid the restaurant, but Simeon did as well. He was one week away from leaving, and his original plan to work up until the weekend before his departure had changed. The culmination of the events—the disastrous end to his party, his friendships hanging on by a thread and now, the only woman he ever loved sleeping with the only person he couldn't stand—took a toll on him and he was feeling rather anti-social. He found it disheartening that he was days away from fulfilling one of his biggest dreams, while the other was slipping away. Anger and frustration seemed to be his reaction to everything and everyone, but to no one more than himself.

Since the party, he'd received numerous calls from family and friends, and quite a few invites from women trying to get their last dose of him before he left. But he was *uncharacteristically* uninterested. The only person he'd had any communication with was the assistant he hired at Gigi's urging. On Thursday morning, he was shocked to see Diego's name pop up on his caller ID since they hadn't spoken since he stormed out of the kitchen. When he answered, his voice was frantic. He told Simeon that he really needed him to come in.

Apparently, Alex needed to take a half day in order to tend to some urgent family business concerning his brother. The sound of his old friend's voice did him some good. He had even managed to make Simeon laugh. They kept it brief so he could pull himself out of bed, and get shaved and dressed. In addition to sulking, he hadn't shaved or showered in at least a day. So he needed a little bit of time to get up to his usual standards. He contemplated whether or not he should call Alana to let her know he'd be coming in. But he decided it would be better if he caught her off guard. History had shown him that if she didn't have a chance to think about what she was going to say to him, he would have a better chance of smooth talking her into forgiving him.

After properly grooming himself, he finally arrived at work and was pleasantly surprised at how normal everyone was acting. Everyone was delighted to see him. After all, it would be the last time they'd get to lay eyes on him in person for quite some time. But even with the kind greetings and the "We sure will miss you!" confessions, the joy amongst the staff could only be matched by their curiosity. Many of them were anxious to see how he would act toward Alex after their royal rumble. There were quite a few theories floating around the restaurant about what the fight was really over. Even more people had more than a few questions about how Alex still had a job, especially since he had in fact attacked one of his bosses. Luckily for Alana, who loved nothing more than her privacy, most of the speculation was only vaguely close to the truth. Only those within their tight-knit bunch were privy to what had really gone down, and none of them had any intentions of telling it.

Things were very quiet and, for all those banking on a dramatic return, they were soon shortchanged as Simeon went on like normal, as if the fight had never taken place. By all accounts, he appeared to have let bygones be bygones as he worked with Alex as usual. Alex was equally puzzled by his ridiculously calm conduct, but he, too, worked with his colleague like it was any other day. He did, however, keep his peripheral vision sharp in the event that he had a sucker punch coming back to him. As they all worked without so much as a glitch in the daily program, Diego thought the rest of the day might actually go on without incident. But, a little after 1 p.m., the unexpected happened.

As Alex prepared to leave, Alana walked through the back door. It seemed that fate would have the business partners return to work on the same day, creating the most awkward exchange in the history of The Cocoa Marra. Diego greeted her with his usual long, drawn out, "Good morning boss." Just hearing that made Alex's head pop up from his station. Everyone seemed a little surprised to see her, even more so because of her appearance. It was rare to see her dressed down during the work week. But there she was, effortlessly pulling off her laid-back look in a sweatshirt two sizes too big, jeans with rips over the knees, and a knit beanie cap.

Her arms hung stiffly by her sides, as if being rigid would protect her from the single-digit temperature. It was clear that she only planned to be there for a moment. But once she saw both men gawking at her, she wondered if she should stay at all. Alex wiped his hands off and rushed to her side to offer her coffee, while Simeon rushed to the opposite side to ask if she wanted something to eat. They both wanted so badly to talk to her right then and there, but they knew better than to bring their personal business around the staff yet again. She looked back and forth between them before giving a nervous, hurried response that let on to just how uncomfortable she was.

"Um, no thanks. I uh…okay…I mean, I'm okay…I mean, okay…um, bye."

She put her hand to her temple, obviously embarrassed by her feeble attempt to form a proper sentence. She swiftly walked through the kitchen and headed to the basement so she could grab an expensive bottle of wine from the cellar. The guys were left staring at each other, unsure of where her head was. Was it focused on her faltering friendship, or her "non-relationship" relationship? Alex looked at the clock and realized he needed to be rushing out of the door to tend to his business. As hard as it was for him to fight his urge to go after her, he knew he had to.

He made his way to his car and, once he was out of sight, Simeon didn't hesitate for a second to ask Diego to take over. If there was a perfect time to seize the opportunity to speak with her alone, it was at that moment. But before he could reach the door, Elizabeth let him know that there was someone asking for him at the bar. Frustration overtook him as he hoped against hope that he could get rid of his visitor before Alana had a chance to leave. But when he burst through the kitchen door and saw who it was, he prepared himself for the second most awkward exchange in The Cocoa Marra. His visitor was Lexa.

She smiled at the sight of him. Although Simeon didn't want to be unkind to her, he was in no mood to be bothered. After joining her, the raven-haired knockout took pleasure in talking about the good time they'd had and how thrilled she was that he finally asked her out. She proceeded on with her compliments, but soon put a stop to the flattery when she realized that his mind was elsewhere. He kept looking behind him into the kitchen window, hoping to catch Alana before she left. But the only thing he saw were the snapping fingers inches from his face.

"Hello! Earth to Simeon. Did you hear a word I just said?"

"What? Sorry, what's up?" he said nonchalantly.

"I said the other night was great! I was starting to think we'd never go out. Anyway, I found the perfect thing for us to do before you go—"

"Listen, Lexa. I don't have a lot of free time in the next few days."

"But you said you wanted to see me before you left. You said we had a connection."

"What? When?"

"When? When you were fingering me on your bed!"

"Look, we had a lot to drink that night—"

"No, *you* had a lot to drink that night!"

"Whatever! I was upset. My mind was clouded. I don't even remember saying that—"

"Well, you did!" she snapped loudly.

"Look, I'm sorry, okay. Lower your voice," he said, pulling her to the corner by the bar. "I wasn't myself that night. Had I been, I would have…"

"You would have what?"

"I would have told you the truth. That I was…that I was just using you to piss off Alana."

She stood in silence leering at him while all emotion drained from her face. She bit her bottom lip, as if it would keep the malicious words in her mind from coming out. Simeon's eyes were unapologetic about his honesty, but they did cast regret for making her an unwitting pawn in his game. He knew that whatever play she was about to make, he would just have to deal with it. "Wow! So, the rumors were true?! I guess I can't say no one warned me, huh? Huh?!" she yelled, causing a few customers to drop their forks. "I really liked you. I really thought you were special, and you used me like I'm nothing?!"

Not only had Lexa's voice gone up a few decibels, but her tiny clenched fists were pounding on his chest. Alana and Elizabeth emerged from the kitchen upon hearing the commotion. But it was Alana who immediately grabbed a hold of her, bear hugging her tightly from behind to restrain her from striking Simeon again. The fiery Latina tried to wiggle free, but Alana's hold was firm. As much as she understood Lexa's hurt, she still had a business to run and calming her down was now first priority.

She whispered in her ear that everything would be okay, which seemed to slow her breathing, but speed up the reddening of her cheeks. It finally hit Lexa that she'd made a complete spectacle of herself. She practically melted in Alana's arms when she asked her to come up to her place so they could speak in private. The ladies disappeared through the kitchen and out of the back door to spare her any further embarrassment, but not before Simeon received a look from his partner that let him know just how badly he'd messed up this time. She tried warning him at The Blue Room that the night meant much more to Lexa than he realized. But he was too wrapped up in his emotions to see it. He was now guilty of the same thing he'd accused Alana of: not caring about someone else's feelings. Simeon stood there mortified, as patrons tried not to stare at him.

He apologized to his "audience" before skulking off to the kitchen as fast as he could. Even the two waitresses, who would have normally got a kick out of seeing him humiliated, put their petty feelings aside to go check on him. He assured the ladies that he was fine and even managed to keep on a brave face as he worked throughout the rest of his miserable day. Orders came into the kitchen as quickly as the thoughts came into his mind, but he made keeping up with it all look easy. There was so much he needed to do before he left. He needed to make things right with Alana, Gigi and now, Lexa.

It was ironic to him: the same intensity women usually had when loving him was the same intensity they now had when loathing him. As night fell and the crowd got lighter and lighter, Diego took pity on him and told him to head home for some rest and relaxation. Simeon didn't dare turn him down the opportunity. He rushed out into the cold and sped off. He drove around in the slushy streets, thinking about what he should do. He wasn't sure where he was going. He only knew he didn't want to go home just yet.

He wanted to go where someone would know exactly how he was feeling, and there was only one person who did. The only problem was that he wasn't so sure he was welcome there. He went against his own judgment and headed over, not knowing whether or not the door would even be opened. Once he arrived, he took a deep breath and knocked on the front door. On the other side of it, he heard the sound of Bilal singing "When Will You Call" loudly throughout the house, before a pair of wild eyes suddenly peered at him through the glass. He stood there with his hands in his pockets, rocking on his heels and bracing himself for the initial reaction.

"Great! This is just what I need right now!" Alex said.

"Look, I'm not here to fight. I just wanna talk to you for a minute."

"How did you even know where I lived?"

"I asked Diego. I promised him and I promise you, it's for a good reason."

"I'll say this. You're brave coming here unannounced!" as he opened the door and walked away, leaving Simeon to enter cautiously.

Alex may not have been thrilled to see him, but he was grateful for the break from his own private hell. Every moment he spent thinking of Alana was like torture. He was fiending for her, like an addict going cold turkey. He used every distraction at his disposal to keep the phantom feeling of her hands on his spine from creeping back in. He wasn't sure what brought the cocky cook to his door, but Alex hoped it wasn't to push his buttons, seeing that he was already on the edge.

Simeon followed him into the kitchen, hoping Alex wouldn't double back and knock his lights out due to the look on his face. He took in the details of his warm, cozy bachelor home and nodded in approval at the layout. Alex went back to making himself a sandwich for dinner as Simeon leaned against the counter and tapped his leg nervously. He stopped once his overly observant eyes noticed a special sauce Alex had prepared and was beginning to spread onto his bread. It was a one-of-a-kind recipe that Alana had concocted one night in college when she was down to only three ingredients left in her fridge. The odd mix had turned out to be quite appetizing and was a delicious secret that she had only shared with Simeon and Gigi—until now.

"She's cooked for you I see."

"A few times I suppose," Alex answered, freezing mid-spread.

"She's good, right?"

"God, yes! I would have never imagined. The first time I tasted her cooking, I wondered why she didn't just become a chef and save herself some money."

"You haven't figured it out yet? She hates to cook! She just happens to be great at it. Funny, right?"

"Not as funny as her living above her own restaurant so that the majority of her meals can be prepared for her."

"That's not funny, either. That's just good old-fashioned laziness."

Both men chuckled lightly before the cold wind came through the cracked window over the sink, reminding them of their iciness toward each other. Simeon went back to observing his surroundings, scanning the kitchen, as he often did when he visited another chef's home. It was his secret way of judging whether or not they were on his level. In his opinion, if the items in his kitchen couldn't be found in theirs, then they weren't *real* chefs. Much to his surprise, Alex owned every single item!

Alex noticed his inspection. But instead of becoming defensive, he simply grinned and cut his eyes, realizing that Simeon couldn't be anything other than himself. It was the first time he understood how Alana had gotten used to certain behaviors from him. He realized that he, too, had actually gotten used to him. He opened the fridge and grabbed two beers, handing one to his unlikely guest. They both took long swigs. But after finishing first, Simeon took one look at Alex and saw that he was the only person more miserable than he was at the moment.

"Have you two spoken yet?" Simeon inquired.

"Not really. You?"

"I don't think you can count our shouting matches as speaking."

"At least she cares enough to yell at you. You know what I get? Silence."

"Maybe you're looking at it wrong. Perhaps her silence means she cares enough to think about what she says before she says it."

"Or maybe she doesn't care at all, and I should get a clue and start counting my losses."

"Or maybe you don't really care as much as you say you do if you're prepared to give up so easily."

"Look, Simeon. I'm sure you didn't come here to alter my perception of things. Why are you here, by the way?"

"I'm here because we need to hash some things out, man to man."

Alex was unsure of what to make of the situation. But he figured Simeon wouldn't have gone through all the trouble that he had unless he was prepared to handle things like grown men. Their bickering, their power struggle, even their mutual love for the same woman had all led up to this point. But as uneasy as he was feeling about their showdown, it failed to overshadow the indescribable emptiness he was feeling. He missed Alana. He had finally told her that he loved her and, not only had she responded coldly, but he was no longer sure where he stood with her relationship-wise. If she'd already decided she no longer wanted to see him, or that she didn't love him in return, was there really anything that needed to be hashed out? He needed answers. He needed to know if he no longer had a reason to vie for her affection. But it was evident Simeon didn't have those answers, and Alana wasn't ready to give them.

He finished his beer and tilted the end of the bottle toward the dining room so they could sit. His dinner was put on pause as he sat across from Simeon at the table, like they were in the middle of arbitration. It was time for them both to let some things off of their chests, which neither was having trouble with.

"Do you really love Alana? Because I do," Simeon declared.

"Obviously!"

"Is it obvious? Because two minutes ago, you were ready to "count your losses," right?"

"Do you really think I would be going through all of this if I didn't love that woman?"

"Who knows? According to my brother, selfishness is a reason, too."

He told Alex about the conversation that had taken place between him and Jirou, which led to the real reason for his visit—and it wasn't just to get his feelings off of his chest. In the process of pondering his brother's question about whether or not he truly loved Alana as deeply as he claimed to, it made him curious as to whether or not Alex's love for her was genuine. Sadly, the words coming from his mouth were of no consequence to Alex, who was struggling not to tell him to mind his own fucking business. He'd rather be talking to Alana, even in the midst of being angry with her. Simeon persisted with the grand overview of their history together in an attempt to be completely transparent. But, with every useless story about how he had come to love her, Alex thought of his own love story.

He thought of the very first time he kissed her lips and how he was aching to kiss them again. He thought of the first time he heard her voice over the phone and how sexy it sounded during their throes of passion. He thought of her eyes and how he could see himself through them any time he caught her gazing at him, and how much he wished they were staring at him from the other side of the table. It wasn't until Simeon finally hit a nerve that he actually began to pay attention to the conversation. Alex cracked his knuckles and gritted his teeth as he listened to Simeon tell him that, out of respect for him as a colleague, and in an effort to avoid the same drama they'd had over Natalie, he had come by to let him know that there were some things he needed to say to Alana, as well. He was going to say them before he left.

In his mind, it was only right for him to let Alex know so that there were no surprises or hard feelings if Alana decided to change her mind about which one of them she wanted. The unprepared host was stunned by his audacity, which he was trying to pass off as honesty. As ice pellets flew against the windows, he kept his cool by focusing on the small tapping sound they made every time the wind blew. Just moments before they left the kitchen, they were on the brink of actually joking with one another. Now Alex was struggling to keep his composure. His ability to remain levelheaded was strong enough to last throughout the remainder of the speech. But once Simeon was done, and assumed he could get up from the table and exit in all of his "boss-like" glory, he was sidelined by Alex's demand that he sit back down and listen to what he had to say in return. He walked over to the bottle of bourbon on his buffet and poured them both a shot, as Simeon turned around and aggressively snatched off his jacket and placed it on the back of the chair. The hit of whiskey was slammed down on the table in front of him as they prepared for part two of their awkward, unpleasant conversation.

Alex didn't hold back as he let him know just how shrewd he found him to be. Simeon cracked his neck and clenched his jaw after every cruel criticism, and it became painfully obvious that he wasn't expecting such brutal honesty to come flying back at him, even though he was owed as much. He realized in an instant that the moment his feet touched the doorstep, he had ceased to be his boss and he certainly wasn't his friend. He was his equal. And that meant taking everything he had to throw his way and not holding a grudge afterward.

"Let me break some things down for you that you obviously don't seem to be grasping! I felt a connection to Alana the moment I laid eyes on her face. The thought of her alone is enough to sustain me through an entire day. I do things for her that I've never even considered doing for anyone else. And when we make love, it's unlike anything I've ever experienced before. She has soul. My heart is hers. I love her! So, say whatever you want to her. It doesn't matter. We were made for each other."

The sound of the fire roaring from the other room was the only thing hotter than Simeon's temper. He didn't want to give Alex the satisfaction of knowing that he was actually starting to feel threatened by him. So, he pretended to laugh off what he'd said, but Alex could sense his insecurity and let out a little laugh of his own. The antique table held them apart as both men looked into the eyes of the other, unwilling to relent or admit how much alike they were. Simeon lifted his glass and gave a small nod to Alex before knocking back his drink.

"Bonne chance!" he sniped in his French accent before slamming the glass on the table.

"Yeah, good luck to you, too!"

Simeon snatched his jacket off the chair and exited before things got heated. As Alex drank his shot and headed to the kitchen to retrieve his dinner, he hoped that everything he said was in fact true. He hoped that Alana felt as he did. He hoped that she loved him, that she wouldn't give up on him, and that he wouldn't end up eating his words, like the sandwich that sat in front of him.

Chapter | 30

It was the night before Christmas Eve or, as Alana and her friends called it, "Eve's Eve," and sleep was evading her. As she lay in bed, staring at the red LED numbers that displayed 6 a.m. on her alarm clock, her stomach was already in knots from the immense amount of stress she'd been under. The days following Lexa's dramatic exit had been quite hard on her and rest was becoming more and more difficult to obtain, and not just because of the holidays. The men in her life were giving her the most grief. She put the drama out of her mind and put on her "Super Girl" cape just long enough to complete her Christmas shopping early, collect rent from all of her tenants and give them each a small gift, donate presents and blankets to the local homeless shelter in the name of her grandmother, and pass out cards and candy to the staff.

In the course of answering "Happy Holidays" texts that seemed to be coming through regularly, she noticed not one was from Alex. It looked like he'd finally had enough of his countless messages going unanswered. It was true. Leaving him in the dark wasn't the best thing to do. But she didn't exactly have a manual on how to deal with the situation. She wasn't sure what *his* silence meant, but she was freaking out. She was mad that he'd outed her. She was happy that he'd said, "I love you," and she was confused about whether or not she should say the same. All in all, she was all over the place! The only thing she was sure of was that the thought of losing him for good was as bad as the reality that the time for Simeon to leave had finally come.

Usually she would call Simeon to talk to him about these things, but he was now a major component of the problem. In all the years they'd known each other, there had never been an issue they couldn't come to some sort of resolve on. They'd fought over everything from money to politics, and even over some of his dates. But nothing had ever warranted them to stop effectively communicating with each other. The thought of him leaving for the next nine months without making up was unfathomable, but she knew she couldn't force him to. The night before, she was pleasantly surprised to hear that he'd gone over to Gigi's to make amends with both her and Brian. Diego even claimed that he'd done the same with Alex.

Although it seemed unlikely that he would be so eager to have peace talks with everyone except her, it was starting to hurt her feelings. She phoned him a few times, hoping to hear his voice. But her calls went unanswered and his voicemail was full. She had every mind to go to his place and demand that they speak. But the blizzard brewing outside, coupled with the memory of how badly things went the last time she popped up on him, made her stay put. For almost two hours, she laid in bed stewing before she got up to get dressed. Around 9 a.m., she emerged from the bathroom with a ravenous appetite and enough energy to make a breakfast fit for a queen.

The meal she made could feed two people. But somehow, she managed to eat it all herself. After cleaning the kitchen, she looked out the window, surprised by the amount of snow that had fallen in the short time she'd been awake. She sat on the old covered radiator under one of the windows and watched the other business owners below as they shoveled and salted the sidewalks in front of their stores. Her cell phone rang in her bedroom, sending her on a mad dash to see if it was him returning her calls. But instead, it was Gigi, who could sense the disappointment in her voice.

"Well good morning to you too, sunshine."

"Sorry, girl. I've got a small case of the winter blues."

"Winter blues or *man* blues? Have you talked to Alex or Simeon yet?"

"No. I don't know what to say to Alex and, as for Simeon, I called him a few times. But he didn't answer."

"That's strange. He said he needed to talk to you before he left. There's still time. I'm sure he's just been busy with everything."

"Or maybe he hates me."

"You have a better chance at winning the lottery than you do at Simeon hating you. He'll come through at the last minute, like always, and everything will be as right as rain. You'll see!"

"I hope so, G. I hate feeling this space between us. He's my best friend."

"I know. Tell you what. I'll blow off work today and come over so we can get Eve's Eve started early. I'm sure the girls can handle the boutique without me."

"Okay, but I gotta warn you. Georgia is coming over this evening. She won't be in town on Christmas, so you know she wants to see me before she leaves."

"Now you know I love me some Ms. Georgia! Besides, someone has to take Simeon's place tonight."

The annual "Eve's Eve" celebration had become sort of a big deal amongst the three friends over the years. It was their way of spending time together before the holidays. Ever since college, the program was always the same: each person had to bring a bottle of wine, wear an ugly Christmas sweater, and bring the cheesiest 80's movie they could find. It was the perfect recipe for a corny Christmas, but one they'd come to love. She was glad that *something* in her life wasn't changing on her.

It was bad enough that her heart was playing see-saw with whom she should be more concerned about, Alex or Simeon. But this was also the first time since her grandmother's passing that she wouldn't be with Georgia and Greg on Christmas. As much as she wanted to pout and be mad about it, she knew she couldn't. Greg was a happily engaged man who needed to bond with his future in-laws. Georgia was headed to Catalina Island with her new beau, who was also a lawyer at the firm. Alana thought to herself that if she had any sense at all, she would have made up with her own beau. But the words, "I love you" had her so afraid of what could possibly change that it was easier for her to pretend she was still mad at him. Was Georgia right? Had she been terrified of commitment all along and not realized it?

To pass the time while she waited for Gigi, she changed into her ugly Christmas sweater, pulled out the old Charlie Brown Christmas tree, put out a few candy dishes filled with chocolates, and strung up some lights to give her place some holiday spirit.

The bright, colorful lights did little to brighten her mood as she continuously looked at the clock, wondering what was taking her bestie so long. After an hour of pacing about the apartment and finding things to do, she retreated to her room and sat down at the end of her bed. She lifted the top of the storage trunk that rested at the foot of the bed and pulled out Alex's Christmas gift. She stared at the beautifully wrapped box sitting in her lap and wondered if he would even want it anymore.

An unfamiliar feeling rose up in her chest and stomach, as if a hole was beginning to form. It caused her to place her hand over her heart, which was beating faster than normal. Before she could panic, the sound of Gigi's key turning in the door quickly calmed her. Alana could hear her in the small coat room, shaking the snow off her coat and hat as she hurriedly put the box back into the trunk. She took a deep breath and closed her eyes until the tears that were forming slowly disappeared. She shook her head and hustled toward the kitchen while Gigi continued to remove layers of clothing.

"Hey, diva! You want some coffee?" Alana shouted.

"Girl, you read my mind. That blizzard is raging outside!"

"Well, thank God you made it safely. Are the roads bad?"

"They're pretty slippery."

"Maybe I should call Georgia and tell her—"

"And tell me what?" Georgia asked as she burst in behind Gigi.

"How?!" Alana yelled as she ran to hug her, almost knocking her over. "How did you know?"

"Well a little birdie called me and told me that my munchkin needed some company ASAP. And since I've officially started my working vacation, I figured now was as good a time as any."

The happy host took the computer bag from her mentor's shoulder and skipped to the kitchen while Gigi helped her out of her fluffy fur coat. As if the arrival of the ladies wasn't already enough to turn Alana's frown upside down, her moping was brought to a screeching halt when she turned to find both ladies posing proudly in their equally ugly sweaters. The girls spent their day pigging out on the couch and laying around with piles of thick blankets as their 80's movies fest rolled on. After watching *The Last Dragon*, *Big Trouble in Little China*, and *Pretty in Pink*, it was obvious that Alana was still knee-deep in mental anguish. She unknowingly checked the time every twenty minutes and, whenever Gigi cracked a joke, her laugh indicated that she wasn't truly listening to the conversation. But when Georgia offered to bake her famous Kahlua-flavored cookies and her response went unanswered, she knew it was time for an intervention. She paused the movie and sat next to her, waiting for her to let it all out.

"Why are you looking at me like that?" she asked Georgia.

"I'm waiting for you to get whatever it is off your chest so that you can enjoy our company as much as we're enjoying yours."

"I'm sorry. It's just that it's almost time for Simeon's plane to take off, so I guess that's it."

"Hardly! He just needed some space. You really think that means he doesn't care about you anymore?"

"No. I just wanted him to know how I felt."

"He's your best friend. He knows how you feel. You wanna know what I think?"

"Do I have a choice?"

"Don't be silly. Of course not. I think you've been using this drama with Simeon to avoid an even tougher topic: the little love bomb Alex dropped on you."

"No, I just have to fix one relationship at a time," she said as her heart started to race again at the mere mention of his name.

"Child, please! Friends fight all the time. Simeon will come around and your relationship will go right back to the way it was because he can't handle not having you in his life in some way. But Alex wants all or nothing. Question is, can you handle not having *Alex* in yours?"

She patted her on the leg and went to the kitchen, leaving her with something to think about. She sat staring out of the window at the snow, which was falling so heavily that it looked like a sheet was being held on the other side of the glass. Gigi had just begun to make some hot chocolate when they suddenly heard the door unlock. They all turned to find a snow-ridden Simeon shivering his way in. He appeared to be freezing as he removed his coat, hat and gloves, which covered his ugly Christmas sweater that was equipped with small bells on Rudolph's antlers and a nose that actually lit up.

Gigi hugged the abominable snow chef before grabbing his frosty hands and pulling him up the stairs. Georgia greeted him while Alana stood with her mouth gaped open, wondering what he was doing there. Apparently, his flight had been pushed back a couple of hours due to the weather conditions. So, he figured he had just enough time to say his goodbyes in person and take their infamous Christmas photo together. His parents, who were waiting downstairs in a town car, told him that he was crazy to squeeze in the unplanned trip, but he felt it was worth the risk. He and Alana stared at each other in silence, which was weird since they'd both been practicing what they would say once they saw each other. Georgia finally broke the ice and suggested to Gigi that they go into the guest room so the two could apologize to each other in private.

"Hey," he said.

"Hey back."

"Sorry we haven't talked, but I—"

"It's cool. It's been a crazy couple of weeks. Listen, Simeon. I'm sorry I didn't tell—"

"Alana, stop! You don't owe me an explanation. I owe you one."

"You don't have to explain anything."

"Just let me say this while I have the nerve. Let me say it so that I can finally say *I* told you, not someone else."

Simeon took her by the hand and led her over to the couch. He explained that the anger he'd been harboring over the past few days was never truly toward her, but toward himself. Over the years, there were so many times he was going to tell her the truth. The majority of their group had even encouraged it, but his fear of losing her friendship always outweighed his bravery. He knew only a fool should have expected her to guess what he was feeling and, unfortunately for him, he had been that fool. Alana's eyes began to water as he told her that there was a place inside of him that only she could touch and that it would always belong to her. For the first time, face to face, without anything else to interrupt him, he confessed the depths of his love wholeheartedly and explained that it was only because of that love that he could let her go.

"When I say that you're my best friend in this whole world, I truly mean it. And I want you to be happy, even if it is with someone else."

"Simeon, I do love you, but—"

"But not the same way that I love you. I know that. And I love you anyway. But down the line, just in case you're ever curious as to if my feelings will have changed..."

He stopped mid-sentence and bolted to the stereo. He searched through a stack of CDs before grabbing one and putting it in. He ran back over to her and helped her up so they could finish the slow dance that had been interrupted at the party. "Just play our song!" he finished as they moved in small, slow circles. Maxwell expressed the words in Simeon's heart as he sang, "Whenever, Wherever, Whatever." The friends held on to each other tightly and let all of the hurt, anger and confusion fall away from them.

Alana listened to the lyrics as she thought about all that they had gone through since the first day they met. She was glad their friendship had survived. Although he hadn't left yet, she couldn't wait for his return so they could start a whole new set of memories. When the music stopped, they held onto each other for a little while longer before he pulled away. A single tear dropped from the corner of her eye, which he quickly wiped away. He went into his right pocket and pulled out his keys, struggling to remove the one to her apartment. She looked at him, puzzled as to what he was doing. But his mission was soon made clear. He grabbed her hand and turned it over gently, placing the key inside of her palm.

"I...I think someone else may need this more than me." Apparently, after his talk with Alex, he decided to step back and let fate decide. She looked down at the cold brass and shook her head negatively, unsure of whether or not she still had a special someone to give it to.

"Maybe you should keep it. I think I may have blown it."

"Trust me. I seriously doubt that. It's not too late, if he's what you want, that is."

Simeon summoned Gigi and Georgia back into the room so they could take their photo. He pulled out his selfie stick as the women surrounded him and snapped the best ugly Christmas sweater photo they'd taken yet. He hugged each of them goodbye and, in return, they wished him good luck, safe travels and a speedy return. Alana walked him to the door and helped him with his coat. He gave her one last hug, closing his eyes and clinching his jaw as he pressed his nose into her hair, hoping to hold onto the sweet coconut smell.

"I promise I'll call you when I settle in."

"You better!" she ordered. But as Simeon turned to leave, he snapped his fingers as if he'd just remembered something important. He unzipped his coat and pulled out an envelope with pretty red ribbons on it, as well as a UPS express envelope.

"The festive looking one is from me. The other one, no clue. I ran into the delivery guy downstairs and I told him I'd make sure you got it." He handed over the items and kissed her on the cheek before closing the door behind himself, leaving Alana to face the coat room and let out a sigh of relief. The snow was beginning to lift just as quickly as the weight on her shoulders. But before her foot could touch the first step, she heard a light tapping on the door.

"What did you forget?" she asked.

"This!"

Simeon burst back through the door and swept her up in his arms, pressing her back against the wooden wall. The envelopes fell to the ground as her feet dangled in the air. He pressed his lips to hers, kissing her hard. He pulled back and kissed her bottom lip, then her top. He kissed her cheek, then her ear and back to her lips for one last, long peck. He loosened his grip and planted her feet back on the ground, leaving her speechless as he once again walked out of the door. In shock, she ran to the door to catch a last look at the kissing bandit as he slid back the gate to the elevator. Just before the cold, steel cage descended to the lobby below, he thought it would only be fair to offer an explanation to the flabbergasted beauty.

"I had to get it out of my system. I mean, just in case you marry the guy."

They couldn't help but laugh as he waved goodbye for the next nine months. She scooped up her items from the ground and returned to her spot on the couch, somewhat relieved. She threw the UPS envelope on the table as the ladies sat opposite of her, waiting to see what his gift was. Alana slowly untied the ribbons and ripped it open right after reading the front, which said, "In case you want to visit." The gift was an open-ended ticket to Paris. Her spectators both gasped at the overly generous gift. As her heart quickened just as it did earlier in the day, she ignored it and blamed it on the present. Georgia and Gigi chattered on and on about how great it would be for her to get out of town. She picked up the UPS envelope from the coffee table, curious as to who'd sent it. But after tearing it open, she found a folder inside with a letter taped to the front of it. It was from Alex! As her guests' voices faded into the background, she moved to the edge of her seat and read on.

Alana, I hate the way things are right now between us. Since you haven't been responding to my texts or calls, this is what we've been reduced to: an ancient form of communication (just kidding). But seriously, I'm sorry I've made you feel like you need so much space from me. I thought we could talk about anything, even the fact that I'm in love with you. But maybe you don't want to discuss it because you don't feel the same. I never expected my feelings for you to grow to this. I only knew after seeing you for the first time that no woman would ever be able to compare afterwards and that has not, and will not, change. I was going to surprise you with this for Christmas, so here it is. Since you took me to the beach at home, I wanted to take you to one a little further away. I still want you to go with me, and I hope that you let me love you. But whatever you decide, I have no regrets. Every moment I've spent with you has been well worth it.

Alana opened the folder and clutched her chest, unable to believe what she was seeing. As coincidence would have it, her eyes widened as she looked over yet another plane ticket she'd received for Christmas--only this one was accompanied by a hotel reservation and an itinerary for a weekend getaway to St. Thomas. She dropped the folder in her lap and slid back onto the couch as she began to breathe heavily with a plane ticket in each hand. What were the odds of the two men she loved the most getting her the same thing for Christmas? Any other time, she would admit that the odds were pretty high. But when it came to Alex and Simeon, their thoughts and actions could be eerily similar. The ladies became alarmed and rushed to both sides of her in an effort to make sure she was alright, but her words wouldn't come out. Gigi grabbed the letter to see what all the fuss was about, while Georgia worried that it might be something more serious. She put her hand to Alana's forehead to feel for a fever as she handed her a glass of water, which she gulped down like she was suffering from dehydration. Her breathing quickened faster as her mind raced around what could possibly be causing all of her anxiety.

"Alana, are you okay? Are you coming down with something?"

"No, I—"

"Oh, she's coming down with something alright: a case of dumb luck! It would certainly take my breath away. These men, these men!" Gigi said, handing the folder to Georgia.

"No, I think I—"

"Whoa! I know I'm usually Team Simeon, but this Alex is tre' romantique! Not that a plane ticket to Paris is shabby. Is this a little too overwhelming for you, sweetie?"

"No, I think I—"

"It's my beauty, isn't it? It's choked up more than a few in my lifetime," Gigi joked.

"No, I think I'm—"

"Do you feel like he's pressuring you?"

"That's not it." she reassured them.

"Then what is it dear?"

Alana stopped hyperventilating just long enough to hold her spectators in suspense. They stared at her as a smile spread across her face, which evolved into her laughing hysterically, like a demented woman. Georgia and Gigi stared at each other, unsure of what to do or of what emotion would pour out of her next. But soon, it would all make sense.

"I think I…No, I know…I'm in love."

Chapter | 31

Alana's heart finally stopped racing. All that she'd been angry about up to that point suddenly seemed so petty, and her confusion seemed to melt away like winter's first snowfall. Without any effort at all, it became clear who was important to her and why. Being true to herself and admitting her feelings gave her a sense of calm that she'd never known before, but it produced shockwaves through the room. Georgia stared blankly into space, unable to believe what she'd just heard. She didn't even flinch when her wine glass hit the floor. In her usual dramatic fashion, Gigi put the back of her hand to her forehead and pretended to faint onto the couch as she fanned herself with the other. The announcement had stunned, but it was something they'd been waiting to hear about as long as Alana hadn't been waiting to feel it.

A montage played in her mind of all the things that those closest to her had taught her about love. Greg was willing to drop everything with just a phone call from Shelby. Diego relished at the opportunity just to cook for his wife, and she was always the first person he wanted to share good news with. Gigi couldn't keep her mind, or her hands for that matter, off of Brian. And then, there was Georgia. Just thinking of the great love of her life could reduce her to happy tears.

Each of them had unknowingly showed her what real love was, and now Alex was becoming her greatest teacher. Whether it was enjoying a movie at their makeshift drive-in theater, spending Thanksgiving in a hospital, letting her guard down and exposing her quirky side, or laying on the floor of his living room and feeling as if they were in the honeymoon suite of some exquisite hotel, Alana knew that he made everything that much better.

"So, he's the one, huh? What makes you so sure?" Gigi asked. Alana took her time before answering. Rather than give a long, drawn out speech, she opted for a more lighthearted response that she knew Gigi would understand completely. She smiled and looked at her best friend, who was eagerly awaiting her answer and satisfied her with an almost comical conclusion.

"Because I want *him* more than sex. I love him more than wine, and I need him more than chocolate."

"Sounds good to me!" Gigi said.

"So, Georgia, any objections?" Alana asked. "I know you always saw me ending up with Simeon, but—"

"But nothing. I just wanted you to be happy. Don't ever choose something or someone because I want you to, or even because it's the safe and comfortable option. Go after what you want, even if it's out of your comfort zone. Even if it's not what everyone else wants. You understand?"

Alana nodded in agreement and kissed her on the cheek before she rushed to the hallway closet and grabbed a small bag from the top shelf, along with her passport. She stuffed it with clothes while simultaneously dialing up Elizabeth, Damien and Diego on a conference call. They were all pleased to hear that she would be taking a vacation, and they assured her that things would be fine while she was away. The snowflakes blowing ferociously outside of the large dining room windows began to lift, as if they were magically making her commute to his house easier. As she chatted on the phone and fumbled with her clothes, Gigi emerged and grabbed her hand.

"Honey, the plane doesn't leave until tomorrow and I hate to point out the obvious, but you haven't even talked to him yet!"

"You know what? You're right! I gotta go," she stated as she hung up the phone and dialed Alex's number. As she placed her toiletries in the side pocket of the carry-on, the call went straight to voicemail. She called a few more times, but each time, she got the same result. By the fourth try, she started to become frantic and wondered if he'd changed his mind. The ladies calmed her and told her that it was never too late for love while pushing her toward the door. After wishing them both a Merry Christmas, she made a mad dash to the stairwell, where she nearly broke her ankle trying to run down the steep stairs with the small suitcase in tow.

Driving on the slick, velvety roads was a nightmare. But she took her time as she tried calling him once more on the Bluetooth in her car. Again, it went straight to voicemail as her fingers nervously tapped the steering wheel. His letter said he still wanted to be with her, so was this payback for all of his unanswered calls? Had his phone died or had he turned it off because he was with someone else? Perhaps Natalie had slithered her way over to his place and surprised him with a kiss, just as Simeon had done to her.

When she finally arrived at his house, she'd barely put the car in park before she bolted for the front door. She nearly slid into the glass as she began to knock non-stop. She looked through the slender glass window next to the door and could see the fireplace going in the living room. When she looked toward the dining room, she saw a concerned Alex peek his head out of the closed, sliding wooden doors, which were embedded in the walls. He slid through the opening and shut them all the way behind him before he jogged to the door to let her in. She rushed in and walked in circles under the chandelier in the hallway, unsure of where to start.

"Alana, what's wrong?"

"Look, I don't know who you have in there, and I don't care because I have to tell you this."

"Okay," he said, crossing his arms.

"I know I handled things all wrong. I know that! But I've never been in a situation like this before."

"You completely shut me out Alana—"

"I know, and I'm so sorry for that. And I know I don't deserve your forgiveness. I mean, when you love someone, you're supposed to talk it through, right? And work at it, and—"

"I do forgive you, wait…you love me?"

"Well, yeah! I was just getting to that. I love you, Alex. I love being with you, and laughing with you, and I love having sex with you, which is always just off the charts, mind- blowing, knee-buckling—"

"Honey, although that's the kind of compliment every guy wants, I think you might want to stop. On the other side of those doors—"

"I don't care who she is! You said you loved me and—"

"And baby, I do love you, but—"

"But nothing! Whoever that is, they don't love you as much as I do. I've never felt this way before in my life. But if someone already had you second guessing us that quickly, then maybe—"

"Sweetheart, stop talking!" he said, as he gently put his hand over her mouth. "If you're thinking there's another woman in that room, you're right. There are a few actually: my mother and my sisters!"

"You're kidding, right?" she asked as her eyes widened with horror and her skin became flushed.

"I'm not. And that's not all."

"Noooooooo!" she whispered loudly. She closed her eyes and braced for the news.

"Don't tell me—"

"Afraid so. You can add my father, my brother, his lady, and both of my brothers-in-law to that list. We just finished having a few pizzas and were about to play some board games. I didn't think you were coming."

"I could see why you would think that. But, just for the record, there's no place on earth I'd rather be."

Alex's hand slid off her mouth slowly before being immediately replaced by his lips. His arms wrapped around her waist, which she began to squeeze tightly. He pretended as if his family wasn't on the other side of the door as he grabbed her butt and kissed her like his life depended on it. Her body felt weak. She had never been more in tuned with another person. She desperately wanted to whisk him away upstairs so that their naked bodies could continue the display of affection. Had the sound of the doors sliding open not been so loud, they could have remained in that position for as long as their legs would have allowed. They paused, staring into each other's eyes, trying not to notice the eight pairs of eyes now staring at them.

"Alana, this is my family," Alex said with his lips still smashed onto hers.

"Nice to see you again!" Sherri said with a big bright smile.

Alana quickly pulled away from him and wiped her mouth. She straightened up her jacket and hair, as if they hadn't already seen her, while Alex massaged her shoulders to help her relax. She waved at everyone, shaking both of his parents' hands while simultaneously apologizing for the interruption.

"Pardon my intrusion. I am so sorry we're meeting like this," she said, obviously embarrassed.

"Oh, don't be silly. I'm happy to meet my son's new love. Besides, it's not as if you weren't here already with the way this one has been pouting all night," his mother said.

"I knew nothing but a beautiful woman could have caused him to be acting the way he was. And I see I was right," his father said. "Okay everyone. I think it's time for us to go around the corner to Eric's house and give these two some privacy."

His father's suggestion was met by, "Boo!" and protest from the rest of the family, who wanted to stick around and dig into the love birds' business, or at least get to know Alana. His brother put up the biggest fight of all. It was his first time out of the house since his accident, and he wanted nothing more than to spend the precious time embarrassing the pants off of his little brother. But his fiancée agreed with the family's patriarch that it was time to be going and gently helped her injured beau toward the door. As the family put on their coats and threw jabs at Alex for still being the spoiled, young brat of the family, Alana covered her face and laughed hysterically. One by one, they hugged both her and Alex, his father even giving him a pound, and said their goodbyes. They piled into his parents' van out front, which Alana couldn't believe she'd missed in her haste, and gave a quick honk before pulling off.

After watching them drive off, Alex leaned against the door and smiled at her for a moment. His eyes exuded a fondness that couldn't be mistaken for anything else. She removed her jacket and threw it onto the banister before she was once again in his arms.

"Oh! I almost forgot," she said, going into her jacket pocket. "I was in such a rush that I forgot your big present, but you can have the small one for now." She pulled the key to her place from her pocket and put it in his hand. He held it up and stared at it as it dangled from white ribbons, making his bright white smile even brighter.

"This is no *small* gift. This is huge, especially for you! I don't know what to say."

"Say you like it."

"I love it!" he answered. "So, what do we do now?" he asked.

"How about we sip some wine, make love, fall asleep in each other's arms, and then tomorrow, we do it all again in paradise?"

"Baby, I'm already in paradise," he said.

They raced each other to his bedroom, where they ferociously tore off each other's clothing. This time, they disturbed the neighbors on purpose well into the night. She enjoyed every inch of his chocolate skin as sweat trickled over every muscle. After hours of indulging on every curve of her body and finally reaching the heights of ecstasy, Alex grabbed the cover, which was now on the floor. He put it over their naked bodies before kissing her forehead and wrapping his arm around her. They held each other tightly and thought about how thankful they were—her thankful that she'd finally found love, and him thankful that it was with him. It didn't take long before they were both drifting off into a sweet, satisfied sleep.

Alex's eyes could barely stay open as he whispered to her, "I'm glad it was me, babe. I'm glad I was the one." Alana opened her eyes and realized for the first time, she had it all: family, friends, success and *love*. Instead of wine being the culprit, she was drunk with love and the sweet taste of a new life replaced her craving for chocolate--well, not *all chocolate*! She rubbed her fingertips over his beautiful thick lips, happy that they were hers before whispering back, "I'm glad, too."

Made in the USA
Middletown, DE
14 March 2018